BOMBSHELLS

T. ELLIOTT BROWN

www.inkoutloud.com

InkOutLoud Publishing
www.inkoutloud.com
A division of Develop Things LLC.

This book is a work of fiction. Names, character, places and incidents are products of the author's imagination. Any resemblance to persons, living or dead, is coincidental. Historical events are depicted as accurately as possible within the framework of this novel.

Edited by Caro Carson
Cover Design by Jonathan Brown and Jason Koi
Cover Photo by Ringo Bartle
Designed by Jonathan Brown

ISBN-978-0-9849258-0-3 (EPUB)
ISBN-978-0-9849258-1-0 (MOBI)
ISBN-978-0-9849258-2-7 (Paperback)

More BOMBSHELLS!

Board the time machine and head back to those tension-filled days of the Cuban Missile Crisis in October 1962

BombshellsBook.com

- Download a playlist of early '60's music to accompany your read. Talk about total immersion, right?
- Listen to President Kennedy tell the nation that Russia is setting up missiles in Cuba and what the US is going to do about it.
- Read accounts of Navy personnel aboard the *USS William R. Rush* as they are recalled from shore liberty during the crisis.
- Wondering what the clothes looked like? The cars? The hairstyles? Take a peek so you can visualize the characters of *Bombshells* as you read.
- What was on television? On the movies? On Broadway?

BombshellsBook.com is the place to go to find all the extras to enhance your reading experience.

This book is dedicated to Margie and Cliff Elliott, who always kept me safe, always gave me love, and always believed in me.

Foreword

The idea for this book came to me first in the form of a poem during a long ago poetry class. The poem, called "Nuclear Granny", is about a woman, rocking in her chair, telling her grandchildren wild stories about ducking under her school desk to avoid being killed by a nuclear bomb. The children laugh and Granny tells them how happy she is that they will never have experiences like that.

Of course, this was before the Persian Gulf Wars began in 1990, before the attacks of September 11, 2001, before nuclear weapons spread from two major nations to countries dotting the entire globe. I now realize the poem is a fantasy. Every generation, ancient or modern, lives with the fear, the real possibility, that peoples and powers far removed from them will determine their fate with violence.

Despite our worries about war, personal bombshells really change our lives. Unforeseen events can destroy families as quickly and more accurately than unmanned drone attacks. This book is about a family that is changed by, but survives, the possibility of nuclear bombs and the actuality of private bombshells.

I've done my best to recreate the world of 1962, including the political tensions and cultural divisions that defined America during this period. While the story is complete fiction, some events mirror my own experience during this time, such as taking rations to school, wearing dog tags, and housing a Navy family evacuated from Cuba. I've taken some license with historic dates and events as I wove this novel.

Here I want to thank the people who patiently stood with

me as this book emerged from that long ago poem, starting with Kristen Lewotsky Hardy, who was there from the beginning, always encouraging me and offering sound advice in story-crafting. There are no words to express my gratitude.

Thanks to critique partners through the years: Lori Johnson, Karen Potter, Lynn Meiseles, Kresley Cole, Elizabeth Grainger.

Special gratitude to my current team: Nancy Robards Thompson, Catherine Kean, and Caroline Phipps. I couldn't write without you. I can barely make it through a couple of weeks without seeing you.

Thanks to my fabulous editor, Caro Carson (aka The Midnight Line Editor), who understood the heart of this story from the beginning.

Last, but certainly not least, my husband and love, David, who stood by me and supported me through this long journey with love and patience. Love to my sons, Matthew, Jonathan and Jeremy, who've all contributed to the richness of my life and therefore to the depth of my writing. My special thanks to Jonathan and Jason Koi for their work on the book cover and the formatting of this novel. Love and kisses to my granddaughter, Alexandra. You keep me young!

Friday
August 17, 1962

Jacksonville, Florida

MELANIE

Yesterday, I turned twelve.

Today, I remembered my birthday.

I woke up this morning and realized that I'm already twelve. I'm not sure how we all managed to forget. Mama had a doctor's appointment yesterday and her blood pressure was high, so the doctor and nurses were worried about the baby she's carrying. He made her stay in the office for a long time. That scared us.

When the doctor finally let us go we did some quick grocery shopping. Mama got tired, but she bought us some Oreos and we all felt happier.

So many things are different this year. The baby coming is the biggest difference. We'd gotten my birthday present, a new red bathing suit, a week and a half before, so I wasn't expecting another gift. And my best friend, Stephanie, is in Philadelphia on vacation with her family. No point in planning a party or spend-the-night.

My birthday ended up as just another day, filled with the usual worries and work. That's what Daddy says when Mama asks him how his day went.

I feel happy and sad all together. How could I forget my own birthday? But what makes me sad is that Mama and Daddy forgot.

As I walk to the kitchen, the speckled floor tile is cool and slick, and because of the humidity, my warm feet leave foggy footprints that fade away quickly. The pale green curtains at the kitchen window flutter in the breeze. I can smell a little bit of salt the air picks up from blowing across the ocean.

Through the window, I see wet laundry hanging on the clothesline, making it sag so low in the middle that the white bath towels almost touch the ground. Mama always hangs the clothes in order of size and color, starting with my sister Birdie's little white socks.

Mama's there, near the end of the clothesline, struggling with a wet bed sheet in the morning breeze. Her white Keds left a flat path in the St. Augustine grass Daddy is so proud of. Sweat darkens the underarms of her pink and blue striped cotton dress. The sheet flaps again before she snags it with first one clothespin, then another.

A Navy jet zooms over, roaring loud and low, and Mama jumps, dropping a clothespin. The end of the sheet floats in the breeze while Mama bends over, her hand pressed to her back as she picks up the pin. Finally, the sheet is anchored to the line.

As I move away from the window, the sunlight glinting on the aluminum cake cover catches my eye. I walk over to the buffet where the cake plate always sits and lift the cover. The rich, dark smell of chocolate blooms all around me, erasing the bacon and coffee scents left over from Daddy's breakfast.

Smooth, shiny frosting is swirling over the top of the cake like waves breaking against the jetty on the St. Johns River.

Mama never really forgot my birthday.

The screened porch door slams and I drop the lid over the cake, snuffing out the sweet smell with a metallic clang.

"Mornin', Mellie." Mama sets down the wicker laundry basket and wipes beads of sweat from her upper lip. She arches her back and rubs her hands back and forth across her hips. "You're up early."

"Yes, ma'am."

Mama reaches for her glass, fills it with tap water, and brings it to her lips.

I go stand beside her and rub my hand across her belly, stretched like she has a watermelon under her dress. "Is the baby moving a lot today?"

She shakes her head.

I kiss her tummy. *Please, God, let it be a brother.* I can't take another sister. And I know Daddy wants a boy.

That's one of my morning rituals—to kiss Mama's tummy and pray. Scooting back a little so I can see her face, I say, "Guess what?

Mama puts her glass back on the windowsill. "What, sweetie?"

"No, you have to guess."

"Um, let me see. Birdie lost another tooth?"

Not wanting to start the day off being sassy, I resist rolling my eyes. "No, Mama." Sometimes it's really hard being the oldest.

"Well, you might have to tell me. I can't think fast enough to imagine what kind of trouble Birdie's gotten into now."

Swallowing a sigh, I say, "It's not about Birdie at all. It's about me."

"Oh, sweetie, no! Don't tell me you…"

Good grief! Was that what she thought? She'd given me the *time-of-the-month* talk last week because my birthday was coming up. I'm still waiting for the one about the birds and the bees. Stephanie's already heard that one. Of course, her sister, Cherie, is sixteen, and tells Steph anything she wants to know.

"No, Mama. Thank God, it's not that."

"Watch your mouth, young lady." Mama points her finger at me. "Nice young ladies don't use the Lord's name in vain."

"Yes, ma'am."

"But, thank God, that's not what it is. I don't think I could cope with that just now."

"Why can you say *thank God* but I'm not allowed?"

Mama pulls out a chair and plops into it like she can't hold herself up anymore. "Like I told you: do as I say, not as I do."

I frown. "Okay. But guess again."

Resting her chin in her palm, she stares at the table. Suddenly she jerks upright, looking at me like I'm a ghost.

"Lord have mercy! We forgot your birthday." She grabs me to her and hugs me up against her chest. "Oh, sweetheart. I'm sorry."

No matter how old I get, I don't think anything will feel quite as good as a Mama hug early in the morning. Right now she smells like bath powder and sunshine and just a little bit of sweat. Her body's warm and soft against mine, and that shaky feeling that's been in me all morning fades away. If I were my new brother or sister, I would try to stay safe inside Mama's belly forever.

"How could we forget your birthday, Melanie Adams?"

I grin and snuggle closer to Mama. A thought zips through my brain, quick as a flash of lightning. Maybe I didn't want to have my twelfth birthday. Somehow, I'm not so sure I'm going to like being twelve. But instead, I say, "I don't know, Mama. Maybe I'm getting old."

Mama chuckles, the sound coming from deep in her chest. It rumbles through me too. Deep and soothing. "Hey now, you can't steal my excuse. How does cake for breakfast sound?"

"Yummy!"

Mama turns me around and pats my backside. "Well, you go get Birdie up, and I'll call Daddy to see if he can come home to have some cake with us." A little frown creases her brow. "Put some clothes on, sweetie. And don't forget your bra."

NORAH

My God, she's growing up so fast.

No wonder the girl frowns at you, Norah.

I shove up from the table, off balance like a horse on a tight rope. How could I forget my firstborn's birthday? And if I forgot her birthday, how in the world will I manage three children? What am I going to do?

Grabbing the phone receiver from the wall mount, I dial the factory's number. I hope Clay can come home from the office for a few minutes, like he used to. When did he *stop* coming home for lunch, anyway? I can't remember, but it's been a while, I guess. Maybe he got tired of bologna sandwiches.

I wait for the switchboard at the office to pick up.

"Reynolds Aluminum, Jacksonville. How can I help you?"

"Clay Adams, please."

"May I say who's calling?"

Shirley's authoritative tone makes those five words sound like a political speech. I answer in the same precise manner. "His wife."

"Oh. Norah. He's on the floor. Everything okay?"

Sighing, I rub my aching back. Shirley and everyone else at the plant knows I'm expecting. She's not really being nosy. "Yes, everything's fine."

"He's really busy this morning. A machine went down. Do you really *need* to talk to him?"

So now Shirley decides if I'm important enough to talk to my husband? I don't think so. "Yes, Shirley. I *need* to talk to him now." Our daughter's birthday is important, too.

"All right. Hold on." The phone clicks, and I know she's connecting and disconnecting lines, paging Clay on the factory floor, and answering other calls. I know all this because that was my job once. Two babies ago. A lifetime ago.

Staring out the window at the laundry hanging dead still on the line, I grab the folded newspaper and fan myself while I wait for Clay to pick up the line.

It gets under my skin that Shirley, and every other woman in that office, knows where my husband is eight or ten hours of the day, and I don't really know anything but that he leaves me at seven-thirty every morning and comes home at six o'clock every night.

Then I think how ridiculous I am. Of course, I know where Clay is. He's working to support his family. So what if Shirley knows *exactly* where he is.

It's the hormones, I guess, making me illogical like this.

I'm thankful he comes home each evening. That he doesn't go out for drinks with the guys. That he only rarely brings home a can of beer in a paper sack. Like he says, we don't have the money for extras like that these days. But he has money for lunch every day? I've got to talk to him about that. We can't afford lunch at a restaurant every day. Even the cost of Krystal burgers adds up.

"He'll be right with you, Norah. Just stay on the line." And Shirley is gone again.

Holding the phone against my shoulder, I turn on the hot water to add to the sink full of dirty breakfast dishes. Not waiting for the water to turn warm, I plunge my hands into the dishwater. The ickiness of slimy eggs and bacon grease makes my stomach roll. The dishrag slips out of my fingers and I close my eyes. How will I endure eight more weeks of this pregnancy?

"Norah." Clay's voice on the line startles me. "What's wrong?"

"We forgot Mellie's birthday yesterday."

"What?"

"Mellie's birthday was yesterday. I had the cake made, but we forgot all about it. I promised her cake for breakfast this morning. Can you come home for a little while?"

"I shouldn't. We had a machine break down this morning."

"I know. Shirley told me. Mellie's already twelve. This is important."

"So's my job, with another child on the way."

"You don't have to remind me of that." I blink against the tears stinging my eyes. Just as quickly, anger simmers up from my gut. "But let me remind you that you were there when we made this baby, just like the other ones."

"Norah."

I hear the frustration in his voice and for a moment I want to take it back. But I don't. I won't apologize, either. "How about coming home for lunch, then? It's been a while since you've had lunch with us."

He's quiet for a few seconds. Is he wondering when I noticed he stopped coming home for lunch? "The broken machine is causing production to drop. It's my job to make sure it's fixed and we're rolling again. I should stay until it's done."

"We'll be fine without you." I'm so upset my words pop like snapping gum. Yes. Yes, we will. "Don't worry about it."

"C'mon, Norah," he sighs.

"Bye, Clay. Guess I'll see you tonight." Trying to contain my hurt and anger, I hang up the phone softly, straighten the long, curly cord, then reach for a tissue to blow my nose.

BIRDIE

"Birdie, wake up." Mellie yells at me. "We're gonna have cake for breakfast."

"Nuh-uh." I lift my chin off my chest and take a deep breath. "Mama never lets us have sweets for breakfast," I yell back.

"Well, we are today." Mellie throws open the door to the bedroom we share. She stares at me for a few seconds, then says, "C'mon, Birdie, get up."

Mellie stares at me because I'm in the middle of my twin bed with both of my feet tucked behind my head. She's jealous because she can't do this. Mellie thinks she can't do it because she's so grown up, but that's not true. She *never* could do this trick.

We used to have regular contests to see who could do the funniest tricks, before Mama, she got 'xpectin'. We'd stand on our heads, or do cartwheels. Mama can do the best cartwheel.

Daddy can do the best handstand. But only I can put my feet behind my head. Daddy says I should join the circus and be a 'tortionist.

He told me a 'tortionist is someone who can move her body all kinds of ways and look like a human knot. Maybe I'll get to wear a sparkly costume when I'm in the circus.

Just to aggravate Mellie, I stay put. I slap my butt four times and sing real loud, "Oh." Again. *Slap, slap, slap-slap*, "Oh."

From my 'tortion knot on the bed, I watch Mellie take her new bra, snowy white with a little pink rose bud in the center, out of the drawer. She turns her back to me and tugs her nightgown over her head. She doesn't want me to see.

She didn't used to care if I saw her. We took baths together, got dressed in front of each other, even slept together sometimes. Nothing was a big deal until a few months ago. About the time Mama told us we'd have a new baby brother or sister.

Please God, let it be a brother, I pray. Then I continue what I'm doing. *Slap, slap, slap-slap*. "Oh."

"What are you doing anyway?"

"Singin'." *Slap, slap, slap-slap*. "Oh."

"You have to sing words to be singing, you idjit. You're just slapping your butt and saying 'Oh'."

"Not if you're singing *Bingo*. And Mama said not to call me idjit no more. I'm telling." I unknot myself and somersault to the end of the bed and stand up, bouncing a couple of times before I land on the floor with my arms straight up in the air. I would be good in the circus.

Since I'm only six years old, I have time to work on my act some more. Heck, I'll probably be ready to run away and join the circus by the time I'm as old as Mellie. Maybe I can be a clown, too. I look in the mirror, roll my tongue and stick the whole thing through the gap where I'm missing four front teeth. I don't even have to open my jaw. When I do that in front of people, they laugh like it's the funniest thing they ever saw.

Yep. I would be a great addition to the circus. Birdie, The Acrobat Clown 'Tortionist. I pick up the hairbrush and run it through my hair. Even after brushing, it stands out like a yellow cotton ball. "Why are we having cake for breakfast?"

Mellie frowns at me. "Cause it's my birthday."

"Nuh-uh. Yesterday was your birthday."

"But we forgot."

"I didn't." I cross my eyes and look at the freckles on my nose so I won't have to look at Mellie. I know she's frowning real hard at me like a grown-up. It's not my fault she forgot her own birthday.

"You remembered? Why didn't you say anything?"

Besides, I didn't remember until after we went to bed. Then it was too late. I was scared for Mama and the baby. Yeah, it wasn't my fault. It was the stupid baby's fault.

I balance on one leg, and do my special one-legged dance as I hop right through the door. Over my shoulder I say, "Well, it wasn't *my* birthday, idjit."

MELANIE

Gosh almighty! Isn't that just like a bratty little sister to let you forget your birthday? I brush my hair into a ponytail and stretch the rubber band around it while I count to ten to keep from yelling at her.

When I reach the number twenty and finally calm down, I remember Mama saying, "What goes around, comes around." I'm sure something like this will happen to Birdie someday, and she'll see how it feels to be invisible.

In the kitchen, the percolator hums and gurgles, filling the house with new coffee smells. Birdie turns on "Captain Kangaroo," adjusts the long silver rabbit-ear antenna to get rid of the static, and sprawls on the couch. The toilet flushes, and I hear Mama singing as she comes down the hall.

"Mama, which plates do you want to use?"

"We'll use the good china. After all, this is a birthday party."

"No, it's not!" Birdie sings from the living room sofa. "Yesterday was her birthday."

"We know, Birdie. But we're going to celebrate today." Mama pours two glasses of milk and fills the cream pitcher. She carries the creamer and sugar bowl to the table, placing them next to the cake plate.

"But it's not a real birthday party. You can't have a real birthday party if it's not your birthday." Birdie's voice sounds kind of whiny, like she's about to cry. Or maybe throw a tantrum. And she would, too, just to spoil my birthday.

Birdie's tantrums are awful. Sometimes she collapses to the floor, screaming and kicking until you think the world is ending. I'll do almost anything to avoid Birdie's tantrums. Mama just ignores her and goes about her business. She says that's what the pediatrician told her to do.

Easy for him to say. Dr. Withers has never seen one of Birdie's tantrums.

"Okay. Calm down. We'll just have cake."

"Well, as long you know it's not real. Nobody's allowed to have two birthdays." Birdie sounds calm now.

Thank goodness. I sure don't want to have my almost birthday completely ruined.

Outside, the brakes on our old blue Ford squeal. Mama drops the cake knife. It clunks when it hits the floor.

"There's Daddy." I try to keep the excitement out of my voice. I just have a feeling that Daddy will do something special for me.

The front door opens, and he stands there with the sun shining behind him. Both his hands are behind his back.

There it is. There's my real surprise.

He looks over my head toward the kitchen where Mama is, puckers his lips and blows her a kiss. Looking back to me, he shouts like an announcer in a parade, "Where's the birthday girl?"

"It's not her birthday!" Birdie yells from the couch. She jumps up and turns Captain Kangaroo louder.

Uh-oh. Here comes the tantrum.

Daddy just looks at her. *That* look. The one that doesn't need any words at all, but says everything.

Birdie, still standing next to the television, snaps the switch off and goes to put napkins on the table.

"Here's something for the young lady of the house." He smiles and shoves the door closed with his foot. "Well, come over here and get it."

I run to him, wondering what kind of surprise he might have for me.

"Oh, no. I get a kiss first." He lowers his cheek for me to kiss. Daddy's face is smooth and smells good, sweet and spicy, with a little tang of cigarette smoke blended in.

"Happy birthday, young lady." He draws his hand from behind his back and hands me a rose, a beautiful, red rose with a long, straight stem. The fragrance, so heavy and rich, seems to hang in the air around the flower. I lower my nose right into the center of the bloom. The petals are like cool velvet on my skin.

The shaky feeling slips into me along with the sweet smell of my "young lady" gift. This is nice, but what happened to skates or records? Even a book?

"I've got surprises for everyone this morning." He reaches into his pants pocket and pulls out a candy bar. "Birdie, this is for you."

"Oh goodie! A Baby Ruth!" Birdie skips up to Daddy and hugs his legs.

Mama stands in the kitchen with her hands on her hips. She raises one eyebrow. "Glad you could make it after all, Big Shot."

Daddy goes over and wraps his arms around Mama, kind of bending over so he can reach around the baby. They look at each other.

Daddy whispers in Mama's ear and kisses her cheek. She smiles and murmurs, "I'm sorry, too." Then he really kisses her.

I always feel invisible when they do that, when they look deep into each other's eyes. I glance at Birdie. She scrunches up her nose at me, but looks back at Mama and Daddy standing there, hugging each other, and I know Birdie feels the same way. For a minute, there's nobody in the world but the two of them, holding each other.

Somewhere inside, that one little speck of me that is looking forward to growing up and becoming a woman tells my brain that this is what love looks like. Aunt Lola always points to Mama and Daddy and says, "Don't you settle for anything less than what you see there."

Isn't it funny how you can have all of this stuff happening in your head and heart while you stand in the dining room, holding a rose and watching your family do everyday stuff?

Daddy holds Mama's face in his hands. "You're going to like your surprise best, Norah."

"Oh, really?" Mama pushes away from Daddy and bends to pick up the knife from the floor, but Daddy beats her to it. He puts it in the sink and gets a clean one out of the drawer.

Mama lifts the lid to the cake plate and says, "You can tell me while I cut the cake."

"C'mon, girls." Daddy pulls out a chair and motions for me. "Miss Melanie, for you."

I sit down, and he pushes my chair in for me. I lay the rose on the table, and, all the while, the scent drifts up to me, reminding me that it's a grown-up gift, not a kid's gift.

Mama puts twelve candles in a circle around the middle of the cake. Daddy takes out his silver cigarette lighter and lights them. Everyone sings "Happy birthday to you! Happy birthday to you!"

Then Birdie climbs in her chair and shouts out, "You look like a monkey and you smell like one too!"

We all laugh, and Mama cuts the cake.

"Remember when I told you about Max's sister?" Daddy asks, while he stirs milk into his coffee.

"The one who does housekeeping?" Mama slides a big wedge of cake onto a plate and hands it to me.

"Yep. Well, she has an opening on Mondays and Thursdays until Thanksgiving."

"That's too bad. I'm sure she needs the work."

"No, she has work."

Mama cuts the last slice of cake for herself. "Good."

Daddy grins really big and grabs Mama's hand. "Yes, it is good. She's working for you."

Mama's fork clatters onto her plate. "What?"

"You need help with the housework since your back and legs hurt you so much. I know Mellie's been a big help this summer, but she'll be starting school soon." Daddy gives Mama one of those winks that means they have a secret. "I'm just no good with those gathered skirts."

Except that's not a big secret. Daddy's terrible at ironing. Period.

"Oh, Clayton." Mama hugs him. "But I'm not sure I'll be comfortable with anybody else in the house. And a colored woman? Nobody else in the neighborhood has colored help."

Daddy shakes his head. "You don't need to worry. Max is a good man. I'm sure his sister is good, too."

"It'll be nice to have someone to do the ironing for me. And you say she can help out until November?"

"Yep. She can start August twenty-third."

"Are you sure we can afford this, Clay?"

He digs his fork into his cake. "Yes, Norah. I'm sure. The budget is tight, but you need help. I've got some overtime coming, and I can sell back the rest of my vacation days. So don't worry, all right?"

Daddy winks at me over the rim of his coffee cup. "And as a special treat, I'm taking all my girls to the movies tonight. The new Elvis Presley movie is playing at the drive-in. It's Dollar-A-Carload Night, too. I expect y'all to have a grocery sack of popcorn ready and be prettied up by six o'clock."

NORAH

"But Daddy said *we* have to do the dishes," Birdie protests.

"I know what your Daddy said, but Mellie isn't going to

wash her own party dishes." Plopping down on the sofa, I sigh. "Just put the dishes in the sink, then you can go outside and play."

"Okay." Birdie clatters the plates into the sink. "But that's not what Daddy said."

Clay not only came home from work for the little party, but he apologized for our spat on the phone, and he surprised me by hiring some help.

I'm still in shock.

When I hung up the phone earlier this morning, I had steam coming out of my ears. And it seemed strange that he couldn't take a little break and run home. We only live about ten minutes from the plant. He used to come home for lunch all the time.

Now, I'm wondering what's going on with him.

No, I won't even think about it.

Besides, he did come home today, *and* he got us a housekeeper. I can't help but wonder what it'll be like to have someone else in the house with me. And a colored woman at that? A new experience, for sure.

"Mama?" Mellie's voice interrupts my thoughts.

"What, honey?"

"Can I put my rose in a vase?"

"Sure, darling. There's one on the top shelf, over the stove."

From the sofa, I can see the stove right beside the open kitchen door. Mellie stands on a chair and reaches into the back of the cabinet. She holds up a bud vase from a long ago florist delivery. "This one?" she asks.

"That's fine." I pick up the newspaper and scan the headlines. *Cuba. Russia. Missiles. Kennedy.* Another story about Marilyn Monroe's recent suicide. The newspapers can't seem to get over the fact that she was nude when they found her. That poor woman is never going to have any peace, even in death.

If this new housekeeper, Flossie, can just take care of the standing chores for me—the ironing, the dishes, some of the laundry—I'll feel like a queen. Mellie's helped out an awful lot over the summer, but she'll be back in school in a few weeks. That means I'll be ironing dresses for the girls as well as Clayton's dress shirts.

My Mellie sits down on the floor beside the sofa, the bud vase on the floor next to her.

I run my fingers through her silky ponytail. She still looks like a younger girl with her hair like that. But she'll want to look older for the seventh grade, I'm sure. "We need to do your hair before school starts, sweetie. How about a permanent wave?"

"Oh, do we have to?" Mellie picks up a section of newspaper from my lap.

"If you have a permanent, your hair will look so nice when we set it with rollers. Don't you want to look pretty for junior high?"

She shrugs like she doesn't care a bit about school starting. But I know that's not how she feels. Mellie tugs at a loose strand of hair and twirls it around her finger.

Her hair is brown like Clay's. Really, she looks so much like him. She's going to be a beauty, but she has no idea of that now.

I wish I could read her mind. She's quiet so much of the time, and I just can't tell what she's thinking.

Mellie is so different from Birdie, sometimes I can't believe I gave birth to both of them. Birdie is like a flashing neon sign telling everything there is to know about her, while Mellie is like a beautiful book you have to patiently study to understand. Will this baby be like Mellie or Birdie, or someone completely different?

What did I think about when I was twelve? I don't remember at all, but I do remember that everything seemed important, urgent, overwhelming. So, what is urgent and important to Mellie? Not a permanent wave, that's for sure.

I guess twelve was when I started learning to dance by practicing with my sister, preparing for the time we could go to the dances at the park.

But, somehow, Melanie seems too serious to be thinking about silly stuff like dancing. In fact, sometimes she seems sad. Am I a bad mother if my child is sad?

That's the $64,000 Question.

"Honey, I'm sorry about your birthday."

"It's okay, Mama."

"No, it's not okay. But thank you for understanding. Things are a little hectic right now."

Mellie turns and rests her cheek against my tummy. "Oh. He kicked me."

I grin. "Maybe she kicked you."

Shaking her head, Mellie says, "No. This is a boy. I just know it."

"Well, we'll find out in about eight more weeks, won't we?"

"Are you scared, Mama?"

"About having the baby? No. I've done it twice before, remember?"

Mellie smiles and slips a loose strand of hair into the corner of her mouth. Her brows dip into a frown.

"What's wrong, sweetie?"

"I don't know." Mellie shrugs and flips a page of the newspaper.

I catch a glimpse of the ads for back-to-school sales. Maybe that's why she's down in the dumps. "Why don't we go shopping tomorrow? Just you and me?"

"Are you sure you feel like shopping, Mama?"

"Listen to you, all worried about me when you're about to start junior high school." I sit up on the sofa. "We'll leave Birdie with Daddy." Pointing to the tartan plaid purse and scarf ad in the corner of the page, I say, "Do you like the plaid? Maybe we can find a kilt for you. Wouldn't that be cute with a white blouse?"

Mellie twists her hair and studies the paper. Is she reading the article about the Kennedy's vacation in Italy? Maybe she's thinking about how we didn't have a vacation this year—or last year. We'll make it up to her soon.

Beginning with a few new school clothes. "What about that shopping trip?"

Melanie shrugs and turns the page of the newspaper. Now she's reading the comic strips. I have no idea what's going on in her mind, but I intend to find out.

Monday
August 20, 1962

MELANIE

I've only got two weeks of summer left. Some days I can't wait for summer to end so I can begin school and see what being a teenager is like. I want to speed things up, to rush through these slow days and get on with my life.

Other days, I want to stop time. I want to keep the days from being sliced away by the cracking lightning in the afternoons. I want the crickets to keep singing at night and the dew to drip off the roof with the same steady beat forever.

This is what I know, this sweet and familiar melody and rhythm.

Stephanie and I count down the days until school starts, making plans and stuff.

"We need to pick out our trademark swear words. Which word do you want?" Steph says, as she reaches under her twin bed and pulls out the dictionary with paper clips stuck in several places.

"I'm not allowed to swear. Mama will wash my mouth out with soap."

Steph curls her lip into a sneer. "Dummy, we won't swear in front of our parents. Just when we're hanging around." She straightens her plaid bedspread before she sits.

"Oh, okay." I've decided that since I have to be twelve, I might as well try to enjoy it. So, I do pretty much whatever my best friend suggests, since she has her sixteen-year-old sister's example to follow.

The trouble is, I don't know many swear words. Daddy only uses one, and then he has to be really mad. I know it's a really bad word, so I would never use it. And Mama doesn't swear at all. At least, not out loud. Sometimes I think I hear her say *shit* under her breath. But she might be saying *shoot* or *sugar*. I can't really tell.

"I like *hell*." Steph gets up off the bed and pauses. "No, that's not dramatic enough." She throws the dictionary into the pillows stacked at the head of her bed. "Hellfire!" she shouts. "Yeah. That's better."

I look toward the door, waiting for Mrs. Starr to come in, but then I remember she's having coffee with the other Navy wives at Mrs. Shultz's house. Steph's sister is on the telephone in the living room.

Stephanie stomps her feet. "Hellfire!" She looks at me with a big grin. "What do you think?"

"That's pretty dramatic. When do you think you'll use it?"

"Oh, all the time. Like when I stub my toe, I'll whisper *hellfire*." She walks to the dresser and pretends to bump her foot against it. "Ow! Hellfire," she mutters, and hops on one foot.

"I see."

"So, what's your word?"

"I don't know yet." I pick up the dictionary and thumb through a few pages. "I need something simple and elegant. A word that won't get me into too much trouble if Mama hears me."

"Well, while you're reading the whole dictionary from front to back, be thinking about another thing. We need to fall in love."

I close the book. "Damn. What did you say?"

"*Damn.* That's a good word for you, Mellie. In fact, it's perfect."

"No, what did you say about love?"

"We need to have some experience with being in love. We don't want to be complete babies in the seventh grade."

"Okay, *damn* can be my word, but I don't know anybody I want to fall in love with." The only boy our age I can think of is Marvin Gordon who lives on the next block. With his surly attitude and pimply face, only his mother could love him. Absolutely not me.

"The boy doesn't have to be someone you really *know*." Stephanie rolls her eyes at me like I'm the biggest dope in the world. My confidence takes a hit. If my best friend thinks I'm hopeless, how will I ever make it through seventh grade?

Steph grabs a bundle of letters tied with pink ribbon and kisses them before holding them to her chest. "I'm in love with Nigel."

"Nigel lives in England," I remind her. "You've never even met him. He's just your pen pal."

"I know that. But we share our deepest secrets in our letters. We have a real bond."

After I think about it for a minute, I decide it's kind of smart to pick someone to love who lives all the way across the ocean. I mean, that way you're in complete control of when you talk to him, and you only have to see him when you pick up his picture. It sounds pretty painless all the way around. I wish I'd signed up for the pen pal program at school the year before. But since I don't have a pen pal, I have to choose someone I actually know.

We hear a lawnmower sputter to life. I walk to the window and peek through the blinds. Robert Taylor is mowing old Mrs. Kraft's yard across the street. His t-shirt's already off, and his brown shoulders are shiny with sweat. My heart does a little flip in my chest.

Maybe I'm already in love.

I know for sure I love the way Robert looks. His brown hair is streaked kind of blond in some places from working outside all summer. His tan makes his eyes shine like clear blue water, and his smile is big and bright. Yes, I love the way Robert looks, for sure. That's a good enough place to start. Except that he's a couple of years older than me.

"Okay," I sigh. "Robert."

"Robert Taylor?" Stephanie looks really surprised. She stands beside me and opens the blinds to look out at the street. "Hmm. Good choice, Mel." She considers a little longer, then turns around and rests her hands on her hips. "Very good."

Robert Taylor is almost sixteen and drives a motor scooter with sparkly blue paint. That makes him a little dangerous. All the other older boys drive jalopies they pretend are hot rods.

Not Robert. He zips around on his motorbike and mows lawns. On the days he does yard work, I ride my bicycle up and down the street so I can watch him. After he cuts a few swipes in a front yard, he'll take off his white t-shirt and stuff it in the waistband of his jeans.

"Robert's shoulders are so brown, his skin looks like a chocolate malt." I didn't think anyone but Steph could hear me, but Cherie came into the room making a big deal of licking her lips.

"Mmm, I'll bet he tastes as good as a chocolate malt, too."
I think she just saw an old Marilyn Monroe movie because she
puckers her mouth and nearly closes her eyes while pushing her
boobies together with her arms. All of the drive-ins play those
movies nonstop since Marilyn committed suicide a couple of
weeks ago.

But Cherie made me think. How does a boy taste? How
does Robert taste? Sweet, like chocolate malt, or salty and hot,
like he looks right now as he mows the lawn? Thinking like
that makes me want to touch my tongue to my arm and see
what skin tastes like.

Of course, I don't. Not in front of Steph and Cherie.
Maybe later.

Deep inside, I know I only have a crush on Robert.
Stephanie thinks love is just giggles and fun. Mama told me
about real love, like when she met Daddy. And I've seen what it
looks like, too. Like when Daddy stretches his arms around
Mama's big belly and holds her tight in his arms.

In the afternoon, we walk down to the corner store to get a
Coke and look at the magazines. Stephanie's hair is set on
gigantic curlers, and she has one of her mom's scarves tied
around it. For some reason, that's supposed to make it look
okay to go out in public. When you see a woman with her hair
like that, you know she's going somewhere. Stephanie's going
to the movies with Cherie tonight. I'm not going anywhere, so
my hair is in a ponytail, like always.

At the store, I take my Coke bottle and lean against the
paperback bookrack and pick up the book I'd started reading
the last time we were in the store. I go right to page fourteen,
where I'd left off. The girl was just about to go in the office to
see her boss about the big mess she'd made of some project she
was working on. I wanted to get to the big kiss, the one on the

cover of the book. I do like to read about love.

Stephanie sits cross-legged on the floor in front of the movie magazines and reads about Elizabeth Taylor and Richard Burton. She keeps flipping the pages back to the picture of Elizabeth Taylor dressed up like Cleopatra.

"Hellfire, look who's coming in," Stephanie whispers around the big wad of bubblegum in her mouth.

I just got to the good part, so I don't even look up. "Who?"

"Oh, my God, he's coming over here." Steph sounds panicked. The curlers in her hair clack together as she stands up. "Sheesh!" She slips off toward the employee's bathroom.

I don't want to stop reading yet, and besides, she'll be back in a minute. Whoever's coming to find Steph can just wait.

"Hi, Mellie."

That voice. It's cool and thick, like ice cream in a bowl on a summer afternoon. Rich, like chocolate ice cream melting slowly from the heat.

I look up and see the tight white t-shirt. A shaky feeling rips through me, and my hands go all cold and clammy.

"Hey, Robert." My voice hardly wavers at all. I can be cool. I hope.

"Your mom wants me to give you a ride home. She needs you."

"What's wrong with Mama? It's too early for the baby to come!"

"Slow down." Robert sees I'm getting upset. "Nothing's wrong with your mom. Birdie fell off her skates and hurt her arm."

A big sigh of relief whooshes out of me, leaving my lungs feeling collapsed. "That's all?"

"Melanie, your dad's on his way home. They're taking Birdie to the hospital."

Now I feel scared again. "Really? She's hurt that bad?"

"Let's go. You can see for yourself." Robert takes my hand and leads me out the door to his motor scooter.

Oh, my gosh, Robert's holding my hand. I have to look down at our hands joined together to be sure it's really happening. It's not like *romantic* handholding, but gee, this is the first time a boy's ever held my hand when nobody told him to. Where the heck is Stephanie? She's got to see this.

Outside the store, Robert puts his extra helmet on my head, smashing my ponytail. The helmet is too big, and he pushes it back out of my eyes before snapping the strap on the side.

Thoughts whiz around in my brain as fast as the electrons and protons they showed us on the filmstrip in science class. Finally, I manage to say, "Why didn't Mama send Caroline?"

Caroline is Robert's older sister. She baby-sits for Birdie and me. Not that I need a babysitter anymore. And actually, I'm glad Robert is here. Glad in a breathless, heart-stopping kind of way.

"Caroline is working at Woolworth's." Robert throws his leg over the saddle seat on the scooter and pats the shiny plastic behind him. "Get on, squirt. I won't bite."

I climb on. Damn, where is Stephanie? She won't believe this. The scooter roars to life, sending vibrations from my butt to the top of my head. I look back and see Stephanie's face plastered to the dirty window of the store, right between the Winston and Marlboro signs. Her mouth is hanging open in shock.

When Robert tugs my arms around his waist, my mouth drops open to match Steph's.

So many sensations sweep over me I can't sort them out. I try to be like a sponge and soak them all up so I can think about them later. I want to remember what Robert's hands feel like on mine, what his back feels like against my chest. Are my breasts even big enough for him to feel them against his back? I stare at his neck for a long minute to memorize the way his hair grows and the pattern of the four freckles behind his right ear. Then my nose bumps into his shoulder blade and all I can smell is white.

I know you can't really smell a color, but some things do smell white or red or blue or brown. White smells like bleach, sunshine, baby powder or fresh milk. A scent so clean and bright that it makes you feel good, and makes everything seem right. That's what Robert smells like.

I really hate that Birdie is hurt. But, riding with Robert is about the best thing that's happened all summer. I make a promise to myself to be extra nice to her for a while.

When we get home, Daddy is carrying her out the front door with Mama rushing out behind them. She slams the door. Birdie whimpers. She has a bag of frozen peas tied around her arm with a dishtowel. I know she's really hurt because she's so quiet. I feel terrible. I slide off the motorbike and suddenly all of those wonderful feelings I experienced on the ride home vanish. I tug off Robert's helmet and hand it to him before I rush toward the car, biting my lip to keep from crying. This is the first time any of us has been hurt bad enough to go to the hospital.

All of the awful things I've ever said or done to Birdie seem to sink to my stomach, making it heavy and sick.

"Mellie." Mama puts both her hands on my cheeks and kisses my forehead. "You stay here, okay? Robert's mother said you could have dinner with them if we're very late. Mind your manners, you hear?"

NORAH

Birdie whimpers in the back seat and my heart just breaks. I wish I could climb into the back seat with her, but my baby belly is just too big. Poor darlin'. "I know it must hurt, sweetheart. We'll be there soon and they'll make you feel better."

"Mama, I don't want a shot."

I glance at Clay. His cheek twitches with a half smile. "Sugar," he says, "we don't know what the doctors will do. But they might have to give you a shot."

Birdie wails.

I mutter, "Now you've done it."

Clay cuts a hard look at me. "What? They may have to give her a shot. She needs to prepare for it."

Birdie wails again.

I rub my temples against a building headache. It's so hot, I can barely breathe. "But you could have let the doctors tell her. She wouldn't be screaming now."

He reaches over and pats my hand. I'm surprised by how much I want to pull away from him. But then he'd ask what's wrong, and I'd have to try to explain something I don't even understand myself.

Clay tries to make me feel better. He tries to understand. But he just doesn't know what it's like for me.

Like today. I let Birdie do something so ordinary—roller skate in our own driveway—and I still can't keep her safe.

And poor Mellie. I think she was about to cry. But Clay said it would be boring for her at the hospital.

I know he's right. She would have been bored. But I think I

would've wanted to be with my family when something like this happened. "We should have brought Mellie with us."

"Why?"

"She'll be worried."

"Yes, and she would be worried at the hospital, too. She's a big girl."

I glare at Clay. "Yes, she's a big girl, and we left her alone with a big boy." Doesn't he remember what it was like when we were young and left alone? For all his talk about letting Mellie grow up, he doesn't realize that she's grown-up enough to get into trouble. Trouble that we don't even want to think about just now.

Clay laughs. "You're worried about Robert? I'm sure he's already taken off again on his motorscooter. She'll be fine, Norah."

How does he know that?

At least I locked the door. I don't have to worry about Mellie and that boy being alone together in the house.

It seems like nothing will be fine, ever again. It must be the hormones making me antsy like this. But then, talking to that crazy Rachel Winston next door doesn't help any.

Her husband's a Navy pilot and I have no idea why they live in our neighborhood. They can afford a better house than they have, or even live on base like most of the pilots. The gossips—who I try not to listen to, but sometimes the gossip just rings true—say Bob Winston doesn't want his wife living on base because there are too many men around. They also say he has alimony to pay to his first wife, so there's not that much left over for a nicer house. But Rachel doesn't do without anything that I can see.

She drives a Thunderbird that's just a year old, she gets that prissy poodle groomed regularly, and her hair and nails are always done. I'm sure she doesn't do any of that herself. The beauty shop must love her.

I don't care about any of those things. I really don't. But when she says stuff like, "*What a shame your poor baby won't grow up,*" and "*I won't have children in a world that's on the edge of nuclear war,*" what can I think but that she's crazy?

Except I have my own niggling doubts. After all, her husband is flying a lot of missions, so she probably knows things we civilians don't. And the newspaper is full of stories about Khrushchev and the Russians.

I rub my temples again and let out a big breath. Birdie has finally quieted down.

Clay squeezes my hand. "It'll be okay, honey. I promise."

I wish he could make everything okay.

He pulls into the hospital parking area and takes a ticket from the parking attendant.

I turn in my seat and reach back to touch Birdie's knee. "We're here, sweetie."

She whimpers. "I don't want a shot, Mama."

MELANIE

I stand in the front yard with Robert and watch until our car disappears. I pull the neck of my shirt up to wipe the sweat off my upper lip, then remember Mama yelling at me about leaving a dingy mark smack dab in the middle of all my shirts. I pretend I was just straightening my shirt after the motorbike ride, but I still rub by face with both hands, just in case any tears leak out.

Robert soft-punches my arm and says, "Want a Popsicle,

squirt?"

I nod. "I think we have some in the freezer."

"No, my treat. Here comes the ice cream truck."

I hadn't even heard the jangle of the music. I always hear the ice cream truck, even blocks away.

"You go on in the house. What flavor do you want?"

"Banana."

"Hey, you've got good taste. Banana's my favorite, too."

The ice cream truck clangs to a stop at the curb, the music sounding scratchy. I turn and head toward the porch. I just want to get inside my cool house where everything can get back to normal. The doorknob is hot and slick under my hand, and it won't budge. Mama must have locked it when she slammed it closed. I walk across the front of the house to the screened porch on the side. I don't slam the screen door, but there is no one here to scold me, anyway.

"Damn," I mutter. Tears burn behind my eyelids again. Louder I say, "Damn it all." That feels better, but the tears are building, and it feels like they're going to burst free any second. It's all too much. Birdie is hurt, maybe dying, who knows? Mama is so PG she can barely fit into the car anymore. And Robert is being nice to me because he knows how pitiful I am.

"Here's your Popsicle, pipsqueak."

"Hey, I'm no pipsqueak anymore. I'm starting junior high in case you don't remember, scooter boy." I hope Robert understands that I'm trying to be cool like he is, because I'm afraid I sounded kind of rude.

But he smiles at me. *Whew.*

"Oh, that's right. I forgot." He shoves the Popsicle at me and drags the other folding chair next to my flattened chaise lounge. "You nervous about it?"

I peel the paper away from my Popsicle and watch the

melted syrup make shiny strings down the sides. I shrug and stick both halves of the two-stick Popsicle in my mouth. I can't think about anything right now except Birdie.

"C'mon. You can level with Scooter Boy." Robert bites off a big hunk of frozen yellow ice and squints his eyes against the sudden freezing feeling I know is seeping into his teeth. Crunching on the ice, he says, "It's okay, Mellie. Everybody's scared."

Impossible, I think. Not Robert. Not Cherie. Not even Stephanie. They all seem to be perfectly content with themselves and the way their lives are going. Happy even. No one can be as miserable as I am.

I suck on one side of the Popsicle and then the other. All of a sudden it seems really important to keep the twin pops even. "I don't think everybody's scared, Robert."

"Call me Rob." He breaks his Popsicle in half and puts one stick in his mouth while he holds the other away from him to keep it from dripping on his jeans. "Yeah, they're scared. Even me. Okay? I'm scared." He looks me right in the eyes then. He lowers his voice a little and says, "But don't say anything, all right?"

I figure he's trying to make me feel better, make me stop worrying about Birdie, so I play along. "Sure thing. But what are you scared of? You're almost out of high school."

"I am out of high school."

I laugh because I know Robert has a couple of years of school to go.

"Don't go nuts on me, like my mom, okay? I turn sixteen in a few weeks and I joined the Navy. I'm shipping out the end of September."

"You quit school?"

"I'm not all that great at books and things, you know. I'm

good at fixing stuff, like my scooter. I don't need a diploma for that, but I do need someone to train me. That's what the Navy's gonna do for me."

"But what about college?"

"Caroline's the one who should go to college, not me. I know what I want to do. I want to work on jets. They're the future, you know."

He sticks the other half of his Popsicle in his mouth, like he needs some time to think.

"Besides, this whole Cuba situation is pretty serious. We don't really know what those Russian commies are doing these days. And I got to thinking about what President Kennedy said. I can do this for my country. My old man is Navy. It's not a bad life, he says."

A jet roars over us, causing the windows in the back door to shake.

"See," Robert—Rob—continues, "those guys need help. I'm going to train to work on the jets on aircraft carriers. I'll probably end up in Gitmo with the Mayfields. Anyway, I'll get to see the world."

He would be in Guantanamo Bay with our old neighbors. Probably cuddled up on a Cuban beach with the beautiful Brooke Mayfield. He'd been kind of sweet on her before she moved. All I can think is that I won't get to see Robert mow lawns anymore. Life really does stink.

"Gitmo, huh? You can tell Brooke and Kevin I said hi."

"Sure thing, pipsqueak." Robert chews on his empty Popsicle stick for a minute before breaking it in half. "So, 'fess up. What're you scared about, Mellie?"

"Oh, I don't know. I'm worried about the baby and Mama." Robert's looking at me with his big blue eyes, and I know I can tell him the truth. "I'm scared about being twelve. I hate it."

I wish I could suck those words back into my mouth like I stop the juice dripping down my Popsicle. Here, Robert is about to join the Navy, and I'm whining about being twelve. Damn, I'm such a goon.

But he just looks at me as though I said something that made sense. "Yeah, I know. It's tough. But, Mellie, you're a good kid. You'll make it fine."

Robert rolls his Popsicle sticks in the wrapper, the broken and whole one together. I suck the last bit of ice from mine. Robert tells me about the good teachers and the bad ones at the junior high. I'm dying to ask him some really important questions, like how do I get a boy to like me? I think Robert would tell me. He's that kind of guy. But I don't have the guts. I don't want him to think I'm a stupid kid.

For a little while, we just sit together on the porch. Steph walks up the street in her going-out-later head scarf and I call to her.

She doesn't even look at my house. I wonder what's wrong with her. In the distance a train whistle sounds. Must be the five-thirty run crossing Beaver Street. Dogs bark and blue jays sing and the sun slips lower in the sky, turning the clouds into spun pink frosting. Marla and Paula, the twins who live behind us, sing "The Lion Sleeps Tonight" and try to cover all the parts.

It's nice sitting here with Robert.

Then I think, gee, this must be what it's like when Mama and Daddy sit on the porch. I always thought it was so boring for them. That they couldn't think of anything to do, so they just sat here. But now I know that they are doing something. Being together.

Our blue Ford pulls into the carport. I jump up and run to

Mama's side of the car.

"Is Birdie okay?"

Mama nods and opens the door.

"How's Birdie, Mr. Adams?" Robert asks as he holds the Ford's door open while Daddy gets Birdie out of the back seat.

Birdie's arm, tucked against her belly, is in a white cast and covered with a navy blue sling. The white strap is loose, draping off her shoulder. Her eyes blink open as Daddy picks her up. She snuggles her head against his chest.

She looks like a soft little baby, not my aggravating sister. My throat swells, and I look away.

"She's asleep, but she's fine. A little fracture is all." They walk through the porch and Mama opens the door with her key. Daddy carries Birdie inside.

Robert stands beside me on the carport. "I'm glad she's okay."

"Yeah. Me, too."

"Hey, we'll splurge and have a Nutty Buddy when I get back from basic training, okay?" He ruffles my bangs and goes to his motor scooter.

Mama comes back to the carport to stand beside me. "Thanks, Robert. Tell your mama I'll call her."

The motor scooter sputters to life and Robert waves. Shredded blades of grass spit out from the back tire.

Mama opens the screen door and I follow her in. She sits on the chaise lounge, making the webbing sag and groan. She picks up my rolled up Popsicle wrapper and sniffs. "Banana?"

"Um-hum. Did Birdie cry at lot at the hospital?"

Mama smiles and pats my back. "Yep, but she was excited about the cast. I'm sure that won't last."

I watch Robert and his beautiful white t-shirt disappear. "I feel so bad for Birdie, especially since Aunt Lola's coming next week, and we'll be going to beach."

"We'll manage." Mama tugs my ponytail. "How did you like riding on Robert's scooter?"

I look at her, and I can't think of a blessed thing to say. Everything that happened this afternoon whirls around in my head. I just keep thinking about how an awful thing like Birdie getting hurt, and a wonderful thing like riding on Robert's scooter happened together.

How am I supposed to feel? I shrug.

A few seconds later, I say, "Mama, you locked me out of the house."

She pats my back and tucks a stray hair into my ponytail. "I know, sweetheart."

"But, why? We couldn't get in."

"You can't be alone in the house with Robert. It wouldn't be proper." Mama pushes herself up and rubs her back for a few minutes before she walks to the back door.

"Why not? What wouldn't be proper?"

Mama looks up at the porch ceiling. "We need to wash this ceiling before too long." Without looking at me she says, "You'll understand one day, Melanie. It's never too early to protect your reputation."

Thursday
August 23, 1962

FLOSSIE

The city bus stops with creaks and groans at the entrance to the Adams' neighborhood. I step up on the curb and wait for the bus to leave before I take a good look around. I never worked in this area before, and I can tell by the houses that these folks aren't used to somebody like me bein' about.

I start walking. It's a nice place, neat little houses, probably ten years old or so, all concrete block with square yards and hardly a tree around. They ripped out nearly every tree to put up these houses. No shade trees at all, only a skinny pine tree here and there. I have a shade tree in my back yard, for sure.

No, these aren't the kind of white folks who hire help. They do the work themselves unless something is happening, like bad health or a baby on the way, like Miz Adams.

Most likely, today I'll be breaking in another white woman who never had a colored woman in her house. Won't be the first time. Most times, it just takes a couple of visits until a white woman relaxes and lets me do my job.

I wonder if Miz Adams has gone and cleaned her whole

house today. First time I went to Miz Grant's house, that's what she did. Plum wore herself out, too. Her son was fit to be tied when he came to visit his mama that afternoon and gave me my check. He finds her stretched out on the sofa having heart palpations. He gave his mama what for, sayin' that's why he hired me in the first place, to keep her from workin' herself to death.

I sure do miss Miz Grant. Once she relaxed, we had a good couple of years. Even got to the point where we'd sit at the table and eat lunch together. Not that either one of us would tell anybody 'bout that.

I don't expect that Miz Adams and me'll be getting too friendly. My brother Max says this job is just 'til Miz Adams gets back on her feet after the baby comes. She's already got two girls, so she'll be wantin' to make sure she sets a good example for the children: whites and coloreds keep separate.

No matter. We'll work things out. I'm glad for the work. I tug my handkerchief out to wipe the sweat off my face. The street is already bakin' hot in the sun.

Since Miz Grant died two months ago, I've had every Monday and Thursday to myself. At first, it was fine. I got my garden going real good, and for the first time in a long while, my own house is as clean as I want it.

Thing is, my pocketbook didn't like me bein' that free. I started sitting in the dark with only my fan blowin', so's to save on the electric. Don't want to use up any more of my savings. Yes, sir, I'm glad for the work.

I check the paper Max gave me with the address and directions on it. I walk up this street and then turn onto Parade Drive. Then, the Adams live on Victory Lane. Seems like strange street names to me, but I'm thinkin' they must be called like this 'cause of the Navy base over here. I don't guess

Cecil Field is too terribly far from this neighborhood, but I don't really know this side of town. I work mostly on the Southside, 'cross the river from here.

Some boys carrying baseball bats come walking out of a house on the corner. I can't help but shiver at the sight. Of course, they've got gloves, too. They're just going to play some ball.

Two years ago, a bunch of white folks took bats and ax handles to those colored folks doing the sit-ins at Woolworth's downtown. Max's boy was downtown that day, and got hisself beat up pretty bad. He's gone off to college now, but the mad in that boy gonna burn him up one day.

Of course, we all got things to be mad 'bout. Yeah, I hope that one day soon I'm gonna eat my Saturday lunch at the counter in Woolworth's instead of havin' to get my hot dog at the backside of the store. One day I'm gonna sit wherever I want to on the city bus.

That day isn't here yet, but I'm not gonna let the mad burn the joy outta my life. No, sir.

I just hope my nephew can find some peace in his soul.

And here I am at the Adams' house. Neat as a pin, it is. That grass so green and trim, it looks like it was painted on. The windows, though, seems to need a cleaning. Lord, I hate those jalousie windows. Those slats of glass catch all kind of dust and my big old hand hardly fits between them. They got the whole front of the house full of 'em, and the front door, too. Lord.

A woman's voice sounds through the open front window. "Birdie, I told you to make sure the Tinker Toys were picked up. She's going to be here soon."

Sure enough, sounds like Miz Adams went and cleaned her whole house up for me. Laws o' mercy. I walk up the driveway and give a knock on the door.

A little girl with hair that's almost white opens the door 'bout soon as I knock. She grins so big, her face nearly splits open. Cute as a button she is, with her two front teeth missin' and a big ol' cast on her arm.

"Mama! The colored lady is here," she shouts, like there's a mile between her and her mama.

Miz Adams rushes up behind the girl and holds onto her shoulders like she gonna get grabbed or something. "Hello, Flossie."

I give her my best smile. "Howdy do, Miz Adams."

We study each other for a minute before it dawns on Miz Adams that she's gonna have to let me inside if I'm gonna do any work for her. It's like that sometimes when I start a new job. Sometimes I wonder what they're thinkin'. They gonna change their mind and decide they don't want help? But no, that doesn't happen.

"Oh," Miz Adams says, like she just realizes all this. "Come in. Birdie, finish picking up those toys."

The little girl grins even bigger then ducks around her mama. Miz Adams says, "That's Beatrice, but we call her Birdie."

"Miss Beatrice." I nod hello and step inside. It feels so good to get out of the heat. Even though it's only nine o'clock, the sun is beatin' down. There's a fan blowing and the air is cooler in the house. I sit my shopping bag down on the floor and reach up to take off my hat. Miz Adams closes the door behind me, rattlin' those dreadful jalousie windows.

The kitchen door is straight ahead of me as I stand there. Another girl peeks out from the kitchen. She's older, somewhere around eleven or twelve. She got that look of a girl about to bust into the teenaged years. I smile at her and she gives me a shy smile back.

Miz Adams turns to look at what I'm smilin' at. "This is Melanie."

Holding my hat in front of me, I say, "Well it's nice to meet you, Miss Melanie and Miss Beatrice. You can call me Flossie, if that's okay with your mama."

"You can call me Birdie," the little one pipes up. She's got a pile of Tinker Toys scooped up in her shirttail, like eggs collected in an apron.

"I'll be happy to, Miss Birdie. Miz Adams, is there somewhere I can put my things?"

"Oh, sure." She steps aside and opens a small coat closet. "Will it fit in here? I can clean a space up for you in a bit."

"No need to clean up for me. There's plenty of room for my bag right here on the floor." I shut the closet door and turn to look at Miz Adams. She's just staring at me.

I know she don't mean nothin' by it. She just don't quite know how to handle this situation. It's up to me to help us get settled in. "Well, Miz Adams, what can I do for you today? My brother, Max—he works with your husband—said you needed some help, so you wouldn't be hurtin' your feet and legs."

She looks over her pregnant belly to her feet like she expects them to be giving her a problem. They do look a little swollen for so early in the morning. But she doesn't say anything.

"Why don't I start with the breakfast dishes and you can think on whatever you want me to do next? I can hang out the laundry, make up the beds, do the ironing, and then sweep up, probably all before lunch. Then we can decide what to do this afternoon. How does that sound?"

"Oh." She looks so relieved. "That sounds wonderful. Melanie was washing the dishes, but if you can finish that up, she can help me fold these clothes." Miz Adams waves to a pile of laundry on the couch. "I'm just not used to having anybody else in the house."

"I understand. After a few of my visits, this will be just like it was always goin' on. You just get off your feet and relax. I'll take care of everything."

She sighs and gives me a big smile. "Yes, I'm sure I'll get used it. Thank you. Thank you for coming."

The older girl, Melanie, is standing in the kitchen door listening to all this. She smiles and slips past me to stand by her mama.

I take about ten steps and I'm in the kitchen. These new houses sure skimp on kitchen space. There's no room for a table, but the dining table is just through the other kitchen door. I suppose that's easy for servin' if a family has to eat in at the big table for every meal. I guess I'll be standin' up for my lunch.

I get to work, scrubbin' at the plates in the sink. Miz Adams and Melanie start folding the laundry. Pretty soon, Birdie joins me at the sink.

"Can I help?"

"You sure you want to help me?"

She nods her head real fast.

"Do you help your mama wash the dishes?"

She nods her head again.

I 'spect she doesn't. She only wants to help me because I'm new. She wants a chance to study me, like. "Okay, then. I'll let you rinse."

"Thank you," she says, nice and polite.

"Birdie, come in here and don't be bothering her." Miz Adams raises her voice a bit, but we can hear her just fine through the open doors. Really, the kitchen, dining room and living room are one big space, with just a corner wall kind of stuck in the middle so you can put a Frigidaire behind it.

Birdie glances up at me and grins. "But Mama. I'm helping."

"She's not botherin' me, Miz Adams, if you don't mind her rinsing the dishes. It'll keep her busy, don't you think?"

"If you're sure she won't be in your way. And Birdie, you've got to keep that cast dry."

The girl tucks her arm against her tummy, like she needs to remind herself not to put it in the water. "I will Mama."

"Don't worry, Miz Adams. We'll be fine. Birdie here will most likely get tired and want to go play soon, anyway."

"You're right," Miz Adams says. "Birdie doesn't stay interested in anything very long. I suppose when you've finished with the dishes, you can hang out the laundry. I've got some mending I need to take care of."

"Yes'm. I'll do that."

Me and Birdie settle in nice at the sink. Maybe it won't be hard to teach this family how to have some help after all.

Saturday
August, 25, 1962

Atlanta, Georgia

LOLA

"C'mon a my house, ah, my house. I'm gonna give you candy."
I splash my hands in the dishwater and sing along while
Rosemary Clooney croons the last phrase.

The record player in the living room slaps down another
forty-five. *Scratch, scratch, scratch*. The needle is stuck again.

Wiping my hands on my shorts, I go to start the record.
Peggy Lee croons "Fever" as I dance back to the kitchen. I have
to have music while I finish up the dishes.

Stan is outside mowing the lawn for me. This little house I
rent is cheap, but I'm supposed to keep up the yard. Good
thing I met Stan shortly after I moved in here. He does a good
job with the lawn and other handyman chores. In fact, he does
a very good job with any *manly* task.

I light one of his Pall Malls and watch him through the
kitchen window. When is he going to pop the question and
make this playing house the real thing? We're pretty good

together.

Unlike that last guy I dated, Claude. What a stick in the mud he was. Of course, Norah and Clay thought Claude was the cat's meow. All sticks in the mud together.

But sometimes I think I'd be real happy with the life Norah has. She stays at home doing a few little chores, and Clay takes care of everything else.

I almost had what Norah has. Almost. But I won't think about Michael now. I only think about Michael when I'm alone and in the dark like he is. It's been five years since the car crash that killed Michael. It didn't kill me.

No. I'm alive, with a bad back and a broken heart.

Checking the clock, I take a long drag on my cigarette. Almost time for another pain pill. I'll make it.

Too bad I won't be able to go to Jacksonville for Labor Day like I usually do. But my back is killing me and that eight-hour drive from Atlanta will just do me in, I know it. Stan could drive, but Norah would probably tick him off by not letting us sleep together at her house. My God, she still thinks I'm a virgin at thirty. So, I'll go to his boss' cookout with him instead of going to the beach with Norah and the kids.

Outside, the mower coughs to a shuddering stop. That's my cue to get the beer mugs out of the freezer and pour Stan a cold one. It's the least I can do for him.

Stan comes through the back door wiping his face and head with his balled up shirt. His bristly blond crew cut stands right back up after the brisk rubbing. I walk over with his mug. He smiles, plants a big smacker right on my mouth, and then directs my hand with the cigarette to his lips. "Baby, you're too good to me, you know that?" he says, blowing smoke over my head.

"You're right. I'm too good for you." Sweat is running

down his bare chest, flattening and darkening the soft gold hair. I trace a pattern with my finger down to his nipple then swirl around it.

He grabs my hips and grinds against me. "Want to get a shower with me?"

"My back is hurting from that twist contest last night." I open my pill bottle and pop one in my mouth, washing it down with the ice-cold beer. I wink at him. "How about you give me a massage when you get out?"

He slaps me on the fanny and whistling, heads for my tiny bathroom.

In my bedroom, I lie down on the bed. Might as well deliver the bad news about Labor Day to Norah and the kids. I pick up the phone and dial her number.

MELANIE

The phone on the kitchen wall rings as I pass by, so I snatch it up. "Hello?"

"Hi ya, sugar." A familiar voice sounds like warm syrup dripping over a stack of pancakes. Anticipation grows inside me with that same warm flow.

"Aunt Lola! When are you coming? We can't wait."

"Well, sugar, I've run into a little problem here."

"Oh, no." All the warm anticipation gets cold and sticky, like dirty pancake plates. "What's happened?"

"Don't sound so serious, Mel. You always take everything so hard."

Lola sounds funny, kind of slow and sleepy. In the background, I can hear the slide and click as her cigarette lighter closes and she makes a blowing sound. I picture the way the smoke wraps around her head and her eyelids droop, but don't quite close. Lola calls it her smoldering look. I think she looks like a smoldering trash fire sometimes, all white smoke and bright colored papers shifting in the breeze while they burn.

"Aunt Lola? Are you all right?"

"I just won a twist contest down at the American Legion Post."

"Neat-o!"

Aunt Lola wins contests all the time. Mama says her sister ended up with all the luck in the whole family. Once, Lola answered a question right on a call-up radio contest and won a real mink stole. When I tried it on, the fur was silky and the satin lining made me feel rich and grown-up, like I should have my hair in a French twist instead of a ponytail. I got to wear the mink stole for ten whole minutes while Mama did some alterations to a dress she'd made for Lola.

"What did you win this time?" I asked.

"You mean besides the heart of my handsome new beau?" Aunt Lola laughs her deep, throaty laugh. She never giggles.

"A new beau? What happened to the last one?"

"It seems he had a previous commitment. But that's old news. I won fifty dollars in the twist contest."

"So, what's the problem? When are you going to be here?"

"I hurt my back, and I'm stuck in bed for a few days." She blows out another breath, and I close my eyes. I can almost smell the way Aunt Lola's "Evening in Paris" perfume blends with the cigarette smoke. It's a heavy scent that can almost smother you, but somehow Lola makes it seem glamorous. "Looks like I'll have to pass on the big end-of-summer shindig this year, sugar."

My heart sinks right to the floor. Labor Day will be a complete flop. Without Aunt Lola, summer is going to close with a whimper and a whine instead of beach parties, sunburns, and shrimp boils. My summer is now officially a total failure.

"Mellie? You still there?"

"Yeah." I swallow my disappointment and remember that Aunt Lola is really hurt. "Gee, I'm sorry you hurt your back."

"Don't worry about me. I've had some real good nursing." That's when I hear a man's voice murmuring in the background.

"Who's that?"

"My nurse checking on me."

"I never heard of a man being a nurse."

"Well, you have now." I hear muffled voices, and then Lola comes back on the line. "So, Mellie, you got any boobies yet?"

My face feels hot as a firecracker, and I'm glad Mama and Birdie aren't around. How am I supposed to answer that question? And what if that man is still there, listening?

I swallow my embarrassment and try for nonchalant. "Sure. I'm almost as big as you."

She laughs real hard at that. Aunt Lola has the biggest boobs you've ever seen in your life. I swear her bra can hold a couple of cantaloupes.

"That's a good one, Mel! How about the curse? Has it paid a visit yet?"

Damn! Can't a girl go through the torture of growing up without everyone prying into her private business? "You know, Aunt Lola, maybe it's a good thing you can't come down for Labor Day. I just remembered I have some big plans."

"Oh, come on, Mellie. Did I embarrass you? Don't carry on so. You'll be a member of the sorority soon enough. I'm looking forward to having you as my pledge. I'm gonna show you all the ropes," she purred. "Get ya started out right."

Mama comes in then. She mouths, "Who's that?"

"Sure thing, Aunt Lola. Well, here's Mama. Take care of yourself." I hand the phone to Mama and stomp off to the bathroom.

As much as I love Aunt Lola, and I really, truly do, sometimes she makes me furious. She can take a little something that you might want to keep a secret, and all of sudden she'll decide she wants to have some fun. It doesn't seem to matter that her fun might hurt somebody's feelings. Now that I think about it, Aunt Lola picks on me a whole lot. Mama says it's just because Lola loves me so much.

I splash water on my face and scrub it dry with a towel.

In the kitchen Mama's still on the phone. Kissing her cheek, I whisper, "I'm going to Steph's. Back in an hour."

"Umm." Mama nods at me and then says, "Lola, that's just like you, you know."

Free at last, I rush over to Steph's. We sit in the old swing set in her backyard. The rusty chains squeak every time we push at the ground with our feet. As the sun sets, the mourning doves coo. Mosquitoes buzz around my head.

"So, Aunt Lola's not coming," I said.

"Too bad." Stephanie pops her bubble gum. "I really had a good time riding in her convertible."

The last time Aunt Lola visited, she let us sit on top of the backseat, just like we were in a parade. Steph and I gave her directions to our friends' houses, especially the cute boys', and she drove us by real slow so we could wave at them. Then we went to the empty field behind the grocery store, and Lola spun the car around, cutting donuts in the dirt until we almost threw up on the leather seat.

"Did she tell you what color her hair is now?"

"Nope. But Mama told me Lola did a hair show for her hair dresser in the last few weeks, so who knows?"

"I'll bet it's red. Or maybe strawberry blonde."

"Honestly, there's just no telling. I guess we'll see when she comes to visit after the baby is born."

Steph and I swing back and forth for a long time, listening to the squeaky chains on the swings and thinking about riding in a red convertible. At least, that's what I'm thinking about.

"Tell me again what you and Robert talked about while Birdie was at the hospital," Steph says.

"I already told you everything." Of course, I didn't. Not everything. Like that Robert said he was scared. I didn't even tell her he was joining the Navy. "We just ate our Popsicles and he told me about the teachers at the junior high. We need to look out for Mrs. Marchman, according to Rob."

"Rob, huh?"

I shrug. "Yea. He wants me to call him Rob." Man, do I love saying things like that. Like I'm the only person who can call him Rob, special privilege for a special person. Sometimes I think Steph is jealous. "How come you didn't come up to the porch that day? You walked right by and didn't even wave or anything."

"I didn't want to interrupt you and your *boyfriend.*"

Yep. She's jealous. "Have you heard from Nigel lately?"

"He sent a new picture."

"Is he still cute?"

"No, he's still as ugly as ever." Steph laughs. "Since Aunt Lola's not coming, maybe you can go swimming with us at the pool on base." Stephanie stops swinging and props her foot on her knee. "Ow," she mutters. "I've got a sticker in my foot."

"Sandspur?"

"No, too small." Steph squints at her foot. "So, you want to go swimming at the pool?"

"Sure. That'd be fun. You know your mom has to call my mom, right?" I stand up.

"Right."

I watch Steph try to pull out the sticker. It's almost dark now, so she'll have to go inside and let her mom get it out with the tweezers.

Steph stands up and hops toward me. "Will you help me get inside?" Suddenly the little sticker in her foot hurts so bad she can't walk.

Steph puts her arm around my shoulder and we go inside her house.

Gee whiz. A little thing like a sticker can become a big deal real quick.

Labor Day
September 3, 1962

NORAH

This Labor Day weekend seems never-ending. It's hotter than blue blazes, and Birdie is driving me nuts because she wasn't invited to go swimming with Melanie and Stephanie. I understand how Birdie feels, but she's got to understand that her sister is six years older than she is. Most important of all, Birdie can't get her arm wet for another few weeks.

Her cast helped me to stand my ground. Honestly, I didn't even want Melanie to go, but Clay said the poor girl deserved to have a little fun before summer ended. That made me feel even worse. But still, I didn't want her to go. Then Clay put his foot down, more or less. He accused me of being over-protective and trying to keep our girl from growing up. I told him, *No, I'm her mother, and I'm doing my job.*

My idea of a perfect nightmare is a crowded swimming pool on a holiday where I can't watch out for my baby. Look what happened to Birdie right in our driveway, for goodness' sake. At least now she's right here in the back yard where I can watch her.

We spent the weekend getting things ready for the baby. Clay got the crib and playpen out of the utility closet and we scrubbed them down yesterday. We put them together today. Hand-me-down baby clothes and new cloth diapers are still flapping on the clothesline. We didn't have too many of Melanie or Birdie's things after six years, but in a neighborhood like ours someone is always giving away used layettes, swearing they'll never need them again. Just like I did.

At least the big items are still usable. Of course, I don't have a high chair or a stroller, but I don't need them right away. Maybe by the time I do, I'll have enough S&H Green Stamps saved up.

Through the kitchen window, I see Birdie playing on the swing set. Her stuffed monkey and two of her teddy bears are tied to one swing with a jump rope, while she dances around in front of them waving her arms, one arm wrapped in a dirty cast, like she's making grand announcements.

The clock on the stove reads four. Melanie should be home in another hour. I fix two glasses of iced tea to take outside. I want to sit with Clay and rest my feet and back for a little while.

The lawn chair creaks as I settle in and hand Clay his tea. "What is Birdie doing now?"

He stubs out his cigarette on the bottom of his shoe and sips his tea. Chuckling, he explains, "She's practicing for the circus."

Birdie skips across the lawn, stopping right in front of me. "Can I have a sip of your tea, Mama?"

"Sure. Are you playing circus?"

She shakes her head while she gulps half of the tea from my glass, then thrusts it back at me. "I'm not playing, I'm rehearsing. I'm the ringmaster today. To be part of the circus, I think I have to know about a lot of different jobs. I know I could be a 'tortionist. But probably, I can be an animal trainer, or an acrobat, or the ringmaster. But not the bearded lady, or the fat lady."

I pat her on her behind. "Maybe I should think about joining the circus with you, huh?"

She grins and kisses my tummy before somersaulting— with her broken arm sticking straight out to the side—to the swing set.

Clay takes my hand and kisses it. "I'm not letting you go anywhere without me, lady."

"You never feel like running away and joining the circus, Clay?"

"Never." His blue eyes are earnest as he says, "I like it just fine right here, with you and the girls."

I study him for a minute, wondering how that can be true. Squirming in my chair, searching for a comfortable position, I think about how great the temptation to run away is, even for me. He must feel that way sometimes, at least. But I'm not going to push him for the absolute truth. The truth might be something I don't really want to know.

Instead, I ask about this lost weekend spent doing baby chores. "Aren't you disappointed about your holiday weekend?"

"Not really." He pauses to light another cigarette. "We needed to get those things done, and this was a good time to do it. How about you? Sorry Lola couldn't come to visit?"

I drain my tea glass and sit it on the grass beside my feet. "No. I'm sure she'll come down after the baby is born. And truthfully, I'm just too tired to keep up with her and the girls." I shrug. "It's just as well she didn't make it. Can you imagine how miserable we would've all been at the beach? Me lolling in the sand like a beached whale. And then trying to keep Birdie out of the water?"

"You've got a point there. About Birdie, anyway." What does he mean by that—*about Birdie, anyway*? I won't ask him. I'm so thin-skinned these days, the littlest thing seems like a criticism. Most likely, he didn't mean a thing except that Birdie is difficult to handle when she goes on a tear.

He takes a long drag on his newly lit cigarette and squints against the smoke, blowing it away from me. He knows it bothers me these days. "I've got to say I'm not sorry Lola couldn't make it this weekend."

Puzzled, I stare at him while trying to read his thoughts. As always, his face is handsome and his expression is about as clear as mud. "I thought you enjoyed Lola's visits."

"It's not that I don't enjoy her. I do. But sometimes, I just want us as a family. And this is one of those times, my dear."

"Oh." That's news to me. He's never said anything about not wanting Lola to come visit us. In fact, he always seems excited to see her. They have a lot in common, really. They both work in factories, Lola in the Atlanta plant, and Clay here. They both like to have a drink every now and then, something I never got a taste for.

Hmm. I guess you learn something new every day. "By the way, where did you put that home permanent I bought at the store Saturday?"

"In the bathroom cabinet. But you don't need a permanent. You're hair is beautiful, honey."

I can't help but blush. "Oh, hush up. It is not. Besides, the permanent is for Mellie, not me." I reach across his chest for his left wrist to check his watch. He nips my ear and I think he'll probably want to have sex tonight. I'm not sure I do. As if confirming my doubts, the baby moves and shoots a sharp pain through my groin.

"Ow," I groan and withdraw my hand to settle back in my chair.

"You okay?"

"Yeah. Baby's just a little feisty this afternoon." We watch Birdie dangle from the swing set's crossbar by her knees. "Birdie! Don't do that! You'll break your other arm." I shift in my chair again. "I hope Mellie's not late coming home. I want to get that permanent done after supper tonight."

"Don't you think that's overdoing it for today, Norah?" His brows are drawn together with worry. He's so sweet to me today. He takes my hand in his.

Yes, he wants to have sex tonight.

His voice is full of concern when he continues. "You've been awfully busy this weekend."

"But tomorrow's the first day of junior high for her and I'm sure she'll want to look her best. Besides, you're doing the cooking tonight, right?"

"That's right. I'd better get the grill going." He puts his hands on his knees and pushes himself up. "Want some more tea?"

"No, thanks. I'll get the clothes off the line so they won't smell like charcoal smoke. Give me a hand up, okay?"

After stubbing out his cigarette, he tugs me up and pulls me into his arms. Humming in my ear, he dances me toward the clothesline. I'm so huge and clumsy I'm surprised he even wants to be close to me.

Clay smells like a man: sun warmed skin and tobacco, sweat and Old Spice. Even though sex is the very last thing I want these days, it feels so good to be in his arms. It's wonderful to feel like I don't have to carry my weight all by myself for a few minutes. His breath tickles my ear and his humming rumbles through me.

Yeah, I'm glad it's just us this weekend, too.

MELANIE

"Your hair will hold a set and look so much nicer when you begin junior high," Mama says. She's putting the mustard and pickles back in the refrigerator. "After all, you're a young lady now, Mellie."

I'm beginning to hate that phrase. "But Mama, I don't *want* a permanent. My pony tail is fine." I smash pieces of hamburger bun into the dollop of potato salad left on my plate.

"Come on, Sweetie. You'll look so pretty."

Daddy picks up the big bowl and grabs the ketchup bottle by the neck to carry them to the kitchen. "Norah, maybe you should listen to Mellie. She doesn't want a permanent, and *you* should rest."

"*You* listen to me, Clay." Mama clutches the jars in her fists like she's put on boxing gloves. She's getting riled up, and that can't be good for me.

Still gripping the jar, Mama pokes her forefinger at Daddy's chest. "I know how important that first day at a new school is, and I am not going to let my daughter down because I happen to be pregnant. This won't take long if we get started right now."

The last thing I want is to start a fight between Mama and Daddy. "Mama, please. I'm fine with my hair just like it is. Why don't we wait until next weekend to put in this permanent?" I cross my fingers behind my back, hoping that Daddy and I will win this time. But it doesn't look good.

Mama's mouth is clenched tight and she has that little line between her eyebrows. When her face gets like that, I think about a pot sitting on a hot stove burner, right before the water starts to boil. The lid gives a little hiss and settles down real tight on the pot just before it begins to dance around from all the bubbling heat inside. I don't think it's good for Mama to get upset, so I decide right then that if she doesn't give up on doing my hair, I'll have to give in.

She doesn't budge.

Instead, she marches to the hall closet and pulls out towels and the box of curlers. Before she even tells me to, I turn on the water so it can get hot.

Daddy turns on the TV and sits down to watch the news. On the television they're talking about how the Russians are going to send weapons to Cuba and how Congress wants the president to attack. I shiver even though the water is hot on my fingers. Talk about Russia and Cuba makes me think about what Robert said about joining Navy. I put my head under the faucet.

Soon I have water in my ears and eyes when all I wanted to do when I got back from the pool was to finish my Nancy Drew book. Instead, here I sit on the last evening before school starts with my sweaty legs stuck to the vinyl chair and my nose pinched closed to keep from gagging on the smelly curling solution.

Birdie comes by every few minutes holding her nose to remind me how awful I smell. My eyes sting so bad, I have to squint to see the clock on the back of the stove. I'm determined not to let Mama forget to rinse the solution out on time. All I need is to start junior high with frizzy hair.

Besides, I really need to go to Stephanie's so we can discuss what we're going to wear and make plans for our first day of school.

But Steph calls instead. We talk for a few minutes before she has to leave to go to the Officer's Club for dinner with her parents.

So, for the last twilight of summer, while thunder rolls in the distance, I sit on the back porch all by myself, with my stinking curls and my nervous stomach.

Atlanta, Georgia

LOLA

"Stan, you don't need another beer." I take the icy brown bottle out of his hand and put it back in the ice chest. He's already so drunk he can barely stand up. We should've left his boss' barbeque hours ago, before we were both so unsteady on our feet.

My excuse is that I didn't eat enough. I subscribe to Scarlet O'Hara's Mammy's philosophy that ladies don't eat much in public, especially at barbeques. Of course, that doesn't apply to drinking, as long as the lady doesn't get nasty drunk. And I'm never a nasty drunk. I'm happy, happy, happy, until I'm not anymore. Then it's time to go home.

It's time to go home now.

Scowling at me, Stan takes the beer bottle out of the cooler. Holding it up like a trophy, he scans the small audience of his co-workers. "Bitch thinks she can nag me."

The women gasp and tug on their pearl necklaces or expensive dangling earrings, then as one body close their circle, leaving me on the outside.

This isn't unusual. Women aren't always nice to me, and I don't give a damn what these snooty priss-pots think. But it hurts like hell to hear Stan call me a bitch.

Stan turns his icy glare on me. "You're not my wife."

He drives the knife even deeper. I'm not his wife. Now, I know that I won't ever be his wife. I swallow the lump in my throat and raise my chin just a bit. They won't make me cry.

The men move forward, arms outstretched to keep their comrade from keeling over, to protect him from further nagging.

I'm left standing alone on the pristine lawn in the orange glow of the late afternoon light. The aromas of sizzling beef and seared chicken swirl in the smoky air. My belly cramps. With a palm pressed against my stomach, I make my way to the bathroom.

Locked inside the beautifully wallpapered powder room, I lean against the door. The hurt has become rage. How dare he call me a bitch in front of his friends, his boss?

His boss who flirted with me so nicely, telling me I looked like Ann Margaret with my strawberry hair and my stylish strapless playsuit with its sexy overskirt. He even tapped the end of my nose and called me sweet.

Of course, now I realize he meant cheap, not sweet. I don't really care. I don't.

I just want to go home. After rinsing out my mouth, and checking my hair, I go to the guest bedroom where we all left our purses. Fishing through my straw bag, I find a lipstick and smear some on. Fire engine red. Suddenly I feel like Scarlett being shoved into Ashley's birthday party by Rhett.

Clark Gable's movie voice roars through my head: "If you're going to behave like a tramp, you should dress like one."

Dropping the lipstick back in my purse, I remember Stan

gave me his car keys. Well, thank you, God, for small favors.

Outside, I walk past the women, who don't say a word to me. I hear the hissing whispers behind me. Ignoring them, I walk over to Stan and his group of friends. Maybe the men are leering at me a bit more, but I disregard them. Their looks can't touch me. *They* can't touch me unless I let them. Nobody can say I'm not choosy.

Holding my head high, I stop beside Stan. He looks at me like I've been gone for days. "Aw, dollface. I missed you. You look so pretty."

I jingle the keys in his face. "Ready to go home, big guy?" I put a hint of smolder in my voice, and the hairs on the back of my neck stand up. I sense the other men inching closer. Standing on tip-toes, I kiss Stan's cheek. Better to put on a good show than to let these creeps know Stan's words got to me. Since they expect a tramp, I'll be the best damn tramp they've seen in a while.

I lean into Stan and slide my fingers between the buttons on his sport shirt, nibble his earlobe.

Stan gulps down the last of his beer and leans heavily on my shoulder. "Good-bye, suckers," he says to the salivating men. Stan's weight makes me stumble like I'm as drunk as he is. I stiffen my back and we lurch out of the backyard, leaving the party behind.

Stan falls asleep as soon as we're in the car, another small favor from above. I don't have to talk to him for the forty-five minutes it takes for me to drive home. I have time to build a sound argument, to put together a solid thrashing for the son of a bitch.

It's dusk when I pull up in front of my little rental house. The yard is trim, the result of Stan's mowing on Saturday, when he was sweet and we played house so nice. The night-blooming jasmine is just opening up; its fragrance teases the warm air.

So serene. So peaceful and clean.

Exactly opposite from the way I feel: hot and restless and dirty.

"Stan. Wake up." I nudge his shoulder. He moves his head and his snore deepens to a low rattle. "Stan." Nothing.

Well, I don't give a goddamn if he sleeps out here all night and is carried away by mosquitoes. I'm not about to lean across him and roll up his window. I slam the car door and go inside.

The house is still and hot, the air stuffy. I step out of my high-heeled red sandals in the living room. I drop my purse on the kitchen counter and pour a glass of ice water from the pitcher in the refrigerator, gulp it down, and drop the playsuit's overskirt on the kitchen floor. With a full glass of ice water in one hand, I go through the house, pushing up the windows to let in the slight evening breeze, stopping in every room to take a sip of water and strip off another piece of clothing.

No lamps, no lights.

I know where I'm headed.

In the bathroom, I turn on the shower and stare at my reflection in the mirror. My hair's light red-blonde seems harsh in the light of the 100-watt bulb over the sink. The hair-do that looked so fresh and keen that morning is limp and weighed down with hairspray and humidity.

Grabbing the cold cream jar, I slather it thickly over my face, changing my features to a white, greasy blur. Using toilet paper, I scrub at my skin, taking away the colors and camouflage until my face is naked and bare. Pale under its tan.

Dark circles beneath my eyes.

Eyebrows plucked in severe, arching lines.

Lips dry and wrinkled from constantly wearing lipstick.

I brush my teeth, hard, scraping the stink of liquor and

cigarettes from my mouth.

God, I'm awful.

In the shower I shampoo twice and stand in the warm spray for a long time, letting the booze ease out of my pores and down the drain. Turning off the water, I step out and stand on the bathmat, dripping. I don't even bother with a towel, except to dry my hair a bit before setting it.

The wafting air dries my body drop-by-drop, tender touches that seem unnatural to me. What feels natural is the hard stab of the bristle rollers and the gouge of the pick that holds them in place. Every two rollers, I drink more water, trying to stave off the hangover I know I'll take to the factory floor with me in the morning.

Soon my hair is set, covered with the black silky hair net, and my skin is dry. I fluff on the scented bath powder Stan gave me for my birthday, three months ago.

After turning on the window fan in my bedroom I slip on a cotton nightgown, the kind my mother always wore. So soft and thin, it feels like a cool whisper.

I lie on the bed and light a cigarette, the red tip the only spot of color in the dim bedroom. Stan is still asleep in the car, and he can stay there all night for all I care.

Bastard.

Aren't we a pair? The Bitch and the Bastard.

Mama, you're probably rolling over in your grave. I never meant to be this way. But you know what happened. You know how it all changed. I'm just glad that you see me through the gauze of heaven instead of the bright light in the bathroom. I hope you know that on the inside, I'm still your girl, no matter what the outside is like.

I stub out the cigarette and arrange my pillow so the hair rollers aren't so prickly.

Later, I wake with horrible cramps and a hot rush between my legs. I stagger to bathroom and turn on the light. My nightgown is stained red and my legs are caked with drying blood. The cramps are worse this time than ever. Maybe because I'm more than a week late. I was beginning to wonder. But no. Norah's having the baby. Not me.

Thank God. Not me. Right?

I clean myself up and put my gown in the sink full of cold water to soak, dig out the belt and the pads from the little linen closet. Leaving on the bathroom light to find another gown, I see that Stan has made his way to bed. He even woke up enough to take off his clothes. He's lying naked on top of the sheet and snoring like a freight train. I'm surprised his snores didn't wake me before the cramps.

The cramps hit with another wave and I head back to the bathroom to take a couple of aspirin and a Seconal.

I lie down, careful to arrange myself just so, making sure my hair curlers aren't shifted, making sure my legs are together. Careful not wake up Stan.

No child, thank God. No Stan's baby. No my baby.

Stan rolls over and nuzzles my neck, his breath hot and sour. "Doll, you okay?"

My face is wet and I swipe my hand over it before pushing him away. "Yeah."

"I'm sorry, doll."

"Yeah, sure."

He cups my breast and throws his leg over my belly.

"Stan, no. I started my period. Go to sleep."

"Oh." He props up on his elbow to see my face in the dim room. His hot breath makes my belly knot up. "It was late, right?"

I nod.

He kisses me on the lips and whispers in my ear. "Thank God, huh? We don't want any brats."

No. We don't want any brats. Certainly not your brat, Stan.

But if Michael were here, I'd be crying for a different reason. I wanted Michael's baby so terribly. I still do. I wish I had a little of him to hug and kiss, to make cookies for, to have dinner with.

Stan rolls on top of me, his erection hard, pressing against my belly. Pushing himself up on his arms, he says, "I'd be happy to get you off. Help those cramps." He starts peeling away the protective layers I put on in the bathroom.

I can't stand it. Suddenly my life is so ugly, narrowed down to rutting like a bitch in heat. I shove him off me. "Get out." My voice is low, steady, determined.

"I said I'm sorry. C'mon. It'll help with the cramps."

"You don't care about me. All you care about is getting your rocks off. Get out, you bastard."

He sits up, moving backward to lean against the headboard. I hear him fumbling on the nightstand. "You don't mean that." He flicks the lid from his lighter and the flame shows his face in shifting yellow light and dark shadows. Inhaling deeply, he studies my face before closing the lighter.

"Damn right I mean it. I want you out of here. Now." I hear a hissing breath, and tobacco smoke winds around me.

"Shit. It's okay, doll. I'll give you a pass."

I shove at his shoulder. "You'll give me a pass? What the hell does that mean?" I turn on the lamp and glare at him as he sits there, naked, in my bed, against my headboard. His lean belly is fish white. His erection seems to be gaining a second life. Just like the sick bastard to get turned on by yelling.

"When I say no, I mean no. You don't *give* me a damn thing."

He grabs my hand and wraps it around his woody. "Okay. You can just get me off."

I yank my hand back and slap him across the face.

He's stunned. His mouth hangs open and he has a fish face to match his fish-white belly. But only for a second. His expression hardens and he stands beside the bed, his balled fists tight against his legs. "If I leave now, I won't be back."

"Good. I don't want you back."

Stan pulls on his trousers and grabs his sport shirt. "You can't bitch at me in front of my pals and then not put out. You tease."

I grab the ashtray from the bedside table and throw it at him. It shatters against the wall, leaving a trail of ashes and lipstick-stained butts trailing across the white sheet. "Go. Now."

"Where are my goddamn car keys?"

"In the goddamn car."

"What? Somebody could steal it."

"That's what I was hoping. For it to be stolen with you in it."

"Bitch."

The front door crashes, then his car roars to life, tires squealing down the street.

Careful not to spill the cigarette mess onto the floor, I roll the sheets up and take them to the bathroom. I get the broom and turn on the overhead light in the bedroom.

Slivers and chunks of the glass ashtray glitter like diamonds on the wood floor. I sweep them up. Dump them in the kitchen trash.

It seems like there should be more garbage to clean up. Everything was so dirty just a few minutes ago.

At two a.m. I finish putting clean sheets on my bed and

climb back in to sleep. I wish I never had to wake up again. I think of Michael. I think of Mama.

I have to get up at five.

Tuesday
September 4, 1962

Jacksonville, Florida

FLOSSIE

It's gonna be another hot day for sure. Last evening's brief thunderstorm didn't do a thing to cool the weather down. There is barely a breeze coming in the open bus windows. Sweat's beading up on my lip. By the time I walk to the Adams' house, I'll be soaked through.

Usually on Tuesday, I'm working at the Samuel's house. They're on vacation, and since yesterday was a holiday, Miz Adams asked if I could help her out today. I don't need four days in row off work, that's for sure, so I told her I'd be happy to help out.

Getting off the bus, I adjust my hat and shopping bag, ready to walk two blocks to the house. About halfway there, shiny, white kids start pouring out the front doors, kissing their mamas, and marching down the driveways like little soldiers going to a parade in their glossy new shoes and stiff new clothes. That first day of school is always a happy day, isn't it?

Lots to learn, new friends to make, nothing bad to carry forward with you.

'Course, Birdie is starting first grade with a clean slate. Don't think it'll take her long to have stories to tell. I swear she's gonna be the star trouble-maker.

A red-haired boy about Birdie's age busts out of his front door, his mama running behind him with a comb. "Tommy, come back here. Your cowlick is standing straight up."

The boy stops dead still and stares at me. "Mama. There's a nigger."

The mama grabs his arm and drags him back toward the open front door, lookin' over her shoulder at me. "Don't use that word. She's a nice colored lady, probably going to clean somebody's house. Get back in here so I can fix that cowlick."

'Course, I smile and keep walking with my head high. Words is words, like they say.

Words is words.

I still got a block to go to get to the Adams' house. Now, what was I thinking about? Oh, yeah. Wondering if Mellie is excited about starting her new school. Last week, she seemed a little nervous.

Now, she's a smart girl, that Mellie. Once she got to know me, she wasn't very shy about things, either. Last week, they were pestering me to tell them stories while I was ironing. So I told them the story of my old slave granny who ran away up North, but hated it so much, she came back home when she could.

Mellie, she's so smart and sensitive, she asked me how I felt about that. Nobody ever asks me how I feel about anything much. I had to think for a few minutes how to put it in words. Finally I said, I didn't like it much, but what could I do about it? What could my Granny do about it?

Mellie sat up straight and said, "I don't know, but I would do something about it."

I had to say, "Melanie Adams, you're a good girl, and a smart girl, too. I know you gonna look around and see what's wrong and try your hardest to make it right. A body can't ask for more than that."

The poor thing looked like she had the whole world on her shoulders. She's too young to be thinking she's got such burdens. There will be plenty of cares and woes for her to carry later on in her life, sure enough.

NORAH

"Birdie, please. Just stand still for two seconds." I swear this girl is going to drive me insane. To provoke me, Birdie starts hopping, first on one leg, then on the other. Calmly, I set the red hairbrush on the back of the toilet. What I want to do is flush the damn thing. "Okay, have it your way. You can do your own hair."

Birdie places her palms on the sink and pushes up so that her feet dangle an inch off the floor. Smiling at her reflection in the mirror, she says, "My hair is just the way I like it, Mama. It's free!" She shrieks and runs from the bathroom waving her arms in the air.

I hear Melanie muttering in her bedroom. Taking a deep breath, I stand in the doorway of the bedroom she shares with Birdie. The sight of her at the dresser in her crisp white blouse and plaid skirt takes my breath away.

My God, she's almost grown.

Her little breasts push against her shirt, a gentle curve in contrast to her ramrod straight back. The skirt's waistband nips her waist and the pleats flare over her hips. Her legs are beautiful—smooth and tanned, shaped like an athlete's.

Tears sting my eyes, but I blink them away. She already thinks this pregnancy is making me crazy. Maybe it is.

Mellie tugs her blue brush through the glossy, extravagant waves the permanent gave her dark, straight hair. "You look beautiful, sweetheart."

She drops the brush to the dresser and turns to face me with a hand on her tummy. "I *feel* sick, Mama."

"Got a few butterflies this morning?"

"Feels like a whole herd." She frowns and rubs her hand in a circle at her waistband. "Do butterflies travel in herds?"

Smiling, I pull her into a hug. "I don't know. But I do know you'll be fine."

She rests her head on my shoulder for a few seconds and I wonder how soon she'll decide that she doesn't need my hugs anymore. Kissing the top of her head, I assure her again. "Sweetie, you'll be fine."

The doorbell rings and Birdie yells, "I'll get it."

Mellie pulls out of my embrace. "What time is it?"

"Early still. That's probably Flossie." We both walk into the living room as Birdie lets Flossie in the front door.

"Good mornin', good mornin'. Don't you girls look pretty as a picture? Ready for school?" With a big smile, Flossie removes the prim little straw hat she's wearing over her slicked back hair.

Melanie responds with a shrug. Birdie with a bounce, shouting, "I don't want to go to school *ever, ever, ever!*"

"Birdie, calm down," I say. "You're going to wear yourself out before the day even starts."

Mellie snorts. "Mama, you know she *never* tires out."

"That's true." I sigh. "Let's get pictures of you both, Birdie's first day of first grade and your first day of junior high. Now, where is the camera? I got it out last night."

Birdie runs to the buffet in the dining room. "Mama, here it is." Grabbing the camera's strap, Birdie careens around the table and heads back toward the front door.

I hold my breath as the camera swings wildly in her wake. "Slow down, Birdie. Be careful with that." As she passes me, I grab her and catch Clay's Argus C-9 before it whacks into the end table. If this camera ends up broken, we won't be able to replace it. I don't even want to think about how disappointed Clay would be.

Me, too. There'd be no way to take photographs of the new baby.

Glancing at the clock on the kitchen wall, I realize we don't have much time before Mellie has to leave. "Come on, girls, let's go outside. Bring your lunch box, Birdie, and Mellie don't forget your notebook and purse. You've got your lunch money in your wallet, right?"

"Yes, ma'am. You already asked me that three times."

"Well, just make sure."

The girls get their things and file through the door Flossie holds open for them. "Why don't I take a picture of all three of you together, Miz Adams? That would be a nice one."

"Okay, thanks Flossie. We'll do that first." I'm glad I put on something decent this morning, though I hadn't thought of having my picture made. I just hadn't wanted Birdie's teacher to think I was a sloppy mother. You never know how first impressions affect the way a teacher treats a pupil.

Outside, I tell the girls to pose so I can set the focus and get the dials where Clay told me to put them. I just hope these pictures come out. "Flossie, all you have to do is push this button. Make sure you hold the camera still until it finishes clicking."

"Yes'm. I think I can do that."

The girls and I line up in front of the bushy green azaleas we always use as a backdrop for outdoor photos. The cloudless blue sky is crisscrossed with the white trails left by the Navy jets. The sun is high and bright, making the reds and greens in Mellie's plaid skirt look like woven jewels. Birdie's pink-checked dress looks like strawberry ice cream: cool and sweet in a shiny white bowl. But the real beauty is in their faces, their skin glowing with health and youth.

Oh heck, those tears are welling up in my eyes again. I swipe at my cheeks, pretending to fix my hair.

Flossie studies the buttons on the camera. "Everybody say *cheese* when I get to three." Squinting one eye closed, she aims the camera our way. "One, two, three. *Cheese!*"

MELANIE

The day I've dreaded all summer has finally arrived. Here I am, standing in my front yard, forcing a smile on my face while first Flossie and then Mama snap picture after picture of Birdie and me. Birdie keeps sticking her tongue out, so Mama tells her to move. "Birdie, stand by Flossie so I can take Melanie's picture. She has to leave in a few minutes."

Thank goodness this will be over soon.

Flossie has her hands on Birdie's shoulders, like she's keeping her from floating up like a balloon. Flossie smiles at me. "Oh, that's a nice one, Miss Mellie. Real nice."

Mama studies the camera like she thinks she can see the

photograph inside. I wish Daddy had bought a Polaroid Instant camera instead of the big one he got. But he said the thirty-five millimeter can shoot slide film, and they'll last longer than the Polaroid photos.

I don't know, but at least with Polaroids you can see them right away and don't have to have a slide projector or a hand-held viewer. Right now, we don't own either one of those.

Hmm. I might never have to look at these snapshots I don't want to have made.

"Okay, Sweetie. I guess we're finished." She turns to Flossie, "Do you really think that was a good one?"

"Yes'm. She was smilin' real pretty."

Mama holds out her arms to me. "Well, give me a kiss, and go pick up Stephanie." The camera dangles from the strap around her neck so that it sits right on top of her belly. She lifts it away and wraps her arm around me.

I kiss her cheek and say, "I love you, Mama."

"I love you, Sweetie. Have a nice day, now."

"I'll try. Bye, Birdie. Bye, Flossie. I'll see you this afternoon."

Flossie smiles and waves. "I'll be waiting to hear somethin' good."

"Bye, Mellie!" Birdie shouts.

Before I get to the end of the driveway, Birdie is beside me. She tugs on my skirt to make me stop. Looking up at me with big, scared eyes she says, "I don't know what to do. Tell me what to do."

"Don't be scared." I lean over and hug her. "You'll like first grade. You'll make new friends, and I bet you have a nice teacher."

"But I don't know what to do without you to show me." Birdie looks like she's about to cry. "You always show me what to do."

Boy, does that surprise me. I never realized Birdie paid any attention to me at all. But I guess she does. Suddenly I feel older, and even responsible for how she behaves today. I stand up straight and adjust my notebook and purse on my hip. With my other hand, I give Birdie's hand a squeeze. "Here's the secret, Birdie. Just keep still and quiet, and do what the teacher says to do."

"Okay. I'll try to be good like you. Bye."

At least I don't have to face the first day of school alone, like Birdie. At seven forty-five, I knock on Stephanie's door.

"Hi, Mel." Cherie, Stephanie's sister, opens the door and stuffs her hands into the pockets of her pink chenille bathrobe. She yells for Stephanie, then looks at me as she cocks her head to the side, making the rollers in her blonde hair click against each other. "Nice hair-do." She sniffs. "Toni?"

I wait just inside the doorway, wondering how bad my hair really smells. I tug one of the curls under my nose. I can't smell it, but then, my nose might be numb after last night.

Mr. and Mrs. Starr sit at the breakfast table. They both have newspapers open and coffee mugs with the Navy insignia on them held in mid-air. Mr. Starr wears his khaki uniform, and his hat sits on the table beside the ashtray, where twin curls of smoke drift upward.

"Good morning, Mr. and Mrs. Starr," I say.

Mr. Starr grunts back at me. Stephanie's mom swivels around and the red leatherette chair squeaks. "Hi, Mellie. Excited about your first day? Where is Stephanie? Stephanie! You're going to be late!"

"I'm going, Mom. Don't blow a fuse." Steph grabs my arm and steers me out the door. She's wearing a new white blouse, a full blue skirt over a stiff crinoline, and a wide, black patent belt at her waist. She looks like a picture in a magazine.

I tug on my blouse. It's a little big across my breasts, and I can see the little pink rose on my bra when I look down at the neckline. Suddenly I feel like the emperor with the new clothes when he realizes he's been tricked. But I do have new loafers with shiny pennies in the slots. Maybe those pennies will bring me good luck.

"What's that smell?" Steph sniffs and curls her upper lip. "That tom cat must have been hanging around last night. Pee-yoo."

The Toni home permanent. *Thanks a lot, Mama.* Gosh, I hope I don't smell like this all day. Steph hasn't even noticed my new hairstyle. I must look like my old, plain self. All that trouble and stink for nothing. I speed up a little and pray she won't get another good whiff of my hair.

"Come on," I say. "We don't want to be late."

The bus rolls to a screeching stop at the corner just as we get there. The other kids had already lined up, so we're the last ones on.

Steph pokes me in the back with her finger, prodding me to hurry down the aisle. "Last seat, Mellie."

The driver hits the gas just as I slide onto the seat. My head bumps against the back window. "Wow, a thrill ride every morning. Just like being at the Grand Prix."

Stephanie takes out a lipstick along with an empty powder compact. "Cherie's. Nice to have a make-up counter in the bathroom." With a sly grin, she carefully fills in her lips, smacks them together, and then offers the lipstick to me.

I shake my head. "I don't like the way that pasty stuff feels on my mouth. Did Cherie say you could have that lipstick?"

"Well, she didn't say I *couldn't* have it." She shrugs and drops the gold tube and compact back in her purse.

The bus is still cool, though the sun is strong in the windows on our side. The bench seat feels stiff and hard. At the next stop, a column of boys with crew cuts comes marching down the bus aisle. "Looks like we might have to move."

"Let me handle this, okay?" Steph folds her hands on top of the notebook in her lap like she's sitting in church, holding a hymnal.

"Sorry, little girls, but you're in the wrong seat." Buzz, the bully from elementary school, props his elbow on the seatback in front of us. The short sleeves of his shirt are rolled twice, and he flexes his stringy bicep for us before leveling an evil grin at Stephanie. The other boys take that as their cue to sneer.

I nudge Steph and gather my purse and notebook, ready to head for higher ground. I don't want any trouble from these hoodlums.

She elbows me back, harder. Tossing her blonde hair over her shoulder, she says, "Shut up, Buzz. We're not going anywhere."

"Oh yeah?"

"Yeah."

"Well, who's gonna keep me from making you move?"

Stephanie flips open her notebook and points to a name and telephone number written in red ink. "This is my sister's new boyfriend. He told me to let him know if anybody gave me any trouble."

I didn't even know Cherie had a new boyfriend. Over Steph's shoulder, I read, *Clint, EV5-4367*. Clint who?

Obviously, Buzz knows Clint. Buzz's evil grin fades and he studies Steph's notebook for a few seconds. Then he backs away, motioning for his friends to move up the aisle to take another seat. Buzz flops in the seat right in front of us. "Tell Clint I said hey, okay?"

Stephanie smiles like she has a buttery after-dinner mint in her mouth. "Sure, Buzz, I'll tell him." She winks at me.

I'm dying to know what's going on, but can't ask with Buzz sitting right in front of us.

I don't get a chance all day. Of all the rotten luck, Steph and I don't have any of the same classes. Not even the same lunch. I never did get my locker open in the morning and ended up lugging all of my books around the whole day.

Now I stop at my locker to try one last time to ditch my books. I sure don't want to carry them home when I don't need them for homework. I fumble with the combination lock again, and tug on it.

It doesn't budge. "Damn." I bang my head against the blue metal locker. At least it's cool against my skin.

Stephanie swishes up beside me. Her new crinoline hasn't lost any of its bounce since the morning. "Hi, Mellie. Wasn't today just the best day ever?"

I stare at her. "Good grief, Steph. Did we live through the same day?"

"Yeah, it was great! I've been asked to join the Beta Club, and Marianne wants to sponsor me for the junior varsity cheerleaders." She pauses to adjust her notebook. "What about you?"

"Okay, I guess. I've got to collect current events from the newspaper for Social Studies. My teacher says," I pause and imitate her voice, "*We are witnessing one of the most challenging, and therefore, one of the greatest, times in the history of our nation.*"

"Yeah. I have to get current events, too. I hate that."

"And my English teacher wants me to work on the yearbook."

"Oh, that's good."

Steph keeps turning her head, like she's looking for someone. "By the way, I've decided that we have to have our first kiss by the end of the Sadie Hawkins Day Dance in three weeks, okay?" She waves at two older girls in straight skirts. "Well, let's go get our seat on the bus."

I slam my locker and catch up with her. "You're not serious about the kissing stuff, right?"

"Sure, I am. C'mon, Mel, you've *gotta* grow up."

"Hey, we're the same age, remember? Twelve. We're as grown up as twelve. Anyway, what's the deal with Buzz and this Clint guy?"

"Oh, Clint just told me to let him know if Buzz gave me any trouble." She dabs a little pink lipstick on, then slips the tube back into her purse. "He's kind of cute, don't you think?"

"I don't know. I've never seen Clint."

"Not Clint." Steph elbows me and motions with her head toward our bus. "Buzz. Buzz is cute."

"Buzz? Really?"

She takes off for the bus, her skirt swishing one way and her hair swishing the other.

Buzz is already on the bus. When he sees us coming down the aisle, he motions for us to take the back seat. "Tell Clint I'm looking out for you, okay?"

"Sure thing, Buzz." As we pass, Steph puts her hand on Buzz's arm where it rests on the seat back. "And thanks for saving our seat." Her hand slips off his arm real slow. I remember some blonde bombshell doing that in a movie.

Plopping into the seat first, I rest my head against the window frame and close my eyes. Having a big sister sure has helped Steph.

I feel like one of those monkeys who ride in the space ships: disoriented, out of my element. I'm definitely not in my regular jungle, and Steph seems to be swinging around with a whole new bunch of chimps.

BIRDIE

"I'm going home. I'm going home. I'm going home." Isn't that what Dorothy says before she clicks her heels in that scary movie with the flying monkeys? I can't remember. But I know she wants to go home through the whole movie, even though she made some good friends, like a lion.

I'd like to have a lion for a friend. He could join the circus with me. We'd be famous. "Presenting Birdie, the Acrobat Tortionist Clown Lion Tamer, and Fred, the Friendly Lion."

Where is Mama? She told me to wait for her right here at the front of the school and we'd walk home together. I hop on one leg, then the other. I have to tinkle. Bad. Maybe Mrs. Higgins will let me go back in the classroom.

"I have to go. I have to go. I have to go." That's my song right now. Singing that and hopping helps me hold it in. One more hop.

Where's Mama?

Debbie Robison from my class walks past. "Bye-bye, Beatrice. Want to walk with me?"

Oh, I have to go so bad. If I start walking with Debbie, I'll get home faster. I'll see Mama on the way. "Okay."

We start walking behind a group of big kids. I watch my feet, thinking hard about holding in my pee. I didn't go to the bathroom the last time Mrs. Higgins lined the girls up. I'm kinda scared of the tiny, dark space when the door is closed, but I can't tell anyone that. They'll think I'm a baby. And I'm not. I'm Birdie who has a lion for a friend. I'm not scared of anything. Nothing at all.

The safety patrol boy stops us at the corner of the school street and the busy road Mama told me never to cross without her or the safety patrol. Well, Mama isn't here but the safety patrol boy is. So I guess it's okay.

He sticks his arms out and walks to the middle of the street. The cars stop like magic. And all he had to do is stick out his arms. Debbie and I walk across the street behind the big kids.

"Beatrice, did you like school?" Debbie asks. She talks kind of funny. Really fast and her words are short, like she cuts the ends off with scissors.

"It's okay." I wish I could be Birdie at school. But my full name was written on a card on my desk. *Beatrice Adams.* It is easier to stay still when I have to be Beatrice. It's like the extra letters weigh me down.

"I got to have ice cream at lunch. Did you?" Debbie doesn't have a neat-o lunch box like mine. She's not carrying anything but some papers in her hand. I put my papers safe inside my lunch box.

"No. I had peanut butter and jelly, and carrots, and a cookie. My mama made it for me." My throat gets hard and tight thinking about Mama. Why didn't she come to school like she promised?

"My brother is in the sixth grade. He's a safety patrol. He'll be at the next corner. He says Mrs. Higgins is a nice teacher. Did you think so?"

"I guess." I can't think of anything else to say about school. All I can think about is how bad I have to pee. I don't want to have an accident. I watch my feet some more so Debbie won't see I'm about to cry. She'll think I'm scared of school. I don't want anybody to know that but me.

Soon, we're at the next corner, and Debbie says hi to her brother, Jimmy, the safety patrol. He doesn't say anything, but winks at Debbie before he puts out his arm to make us stop. While we wait, I look around. But I don't see the yellow house with the fence and the big dog that was on the corner this morning when Mama brought me to school. This corner has a blue house with no fence, a yellow house with a big tree in the front yard, and a white house with red paint around the edges. This isn't the same corner at all.

I'm so scared. Where is Mama? Why didn't she come to the school like she said?

I don't know what to do. Suddenly, my belly feels like it's exploding and hot pee floods down my legs. I can't stop the tears from running down my cheeks.

"Eww. Beatrice peed in her pants." Debbie Robison points and laughs. "Baby Beatrice peed in her pants."

I cry harder. "I'm not a baby! I'm not!"

The other kids all laugh and step around me as I stand in the puddle of my own pee. I can't stand it anymore, so I start to run back to the school. Jimmy yells at me to stop, but I run across the street all by myself. I put my both of my arms, even the heavy one with the cast, straight out to stop the cars just like the safety patrol boys. A car screeches to a stop right beside me and my lunch box clunks against the front of the car. There's no air in my chest. My heart is beating so hard I think I must be about to die. But I keep running and running.

The second safety patrol boy is in the middle of the road stopping cars. I run through the kids, the other way from them, toward the school. When I get there and see a teacher, I'll have to say those baby words: *I'm lost.*

But what if all the teachers are gone? Don't they go home

when we do? I don't know. I don't know. I don't know how to get home.

FLOSSIE

Miz Adams told me to wait for Birdie in front of the school office. Well, I'm standin' here and there's hardly any children around. The teachers are locking the classroom doors and heading my way, I guess to check out and head home. Should I go inside and ask about Birdie?

No.

Those teachers are lookin' at me like I'm gonna pull out a switchblade and cut 'em up where they stand, even though I wore my apron for this walk through a white neighborhood. That should be like a badge sayin' *It's all right, folks. I's jess a housekeeper.* But I'm still gettin' those looks.

Standing up straight and smilin' at everyone who passes me by, I make sure my hands are in front me, fingers wrapped together, loose and safe.

Then I see her.

Poor little Birdie, runnin' like a scared rabbit, pumping her arms, the white cast on her arm seeming to weigh her down. She's headin' straight towards the school office, her shiny new lunch box bouncing around like a live creature caught in her white-knuckle grasp. She doesn't even see me. The tears are wet on her face and her eyes are wild with scared.

"Birdie! Birdie, sweet baby. Here. I'm here."

She slides to a stop in front of me, gulping air into her skinny chest. I'm not sure she sees me, knows who I am.

"Birdie. Birdie. It's Flossie. Your mama sent me."

The girl flies into my arms like she is the veriest lost little bird. I pick her up and her little fingers dig into my shoulders like she's never gonna let go. Her whole body is flutterin'. Poor baby.

It's then I notice the wet and the stink. Oh, my poor baby girl. She had an accident and wet herself on top of whatever made her so scared.

"Is there something I can do for you?" a white lady dressed in a sharp lookin' red dress and black high heels says.

"No, ma'am. I'm just here to bring Miss Birdie back home."

The lady acts like she's used to being in charge. She must be the principal. She touches Birdie on the shoulder, but Birdie won't take her face from where she's buried in my neck. "Birdie? Is that your name?"

Sweet baby girl nods into my shoulder.

"And do you know this woman?"

Again, Birdie nods.

"I work for the girl's mama. She couldn't come to school this afternoon because she's expectin' and was feelin' poorly."

"All right. Is the girl okay?"

"I don't rightly know, ma'am. She seems scared, and she had a little accident. She came running toward the school from the other direction."

"First day frights. Happens every year, I'm afraid. You can go ahead and take her home." The lady principal opens the door to the office and walks in, leaving us standing there on the sidewalk.

"Let's get you cleaned up a little bit, sweet baby." I open the office door myself and walk in. The same lady is standing beside a desk, looking through some papers. The nameplate says Principal McKinney.

"Yes?" Principal McKinney asks.

"Could I clean Miss Birdie up before we go home to her mama?"

The principal wrinkles her nose and nods. "I'll call the janitor and see if she can help you." She picks up a microphone and speaks into it. "Jestine. Jestine. Come to the office please."

After a few minutes, a short, round colored woman wearing blue pants and shirt with her name sewn on it comes through the door, pushing a mop bucket. "Yes'm?"

The high-heeled lady glares at us through her black-rimmed eyeglasses. "Jestine, can you help this child get cleaned up? She had an accident on the way home."

Jestine makes eye contact with me, and we say lots with no words. "Yes'm. Y'all come on with me. We'll get things right, quick like."

Outside, Jestine reaches over and pats Birdie on the back. "'S okay. We'll take care of you, honey."

"Much obliged, Jestine. I'm Flossie and this here's Birdie Adams."

Jestine leads us to the janitor's room in the rear of the cafeteria. The smells of bleach and sour milk 'bout slap me down as we walk across the still-wet tiles to the open door in the back.

Inside is a big sink and faucet for filling mop buckets. Jestine turns on the hot water and reaches up on the shelf for a big bar of Ivory soap. "Can't use nothing but Ivory on my hands. They get burned so bad from the bleach and all. It'll be good for this little girl's behind."

Birdie starts to cry again. "I didn't mean to. I tried to get home, but I got lost. This girl, Debbie, took me the wrong way and I got lost. Where is Mama? She didn't come."

I untie Birdie's oxfords and roll away the wet socks from

her feet. "It's okay, Baby. Your mama is fine. She just didn't feel like she could make the walk. She's fine, though. Don't you worry."

"Are you gonna give me a bath in that sink, Flossie?"

"We're just gonna pretty you up afore we go see your mama. That all right with you?"

"Yes, ma'am." Birdie puts her sweaty hands on both sides of my face and makes me look at her. The edge of her cast feels rough on my cheek. "Thank you, Flossie. I tried all day to be like Mellie. I was a good girl until the very end when Mama didn't come." The tears well up in her eyes again.

I have to look away so she can't see my eyes fillin' with water. "I know you did, baby girl."

Jestine hands me a sparklin' white washrag and a worn towel. From a box on the shelf she tugs out a pair of white drawers. "I collects a few things for the chil'run. They's clean, don't worry."

"I'm sure grateful. So's Miss Birdie. I'll send something back for you with her."

"Gotta take care of the little ones. I'll be out here 'til you get done."

When I finish washing up Birdie, Jestine walks out of the cafeteria with us. "Again, we're grateful to you for your help, Jestine. I'll make sure we send some clothing items for you to keep."

"Appreciated, I'm sure. Sorry the little girl had to come to the janitor closet. If her mama had been with her, she'd a been able to go in the clinic. But the nurse don't keep no clean drawers in there. I don't understand it, myself."

"Hardly anythin' makes sense." I squeeze Birdie's hand to reassure her.

Jestine walks on toward the office, pushing her mop bucket

and whistling between her teeth. Birdie and me walk home. The neighborhood is noisy with kids runnin' and playin', workin' off all that energy left over from a long school day.

Birdie doesn't say a word. And she doesn't let a-loose of my hand until we step onto her concrete driveway. Then she flies to the house.

When I walk in, Miz Adams has Birdie in her arms and they's rockin' back and forth. Birdie's story spills out in jumbled words and sobs. Miz Adams looks at me with tears in her eyes.

"Thank you, Flossie. Thank you."

A little choked up myself, I nod, then pull out my kerchief to mop the sweat off my face.

"There's some iced tea on the counter for you. I thought you'd be hot and thirsty when you got home."

"Why thank you, Miz Adams. I appreciate it. It was a little warm walkin' home, wasn't it, Miss Birdie?"

MELANIE

The walk home from the bus stop is long and hot and chatty. At least Steph is chatty. I don't have much to say at all. Honestly, it's a relief to tell Steph good-bye at her driveway and walk the rest of the way home by myself.

Sometimes I have to be alone. I need to be able to hear the voice in my head instead of other people talking all the time. When I'm alone, I can sort things out better, and I have a lot to sort.

How does Steph expect me to get someone to kiss me, let alone do it in three weeks? And who?

Robert? In my dreams.

Things are changing real fast. I have this feeling that nothing is going to be the same for me.

I've got to face this change on my own, I think. I might be completely on my own if Stephanie keeps heading the way she's going.

Stolen make-up? Buzz is cute? We have to get a kiss whether we want one or not? I'm just not sure about Steph anymore. And that makes me not sure about *myself* anymore.

A jet roars overhead, stealing my breath and ripping the air with sound, leaving a long white scar in the sky.

When my breath comes back to me, I focus on putting on a happy face for Mama.

My house is quiet and the fan is bouncing hot air around the living room. Mama and Birdie are sitting at the dining room table while Flossie stands at the kitchen sink, washing dishes.

Birdie looks up. Her eyes are red and swollen. Her first day of school must have been even worse than mine. Poor Birdie. It must have been really awful.

Mama smiles, but it looks like she's working really hard to do it. "How was your day, Mellie?"

"Oh, pretty good, I guess." I hope she can't see the little white lie I'm telling. Okay, a big fat lie, but it doesn't look like Mama or Birdie can handle any more bad news. I put my notebook on the table. "Birdie, how was your day?"

Birdie looks away from me, and shrugs. She doesn't say a word, while Mama wraps her arms around her.

"Birdie's fine. She likes her teacher, and she didn't get into trouble at all. The only problem she had was getting a bit lost on the way home, because I couldn't meet her at the school. When Flossie got there, Birdie had already tried to find her way home and had run back to the school, scared."

Mama hugs Birdie again, and I can tell Mama feels like it is all her fault.

Flossie comes in from the kitchen and hands me a glass of iced tea, cold and dripping. I gulp it down, like I hadn't had a drink all day long. A carton of milk and a few sips at a water fountain aren't a lot to drink, now that I think about it.

"I just couldn't make it today, and the baby will be here soon, so Birdie will have to be able to go back and forth to school on her own. We've been working on a plan, haven't we?" Mama gave Birdie a squeeze and special smile.

I go to pour myself some more tea. "What's the plan?"

"We drew a map for me to carry." Birdie holds up a piece of notebook paper with lines and names and dots.

"And I've got a special job for you, Mellie." Mama grabs the empty mayonnaise jar sitting beside her on the table. "You're going to paint some dots on the road for Birdie to follow."

"On the road?" Birdie asks with big eyes. "Mama, are you sure that's not against the law?"

"I don't know, and I don't really care. This is how I'm going to make sure you're safe, Birdie."

"She could just walk with the other kids who live on the street," I say. "They'd look out for her."

Shaking her head, Mama thumps her palm down on the table. "Birdie is not going to depend on anyone else to find her way home. These dots will help her for a few days, and then she'll know her way around."

I know this look of Mama's and realize that no matter how I protest, it's no use. Just like I got a home permanent I didn't want, I'm going to paint dots on the road. What will my friends think when they see me painting dots on the road all the way to the elementary school? That's five blocks away. And it's hot. And I already feel like I'm part of the freak show at school.

Maybe there's still a little hope. "But we don't have any paint, do we?"

"We have some house paint in the utility closet. While you change your clothes, I'm going to fill up a jar. You don't have to use a paintbrush, just pour out a circle of paint and let Birdie step in it to make footsteps across the street. I drew it all out for you on the map." She hands the paper to me.

Sure enough, she's drawn the streets and crossings, all with a big circle at the intersection and footsteps going across and pointing in the direction Birdie needs to go. While I don't want to be out making paint circles and footsteps on the road, I have to admit it's a good idea.

Mama pushes away from the table. "And don't forget your flip-flops, Birdie. You're not going to ruin your new school shoes with paint."

"Yes, ma'am." Birdie walks to the bedroom like a normal person. That tells me she's really upset about this whole thing. While she digs through the closet, looking for her flip-flops, she doesn't make a sound. She's really, really feeling bad. I'm not sure what to say to make her feel better.

Mama's waiting for us outside on the carport with a mayonnaise jar full of green paint. The dots and footprints are going to match the wood on our house. I wonder how many other houses have that color? Right now, I can't think of any. But *somebody* has to have a green house besides us. If ours is the only one, this is just too embarrassing.

Mama pushes the jar at me, along with a paint-stained rag. "Just mark the roads like the marks on the map, and come straight home. I don't want y'all stopping to play or anything."

There's no way I'd stop to talk to anyone while I'm painting circles on the street for my baby sister. In fact, I've got my fingers crossed that everybody is inside their houses watching *The Skipper Ed Show* and laughing at *Popeye* cartoons while they have after school cookies and milk. But then I hear all the yelling and laughing and the dogs barking, and know they aren't. "Don't worry, Mama. We'll come home as soon as we finish."

Birdie slips her sweaty little hand in mine and we head down the sidewalk. The map doesn't have any markings for our street, but there's a circle at the corner where our street ends and we have to turn right onto March Street. I pour out a blob of paint on March Street and the fumes rise quickly in the hot air.

"Okay, Birdie. Here's the first one."

"I don't want to walk in it."

"But Mama said that's what you're supposed to do."

Birdie puts her fists on her hips, and I see a tantrum building up in her face. "I don't want to."

"Why are you mad at me? I'm just trying to help you."

"But what if we *do* get in trouble for painting on the road?" Birdie asks. "How does Mama know we won't get arrested or something?"

"So many kids will be walking on those dots, they'll be worn off before too long. Besides, we won't get in trouble at all. If the police come, we'll tell them Mama told us to do it. Then they can go talk to her, like she said. C'mon, Birdie. Let's get this over with."

"No. I'm not a baby, and I'm not making footprints to follow."

"You'll have to tell Mama you wouldn't do it."

"Maybe she won't find out. You won't tell her will you?"

I shrug. "Depends."

Birdie grabs my hand again and we start walking. A yellow cat slinks across the road in front us.

"Depends on what?"

"Depends on if you make me mad or something."

Birdie stops walking for a minute and looks up at me. "Do I make you mad all the time, Mellie?"

Damn. She looks like she's going to cry, and I know if she starts, then I'll cry, too. Then we'll be walking through our neighborhood, pouring green circles of paint on the road and bawling our stupid eyes out.

So, she can't cry. That means I can't tell her how often she makes me angry. "No. You don't make me mad all the time. Like right now, I'm not mad at you." And I'm not, now that I think about it. Birdie had a much worse first day of school than I had. How can I be upset with her?

"Well, I'm mad at someone. Debbie Robison."

"Is her brother Jimmy? He's a safety patrol this year, isn't he?" I remember him from the ceremony at the end of school last year.

Birdie nods, still looking angry. We stop at the next corner: March and Champion. I spill some more paint and look at Birdie. She shakes her head. "I'm not making footprints."

"Okay. It's your map we're making."

After a few minutes Birdie says, "I'm mad at every kid who was at that corner."

"I can understand that." Some boys are throwing a ball around in front of Mark Mitchell's house. I make sure the jar is hidden between me and Birdie. But they ignore us. After all, Mark Mitchell is still in sixth grade.

Birdie sighs. "But really and truly, I'm mad at Mama."

I look down and see that Birdie's face is getting red like she just ran around the house five times. I don't know what to say. I get angry with Mama, too, but I've never said it out loud. In fact, I was upset all day because of Mama insisting on giving me that stupid home permanent. Still, I can't tell Birdie it's okay to be mad at Mama, because it isn't.

Is it?

"I keep thinking that if she wasn't going to have that stupid baby..." Birdie stops walking and looks up at the sky. "I'm sorry, God. I know the baby isn't stupid, at least not yet." She skips to catch up with me and says, "Then Mama would've come to school on time. And none of this would've happened."

"I guess so." I'm surprised at how much sense Birdie's making. And I sure understand what she feels about the baby, though I don't think I've ever even admitted to myself that I think the baby's stupid.

Gee, we're terrible sisters, aren't we?

A car full of laughing teen-aged girls drives past us. They have their elbows sticking out of the open windows and the radio is playing. I wonder if I'll ride in a car and laugh like that with Steph one day? The thing is, I'm not sure if Steph will still be friends with me if I don't start wearing make-up and kissing boys.

Birdie and I don't talk for a while. There's nothing left for us to say. We keep walking and pour circles at Champion, then at Triumph and Ally Boulevard, where the school is. Thankfully, we don't see any more kids around here. It's like they're staying as far away from school as they can.

At the intersection of Ally and Triumph, Birdie stops and looks around. "This is where I got mixed up." She points to her left. "Debbie crossed that way instead of this way, and before I knew it, I was far away."

"So we need to make sure you remember to turn this way when you leave school, right?"

We cross to the other side of Ally Boulevard and I pour out three circles this time. "With three circles you'll know this is the important corner."

"Yes." Birdie points to the wide drainage ditch that runs beside Ally Boulevard. "I need to remember that deep ditch over there and then the yellow house with the fence and the big dog."

"Yep."

The German shepherd barrels toward the fence, barking his head off. He runs back and forth on the dirt path he's worn next to the fence.

I take Birdie's hand and we walk toward the fence. "Hello, Heinzie." Heinzie sits and waits for me to come pet him through the fence. I put the mayonnaise jar and the rag on the ground. "He's always lived here. He won't bite or anything, he just likes to run and bark at people. I think he wants to play with us, but he never gets out of the fence. His owner said we could pet him, but not to let him out."

Birdie puts her hands behind her back and watches while I rub Heinzie's head through the fence. His tongue is flopping around and he looks like he's got a silly grin on his face. "Heinzie, this is Birdie. She's my sister. You take good care of her and make sure she comes by to pet you every day, okay?"

Heinzie lowers his head and sniffs at the ground like he's trying to smell Birdie's flip-flops. She takes a step closer, right up to the fence, and Heinzie licks her toes. She giggles and smiles for the first time all afternoon.

"Hi." She puts the tips of her fingers through the fence and touches the dog's nose, before snatching her hand back. "Ew! His nose is wet." Heinzie barks, and Birdie jumps away.

"It's okay, boy. It's okay," I say, and the dog calms down. "You have to move slow and certain around him, or he'll think you're going to hurt him." I put my hand out in front of me and hold it still for a second, then slowly reach through the fence. "Like this." Heinzie puts his ear right under my fingers for a good scratch. "See?"

Birdie looks up at me. "He likes brave girls, doesn't he?"

I look back to see Birdie watching me with her big blue eyes full of wonder. She thinks I'm brave? I guess that shows what a six-year-old knows, huh? "He's just old and fidgety. See how his eyes are cloudy? I don't think he can see very well, so he likes things slow. You try again."

Birdie does exactly what I did: holds her hand out in front of her, really still for a few seconds, and then puts her fingers through the fence. Heinzie dips his head under her fingers and moves it back and forth, like he's helping her give him a rub. Birdie giggles and says, "I'm a brave girl, too, Heinzie."

"Hi, girls."

I recognize that voice, that smooth, melting chocolate voice.

Robert.

BIRDIE

I skip over to meet Robert as he walks toward us. Heinzie starts barking and running all over again. "Hi, Robert. Do you know Heinzie?"

"Yep." Robert smiles and puts his hand on my head. His palm is hot. "Old Heinzie's been running behind that fence for a long time. Did you pet him?"

"Of course. I'm a brave girl."

"Sure you are. How's the arm?"

"Got some new names today." I wave my cast around. "It doesn't hurt anymore, but it itches like crazy." Just saying that makes me itch, so I rub it against my belly, but that doesn't do much good. I look over to see where Melanie is. She's still standing beside the fence, with the jar of paint by her feet. "C'mon, Robert. Say hi to Heinzie." When Robert and me get to the fence, the dog stops running and waits for Robert to give him a pat.

"Hi, Melanie."

For just a second everything is quiet. Heinzie isn't barking. No cars are driving past. I can't even hear any birds singing. I watch Mellie, waiting for her to answer Robert. She's taking her sweet time.

"Hi, Robert."

Finally. I was beginning to think she didn't want to talk to Robert.

"How was the first day of school?" Robert is still looking at Melanie, not me, so I don't have to answer. I'm so glad.

I hear the rumble of a jet that sounds far away, and look up. The plane is so high, it's just a speck of shining silver in the sky. The long white cloud behind it is puffing up, changing from a straight line to a dotted one. When I look back at Melanie, her face is kind of pink. She shrugs and says, "Okay, I guess. I have Mrs. Marchman for math. Did you have her?"

Robert nods and grins. "Sorry 'bout that."

"Sure you are." Melanie picks up the paint jar and rag. "Come on, Birdie. Let's go home."

"Mind if I walk with you? I'm headed home, too."

Melanie looks at him like she's surprised, but she never answers. So I decide to take charge. I grab Melanie's hand with one hand and bump Robert's leg with my cast. "Let's go."

After we walk across the newly painted dots on the street, Melanie starts to talk. "What are you doing over this way, Robert?"

"Just checking on a few yards to mow. I need some work until I leave in a few weeks. By the way, my folks are giving me a going away party next Saturday. Will you be able to come?"

I look up at Melanie and she's quiet, her lips closed like she's never going to talk again. I have to take charge once more. "Sure, Robert. We'll come. Are you going to have ice cream and cake?"

He laughs. "I'll make sure we do."

"Oh, goodie. Where are you going, anyway?"

He looks over my head at Melanie. "I'm going into the Navy. I have to go to Michigan for basic training."

"You're really going?" Mellie says.

"Yes. I'm really going."

This is a grown-up conversation we're having, so I stop swinging my arms and just hold hands with them both, all connected together. We stop at the corner and wait for a car to go by. Robert looks down at the green dot on the road and then at the jar of green paint Mellie is holding. He says, "Are you two painting graffiti on the road?"

Mellie smiles, and I think for a minute I'm looking at someone else, a girl much older and a lot prettier than my sister.

But I'm holding my breath, because I don't want her to tell Robert what we're really doing. She might tell him I wet my pants. I don't want anyone else to know. So I have to take charge one more time. In a rush, I say, "Mama told us to come paint some graf-a-tee-tee on the road. She said it needed some."

Robert and Mellie laugh really hard, and sound kind of like Mama and Daddy laughing at one of my circus tricks, except I don't remember doing a trick.

Robert leaves us when we get to his driveway. As soon as he is in his house, I ask Mellie, "What is graf-a-tee-tee, anyway? Just dots on the road?"

"Graffiti is when kids go paint things in places where they aren't supposed to. You know those words painted on the trains? And the black paint on the highway bridges? That's graffiti."

"Uh-oh. Robert knows that, doesn't he?"

Mellie laughs again. "Yep."

Hmm. I don't know what kind of trouble I'm in now. Is it worse to tell a lie, or worse to do something bad, like painting graf-a-tee-tee? I'm not sure, but I think Mama will think telling a lie is the worst. But maybe she won't find out.

"Are you going to tell Mama I told Robert a lie?"

"Depends."

"Depends on what?"

Mellie frowns like she's thinking really hard about something. I get those rolling waves in my stomach. I wonder what I can do to make her not mad at me. "How about if I make up your bed in the morning?"

"Okay." She opens the front door for me. "And you have to do a good job."

I run in and tell Mama, "Robert thought we were painting graf-a-tee-tee on the road. Isn't that funny? He also said he was going to have ice cream and cake at his going-away party. Hi, Flossie. Is it time for you to go home?"

Flossie nods her head and unties her apron. I go over to stand by her. I want to say something about her being so nice to me after school, but I'm not sure what to say. Instead of talking, I hug both of her legs. She drops the apron over my back and rubs between my shoulders. "It's okay, Sweet Baby. Tomorrow will be better."

I nod against her white dress. She smells good. Warm and sweet, like those white flowers that turn brown if you touch them. Just like she did at school today when we were in the janitor closet. She pats my back and lets me go.

Behind me, I hear Mellie say, "He joined the Navy. Did you know that, Mama?"

"Yes," I say. "Robert joined the Navy." I'm holding Flossie's shopping bag for her to put her apron in.

Mama nods. "When's the party?"

Mellie puts the jar of paint on the kitchen counter. "Next Saturday."

"How would you like a new dress to wear, Mellie?"

"Really?" Mellie sounds a little out of breath. Is she excited about a new dress? I guess so. Maybe I should have a new one, too.

"I want a new dress for the party, too."

"I'll see what I can do about that. I have some purple fabric that will work for you, Bird-girl."

"Yay! I get a purple dress. I get a purple dress." I dance around the kitchen, watching Flossie put on her straw hat.

"Mellie," Mama says, "what do you think about a jumper made out of that polished navy cotton? You can wear it without a blouse under it for the party, and then still get some use out of it during the winter."

"Yes, ma'am. That would be nice."

"Navy blue always looks sharp and neat, Miss Mellie," Flossie says. "It sure does. Well, Miz Adams, I'm gonna be headin' to the bus stop, now. Y'all have a good evenin'."

"Okay, Flossie." Mama gets up from her chair and shakes

Flossie's hand. "Thanks for everything today. I don't know what I'd have done without you."

"No trouble. No trouble at all. I'll see you on Thursday."

We stand at the door and watch Flossie until she gets to the end of the driveway. I've got a knot in my chest from thinking about how awful the end of school was. "I wish Flossie could live with us, Mama."

Mama closes the front door, and goes in the kitchen to wash her hands. "Where would Flossie sleep? We'll be out of room when the baby comes."

That darned ol' baby is messing up everything. Mama takes a head of cabbage out of the fridge. Oh, no. We must be having coleslaw for supper. Yuck. "Flossie can sleep with me in our room, right Mellie?"

Mellie just wrinkles her nose at me, and I can tell she thinks that's a bad idea. Well, I don't care. I think it's a terrific idea.

"Mama, can I wash my hair?" Mellie tugs on her ponytail. "It smelled bad all day today."

"You have to wait three days unless you want frizzy hair." Mama motions for Mellie to come stand beside her while she grates the cabbage. Even though I don't like slaw, I like to watch the cabbage turn into little specks of whitish green. The shush-whush-shush sound is like an instrument we played in school today. I forget what it's called, but it makes me want to wiggle in a little dance.

Mama sniffs Mellie's hair. "It doesn't smell bad. You'll be fine."

Gee. Mama's smeller must be broken, because Mellie's hair does smell bad. Almost as bad as cabbage.

Thursday
September 13, 1962

NORAH

The girls have been in school for almost two weeks now, and everything seems to be settling down. Birdie hasn't had another accident, and she seems to be adjusting. The only thing I'm worried about with her is she's chewing on her bottom lip. It's red and raw. Something must still be bothering her, but she won't tell me. I'm going to send a note to ask about having a parent-teacher conference. I need to do that before the baby comes in a few more weeks.

Right now, Birdie seems happy enough. She's coloring and humming a new song.

Melanie comes through the door, looking hot and tired, like she has every day since school started. "Hi, Mellie. How was school, sweetie?"

"Okay, I guess." Melanie leans over and kisses me on the cheek. I'm resting on the sofa with my swollen feet propped up on two bed pillows. The doctor told me to make sure to put my feet up for at least an hour every morning and an hour every evening. My blood pressure is still running high and my feet stay swollen.

Having Flossie coming to help me out was strange at first, but honestly, I don't know what I'd do without her. She's noticed how wilted Melanie looks and is heading to the kitchen in my place, so I can stay here with my feet up.

"Melanie, would you like some iced tea?" she asks. "I made some for your Mama's lunch today." Flossie words sound round, like bubbles floating up from her throat then drifting through the air. Her voice is smooth, with no sharp edges at all.

"Yes, ma'am. I'd love some iced tea," says Mellie, my good girl.

Flossie hands Melanie a cold glass of tea and then resumes ironing Clay's shirts. I haven't had to iron anything for several weeks now. She does a real fine job.

"Do you have homework, Mellie?" I ask.

"Yes, ma'am. I need a current event."

"The newspaper is on the end table. I noticed there was a big article about President Kennedy's visit to Cape Canaveral yesterday. They say we won't be behind the Russians in the space race much longer. That should be good for current events, right?"

Melanie picks up the paper and spreads it on the dining room table. "I have some more forms for you to fill out."

"I thought I'd already filled out all those forms the first day of school."

"There are some different forms this year."

"Put them on the buffet, okay? I'll fill them out later."

She takes some yellow papers from her notebook and studies them. With a frown, she says, "Mama, are we C or P or J?"

"What?"

"This form." She waves the yellow paper in the air. "It says: Religious preference, choose one. And then there is a C or P or a J. But there's no B for Baptist."

I laugh. "C stands for Catholic."

"So we can only choose between Catholic and Presbyterian? What's the J stand for?"

Rolling off the couch, I go stand beside her. "P is for Protestant. If you're not Catholic, you're Protestant. And J is for Jewish."

"But what about us? What about the Baptists?"

"Baptists are Protestant. What is that form for, anyway?"

"We have to order identification tags to wear to school. Mrs. Wallace, my social studies teacher, said they are real dog tags, like the GI's wear."

"What in the world?" I snatch the yellow paper out of her hands. "Flossie, would you ever in your life believe this? They're going to make my girls wear dog tags to school. Dog tags." My head starts to pound as my blood pressure climbs. "What is happening to this world?"

Flossie shakes her head and clucks her tongue. "I don't know, Miz Adams. I swear, I just don't know." Flossie sets down the iron and the steel plate hisses.

I pick up the second form and sit down. "Good Lord. Mellie has to have canned food, like rations, and a blanket to leave at school. A gallon of store-bought water."

My hand trembles as I scan the third form. "This is an evacuation notice." Hysteria bubbles up from deep inside me. "They want permission for Mellie to be transferred from school to an approved bomb shelter in case of attack!" I jump up from the table and knock the chair over. Before it stops making a racket on the tiled floor, I have the phone in my hand and am dialing Clay's office number. "Clayton Adams, please." I'm out of breath.

Flossie hums as she irons. If I can just concentrate on those sounds instead of the panic welling inside me, I'll be okay. The phone line rings again and Shirley answers.

"I need to speak to Clay right away."

"One moment, please." Shirley pauses, and I think she's putting me on hold. Then she comes back on the line and says, "Norah? Are you okay?"

"Yes." But I'm not, not at all. The hold-tone sounds in one ear and Flossie's voice floats up and down and all around me, like ripples on a pond, calm and peaceful even though something has fallen out of sky and disrupted the still surface.

I take a deep breath. I realize that Clay can't do anything. There's no point in asking him to come home. He can't change the forms. He can't change the reason for the forms.

Unsettling news stories come to me, chaining together with frightening solidarity: Cuba, Russia, missiles. Navy patrols. Sailors getting sea orders when they were supposed to be on long shore duty. The jets roaring over all day and all night. Our safe little world seems to be slipping away, one link at a time.

I hang up the phone before Clay comes on the line. Trying to steady my hands, I take my time fixing myself a glass of tea. I have to get control of myself. The girls don't need to see me go to pieces.

MELANIE

In bed, I toss and turn until the sheets wrap around me like a mummy cloth.

Seeing Mama's reaction to those *damn* yellow forms made

me realize that there is something to worry about. That shaky feeling is back. Thinking of the forms and what they might really mean keeps me awake.

On the other side of the nightstand, Birdie lies snug in her twin bed, her breath huffing in and out, sleeping softly. Finally, I flop onto my back, fold my hands across my chest and force my eyes closed. *Come on sleep, sleep come on*, I chant in my head.

Just as the edge of sleep begins to slide over me, a jet roars so low the windows seem to crash in their frames and my bed shakes from the vibrations. I bolt up, clutching the sheet against my chest. Birdie screams and leaps out of her bed, pulling the sheet with her until it twists around her feet and drags her to the floor.

I untangle her and we rush out to the living room where our parents sit watching television. Birdie flies into Mama's arms and I land in Daddy's lap, sobbing.

I see the worried look on Mama's face before she buries her face in Birdie's hair.

Daddy pats my back. "Hush, it's all right, Mellie. It's just one of those Navy jets."

Sobbing in a breath, I manage to say, "But it was so loud this time." I can't stop crying, even though I know it's silly. Those jets fly over all the time. They've been flying low like that for months now.

It's those dumb forms.

Birdie sits on Mama's legs, straddling her bulging stomach. Mama rests her chin in Birdie's fluffy hair and closes her eyes. The television murmurs in the background, but Daddy's heart beats strong and steady beneath my ear. He smells warm and spicy and I want to stay there. Maybe forever.

But eventually, we have to go back to bed. Mama

straightens my sheets and smoothes them over me. She kisses me. She doesn't say a word. She doesn't really need to.

I know she feels the same way I do.

As soon as Mama leaves, Birdie slips into my bed. She doesn't say anything. I just tuck her in the crook of my arm. She puts her thumb in her mouth and rubs my pajama top between her fingers. I haven't seen her suck her thumb for more than a year.

The television clicks off. The lamps go out. My parents' voices are soft as they go to bed. I stay awake for a long time, watching the wavering lights of night float through my room. Finally, I slip into Birdie's bed, leaving her sound asleep on mine.

The room seems different from her bed, a little out of balance. Sleep finally comes.

The roaring comes loud. Long and low, followed by a high whine and then a ka-boom, just like in a cartoon. I run through the halls of the Junior High. Instead of School Board green and beige on the walls, ash gray covers everything. Only black, charcoal, blue gray, and white ash. None of the walls reach the ceiling because the ceiling has disappeared and black and gray clouds hang low enough to touch the walls. Stephanie is gone. The teachers are all absent, lost in the whine and ka-boom.

Only me, by myself.

I run until, finally, the crumbling cinder block walls of the school are behind me. Going home, I run past the stark skeletons of leafless trees and grass burnt to dust. My street is a long tunnel of black smoke. The smoke has to be hiding the houses. I can't see them. Can't find my home.

"Mama, Daddy, wait for me. I'm almost home. Wait! I'll be there soon!" I cry and cough from the smoke. Tears stream down

my face, tasting salty and ashy in my mouth.

When I find my house, I open the front door and see the familiar shapes of our furniture, now only ashes waiting to blow away in the howling wind that comes roaring down the street.

I jolt awake. I stare with wide eyes, trying to recognize the shadowy shapes of furniture. The blinds stripe the windows, letting in the soft blue night. Birdie sprawls on my bed, her wet thumb glistening in a strip of moonlight.

It was a dream, a horrible dream. My breathing slows and my hands relax their death grip on the sheets. I listen until I hear my father's snores.

I go to the closet and dig in the box of toys hidden there. Heidi, my stuffed rabbit, is crushed on the bottom of the box. I tug her out. Her fur is matted and flat in places. She smells musty, but feels so comforting.

Back in bed, I keep her clutched against my chest. I'm afraid to close my eyes.

I'll just wait for morning.

NORAH

"I'm surprised Birdie went to sleep so soon. I expected to be up with her most of the night," Clay says, as we fold back the bedspread.

"I peeked in. Birdie's in Melanie's bed and they're both asleep. At least Birdie is. But she has her thumb in her mouth."

Clay is pulling his undershirt over his head. "Our little Birdie has had a lot to adjust to."

I tug the hairbrush through my hair, lifting it up off my

neck so I can cool off a bit. "She was just getting back to her old self."

"Those damn jets." Clay's belt snaps as he rips it through the belt loops. "I sure wish the Navy would stop them from breaking the sound barrier every time they come and go."

"Rachel Winston told me the pilots do that to signal to their wives they've made it home safely from another mission." The attic fan is still pulling a strong breeze through the open windows, and I wait for Clay to turn off the lights so I can open the blinds and curtains to let in more air. "She wouldn't tell me what missions they were running, or why the wives might think they wouldn't make it back. It's not like we're in World War Two."

"I'm sure there are things going on that we don't know about." Clay stretches out on the bed with a sigh. "Hell, there's enough to worry about with what we do know. Last week, the newspapers were saying the reservists are going to be called to active duty, and tonight, Kennedy had a press conference about how he's going to do whatever it takes to protect our security."

"What do you think that means?"

"I'm not sure. I'm not even sure I want to know, but it's got to be serious."

I lie down next to him and curl against his side, even though the night is still warm. I just need to feel him there, the solid certainty of him. "The president won't let anything happen, will he?"

Clay's shoulder moves beneath my head. "He's got some hard decisions to make. Castro and Khrushchev are bullies, and you can't let a bully win. Ever."

I shiver, recalling the *Times-Union's* many headlines about Castro preparing to defend against a U.S. invasion, about missile launching sites in Cuba, about the Army trucks rumbling through Jacksonville with supplies to build nuclear fallout shelters. "What do you think I should do about ordering those dog tags for the girls?"

"You should probably order them, sweetheart." He kisses my forehead. "Goodnight."

That's my cue to move so Clay can roll over onto his side. I stare at the ceiling, trying to round up my scattered thoughts. The girls were so scared tonight, they were shaking. Crying and shaking, yet Clay and I didn't really do anything to make them unafraid.

The fear pulls us together, and at the same time, sets us apart from each other. We want to huddle in each other's arms and feel safe, but if we do, then we have to admit that we're scared.

So I stay on my side of the bed. Clay remains on his.

MELANIE

"Melanie, wake up."

Mama's voice slips through the heaviness in my head.

I jerk upright, expecting to see the grayness of my nightmare. Instead, living color floods every surface, from the muted cabbage roses on our bedspreads to the bright white eyelet of our curtains. Our bedroom walls glow pink in the brilliant, early sunlight. The humid air hums with a melody of normal.

Relief pours through me.

Mama kisses my cheek. "What happened here? Were you playing musical beds last night?"

Fingering the sheet, I think about telling Mama my dream,

but that would make the nightmare more real. My heart races just thinking about it. "No, Birdie had a hard time getting to sleep." I sit up. "I let her come to bed with me, but then my bed was too crowded."

"I'll bet. Birdie's a rambunctious sleeper." Mama crosses to the other bed to wake Birdie. She leans over and kisses her on the forehead. "Wake up, Beatrice, darling."

Mama always uses our given names to wake us. It's like she has enough energy in the morning for our full names, but soon after breakfast she's back to calling us by our nicknames. Sometimes they become even shorter as the day goes on.

I wonder what she'll call us after the baby's born.

Birdie opens her eyes. After a second, she latches her arms around Mama's neck and holds on for dear life. Mama giggles and falls down on the bed with her. Mama stands, yanks the sheet off Birdie and tickles her. "Get ready for school now." She pats Birdie on the bottom and heads for the door. Over her shoulder, she says, "Hurry, hurry."

Birdie jumps up and runs to the closet. "I'm going to wear my green dress today." Tossing the dress onto the bed, Birdie spins around three times before she tugs her pajama top over her head. She spins three more times and pulls her bottoms off.

"Why are you spinning around, Birdie?"

"'Cause."

I stretch my arms over my head and swing my feet over the side of the bed, feeling the sleepy pull in my calves. "Okay, I'll play along. 'Cause why?"

"Jeepers, Mellie. Don't you know anything?"

"More than you."

"Well, you don't know that spinning in the morning will take away bad dreams, do you?"

I stare at Birdie. Did I scream in my sleep? Maybe she had

her own nightmares last night. "You're just making that up."

"Am not."

Birdie stands with her hands fisted on her waist and her white cotton panties ballooning over her skinny thighs. She looks like a fluffy little chick ready to fight. I just don't feel like arguing this morning. My fighting energy might be needed for something more important.

I shrug. "Okay, you're not making it up. Thanks for telling me."

"Well, it probably won't work for you, anyway."

"Why not?"

"'Cause you're not in the magic world anymore."

Birdie pulls on her green dress and dances out of the room like a fairy, her feet skipping so lightly they hardly touch the floor.

Sometimes Birdie makes no sense at all, and sometimes, even when she shouldn't make any sense, she says things that are too true.

Saturday
September 29, 1962

Jacksonville, Florida

MELANIE

"Stupid hair," I mutter, throwing my comb into the bathroom sink. "Damn, I'm never going to be ready for Robert's party."

My reflection glares back at me from the mirror, my hair just as lopsided as it was five minutes before. The right side flips perfectly, a beautiful curve and curl that rests on top of my shoulder, but the left side hangs straight, with no hint of a curl anywhere. My Toni has failed in less than a month. That has to be a record.

"Melanie, come on. We need to leave now," Mama calls out from the kitchen.

Birdie stops on her way to the living room and leans against the bathroom door. "She's still staring at herself in the mirror."

My eyes burn like I'm about to cry, but I won't. Birdie doesn't understand why I cry all the time anymore than I do.

Mama says these spells will pass, but I feel like I live every day with a flash flood of tears ready to spill at the least little thing. And sometimes—no, a lot of the time—Birdie is the "least little thing" that sets loose the waterworks.

Mama and Daddy come to stand by Birdie. They all stare at me in the bathroom. Trembling like a leaf in a hurricane, I turn and shout, "Can't y'all just leave me alone for a few minutes?"

Like a group of dancers, they all take a giant step backward. Daddy clears his throat. "Mellie, don't talk to your mother like that."

Mama pats his arm and then steps into the bathroom. "It's okay, Clay. This is Mellie's first big party." Daddy and Birdie slip away.

I close my eyes and wait for the scolding I know I deserve, but Mama just hugs me. That's the thing that makes me cry and cry.

Mama rubs my back and whispers, "Shush, baby. It's all right." Then she holds me at arm's length.

"Wash your face, sweetheart, and come on down to the Taylor's in a few minutes. We'll go ahead and take the dish of beans. Can you bring the cupcakes?"

"S-s-sure, Mama." I gulp back another sob and kiss Mama's soft, powdered cheek. "I'll bring the cupcakes."

"Okay." She leaves me alone in the bathroom.

Birdie's voice trills through the house. "Mama, why is she crying this time?" The front door clicks shut behind them, muffling Mama's answer.

I'm really alone. I put a washcloth soaked in cold water over my face and sit on the closed toilet. The cool cloth takes all the steam out of me. I grow quiet inside. The trembling stops and the tears slip back to their hiding place.

When I take the cloth off my face and look in the mirror again, I know what to do with my hair. I pull the straight side up and sweep it over to the right, stab a couple of bobby pins in to hold it while I dig around for one of Mama's old hair combs. I put the comb in without looking, and hope that I won't be right back where I started, only more lopsided.

I look up and see a young lady, not a scruffy little girl. The upward sweep of hair makes my face look soft. My cheeks glow light pink and my lips look...well, I guess they look like they are ready to be kissed. I run my tongue over my lips and think about what it must feel like to be kissed by a boy. Not a parent.

In Mama's room, I open her precious bottle of Chanel No. 5. Dabbing my finger to the top of the bottle, I gather just a circle of the golden scent on my fingertip, and touch it behind my left ear, where the skin is exposed by my upswept hair. Then I dab behind the other ear. The last touch I sweep across the skin at the top of my dress.

Carefully placing the perfume on Mama's dresser, I remember when Lola gave it to Mama for Christmas, saying, "Coco Chanel herself says to wear Chanel No. 5 if you want to be kissed." And I definitely want to be kissed. Tonight. By Robert. So I don't have to worry about that stupid pact with Stephanie anymore.

From the Taylor's backyard, music and laughter roll in waves like the rhythm of the breakers at the beach, first loud, then soft, then loud again. I weave through the cars lining the driveway, but stop when I hear voices coming from the carport.

"C'mon, Mrs. Winston."

Robert's voice, but not melting and smooth like usual. He sounds tense, maybe excited. I wonder what he wants from Mrs. Winston.

"Rob, my name is Rachel. Say it." Mrs. Winston sounds

like she's out of breath. Or whispering. She's standing really close to him.

"No." Robert's moves backward and Mrs. Winston tilts forward, leaning into him.

I don't want to hear anything else. I don't want to see anymore. I back down the driveway, and crouch behind a big, red Chevy, balancing the tray of cupcakes on my knees. The waxed paper covering the plate shimmers with iridescence in the early evening light. I squint at the shifting colors and try to make sense everything. They've stopped talking and I can't resist looking over the hood of the red Chevy to see what's happening.

Mrs. Winston puts her hands on Robert's chest and pushes him back against the wall with a slight thud. Robert's palms flatten against the rough gray cinderblock wall on either side of him.

"Well, when you get back from training, then." Mrs. Winston lifts Robert's hand and leans up against him, her breasts pressing into his chest. She kisses him right on the mouth. As she pulls away from him, she takes his hand and places it on her breast.

Robert's eyes grow huge and his mouth gapes like a drowning man gasping for air. Just as suddenly his lids droop and he leans toward Mrs. Winston. His mouth closes slightly.

Mrs. Winston draws one finger over Robert's lower lip and squeezes his hand on her breast. "I'll miss you while you're learning to fight those horrible Commies."

Then she walks away, leaving Robert alone on the carport. Is that how a woman gets kissed by the man she likes? She just takes it?

Robert pushes away from the wall and tugs on his navy blue slacks a little before looking up to see me peeking over the red car's hood.

I clear my throat and stand. "Hi, Robert."

Sweat dampens the hair at his temples and his face glistens. He wipes his hand across his brow and then drags it across the leg of his trousers. "Uh, hi, Melanie." His voice sounds thick and the exposed skin at the collar of his shirt is blotchy red.

"What do you have there?" He nods at the platter which I quickly level. It had been tilting dangerously toward the driveway. "Cupcakes. I made cupcakes."

He walks over to the car. "They look good. You made these yourself?"

"Yes." I didn't realize I was trembling, but now I feel it all the way through me. The waxed paper rattles in my shaking hands. I struggle to think of something to say. "Sounds like a good party. Are lots of your friends here?"

Robert looks up at the sky, now turning a soft shade of violet, the color just before blue, just before dark. He takes a deep breath and exhales slowly. "Yeah. All of my friends are here." He takes the cupcake platter, and we weave through the cars together.

"There's the man of the hour," Stephanie's dad shouts when we come around the corner of the house. The back yard is filled with smoke from the burgers and hot dogs sizzling on the grill. The spicy scent of boiling shrimp roils up from the steaming kettle.

Kids chase each other across the lawn. Grown-ups sit in folding chairs or stand on the brick patio beneath the Japanese lanterns strung from the awning. Mrs. Winston is perched on the edge of a lawn chair with a tall glass in one hand and a cigarette in the other, her gaze locked onto Robert.

Marvin Gordon sits alone by the record player and thumbs through a stack of forty-fives. A guitar lies across his legs. He slips a record on the spindle and Joey Dee's "Peppermint Twist" fills the air.

Stephanie's dad takes Cherie's elbow and pushes her toward Robert, who is putting my platter of cupcakes on a table already loaded with food. "Here ya' go, son. Dance with the most beautiful girl at the party."

"Oh, Dad, stop." Cherie shrugs out of her dad's grasp but continues to move in Robert's direction with a sly smile on her face.

"Thanks Mr. Starr, but I'm going to dance with Melanie."

Cherie's smile freezes and she smoothly changes directions so she's facing Robert's friend, Doug, instead. Doug holds out his hand. They start to twist while all the grown-ups look on.

"You should have danced with Cherie. I'm not very good at the twist."

"I don't want to dance with Cherie. Come on." Robert walks to where a few couples are dancing. "The twist isn't hard."

I put my foot out and pretend I'm crushing a cigarette. Then I move my arms back and forth like I'm drying my back with a towel. I'm doing the motions that make up the Twist, but I look nothing like Robert or Cherie or even Doug. "I just don't have any rhythm."

"You're doing fine. Just loosen up a little. Relax and have some fun." Robert moves a little nearer, closing the distance between us, and bends his left knee so that his face is level with mine. "How long were you standing by the Chevy?"

I manage to shrug while yanking my imaginary towel back and forth across my back.

"That was nothing with Mrs. Winston. You know that, right?"

I glance over my shoulder. Rachel Winston is glaring at us

like she can hear what Robert's saying, but that's impossible with the volume of the music. Maybe she can read lips. When she notices that Robert's looking her way, she takes a sip of her drink and leans in closer to Mr. Schultz and the young man with him.

What could I say? Maybe Robert wanted to be kissed tonight, too. Maybe Mrs. Winston was his prize, just like I want him to be my prize. Except, I don't want to think about that. Instead, I shrug. "Sure, Robert. Whatever you say."

"Hey, you can keep another secret, can't you?"

I look into his big blue eyes and see something I can't put my finger on. What is the secret he wants me to keep? Is he scared of Mrs. Winston like he said he was scared about joining the Navy? No, I don't think that's it, exactly. "Yeah, I can keep a secret for you."

I wait a second and realize he's not going to say anything else. I guess the secret is not to tell anyone about Mrs. Winston kissing him. Yeah. I can understand why he wants to keep that a secret.

Robert seems relieved. He smiles and relaxes into the dance. His body moves like it is all one piece instead of jerking around like sticks glued together the way mine does.

Soon, Mrs. Winston and the young man she was talking to join us on the makeshift dance floor. Rachel Winston does the twist like no one I've ever seen. Where I put all the effort into crushing my foot into the floor, all of Rachel Winston's movements come from her hips. The young man moves closer to her until they're almost touching.

I don't understand why she's dancing like that. Everyone knows the partners don't touch during the Twist. But somehow, Mrs. Winston makes it look like everybody else is missing out on something.

Finally, Mrs. Schultz steps forward and taps Mrs. Winston on the shoulder. "Let me," she pauses to clear her throat, "cut in, dear. Davy promised a dance to me, too."

Mrs. Winston sways over to the drink table. She pours herself a tall glass of Coke and splashes some rum into it. She stands alone by the table while the music plays and conversations resume.

Mrs. Schultz is even worse at the twist than I am. She grimaces and moves like she's afraid she'll strain her back. Davy keeps glancing at Mrs. Winston, who's staring at him over the rim of her glass.

It dawns on me this is Stephanie's advice about getting a boy to kiss you acted out in real life. During a three-minute song, Rachel Winston made sure Davy knows she likes him. She convinced him that he wants to kiss her. Even I can see that hungry look written all over his face. Over the rim of her glass, her eyes promise that she'll make the opportunity happen.

It looks so simple. Somehow I know what I just witnessed is more than just getting a boy to kiss you, though. It scares me a little and thrills me a little more.

The music ends and Steph runs up beside me. "Hey, Robert. Will you dance with me, too?"

"Sure, kid, but I need to get something to eat first. Later, okay?" Robert walks backward to the table. "Thanks for the dance, Mel. And everything."

"Sure." Now Robert and I share two secrets. The first one I understand, the second is a mystery I don't really want to solve. But we share them, and that's all that matters.

"Wow, did you see that?" Steph whispers. "Everyone's talking about it."

"What?"

"Mrs. Winston. You know her husband's on duty."

"Yeah. So what?"

"Dad says he's flying over Cuba. The Navy's keeping an eye on things since the Russians said they were going to help Castro more."

I'm having trouble following Steph. What does Cuba have to do with Mrs. Winston? "So everyone's talking about Castro?"

Steph rolls her eyes and groans. "How can you miss what's right under your nose? I'm talking about Mrs. Winston and that boy, Davy."

"Oh. I saw that." But I don't feel like talking about it. Confusion and tension flare like little explosions in my queasy stomach. I want to be like Mrs. Winston in some ways. I want to be looked at the way Robert and Davy look at Mrs. Winston in her tight white dress and high-heeled sandals. But I know I don't want to be talked about the way people talk about Mrs. Winston.

And I never want someone nice like Robert to push me away.

NORAH

Melanie stands beside me, leaving Stephanie looking at records with Marvin. I reach up and tuck a stray hair into the pretty comb she's put in her hair. "Did I tell you that you look real pretty tonight?"

"Thanks, Mama." Melanie leans over and kisses my cheek.

In her new dress with her hair swept to one side, she looks very grown up. Especially when she was dancing with Robert.

I'm a little uncomfortable, since they seem to be becoming close friends. No, it's nothing to worry about. Robert's leaving in a few weeks and when he returns he'll be a worldly sailor and Mellie will still be my little girl.

"Daddy, come dance with me," Birdie shouts, as she runs through the groups of people clustered on the lawn. "Marvin said he'd play the 'Hokey Pokey' on his guitar if all of us kids get a grown-up to dance."

Clay hands me his beer bottle. "Okay, okay. You don't have to drag me across the yard, Birdie."

The kids and their grown-up partners form a sloppy circle around where Marvin sits beside Stephanie. She's grinning like she's the special guest on the "Queen for a Day" television show. Soon everyone in the circle is sticking out a foot and shaking it all about.

For a few seconds I think about joining the circle, but then a pain shoots through my hips. I'm just fine where I am. In fact, I'll be a lot better when I can get home and put my feet up and rest my aching back.

Sara Matthews comes over to stand beside me. "It's just disgraceful, isn't it Norah?"

I take a sip from Clay's beer and put it down on the table behind me. "I never thought the 'Hokey Pokey' was disgraceful."

Sara nods her head toward a group of boys standing around Rachel Winston. Her head is thrown back and she's laughing that deep smoky, laugh of hers. The low V-neck of her dress shows a good bit of shimmying cleavage. The boys didn't seem to get the joke.

"I feel sorry for poor Bob. He's such a good man. He deserves someone better than that hussy." Sara leans closer and lowers her voice. "You know Bob had to take her to the doctor last month, don't you? My Mitch said he heard it was nerve pills, but I think it was liquor. I mean, look at her, she's drinking like a fish tonight."

Even though I have my own opinion about the woman's behavior, I just don't like gossip. I never have. Besides, Melanie is still standing beside me, and I don't want her to hear anything more about our neighbor. "Sara, we don't know what really happened, do we? You know I had to go to the doctor last month myself. Did you hear what was wrong with me?"

Sara glances at my bulging belly then looks up at me with a smile. "Why, Norah, the rumors are true? You *are* expecting?"

We both laugh and Melanie looks at us like we're crazy women. The "Hokey Pokey" circle breaks up and Clay comes over with Birdie riding on his shoulders. "Well, girls, are we ready to call it a night?"

"I just need to get my dish, honey."

"I'll get it, Mama," Melanie says.

"Thanks, sweetie."

"You've got three lovely ladies, Clay." Sara pats me on the back. "You call if you need anything, you hear? How much longer 'til the baby comes?"

"Just a couple of weeks, I hope."

Melanie walks up, holding my casserole dish, with Robert right behind her.

Clay claps Robert on the shoulder and shakes his hand. "Rob, my boy, congratulations. I hope you'll be happy with your decision."

Two jets roar over, drowning out all the sounds of the party. Robert and Clay look skyward, even though they can't see anything in the black night. I notice some of the children stop their games and glance to see what their parents are doing.

Robert says, "Thanks, Mr. Adams. I'm sure I'll be fine."

"I'm ready, Clay. My back's killing me. Did you get the tray for the cupcakes, too, Mellie?"

She shakes her head. "There are still some left."

"Okay, we can get the tray tomorrow. Let's go home."

"Does Melanie have to leave now?" Robert asks, looking from me to Clay.

I reach over and tuck that same strand of hair back into Mellie's comb. Why does Robert want my girl to stay? Of course, she's the prettiest girl here. Still, my gut reaction is to say no, but she has such a hopeful look on her face. And Stephanie and her parents are still here. I'm so tired I've got squirrels in my head. Clay should make the rest of the decisions for tonight. "What do you think, Clay?"

"I'll walk her home, Mr. Adams," Robert says. *How sweet*, I think, even though we only live five houses away.

Birdie bounces on Clay's shoulders. "Let's go, let's go. I have to potty."

Clay reaches up to bring Birdie down, but she giggles. "Not really, not really."

"Sure, Rob," Clay says. "Have her home in an hour or so."

"Yes, sir, Mr. Adams. Thanks again for coming."

"G'night, Robert." Clay wraps his warm hand around mine, and I feel more relaxed. Mellie will be fine. I have to let her grow up. I know that.

I lean over, kiss Mellie's cheek and take the dish from her. "Mind your manners. Make sure to thank Mr. and Mrs. Taylor."

"Yes, ma'am. I'll see you at home." She turns and follows Robert over to the record player, where Stephanie and Marvin are still sitting together.

With Birdie riding on Clay's shoulders and her fingers clutching his wavy hair, we wind through our groups of friends while saying goodnight. It's dark on the street. Only the neighbors' porch lamps and a pale moon light our way. Already the noise of the party is fading. Clay and Birdie are singing. It's been a good day, but I'm glad it's over. I'm tired and want to sleep.

We arrive at our yard and Birdie begins chanting, "Do the trick, Daddy. Let's do the trick."

"Birdie," I say. "It's late and it's dark. We should get you to bed."

"Please? Please, please, please? Daddy, you're not sleepy, are you?"

Clay gazes at me a grins. "She's growing up fast, Norah."

I understand that he wants do this trick he and Birdie have worked out, and he's right: she'll be too big to do it soon. In fact, I think she's already too tall and lanky. "I wish you wouldn't."

"Please? Please?" Clay and Birdie chant together.

"Oh, all right. Then we all go to bed, okay?"

"Yeah!" Birdie shouts and kicks her shoes off.

Clay grips her calves. "Ready?"

"Of course. I'm Birdie the Acrobat Tortionist Clown." She wraps her arms around her daddy's head and eases upward until her feet are on his shoulders and her toes curl down like a monkey's to help her balance as she stands. She stretches her arms and takes a deep breath.

Clay's legs are braced and his biceps are tight as he holds our daughter on his strong shoulders, a huge grin on his face.

This is the point where I always hold my breath and think I should stop them. This is dangerous and I shouldn't allow them do something so foolish.

Clay says, "Now!"

Birdie falls forward, almost like a diver. The skirt of her

dress inverts as she drops forward, forward, forward, until about six inches from the ground Clay stops her fall with his grip on her ankles. Birdie's giggles sound breathless with excitement.

Clay gently lays her down on the grass. She does a somersault and rises from her curl with her arms raised over her head. "Ta-da!" Father and daughter take a bow, while I exhale a deep sigh of relief and applaud. Birdie runs to the front door and Clay puts his arm around me.

"That's the last time, Norah. She's too big. It's not safe anymore."

MELANIE

"Do you want something else to drink, Mellie?" Robert asks.

"No, thanks." I look around the group dancing and laughing beneath the Japanese lanterns. Stephanie and Marvin are sitting closer together. He's putting her fingers on the strings of his guitar, showing her how to make a chord while he strums. Nerves tingle in my scalp. This is it, my first adult party without my parents. And I'm here with Robert. He wanted me to stay, so it's almost like a date.

Awareness slips over me like a new skin. The air feels thicker somehow, like it actually touches my bare shoulders and leaves invisible, feathery fingerprints. Night-blooming jasmine and heavy-sweet honeysuckle perfume the darkness, while cigarette smoke drifts over the heads of the men standing near the fence. Their voices rise and fall. I hear the words Castro and Russia. They talk about planes and make guesses about what kind of missions their friends have been flying.

Robert stands beside me. Has he noticed the same things I have? I wonder if he hears the men's war talk. Does it frighten him, or make him more eager to join them? His face shows no emotion, except when Mrs. Winston rises like a graceful white bird from her chair. His brows draw together, and he looks down at his shoes.

She sways through the middle of the party, clearing a path until she stands in front of Robert. He steps back and bumps against the drink table, making the bottles rattle.

"Goodnight, Rob. I'll see you when you get back, right?" She kisses his cheek and lets her fingers drift over his forearm. "Good luck."

I swallow the lump of jealousy clogging my throat. I really don't like Mrs. Winston.

"Uh, thanks for coming." Robert shakes her hand, like he shook my daddy's.

Mrs. Winston's hand slowly leaves Robert's. "I always do, Rob."

Robert looks embarrassed, but I don't know why. It's a fact Mrs. Winston comes to *all* the parties.

Then she's gone, leaving her heavy scent to cloud our breath. "Want to dance again?" Robert asks.

For the second time in one night, I'm paired with Robert on the dance floor. Only this time the song is a ballad, so his hand is on my waist and mine rests on his shoulder. I think I'm in heaven.

The next hour passes so quickly. Too soon, Robert and I weave our way through the cars parked in the driveway. It's very dark. Music from the backyard sounds softer and higher, as if it comes from way up in the sky rather than behind the house. That tingling awareness lingers with me, magnifying every scent, every sound, every touch. I trip on the edge of the driveway and Robert catches my arm. His fingers feel warm on my skin. He smells like earth and strength and heat in the night.

I want to bury my face in his shoulder again, like when I rode behind him on his motorbike. But we walk side by side down the shadowy street, in and out of puddles of porch light. Robert is carrying the empty cupcake platter, letting it bounce against his leg with a thump every now and then. We pass the five houses between Robert's and mine without saying a word, swatting mosquitoes with exaggerated movements, a strange, silent dance.

At the end of my driveway, Robert stops abruptly and steps in front of me, blocking my way.

Was Robert going to kiss me? Me?

Suddenly, I feel like I've run a mile. There's no air in my lungs, no thoughts in my head, only my blood rushing through my body.

He steps closer, his breath warm on my cheek. Then magically, without thought, our lips came together. He moves his lips, covering mine with more heat, more wetness until I feel the rest of my body disappear. Only his lips on mine. Nothing else in the world exists.

Just this kiss. Just this moment.

I move my mouth against his, following his lead, kissing him back. This is even better than I thought it would be. I want to keep kissing Robert forever.

"Mellie." He touches my lips with one finger. "I shouldn't have kissed you."

"Why? I wanted you to kiss me. I wanted you to be my first one."

"Your first?" Robert slides his hands to my arms once more.

"You're sweet, Melanie. Don't ever change." He touches my forehead with his closed mouth. It isn't a kiss.

Now, I know a kiss.

He steps around me, and turns toward his house. "'Night, Mellie."

He walks up the street, his back straight, head held high, like he's already a sailor.

I cover my mouth with my hands to hold onto the kiss. My whole body sings. Deep inside, in the place my soul must rest, a tiny pulse throbs and grows until it echoes all through me, from my scalp to my toes.

Thursday
October 4, 1962

NORAH

"Cherie is grounded, Mama," Melanie says. "Steph told me her parents really hate her boyfriend, Clint."

I shrug and focus on the blue booties I'm crocheting. Everyone is hoping for a boy now, even Birdie, who's coloring blue pictures for the baby's room.

Melanie sits beside me on the couch. She rubs a thread of yarn between her fingers. "Why do you think they grounded her? She and Clint only go to the movies and stuff."

"Parents have to make decisions about what's best for their children. Sometimes the children don't like it, but it's still the best thing for them."

"But what's wrong with going to the movies with Clint? Cherie's parents let her start dating a couple of years ago. She's had a few boyfriends."

I study her serious face, thankful that she's still so innocent. How long will I be able to keep her that way? I might as well take this chance to teach my girl a little about men. "There are different kinds of boys, Melanie. A girl has to be careful which kind she chooses. I think Clint might be, well, a little rough. I wouldn't want you to date him."

Flossie continues to dust, arranging the china shepherdess and her sheep on the bookshelf. She glances at me and smiles. She understands what I'm saying. It occurs to me I don't even know if she has children.

Melanie looks from me to Flossie. "How can you tell, Mama?"

I can tell Mellie's confused, wondering what kind of special x-ray vision grown-up women have that girls don't.

"Experience, sweetie." I can't help but shake my head, hoping that she has an easy time of it, but knowing that learning about men and love is never easy. "Just experience."

"Is it because Clint's hair's a little too long?"

"No. It's more in his attitude. Like he rules the world and everything in it. And, of course, that means he rules Cherie, too. You don't want to get involved with a man who wants to control you, sweetie. You want to love a man who loves you and thinks of you as a partner."

Flossie picks up her dust-rag and runs the cloth over the piano's smooth walnut finish. She lifts the keyboard cover and dances the rag over the keys, making nonsense chords from high to low.

"Let's play our duet, Flossie." Melanie slips onto the piano bench and pats the space beside her. Flossie glances at me and I nod. She scoots in next to Melanie.

They position their fingers on the keys and Flossie begins a blues rhythm in the bass register, the notes rich and dark like her fingers on the keys. Melanie tinkles a melody high in the treble notes.

It isn't really a song, at least not one Melanie's piano teacher would play, but it sounds like music to me. Mellie loves to play it with Flossie.

Sometimes Flossie sets the tempo faster, like a boogie-woogie, and sometimes it's slower like a ballad. Today it's really mournful, like the blues.

While they play, Flossie makes up words. "Sometimes a man cain't find no peace in himself," she sings in rhythm to her chords. "So he looks for a woman to make him quiet inside, so he can stand himself. But cain't no woman do that for him. Just like no man can do that for a woman."

The words pause here and Flossie plays a sad, melancholy melody. She rocks on the bench and sings, "Every person got to find his own peace. Every person got to make his own happiness, child. It don't come from outside." She pounds out the final notes, and Melanie's fingers do a run in the high keys.

Flossie nods and folds her hands over her heart and sings, her voice clear and true. "It comes from here, inside."

Melanie tinkles the piano keys a little more. "Flossie, how did you learn to play piano like that? My teacher doesn't play that way."

"I just picked it up here and there. Mostly at church. I had some music lessons at college, too."

"You went to college, Flossie?"

"Yes, ma'am. I sure did."

Flossie rises from the piano bench and takes up her dust rag again. Her shoulders are back. Her head is held high.

I know that she knows that I didn't go to college, but she doesn't say anything.

Does it embarrass Melanie to know that the colored woman who dusts her house went to college and her mama didn't?

Just the other night we talked about that mess up at the University of Mississippi where that colored boy wants to go.

Well, he's going there now, despite all the fighting and the National Guard being there. What a mess.

I told Melanie that if she decided to go college I wanted her to stay close to home in case trouble broke out like that. And it's a fact there's going to be more trouble. Once the gate is open, there's no stopping the trouble from rushing in.

Melanie sits silently on the piano bench, her gaze on the keys, her hands in her lap. I can tell her mind is going about a hundred miles an hour, thinking about all the different choices people can make in their lives.

I watch Flossie continue her dusting, humming under her breath like she's just the happiest person in the world. I wonder what choices she made that led her to cleaning my house with a college education behind her. Surely, being a maid wasn't her only option. Was it?

But then, how many options do women really have, black or white?

I wrap more yarn around my finger and begin the next row of crochet stitches.

I started working in an office, but I sure didn't want to end up like Miss Jacobs, the old maid office manager. She'd worked for the company for nearly forty years. She couldn't move up any higher in pay grade. Miss Jacobs didn't have a choice, because she never got married.

Even I had more choices than Miss Jacobs. I pause to count my stitches again and look at the pattern. Two more rows like this. Birdie jumps up to show me her picture.

"That's nice, Birdie. We'll put it on the wall later, okay?"

What kind of choices will Melanie make? All I can hope for is that she'll make decisions she'll be happy with.

That's probably the most any of us can hope for. I look at my girls, peaceful and happy, and realize that I've made a lot more good choices than bad.

"Mama?" Melanie's voice interrupts my thoughts. "Is it all right if Steph and I go to the store for a Coke?"

"Sure. Bring something back for Birdie, okay?"

"All right. What do you want, Birdie?"

Birdie squeezes her eyes closed. "I can't make up my mind."

"Let Melanie surprise you," I suggest.

Birdie shrugs her shoulders. "Okay. I like surprises."

"See you later, Mama." Melanie kisses my cheek and goes out the door. For now, her choice is simple: choose a piece of candy Birdie will like. Birdie likes all kinds of candy. Melanie can't go wrong.

Wednesday
October 9, 1962

Jacksonville, Florida

MELANIE

Mad Math Marchman's voice stops. In fact, the whole classroom gets quiet. Too quiet.

I understand why people believe in fortune-tellers, because I know what's going to happen next. Behind my closed eyelids, I see Mrs. Marchman standing beside my desk with her arms folded across her chest and her long wooden pointer dangling from her hand.

I open my eyes and there she is for real, just like I'd seen her in my head.

"Melanie, should I have marked you absent from this class?"

I rub my cheek, hoping there are no ink stains on it, or worse, strings of drool. "No, ma'am." I swallow hard and try to ignore my rolling stomach.

Mrs. Marchman lays her pointer across my desk and rests her palms on top of my blank notebook. "Can you explain to us how to solve for x?"

I scan the chalkboard, searching for a clue, but see only a new equation. Every face in the class is turned my way. Some express pity, others gloat. My stomach pitches again and I clutch the front of my dress to try to stop the inevitable.

The future looms dark before me once again, and I foresee my half-digested school cafeteria cheeseburger all over Mrs. Marchman's brown orthopedic shoes.

She must have caught a glimpse of the future too, because she backs away from me, and heads to the blackboard. Thank goodness both of us are wrong. My cheeseburger stays put.

"For the benefit of Miss Adams, we will solve for x once more, class."

The emergency alarm clangs. My heart stops. Mrs. Marchman freezes, her pointer rigid against the blackboard. The loud speaker crackles while we sit motionless.

I glance to where the blankets, bottles of water and cans of food brought in by Marchman's homeroom await disaster in neat stacks. Instinctively, we shuffle our feet and shift in our chairs, ready to duck under our desks. The alarm had sounded twice last week, and we were instructed to scoot under our desks and cover our necks with our hands.

This would prevent serious spinal injuries in the event of a bombing.

That bit of information became great material for the class clowns. Grotesque jokes seemed to be the preferred method for dealing with fear after these drills.

I had to admit that even I saw the comedy when I glanced down the aisle and saw butts of various sizes and shapes protruding from beneath the ancient metal desktops. These were supposed to protect us. These desks barely remain upright through a standard dismissal bell. No one believed they would withstand Russian missiles.

I try to swallow past the knot in my throat.

Finally, the principal's voice booms over the loud speaker. "Remain calm. This is a drill only. Teachers, proceed with the planned evacuation drill at this time."

Mrs. Marchman claps her hands. "Quiet. Quiet. Don't move until I motion for your row to stand."

I have to admit that I feel better in Mad Marchman's care than if I had been stuck with Mrs. Carlton, my English teacher. She'd probably make us recite one of the poems she loves so much to give us inspiration.

Marchman stands at attention behind her desk, her grizzled gray head upright and her arms rigid at her sides. She slaps the pointer against her desk, signaling each row, one at a time, to file out.

Lines of students exit every doorway of the school building then snake down the driveways. Cars wait, manned by cafeteria staff and janitors and coaches. They drive past us slowly, like a funeral procession, while we are counted off by fives and then turned back toward the school building.

Mrs. Marchman prods each student with her pointer, repeating over and over again, "In case of actual evacuation, you will enter this car and be taken to a safe shelter." Her voice never wavers. Neither does her pointer.

All I know is I'm not going to any *safe shelter*. While waiting in line, I plan routes from school to home. I ride the bus because of the busy highway, not the distance. I can easily cut through the neighborhood by the school and enter my own neighborhood through the field bordering the elementary school. It will only take about ten minutes at a nice run. Then I can pick up Birdie from first grade and we can be home with Mama in only fifteen minutes.

I need to run the route to make sure there are no fences or bad dogs. And to get into shape. Maybe that's why President Kennedy started the physical fitness program last year. He wants us all to be in condition for evacuations.

It doesn't seem possible that it can be so quiet with the entire student body outside. The only sounds are the murmur of teachers' instructions, the soft hum of the car engines, and the happy song of the birds.

How strange it is to be planning for disaster on such a bright October afternoon. The sun dazzles gold in a brilliant blue sky. Wisps of clouds glow silver. A slight breeze catches a few dry leaves and sends them dancing across the lawn in front of the school.

Everything seems so normal.

Except I'm in a line pretending to get into a car, practicing to escape from a bomb.

Sweat beads on my forehead and upper lip. My head pounds fiercely and my stomach heaves again as I walk up to the door of a faded beige station wagon driven by the baseball coach.

Never, never, will I get into one of these cars. I'll make a run for it and get home.

The wooden pointer directs me to turn back toward the building. "Chin up, Adams."

The bell rings as soon as we get inside. I go straight to the restroom and splash cold water on my face. I enter the nearest stall and slam the door. My insides are still clenching, but I no longer feel like I'm about to throw up.

There it is: the red stain in the center of my white cotton panties.

I can't believe this is how *The Curse* has made its first appearance.

It seems much worse than Mama said it would be. I can't believe there's so much blood. She didn't tell me there would be so much. Tears burn my eyes. All I want is to be home with Mama.

I go to the machine on the wall and with trembling fingers, slip my emergency dime in the slot. I crank the handle and it freezes. I hear a thump and stick my hand up the big slot at the bottom of the machine.

Nothing.

I bang the front of the machine, then listen, hoping to hear the thump sliding down and out of the machine.

Silence.

Back in the stall, I'm shocked to see how much more blood there is than just a minute before. How am I ever going to make it home without a disaster? Tears pool in my eyes as I try to blot some of the red from my panties.

Crying won't help now. Think, think.

Grabbing toilet paper until my hand is full, I roll it into a bundle and stuff it in my pants. This will have to work.

Thank God, school is over for today. Just let me get home without embarrassing myself. After washing my hands and face, I start down the hall toward the bus area.

"Where have you been?" Steph runs up and grabs my arm. "We're gonna miss the bus." She tugs me along beside her.

I walk carefully, trying not to disturb my emergency arrangement. She practically drags me onto the bus. In our usual seat, Steph eyes me. She leans over and whispers, "What's wrong, Mel?"

I sure don't want to talk about this on the bus. Already, I feel like a marked girl, like everyone can see what happened to me today. If Steph and I start whispering, it will be obvious to the whole bus that *The Curse* has now visited Melanie Adams.

Shrugging, I try for a relaxed, normal voice. "Old Marchman just gave me a hard time in class, that's all. Not a big deal."

Steph leans back against the seat. I feel her gaze on me while I look out the bus window.

"The drill shook you up, didn't it? You don't need to worry. I told you, my dad says the Russians will never do anything."

I stare at Steph for a second. She worries more about getting kissed than being bombed. My metal identification tag shifts beneath my dress, moving body heat from one spot to another.

How can she not be afraid? Her dad's jets are part of an aircraft carrier crew. He'll be one of the first to ship out if the Russians dare to come across the ocean. I shake my head in amazement.

Even Robert had been a little scared.

Not Steph, though. "Dad says they're big talkers, but they don't have any bite. Don't worry." She picks at a hangnail. "So, what do you think about my plan?"

I shrug again.

"C'mon, Mel. The dance is tomorrow. What's wrong with you?"

Suddenly, I am fed up with her always telling me what to do, what to think, how to behave. Like she always knows everything that's going on. What gives her the right to treat me like I'm her little sister?

"If you're so damn smart, then you can figure it out."

Steph's mouth flies open for an instant, then she scowls and folds her arms over her chest. I turn toward the window. We reach our bus stop without saying another word.

Rounding the corner of our street, I see Mr. Starr's car speed into his driveway.

Shocked, Steph leaves me on the street and runs toward her house. Her mom bolts out the front door crying and waving a piece of paper at her husband. He snatches it out of her hand. I catch up with Steph, and we stand in the front yard, watching.

"What's happened?" Steph voice is barely a whisper.

Mr. Starr wads up the paper and throws it to the ground. He faces his wife, a dull red flush rushing up from his collar. He thrusts his finger under his wife's nose. "This is your fault, Delores. You let her go out with that hoodlum."

Mrs. Starr swipes at her eyes, and then she shoves Mr. Starr with both hands. "My fault? My fault!" She shouts back, her voice shrill as a siren. "I'm the one who made the rules you never enforced, Harold." She shoves him again. "I'm the one who sent her back to her room to change into decent clothes all the time."

"Are you saying I'm not a good father? Is that what you're saying?"

"Oh, my God!" Stephanie whispers. She grabs my hand. "Something's happened to Cherie. She acted kind of strange this morning."

Tears stream down Mrs. Starr's face. "You're the one who was always pushing her, telling her she was beautiful. Telling her how she would have the young men drooling over her."

Mr. Starr balls his fists at his side and looks around, noticing Steph and me. He glances across the street. Following his gaze, I see the neighbors peeking through slits in the blinds. Stalking to the car, he climbs in and slams the door. The tires screech as he leaves in a cloud of exhaust.

Mrs. Starr covers her face with her hands. Her shoulders shake with sobs.

"Mom?" Stephanie drops her books and races to put her arms around her mother. "Mom? What's happened?"

Mrs. Starr buries her face in Steph's shoulder. Finally, she chokes out, "Your sister ran off with that boy. They've gone to Georgia to get married."

Steph faces me, her expression blank. "I wonder if Dad knows where to look for them? I hope he doesn't kill Clint." Then she picks up her books. She walks to the front door, then turns. She stares at me for a long minute.

Gnawing cramps crawl inside me. I clutch at my stomach.

She shakes her head just a little, like you do when you just figure something out. "You got your period today, didn't you?"

I nod.

"You could've told me, you know."

I guess Steph does know more than I do.

BIRDIE

I'm dancing from one foot to the other, bouncing Mama's overnight case with each step. I ran like the wind when she told me to get her suitcase while she called Daddy. She said the baby's coming today! I can't believe it.

Mama's got the phone pressed to her ear and is leaning on the kitchen sink like it's hard for her to stand up. "Clayton, the pains started. I called the doctor." She takes a deep breath. "He said to get to the hospital. He's afraid the baby's going to come quickly, like Birdie did."

I came fast? I guess I've always done things fast. Maybe I'll be the fastest baby Mama ever had! That's why I'll be great in the circus. They'll call me Fast Flying Birdie. Gee, that sounds good.

"Hurry, Clay." Mama stops talking. She rubs her belly with

her hand and smiles at me. "Okay, I'll tell the girls."

"Tell us what, Mama? Is the baby coming now?"

Mama puts the phone on its hook on the wall. "I sure hope not. Not right now, but soon."

Mellie opens the front door. I drop Mama's suitcase and run to grab Mellie's hand. "The baby's coming! The baby's coming!"

Melanie looks real surprised. Her face is white like she might be scared. She drops her pocketbook and notebook on the couch as she rushes into the kitchen. "Really, Mama? Right now?"

I stare at Mama's belly, in case the baby pops right out of her belly button. But doesn't the doctor have to catch the baby? Now I'm scared, too. I look at Melanie. She should be in charge. She's the oldest. But she's just standing there staring at Mama's belly, too.

Well, if Melanie isn't going to be in charge, then I'll have to be. After all, Mama can't have the baby right here in the kitchen. "Mama, you said the baby wouldn't come until you go to the hospital. So don't let it!"

Mama chuckles. "The baby's not coming right this minute, silly." But she grabs her belly with both hands and screws up her face like she's hurting all over.

Melanie grabs Mama's elbow and says, "Move, Birdie. Let Mama sit down."

Finally, Mellie is realizing this is an emergency and she needs to do something. I jump out of the way.

But Mama doesn't budge. She just stands there with her eyes closed and all of a sudden pink water gushes from between her legs.

I scream and hug Mama's legs. "Don't die, Mama. Please don't die."

"Don't worry, girls." Her face is relaxed now, but I'm so scared my teeth are clicking together. "That's normal. I'm not going to die." She pries my arms away and walks carefully to the dining room chair to sit down.

Mellie sucks in a deep breath. "But what happened?" Her voice sounds as shaky I feel, but she keeps talking, sounding more certain with every word. "Is the baby coming right now? What do you want me to do, Mama?"

Mama sighs real hard and rests her hands on her knees. "My water just broke."

"It broke?" I scream. "How do you fix it?"

"Birdie." She puts both her hands on my cheeks and dries my tears with her thumbs. "Birdie. It's okay. I'm fine."

Melanie stands by the puddle in the kitchen floor like she's frozen there. At least I'll be right next to Mama, touching her if she dies.

"Melanie, would you clean that up, please?" Mama says. "I don't want anyone to slip and fall."

"Yes, ma'am." Mellie grabs paper towels and drops them on top of the water. Quickly, they turn pale pink and Mellie's face looks even whiter than it did before.

Mama slides her feet out of her sopping wet bedroom slippers. "Birdie, go get my sandals for me, sweetheart. And bring the dress that's hanging on the bathroom door."

I choke back a sob and run through the house. Right now, I really want to run away. Things have to be calmer in the circus.

MELANIE

Mama takes another deep breath. "I'm sorry, Mellie. What a mess I made for you. My water's never broken this early before."

I can't look at her. I don't want Mama to see my tears. I don't want her to see how terrified I am. Not just about Mama and the baby coming, but how everything's changing so fast.

What am I going to do about my period while Mama is in the hospital? I can't tell Daddy.

The car door slams. "Norah!" Daddy shouts, as he rushes into the house. "Are you all right?"

She smiles at him, and he leans over to kiss her. When he lifts his head, he's smiling, too. Birdie runs back into the dining room with Mama's sandals and dress.

"Daddy, the baby's coming right now," she shouts.

No, God. Please, no. I can't even imagine having to deliver the baby here. *Please, God, no!*

"Not right this minute, sweetie," Daddy says. "You girls are real troopers for taking such good care of Mama."

I can't believe all this pink water just exploded from my mother. Is this what my period is going to be like? It didn't seem like water earlier today, but maybe it changes. Gosh, I wish Mama had time to talk to me about this.

But Daddy's helping her stand up and tells us to turn around so she can slip on the dry dress. I toss the bundle of wet paper towels into the garbage and wash my hands. Birdie grabs the overnight case and runs ahead of them to the front door. With Daddy's help, Mama waddles to the car. I'm right behind them, holding my hands out so I can catch Mama if she starts to fall.

Daddy opens the car door and helps Mama inside. She has to sit still for a minute with her face tight with pain before she can swing her legs around. Daddy closes the door.

"Mellie." He turns and grabs me in a big hug. He kisses my forehead and holds my shoulders. "Max is bringing Flossie over to stay with you girls. She'll spend the night, because we don't know how long this will take. She'll be here to help you get ready for school tomorrow, okay? You need to watch Birdie until Flossie gets here. It might take about an hour. Y'all stay in the house and everything will be fine. Understand?"

"Okay, Daddy." I look around him to see Mama resting her head on the back of the car seat, rubbing her hand in circles on her tummy.

Birdie climbs in the back seat on the driver's side. "Daddy, I want to go, too. I don't want to stay here." She's clutching the overnight bag with white knuckles.

He frowns. "Time to get out, Birdie."

Birdie starts crying again, like she's winding up to throw a temper tantrum.

"Not now, Birdie." Daddy reaches for her and she stops crying immediately. "Get out of the car." She looks from him to Mama. Mama blows her a kiss, then Birdie climbs out of the car.

I lean in through the open window and give Mama a kiss. Daddy cranks the car. Mama says, "I'll be home soon. Love you."

Birdie stands next to me like a wooden doll as we watch our parents drive away. I put my arm around her shoulders and offer the only comfort I can think of. "They'll come back with our baby brother."

"I don't want him anymore." Birdie turns around and

stomps into the house.

"Too bad," I mutter to myself.

Inside, Birdie parks herself in Daddy's chair and cuddles with her blanket while she watches afternoon cartoons. She's scowling so fiercely, I think her face might freeze like that. At least, that's what Mama would've said to get her to stop being so pouty.

But Mama isn't here. It's just me, and I'm not about to tackle Birdie's mood when I have my own problems to cope with. Like, where does Mama keep the *girl stuff*? She'd forgotten to mention that during her *time of the month* talk. Plus, I don't guess she's needed any girl stuff since she's been pregnant. But, I sure need greater protection, or Birdie will be crying and asking me if I'm going to die.

I feel sick and achy like I did in math class, but I trudge to my parent's bathroom to begin my search for supplies. I kneel in front of the cabinet, and the doorbell rings. Maybe it's Flossie. Maybe she's early.

Birdie opens the door.

"Hey, Birdie." Steph's voice rises over the cartoon *boinks* on the television. "Where's Mel?"

From the hallway door, I see Birdie wave her hand my way and crawl back into Daddy's chair, pulling her blanket up around her.

Steph nods in my direction. Walking toward me, she mumbles, "What's her problem?"

"Mama and Daddy have gone to the hospital. The baby's coming."

"Really? Neat."

I motion for her to follow me back to the bathroom. She leans against the door as I kneel in front of the cabinet again. "What you lookin' for?"

"You know, some stuff."

Steph sits on the bathroom floor beside me. "Hellfire, Mellie, are you too embarrassed to even say *pads*? No wonder you couldn't tell me you got your period. What in the world did you do about it at school today?"

"I made do, but I need something better now. And pretty quick, too."

Setting aside hemorrhoid treatment and cocoa butter lotion, I finally pull out a dark box with what looks like a Greek soldier's head on it. I open it to find a jumble of foil wrapped packages.

Steph looks over my shoulder and laughs. "Well, I guess your folks haven't used those for a while, huh?"

I pick one out of the box. "What are they?"

"Rubbers."

Oh, my gosh. I toss it into the box like it might burst into flames.

Steph pulls out one of the foil wrapped packages. She examines it, holding it between her fingers, squeezing it gently, but she doesn't open it.

A scarlet blush burns my face while I watch Stephanie fingering my dad's rubbers. Rubbers meant that Mama and Daddy did IT. *Of course, they did IT, Melanie, you idiot.* But they must have messed up, because they're at the hospital right now.

Casually, like it was an old Kleenex or something, Steph slips the rubber into her pants pocket.

I pretend not to notice. I don't want to know what she's thinking.

Honestly, the amount of embarrassment for me to experience in one day seems infinite. Then I think, what a stupid way to finally understand an abstract algebraic concept:

unlimited mortification with no boundaries, humiliation expanding as far as the universe and beyond.

Steph pushes up from the floor. "Looks like your mom ran out of pads. She hasn't needed them for a while, you know."

"I know. That's what I was afraid of." I sit on the toilet and rest my chin in my hand. I need to think. "What am I going to do, Steph? I can't ask my dad to get me some pads, for goodness' sake."

"Why not? It's not like he doesn't know what they are." Steph picks up one of Mama's lipsticks and slides it over her lips, holding her mouth open while she looks in the mirror.

"Don't do that. It's not yours." I groan and clutch my belly.

She shrugs and puts the tube back on the shelf. "Cramps, too?"

"Yeah, they hurt bad."

"I know. Cherie complains about them all the time." Steph tucks the lipstick-marked paper into her pocket along with the rubber. I have no idea why she's collecting these things.

Then it occurs to me that Steph's never said anything about having periods. "Have you had your period yet?"

"No, but I'm sure it'll come soon now. Cherie says that friends always get their periods together. Some mysterious female bond that we share or something."

"Probably more like misery needs company."

"Maybe." Steph shrugs again, so nonchalant. "Listen, come home with me and I'll get some pads. We have lots at our house." She leaves the room, as if she expects me to follow. I do.

"I can't leave Birdie. Daddy said for us to stay in the house until Flossie gets here."

"Flossie's coming? Neat. She gonna spend the night?"

"That's what Daddy said."

"All right. I'll go get some stuff for you and come back. I guess you can't go over to Marvin's with me, either."

"Why are you going to Marvin's?"

"Oh, Mom's still crying and sitting by the phone. I can't stand it anymore. She even said I wasn't allowed to go to the dance tomorrow."

"Really? Why?"

"I guess she thinks I'm going to run away from the dance and get married or something. Boy, am I going to let Cherie have it when she finally shows up. If things keep going like this, she's gonna ruin my whole life."

Steph opens the front door and pauses. "Take some aspirin. It will help with the cramps. Want me to bring the hot water bottle, too?"

"We have one of those, I think."

"It's in the hall closet," Birdie says. "What do you need the hot water bottle for?"

Count on Birdie not to miss a thing.

Smooth as silk, Steph says, "She has a tummy ache. You will too, Birdie, once you start eating junior high school cafeteria cheeseburgers." Steph winks at me then heads out the door.

"You get cheeseburgers at junior high?"

I nod.

Birdie sighs. "I can't wait. We had meatloaf for lunch today, with peas. I hate peas."

"Yeah, I know." I motion for Birdie to scoot over and I sit beside her in Daddy's chair. She tosses the corner of her blanket over my lap.

"I'm hungry." Birdie puts her head on my shoulder. "Do you think Flossie will make us some fried chicken for supper?"

"I don't know, but fried chicken sure would be good,

wouldn't it?"

"Mashed potatoes, too." Birdie turns her attention to the Popeye cartoon.

Today added a bunch of stuff to the long list of things I need to sort out. Now I'm worried about Mama, the new baby, and Cherie, wherever she is.

There's at least one thing I can be relieved about: I don't have to worry about the stupid Sadie Hawkins dance. If Steph can't go, then I don't have to go. I haven't told her about Robert's kiss. It's too special to talk about. I don't know if I'll ever tell her. And, now I don't have to worry about her pressuring me anymore.

The second thing is, I got my period before Steph. I feel almost like I scored a point in some kind of big game. I probably have two points already, now that I think about it. I doubt Steph has gotten Buzz to kiss her yet, or she would have told me.

Two points for me, zero for Steph. Even though I can't tell her. Still, not bad.

Birdie and I sit staring at the television for a while. In kind of a trance, I watch Popeye and Olive Oil and Bluto fight and kiss and make up. For the first time all day, my mind is a complete blank, like I've thought every possible thought.

The phone rings, making me jump. *Oh, no. Something's happened to Mama or the baby.* I run through the kitchen to snatch the phone off the wall.

"Hello?" I'm trembling.

"It's just me."

Stephanie. I let out a big sigh. "Thank goodness. I was afraid something had happened to Mama."

"No, but something's happened to *my* mom." Anger squeezes her voice tight, like it's being pushed through a tiny tube. "I swear she's lost her mind." She huffs into the phone. "Now she won't even let me out of the house. I'm gonna kill Cherie when she gets home." Steph sucks in a deep breath. "So, you're gonna have to come over here to get the stuff."

"Really? She won't even let you bring it to me?" It does sound like Mrs. Starr has a screw loose.

"Nope. It's like I'm living in a concentration camp now."

A car pulls into the driveway, its headlights shining through the twilight gloom of our living room. I hadn't even remembered to turn on the lamps. Birdie jumps up from the chair and runs to throw open the front door.

"Flossie's here," I say to Steph. "I'll be over in a few minutes, okay?" I slam the receiver down. Standing in the front door, I watch Flossie and her brother, Max, hand small paper bags to Birdie, then load their own arms with larger items and Flossie's ever-present shopping bag.

"So, how are the big sisters this fine evenin'?" Flossie sings out.

Max tips his hat to me, and I open the door wider. He walks in behind Birdie.

"Can I help with anything?" I reach out to take a bag from Flossie, but she shoos me away.

"I can manage this, sugar. You just close the door behind us. I swear, sometimes Max still thinks he was raised in barn." Flossie chuckles. "C'mon girls, we're gonna fry us some chicken and make us some biscuits."

Birdie dances in the kitchen. "How did you know I wanted fried chicken, Flossie?"

"Well, now, most of the time little birds don't eat fried chicken. But I knew me and Mellie would be wantin' some."

Birdie dances faster and claps her hands together. "But this little bird l-o-v-e-s fried chicken."

"Gracious me, and she can spell, too."

"Y-e-s, ma'am."

"All right then, fried chicken for everybody." Flossie tugs a clean white apron out of her shopping bag and ties it over her red print dress. She carefully takes off her hat, sticking the hatpin through the crown before placing it on top of the other items in her bag.

Max clears his throat. "Flossie, you all set, then?"

"Yeah, I'm fine. We're gonna have us a time, aren't we, girls?"

Max twirls his ball cap around on his finger. "Birdie, don't you let this ol' gal talk you into any trouble now." His wide grin crinkles his eyes at the corners. Even his ears wiggle just a smidgen from the force of his smile. "'Less I hear different, I'll pick you up tomorrow evenin'."

It seems like Max is never going to leave, and I'm never going to get to Steph's.

Flossie nods and waves her hands in the air like she's scattering flies. "That's right, Max. Now go on home to your wife. We got some chicken to fry."

"Bye, Max." Birdie dances to the front door with him and waves until his headlights lead him down the street.

Finally, I can get going. "Flossie, is it okay for me to go to Stephanie's house for a few minutes? I need to get something." I pull the last item out of the grocery bags on the table and put the buttermilk in the refrigerator.

"It's mostly dark outside now, Mellie."

I swallow. What if she won't let me go? What will I do then? "I know, but this is important. I'll come straight home."

Flossie rubs her hands down the front of her apron, like she's still thinking about whether or not to let me go. "What on earth is so important?"

All I can think about is I need to get some better protection soon. I've already used up half a roll of toilet paper.

I don't want to lie to Flossie, but I don't want to go into all the details either. The best I can come up with is, "I forgot something from school." And I did, in a way.

With a sigh, Flossie says, "No messin' round, now. I'll need some help with the biscuits if we're gonna eat before midnight."

I'm about to burst with relief when I say, "Yes, ma'am."

"Hurry, Mellie. I'm starvin'," Birdie says while she drags a chair into the kitchen to help with the chicken.

FLOSSIE

The girls and me are sittin' on the screened porch lettin' our suppers digest a bit before bed time. I've never seen a tiny thing like Birdie eat so much. I'm surprised she doesn't have chicken and biscuits and mashed potatoes comin' out of her ears. But then, I ate my share. Mellie, she didn't put a dint in her dinner.

Can't quite figure out what's troublin' her. I'm thinkin' it's more than just worry about her Mama and the baby. Well, if she needs to, she'll tell me what's the matter. Not my business to go messin' in hers.

I'm enjoying my last cup of coffee and humming as Melanie and me push the glider back and forth with our feet. Birdie's gone quiet. I think she might be asleep. She's wrapped in her blanket and tucked up under my arm like a little chick.

The night is black as pitch and the earlier storm has settled into a steady rain, its rhythm only interrupted by an occasional distant rumble of thunder. The quiet is soft and settled around the three of us like Birdie's blanket.

Melanie lets out a big sigh from her end of the glider, and I sense the restless anxiety easing out of the girl a bit.

"I didn't have a chance to ask how your visit to Stephanie went. Is everything okay?"

"Yes, ma'am. I just needed to borrow something from her."

"I didn't even think that you girls might have some homework. Do you?"

"No. Birdie doesn't have homework yet. And we had an evacuation drill in school today, so I don't have any either."

"Say what? Evacuation drill?"

"Yes, ma'am. They made us line up like we were getting into cars to leave school."

"Umm, umm, umm. You had to do that before?"

Melanie shakes her head. Now, that would be enough to make the girl tense-like. But I still have a feeling something else is bothering her. "Well, I'm glad you didn't have homework tonight. You girls got enough on your mind without havin' to worry about such as that."

The lightning keeps up the show, but the thunder is a shadow sound. Birdie sleeps on. I'm just about to suggest we head to bed when Mellie says, "Flossie, you remember that day we were talking about Cherie and you sang that song with me?"

"I sure do. Remember it like it was yesterday."

"Cherie ran off today and got married."

"Umm, umm, umm. How's Stephanie and her Mama and Daddy takin' that news?"

"Not good. It was strange being in Steph's room with most of Cherie's stuff gone. The room looked empty and Stephanie seemed real sad. Except she acted like she was mad at her sister."

"Well, sometimes we just don't want folks to know what we're really feelin' inside. Sometimes mad is better than sad."

"Maybe so. But I think Steph's mom is going to be sad for a long time."

"Probably not for that long. Soon as Cherie comes back and explains things, they'll get back to normal."

"Do you think so? Can you really get back to normal?"

"In this case they will. Cherie getting married happened before they all planned on it, but it would have happened sooner or later."

"But when Mama comes home with the baby, that won't be normal. When we have more drills and stuff at school, things aren't normal."

"Mellie, you just have to let things happen as best you can. Life goes on. Things become normal again."

'Course, that's not exactly true. Sometimes you just limp on through the change and make the best of it.

Lord knows, that's what I've had to do. After my Clyde was killed, I spent years hoping for normal to come back. Sometimes, it just never does.

The jangle of the phone sends Mellie rushing to the kitchen. I pick up Birdie, and we follow just in time to hear Mellie say, "Really? A boy?"

Birdie jumps down from my arms, wide awake. "It's a boy, Flossie. A boy."

All serious now, Mellie says, "How's Mama?"

Birdie dances around, tugging on the phone cord, wanting her chance to talk. I pull her back against my legs so Mellie can finish talking to her Daddy.

"Three days before Mama can come home? That seems like a long time."

Three days without their Mama will seem like a really long

time to these girls. After a few minutes, Mellie says, "Bye, Daddy. I love you. Give Mama and David Clayton a kiss for me."

She hands the phone to Birdie, who paces the kitchen, twirling the phone cord around her fingers like her mama does. "But, Daddy? If Mama has to stay in the hospital, who's going to take me to get take my cast off?" She pauses for a minute. "You? You're going to take me to the doctor? Okay, I guess."

Melanie really smiles at me for the first time all evening. "Daddy said for us to go to bed. He wants to talk to you."

"I 'spect he does. Why don't you go ahead and brush your teeth and hair, sugar? I'll send Birdie in a minute, then I'll tuck you girls in."

Another hour passes before I have the chance to rinse my coffee cup and turn out the kitchen light. Tiredness creeps into my bones like the moist air seeping in through the windows. I wish I was home, gettin' ready to crawl into my own bed. Instead, I unfold a sheet and spread it on the sofa in the living room.

"Flossie."

I 'bout jump out of my skin before I realize it's Melanie standing behind me in the dark. "You scared the life outta me, child. What's the matter?"

She steps up beside me. In the bit of light coming in between the blinds, I see she's got tears in her eyes. I want to hold her in my arms so bad. But she's a young lady now. I can't do something like that. It's just not done. "What's wrong, baby?"

"Um. I got my period today, and my stomach hurts something awful. Can I have some aspirin?"

Besides everything else that happened to the poor girl today, she gets her monthly. "'Course you can have some aspirin. Want me to fix up the hot water bottle for you?"

"Will it help?"

"Most times it does help. It can't hurt, can it?"

"No, ma'am. Thank you."

"You go on back to bed, and I'll bring you a glass of water and that hot water bottle."

After I wrap a towel around the water bottle and get Mellie all settled in bed, she still looks like a lost lamb. She raises her arms toward me and much as I know I shouldn't do it, I lean down and hug her. She wraps her arms around my neck and hugs me somethin' fierce.

Those things that are so different about us don't matter much just now. Not to me. Not to her.

Monday
October 15, 1962

NORAH

"Hi, Mama."

Melanie stands at my bedroom door with her arms wrapped around her books. "Hi, Sweetie." My new baby boy, DC, relaxes, his lips going slack on my nipple. I bring him up to my shoulder.

I haven't seen her since I left for the hospital on Wednesday. It seems like forever, not just five days. She looks so much older. Maybe it's because I've only seen DC and other babies lately. Even Birdie looked all grown up. "I swear you look like you're a year older."

She darts her gaze away from me, like she does when I've discovered something she wanted to keep secret from me. What have I missed in the days I've been gone?

But she recovers her composure and puts her books on the dresser.

"Come here and give me a hug," I say.

She stands beside the bed. "Is it okay when you're…?

"Of course, it's okay." I reach for her hand and tug her to

me for a kiss and a hug. "We won't break, Sweetie."

My oldest girl feels so strong and solid against me. She smells like AquaNet and perspiration and Secret roll-on deodorant, a mixed bag of childish and womanly scents. Just knowing that babies can grow up into fine people like my Mellie gives me confidence. Before I can get all teary, DC huffs small breaths and pushes at Mellie's stomach with his feet.

I pat the bed beside my hip, motioning for her to sit with me for a while. "So, how was school?"

She shrugs. "Okay." Her brows pinch together and she looks away. "Are you all right, Mama?"

"I'm perfectly fine, Sweetie." I adjust DC so he's resting on my left side, facing Mellie. "And so is your brother."

She smiles and looks down at her hands.

"You can touch him, you know."

She takes her baby brother's hand. "He's so tiny." When his fingers wrap around her index finger she sucks in a breath. "Look at his little fingernails," she whispers. His lips move in a half smile. "Oh, he smiled at me. Hi, David Clayton."

DC yawns and nuzzles my breast. "I think he's a little tired from Birdie's after school inspection. He's also ready for his second course."

Mellie's staring at the baby's mouth fixed around my nipple like it's the strangest thing she's ever seen. Maybe I should've covered up. There's nothing like a maternity ward to make you forget about modesty. I reach for the extra receiving blanket beside me so I can drape it over DC.

"Does that…?" She pauses, a blush reddening her cheek.

"Does what?"

I finish covering up and glance at her, but she's looking away. "Go ahead, Mellie. Ask me whatever you want."

"Well, I was just, you know, wondering what it felt like

when DC…" She shrugs, unable to force the rest of the sentence out of her mouth.

I understand how she feels. I remember wondering about things like that when Lola was born. "What does it feel like to nurse DC?"

"Yes, ma'am."

"Melanie, having your baby at your breast is one the most wonderful sensations in the world. Mothers always want to be able to give their children what they need, but it seems that we're only really good at it when they're very young. They grow up way before we're ready, like you did. They find other things to make them happy." I stroke DC's cheek and think this will be my last chance to give everything to a baby, to be the most important thing in a child's life. "For this little period of time, though, I can take care of everything DC needs and wants."

"But, does it hurt?" She shivers and I can imagine what she's thinking.

I can't help but chuckle. She has no idea that breasts can give a woman pleasure and pride and satisfaction instead of the discomfort I know Mellie feels now. "Not really. I know what you're thinking, but you won't always be this tender and sore." I pick up a strand of her ponytail and let the softness flow through my fingers. "When DC nurses, it feels like he's tugging on a string that runs from my breast to the heart of me. Every nibble and suck is another tug on that string that makes us closer, ties us to each other. Just like when he was inside me and he got his food through the umbilical cord. Remember when we talked about that?"

She nods.

"From the very beginning of your life, we've been tied together, first by the cord, then by this invisible string that we create by nursing. Mamas and their babies are always connected. Like you and I are connected."

Tears glisten in Mellie's eyes but she smiles at me, a wistful kind of smile, full of love and hurt and hope and fear. I take her hand in mine. "So, why don't you tell me what's happened?"

"Mama, I started my period on Wednesday."

"Oh, Mellie, I ruined your special day. I'm so sorry."

"Special? It felt pretty awful to me."

"It does, doesn't it? But it's not really awful. You're truly a young woman now."

"I guess so."

"Did you have cramps?"

"Awful. And I was sick to my stomach. It happened during Math class, while we were having an evacuation drill." The whole awful story spills out.

I feel so bad that I wasn't at home to take care of her when she needed me. Her hand clutches mine so tightly, I can guess how scared she must have been. "I'm so sorry I wasn't here."

She shrugs and pulls her hand away.

"I'll make this up to you somehow."

"It's okay. Stephanie and Flossie helped me out." She hesitates, twisting her hands in her lap. "But I'm worried about the drills."

How do I ease her mind about *this* terrifying thing? I know how to comfort her when she has cramps. I know what to do when that inevitable first heartbreak comes along. My mother gave me a good example in those instances. But Mama never talked about how her mother comforted her during World War II. What was their conversation like after Pearl Harbor?

Of course, this Cuban situation isn't going to get that bad. We don't even have to worry about that. These are just precautions. All I can think to say is, "It was just a drill."

Mellie looks at me like I've been locked away from civilization for month.

"But what if it really happens? What if we are attacked? I don't want to go to some other place. I don't want to be away from you and Daddy."

I glance away from her searching gaze, looking down to my sweet, helpless little boy. Those crazy things Rachel Winston said about bringing a child into this dangerous world suddenly don't seem so far-fetched. But I can't show my fear. I have to be strong. I have to use common sense. That means I have to make sure my children are safe. If safety means we're separated for little while, then…

Besides, the Russians are bluffing. I take a deep breath. "The important thing is for you to be safe. The school knows what's best. But nothing is going to happen. Do you hear me? We're all going to be fine. This is all just a bunch of talk."

Mellie looks doubtful, and my heart sinks. Is this where we begin to drift apart? So early? Is this the thing that makes my girl doubt that I can take care of her? I can't find my way out of these thoughts to the words that will comfort her.

DC kicks his feet and wails his newborn cry. I know how to solve this problem. I'll teach Mellie. "He needs to burp. Do you want to do it?" I lift the baby toward her.

She stares down at his little mouth, opened in a squall, milk pooled in the corners of his lips. He twists in my hands.

Mellie looks unsure. "I don't know what to do."

"Just hold his head and put him against your shoulder. He'll snuggle into you. Then you just pat his back until he burps." I drape a diaper over her shoulder and help get him settled. He snuggles into her like he was made to fit there.

"Like this?" She pats his back, barely touching him. His little legs jerk.

"You need to be more firm. He needs some help getting the air bubble up."

She pats a bit harder and his legs quit jerking. "Just like that, Sweetie."

I rest against my pillow and think into the future. Think about my Mellie holding her own baby, my grandchild. DC has stopped squirming and is resting peacefully on Mellie's shoulder. Now she knows. She knows how to do the one thing a woman has always been able to fix, throughout wars and peace and everything in between.

"When I put him on formula in a few weeks, you'll be able to feed him and burp him. You'll be a big help to me."

"Okay." She smiles at me, looking so very grown up.

The quiet in my room is soothing and my eyes drift shut.

Then, I hear Birdie slam the front door.

BIRDIE

"Do you have your nickels?"

My best friends, Mary and Ramona, each hold out a nickel. Mary's is shiny new, but Ramona's is so dingy I have to make sure it's really a nickel. Yep. I put them in my pocket. If I can get two nickels a day, I'll have enough money to buy ice cream at school every day.

"Okay. You remember the rules, right? You have to be quiet."

I keep my finger against my lips while we walk through the house. Mama must be in her bedroom. I put up my hand so Mary and Ramona will stop to wait at the door. They have their hands folded behind them just like I said.

Mama is propped up against some pillows and Mellie is holding the baby. I didn't get to hold the baby like that. Mama made me sit beside her on the bed, and she kept her hand behind his head the whole time. Oh, well. I've got business to take care right now. "Mama, can we see the baby? Don't worry," I rush on. "I told them what to do since they don't have any babies at their houses."

"You and your friends can see DC this time. But, Birdie. Honestly." Mama's lips go flat and I know she's not happy with me. I'm not sure why, though. Why doesn't she want to show off my new brother?

"From now on, ask my permission before bringing your friends inside."

"All right. But can we see him?" I fold my hands in front of me like my teacher does, and I talk in a soft, but grown-up way, to Mary and Ramona. I'm teaching them about babies. All girls need to know about babies. "See, this is what a baby really looks like. He's much littler than we always think. No chubby legs." I point to his legs dangling from the blanket. His socks droop off his toes like empty balloons. They are always falling off. I wish I got a nickel for every one I found on the floor. Then I wouldn't have to worry about having money for ice cream every day.

But I have to keep talking so we can get to the good part. "And, see? No big eyes." I push at Mellie's shoulder. "Uh, Melanie? Turn around so they can see his face."

She looks at Mama, who winks at her and nods. That means it's okay for her to move and let us see DC's face. What's she waiting for, then? "Turn around. They want to see."

Mary and Ramona come stand beside Melanie. Ramona adjusts her glasses so she can get a good look. Mary pulls out her handkerchief to wipe her nose. Uh-oh. "Mama, Mary doesn't have a cold. Her mother said it's hayfever. She gets it every fall."

"Maybe Mary should keep her handkerchief over her nose and mouth. Okay?"

"Yes, Mrs. Adams. I will."

"You still haven't seen the best thing." I prop my elbows next to Mama's pillow. "Mama, aren't you going to change his diaper now?"

Mama and Mellie burst out laughing.

"What's so funny?"

Mama puts her hand over her mouth and makes her eyes serious, though her cheeks are still smiling. "No, Birdie. I'm not going to change his diaper now."

That's a surprise. She changes his diaper every time she holds him. Besides, I've got two nickels in my pocket. "But, Mama. I promised."

"Sorry, Birdie. DC is your brother, not a zoo exhibit."

Just then DC lets out a scream. He jerks his head and kicks his feet. Melanie hands him back to Mama.

Over the screaming, she says, "Y'all go back outside and play."

"Okay, we're going." I motion for Mary and Ramona to follow me. "See? He's just as loud as I told you."

Mary says, "Birdie, I want my nickel back."

Thursday
October 18,1962

MELANIE

Stephanie came home with me after school. Since Cherie ran away, Steph's been at my house a lot. Mama doesn't mind. We do our homework, watch TV, and sometimes Steph will help me do chores. But today, when Mama tells me to fold the clothes, Steph announces she's going to Marvin's.

"Stephanie, make sure you call your mother and tell her where you are." Mama has reminded Steph to call home for the last three days.

"I will Mrs. Adams. Bye." Steph grabs her books and leaves through the screened porch to cut across our back yard to Marvin's house. She hardly ever talks about Buzz anymore, especially since her big plans for the Sadie Hawkins Day dance were cancelled by *Cherie's Adventure*. That's what she calls it, *Cherie's Adventure*, like the title of a book. She says it real sarcastic like.

There's a knock at the front door. I'm surprised to open the door to see Cherie standing there, holding a little package wrapped in blue paper printed with booties. I guess *The Adventure* is over already. Cherie smiles at me more sweetly than she ever has before.

"Hi, Melanie. Is your mother busy?"

Mama comes up behind me, with DC in her arms. "Cherie, come on in. How are you?"

Mama and Cherie settle on the sofa, while I close the door.

"Oh, he's so beautiful," Cherie whispers. Her hands seem to reach out to touch DC without her moving.

"Do you want to hold him, Cherie?"

"Oh, could I?"

She looks so different, I can't believe she's only been gone a week or so. Almost everything about her has changed. She's wearing a lot less make-up and her hair is softer. I never realized how pretty Cherie really is until today. She has the clear and glowing complexion the teen magazines write articles about. Her eyes are a nice green.

She holds DC in her arms like she's afraid he'll break. When she glances up at Mama, Cherie's eyes glisten with tears. She looks like an angel, a sad, pretty angel.

Mama wipes a tear from her cheek, too.

"Melanie, why don't you get us some iced tea? And how about bringing some of that cake that Flossie made today?"

"Yes, ma'am."

In the kitchen, I pour three glasses of tea. I look out the window to watch Flossie taking the clean laundry off the clothesline, but I'm listening to Mama and Cherie talking in the living room.

Through the open kitchen door, I hear Mama say, "So, how do you like married life, Cherie?"

"Okay, I guess." Cherie's voice is barely a whisper.

"Be patient, honey. Everything will settle down soon."

Cherie's voice changes, like she's answering a question in class, one she's certain she has the right answer for. "Don't get me wrong, Mrs. Adams. Clint is terrific. We have a nice little apartment near his work. It's just that Mama and Daddy don't understand. They can't remember what it's like to be in love."

"Are you sure that's it, Cherie?"

"Sure, why else would they be so mean to Clint? They treat him like he's a criminal."

I don't quite understand what's going on, but Mama looks at Cherie as a friend now, someone with the same interests as herself. How has Cherie suddenly gone from a teenager to a woman, someone who could be Mama's friend?

Flossie stoops over and lifts the wicker clothes basket to her hip. Tilting back her head, she scans the sky and smiles before turning toward the screen porch. I cover the pound cake with a clink of aluminum against the glass cake plate. Mama and Cherie are laughing at something I didn't hear.

"Here's the mail," Birdie shouts, startling me back to my task. As I carry the tea to the living room and put it on the coffee table, Birdie tosses the mail onto the table with a thump, sending the envelopes sliding to a stop against the side of the tray.

"Gotta go, gotta go bad." The bathroom fan whirs on and the door clicks shut. Sometimes Birdie is just plain embarrassing.

DC squirms and cries. Cherie hands him back to Mama. I glance at the mail and see, right on top of the *Life* magazine, a letter addressed to me.

From Robert.

My heart stops for a second, then begins to kick against my chest. I snatch up the envelope and tear open the back flap. A snapshot slides out from between the folded sheets of notebook paper. I swoop down to snatch it, but it lands at Cherie's feet.

She picks it up. "Oh, it's Robert Taylor and Brooke Mayfield. I haven't seen her since her father got stationed in Cuba last year." She holds the photograph so Mama can see and then Cherie studies it some more.

I'm dying to grab it away from her. Anger surges through me. It's my picture. It came in a letter addressed to me. Me. Not Mama or Cherie, but me.

"Robert looks good, doesn't he, Norah?"

I stiffen. Since when does Cherie call my mama "Norah," like they are best friends?

Cherie seems oblivious to the anger I direct at her. "And Brooke looks so cute. I was just thinking about her the other day and wishing she'd been able to stay here instead of going to Cuba with her parents. We were really good friends, remember?"

Cherie's voice has changed once again, from pretend woman to sad teenager who misses her best friend. Finally, Cherie hands the picture to me.

I don't hear anything else they say. My whole world focuses on the image of Robert and Brooke, posed side by side on a golden beach. Their bronzed skin glistens with oil. Brooke's corn silk hair is lifted by the breeze. Both of them smile so brightly, they seem to outshine the sun.

I'm so jealous, my stomach burns like I drank a Coke too fast. I hate seeing them together like this.

But, Brooke looks like I remember her—pretty in a soft, frail way. Her thick, pale hair makes her skin seem fragile, even though she has a tan. Her eyes are still so big behind her black-rimmed cat-eye glasses. I really don't like her anymore.

But Robert has changed a whole lot. His hair is buzzed short. He seems bigger. Well, he is bigger.

His arms bulge with new muscles, and his chest looks different from when he mowed lawns during the summer. A beer bottle dangles from the hand he has draped over Brooke's shoulder. He pinches a cigarette between his forefinger and thumb. I've never seen him smoke before.

I swallow. Robert looks like a man, completely different from the boy who bought me a banana Popsicle and told me he was a little scared.

This Robert looks like he would have followed Mrs. Winston home from his going away party, instead of walking with me.

This Robert would have never kissed me.

Tears sting my eyes, but I remember I'm standing in the living room with Mama and Cherie watching me.

"So, what does Robert have to say?" Mama sits her glass down and picks up the plate with slices of pound cake. She offers some to Cherie.

"No, thank you. My stomach's still queasy sometimes."

"Eating something helps that. Are you sure you won't have some?"

Cherie shakes her head. "Does Robert say whether he likes the Navy or not?"

"Uh, I haven't gotten that far yet." I haven't even read the letter's first line. All I want to do is go to my room and close the door so I can read every word by myself. Instead, I scan the page quickly so I can answer Mama and Cherie. "He says he's fine and likes what he's doing."

The telephone rings, and Flossie picks it up. "Adams residence."

Birdie skips through the living room, stopping to grab a piece of cake from the plate.

Mama catches her wrist. "Did you wash your hands, young

lady?"

Birdie rolls her eyes. "Yes, Mama."

"Well, what do you say then?"

"May I have some cake, please?"

"Yes, you may. Stay in our yard. You'll need to come inside soon."

"Okay. Bye, Cherie." Birdie slams the front door behind her, this time waking DC and making him scream.

Cherie jumps to her feet. "I think I'd better go now. Mother didn't want me to stay gone too long."

"I'll save all of DC's things for you, Cherie. Take care of yourself."

"Thanks, Norah. Good-bye, Melanie. Flossie."

After the front door closes Flossie says, "Was she in trouble like we thought?" She's covering the phone's receiver with her hand.

Mama nods.

Oh. That's why Cherie seemed so grown up and why she was acting like Mama's friend. Running away to get married and being in trouble means one thing: Cherie's going to have a baby. I wonder if Steph knows?

"Told you she'd be in trouble 'fore Christmas. Turns out, way before." Flossie shakes her head sadly and lifts the phone toward Mama. "This is for you Miz Adams. Want me to take the baby?"

Mama pushes up from the sofa with a sigh. She takes the phone from Flossie and hands over the crying DC. "Hello?"

Flossie carries the baby back to Mama's room to change him. I flop on the couch, letter in one hand and snapshot in the other.

While I stare at the blank television screen, digesting this new information that Cherie is in trouble, Stephanie appears at the back door. "Can I come in?"

"Sure. You left your math book on the table."

"Mellie, you'll never guess what just happened." Stephanie sits next to me on the couch and preens like the cockatoo I saw at the zoo, stroking her ponytail with her fingers.

You'll never guess what happened either. Some news is better coming from home, I decide. I'll let Cherie or her mother tell Steph she's going to be an auntie.

"Well, aren't you going to try to guess?" Steph asks.

"No. Tell me."

She leans over. "Marvin kissed me." She stretches like a cat, nodding at me like she's trying to convince me it's true.

"Really?"

"Yes. No wonder they write songs about it. You can't imagine how wonderful it is."

Yes, I can. I know how wonderful it is. But I wonder if I'll ever have another kiss from Robert, especially this new Robert in the photo.

Mama comes back into the living room. "Oh, hi, Stephanie. Your sister just left."

"Cherie's back?" Stephanie's voice squeaks with surprise. She looks happy and a little frightened. She gives me a dirty look that says I should have told her.

I shrug. I've got other things on my mind. Like why is she so sure she's the only one who's experienced a kiss?

"I'd better get home then. I'll call you later." She grabs the math book off the table and darts through the back door.

Mama sits next to me on the sofa and props her feet on the coffee table. She rests her head against the back of the sofa. "Turned out to be a busy afternoon, didn't it?"

"Yes, ma'am." I stare down at my letter, which I still haven't read completely. "Who was on the phone, Mama?"

Her eyes drift closed. "Aunt Lola. She's coming down tomorrow after work. She'll be here about midnight."

"Midnight? That's awful late. Are you going to be able to stay up that late?" Mama's been going to bed at the same time Birdie and I do, and she's still tired all the time.

Mama sighs her breath out. Right now, it sounds like she's almost too tired to suck one back in. "Yeah, it'll be good to see her."

"I know. I miss her, too." I lean over and kiss Mama's cheek. "Don't worry, I'll help out with the extra work. I'll do whatever you need me to do."

A smile lifts the corners of her mouth, but Mama doesn't open her eyes. "I know. You're a big help to me."

As Flossie sings a lullaby for DC, her voice drifts through the house. Soon he quiets down, and Mama's breathing settles into a steady rhythm as she dozes off, too.

I slip off to my room. Finally, I can read Robert's letter again, slowly this time, and savor every word. But I'm bothered, thinking of Stephanie and Marvin kissing. It makes me feel a little queasy, because I know Stephanie doesn't really like Marvin. Sure, she thinks he's interesting because he plays the guitar and stuff, but she still makes fun of him. If she thinks she'll get a laugh from the crowd, she'll mock him by pretending to be a beatnik.

I guess that kissing Marvin was just a new experience, so it was exciting to Stephanie because she wanted to be kissed so badly. How can she think a kiss from someone she doesn't really like is wonderful?

I know what wonderful really is. I just haven't told Stephanie about it.

I tuck Robert's picture under my pillow and settle down to read his letter for the second time.

Friday
October 19, 1962

NORAH

It's eleven o'clock now. I want to be in bed. But Lola should be here soon. I feel like I've been in these same clothes for days. Birdie, snug in her pajamas, is sleeping with her head in my lap, so I can't really get up. Besides, I don't want to greet Lola in a nursing gown. Still wearing her rumpled school clothes, Melanie sits between Clay and me. I focus on the television, fighting yawn after yawn.

The local anchorman uses his best Walter Cronkite voice as he shows the photos of the Russian missiles based in Cuba—ninety miles from Miami. Now he displays a map. This is the same map used on the evening CBS news, showing where the missiles might be aimed and how far they might travel. There are big red circles around Miami, Jacksonville, Atlanta, Washington, D.C., and the coast of Virginia. They've even got a warning around New York City.

Unease creeps over me. All the things I didn't want to accept: the dog tags my children wear to school, the constant roar of Navy jets returning from spying, the reasons why

Melanie has to worry about having to evacuate her school.

I glance at Clay. The flicker of the TV casts his face in shadows, his eyes dark as he stares at the set. His cigarette sends smoke curling toward the lamp like a fog is settling in. He's hunched forward with his hands fisted together between his knees. I wonder what he's thinking. Does he worry like I do?

His fingers knot together, and I realize that he's feeling the same fear and frustration I am.

Melanie tugs the band from her ponytail and stretches the rubber band between her fingers over and over. She's biting her lip.

"Daddy?"

"What, sugar?"

"What's going to happen?"

"I'm not sure. But we'll be fine. We'll be safe. You don't need to worry."

"How do you know?" Her voice sounds so fragile, frayed around the edges.

Clay stands up and puts his hands in his pockets, and paces over to look at DC, sleeping in his bassinet. Glancing toward the television he says, "I figure the president loves his children, too. He'll stop this. We have to believe that."

Mellie leans against my shoulder. She shivers, even though the house is only cool. The weatherman says this rain is bringing in a cold front. I wrap my arm around her and wait for the heater to kick on. For the next two days the temperature will be lower than normal, and then we'll warm up again, getting back to our usual mild October weather.

Clay walks into the kitchen, and I hear him getting the whiskey bottle from the top cabinet. The liquor was a Christmas gift last year from his boss. Clay's only had a couple of drinks from it, but I can't blame him for having a shot now.

"Honey, make one for me, too."

Mellie is still curled against me. There's a desperate part of me that wants to give her something to make her feel better, something to make everything seem normal. "Want Daddy to bring you a Coke?"

She nods and sits up. She wipes her eyes real quick, like I won't see. My heart just breaks. I wish she were as young as Birdie, young enough to sleep peacefully through a newscast that declares the world is changing by the second.

Clay comes back and hands me a tumbler filled with a couple of ice cubes and amber liquor. I don't usually have a taste for it, but it seems the right thing tonight. He hands Mellie a Coke bottle. After going back to the kitchen to get his drink, he changes the channel to *The Tonight Show*.

I'm hardly ever awake to see it. Of course, if it was on at two o'clock in the morning, I'd be able to enjoy it while I fed the baby. At least tonight I'll get to see the new host, while we wait on Lola.

Why is she so late? I guess the rain has slowed her down. I hope she's driving carefully.

Melanie puts her Coke bottle on the coffee table and leans against my shoulder again. After Johnny Carson's monologue, I feel the tension draining out of Melanie. The whisky and the humor are settling my nerves, too.

I wish I could sleep for a couple of weeks. Every day seems to be longer, with more chores left undone, and more demands on me. Sometimes I wonder if I could've prepared better. Maybe I should ask Clay if Flossie can come another day a week. But, that's selfish. She's already here on Mondays and Thursdays. We don't have the money, and I don't want Clay to work more overtime than he's doing now.

Soon, the voices on the television are just noise in the

distance. I drift in and out of sleep, feeling trapped by the weight of the girls asleep on my lap and my shoulder, then by my own heavy tiredness.

I open my eyes when Clay takes the glass from my hand, focusing on the TV for a few minutes before my eyes drift shut again.

The doorbell sounds like an alarm. I jerk at the sound, and Melanie tenses, then opens her eyes. Birdie sits up, rubbing her fists across her face.

When Clay opens the door, Lola blows into our house like a tornado.

"Hey! Y'all weren't sleeping, were you?"

Clumsily, I struggle up from the couch, the darn stitches pulling uncomfortably. "We just dozed off for a bit."

Lola's arms wrap around me. She's cool from the night air and raindrops glisten in her blonde, lacquered beehive. Smelling like too many cigarettes and too much coffee, she's all laughter and bright, swirling colors as she sweeps through the living room in her narrow orange pants and her yellow, green, and orange cropped sweater. Her creamy, flat tummy flickers at me with every sweeping motion of her arms.

Was my belly ever that flat? I don't think so. Certainly, it isn't now, and probably never will be like that again.

"Lola, you look beautiful, like always," I say, studying her face. "How was the drive?"

"Good as can be expected. You know they're still working on the stretch of highway north of Folkston. That took forever, so I tried to make up some time after that."

Standing by the television, Clay rattles the change in his pants pocket. "Uh-oh. What does that mean?"

Lola looks sheepish for a second, then tosses her head back and laughs. "That means, dear somber Clayton, the cracker sheriff in itty-bitty Folkston had that damned speed trap set up again. This time I had to hand over twenty-five dollars and have a cup of coffee with him. He offered me a get-out-of-jai-free-card, but he was just too damn ugly."

"Lola..." I scold.

"You were playing Monopoly?" Birdie asks.

Everyone laughs, even Mellie, and Birdie looks at us, trying to figure out why that was funny.

"But you still made good time from Atlanta," Clay points out.

I frown. Lola should know better that to drive so fast in bad weather. And she should be ashamed of herself for flirting her way out of a ticket. "Lola, you are bad."

Grinning at me, she says, "Only in the best way. Clay, I swear I pegged the speedometer at about ninety miles an hour. You've got to take my Bel Air for spin before I go."

"I'd love to, Lola. I haven't driven a fast car in the longest time."

"Yep, you've been stuck driving the family buggy too long. You need to break away and have a little fun." Lola winks at him and kicks off her striped flats.

I look between her and Clay. It never occurred to me that Clay would like to drive fast. Had he been lying to me on Labor Day, when he said he never wanted to run away? Is he feeling as much pressure as I am? Of course, he must be. I need to be more sensitive to that.

I'll try, I really will.

I just need to find something extra inside me to give him. Feeling a chill, I rub my arms. Finally, the heater to turns on.

Lola spreads her arms wide. "Now, don't I have some other hugs coming my way?" She grabs the nearest person for a hug. That happens to be Birdie, because she flies from the couch.

Lola practically catches her in mid-air.

"Did you bring me a present?" Birdie giggles as Lola spins her around and around.

"Birdie. I told you to mind your manners."

"But, Mama," she whines.

Lola winks at me and gives Birdie a smacking kiss on the cheek. "Now, why would I bring you a present? You aren't the new baby, are you?"

"No."

"You didn't give birth to the new baby, did you?"

Birdie looks surprised then she giggles. "You know that's not right."

"So why should you have a present?"

"Because you love me?"

"Of course, I love you, Li'l Bird. And I did bring you a present. You have to wait until it stops raining, so your Daddy can help me bring in my suitcase. Okay?" Lola puts Birdie down.

Birdie jumps up and down, clapping her hands. "I can't wait. It's been so long since I've had a present."

"Mellie, are you awake now and ready to give me a hug?"

"Hey, Aunt Lola."

She dances Mellie in a circle in the center of the living room. I wish I had just a tiny bit of Lola's energy.

"Now, where's that baby boy? He needs to see his Aunt Lola."

All the commotion has DC stirring in his bassinet. I try not to be irritated as I pick him up and hand him to her.

After the flash and noise of her greetings for everyone else, Lola's quiet as a church mouse as she holds David Clayton. Her expression is soft, and I swear there are tears welling in her eyes. Her voice sounds almost like a prayer. "He's beautiful,

Norah. Just beautiful." She sits on the edge of the sofa and stares at the baby's face, taking his little fingers from the beneath the blanket he's swaddled in.

Birdie interrupts the quiet. "What about my present?"

Lola convinces Clay to dash outside in the rain to bring in her huge, red suitcase. Even after he comes back inside, she's still holding DC, refusing to put him down so she can fish through her suitcase for presents. She has Birdie and Mellie open her suitcase instead.

"I had to sit on the damned thing to get it to close."

"Lola, I wish you'd watch your language," I say. "We need to set a good example for the girls. And besides, if Mama could hear you, she'd be rolling over in her grave."

"I'll watch my mouth for the girls. But I told Mama a long time ago that I was going to be myself, no matter what she expected." Lola turns her cheek to rub it against DC's head, like he's a lucky rabbit's foot. "We came to a truce, Mama and me, so I expect she's not paying much more attention to me now than she did back then."

I stare at my sister. What on earth is she talking about? Lola was the light of our mother's life, her very heart and soul. Before I can contradict her, Birdie releases the snapping closures on the suitcase and it pops open with a whooshing sound.

A gigantic stuffed ostrich seems to draw breath and unfold out of the suitcase. Birdie snatches it. The bird cranes its neck and stretches its legs until it stands almost as tall as Birdie. She's so excited she jumps around the big gray and white monster, but its legs start to sprawl wide apart on the tile floor. The fuzzy gray head droops like the bird is ashamed of its behavior, but helpless to change it in any way. The poor ostrich simply accepts its lot in life and allows its legs spread until it slumps to the floor.

Its resignation is about the saddest thing I've seen in a while.

Lola nudges Mellie with her elbow. "Hey, what's that long face about, Sweetie? Did you think I forgot you?"

Mellie shakes her head. "C'mon, I'm too old for presents now."

"Baby doll, you never, ever get too old for presents. And don't let anybody convince you otherwise." Lola glances at me. "Especially a man. Never let a man get away with not giving you presents."

Tucking DC closer to her chest, Lola leans over her suitcase and withdraws a small package wrapped in shiny pink paper. She hands it to Mellie with a sly grin. "Go ahead. Open it."

MELANIE

Carefully peeling away the shiny paper, I hold my breath, wondering what the glossy white box contains. Maybe it's a diary. Or jewelry. Aunt Lola finds really great necklaces or bracelets.

I lift the lid and tenderly separate the tissue paper to reveal–

The breath rushes out of me like I've been hit in the stomach.

Birdie dances around her giant bird. "What is it?"

I can't take it out of the box. I'm too embarrassed, too mortified. And a little bit thrilled, but I can't let that show. Especially not to Mama.

"Come on, Mellie, let us see." Mama leans forward, resting

her elbows on her knees.

Pinching my fingers together, I lift out the satiny red panties with a black cat embroidered in the front.

"Oooh! Pretty," Birdie exclaims. "I love pussy cats. Did you bring a pair for me, Aunt Lola?"

My face heats until I know it's the exact shade of the scarlet panties. I want to drop them in the box and shut it up tight, but I look up and see the look on Lola's face. Then I see Mama.

She puts her hand over her mouth. Her brows draw together in a ferocious frown and she glares at her sister. "What were you thinking? Melanie is only twelve years old."

I stuff the panties back in the box and close the top.

Birdie crosses her arms over her chest. "Yes, What were you thinking? You didn't bring me any kitty panties."

"Hush, Birdie," Mama says.

Lola's expression is hard, like a grown-up version of Birdie's face when she gets in trouble but doesn't really believe she did anything wrong. "Yes, she's twelve and old enough for matching underwear. Mellie, show your Mama the matching bra."

My stomach clenches. I don't want to take the bra out of the box. It's both awful and beautiful at the same time. The tiny padded cups looked like a bad science project on volcanoes: pointed little mountains oozing red satin.

"Don't you just love it, Mellie?" Aunt Lola's voice is determined, like she wants to convince us all that this is the best present ever. "That red will look so pretty with your hair and skin."

"Lola, no one will ever, ever see these things." Mama stands up and takes the box away from me, shoving the top back on.

Now I'm afraid Mama and Aunt Lola are going to fight, and the whole weekend will be ruined.

"Come on, Norah." Lola heaves a sigh. "Loosen up a little. I thought these would be fun for her. Let me have them. I'll send her something else."

I'm not sure if Lola's really surprised at how we all reacted, or if she actually expected Mama to get upset. Maybe Lola wanted to get a rise out of Mama.

Daddy clears his throat. "Girls, I think we'd better turn in. Believe it or not, I have to go to work in the morning."

Relief rushes through me. This is over. Daddy's said we all have to go to bed.

Mama reaches to take the baby out of Lola's arms.

"Let me tuck him in, please." Lola pleads, rising from her chair with DC held against her chest. "I might not know how to pick out underwear for a twelve-year-old, but I do know how to put a baby to bed."

Mama pushes the bassinet toward the hall and Aunt Lola follows. I can tell by the way Mama's holding her lips together that she's still mad. "Birdie," she snaps, "time for you to go to bed."

Daddy and I are left alone in the living room. I look at him. He shrugs and shakes his head, without ever making eye contact with me. "I don't understand your Aunt Lola sometimes."

Suddenly, I think of Brooke and Robert on the beach and I wonder if Brooke has red satin underwear.

LOLA

In the dark, small middle bedroom that will be David Clayton's very soon, I stub out my last cigarette and fold back the covers. Rain is still dripping outside the slightly open window. The air is chilly, but not as cold as the weather in Atlanta. Night sounds different here: not much traffic, a distant train whistle, a solo bird call.

In Atlanta, I'm close to the highway and cars whiz by all day and night. Strange how I never think about it when I'm there, but here, the quiet seems as heavy as the damp atmosphere, more oppressive than the traffic at home.

I lie on the bed and pull the blanket up to my chest. The foldout sofa is smaller than my bed, but I feel so alone it might as well be a giant bed in the isolated tower room of a castle.

Oh, God. I've already screwed up this visit. I didn't expect Norah to react so strongly to Mellie's gift. It's not like I expected the girl to wear them to school or anything. I just thought they'd be fun for her, give her a little taste of the exciting things to come in her life. I thought they'd teach her to enjoy being a girl.

But no. Norah completely lost her cool, blowing everything out of proportion. Just like she did when Claude and I came to visit and we had to get a hotel room because she wanted him to sleep on the couch. I guess I forgot exactly how straight-laced my sister is.

But I'm still glad I'm here. Norah and I'll make up. I'll do something special for her, and make sure the next present I buy for Melanie is completely sweet and *appropriate*.

I'm certainly not leaving because of this *faux pas*. I'd do just about anything to hold that sweet baby in my arms. I didn't want to leave him in his bassinet in Norah's room. She refused to let him sleep in his crib in the room with me. Even my argument that she needed her sleep and I could get him started on formula by giving him his two o'clock bottle didn't budge her.

Here in the dark, my arms ache to hold him. Tugging the pillow to my chest, I try to fill the emptiness, but there's no warm, sweet breath against my cheek. No soft, new hair under my fingers.

Through the wall, I hear Norah and Clay's muffled voices. I can't tell what they're saying. Maybe Clay is complaining about the gifts I brought the girls.

It doesn't matter what the words are. Norah is so blessed to have someone to talk to in the soft hours of the night.

Their bedsprings give a deep sigh, and I imagine them settling into each other's arms for the night. In my mind's eye, I see Clay holding her. It's too soon after the birth for sex, but he'll rub her aching shoulders, kiss her temple as she falls asleep. He'll make sure she knows he loves her.

I roll to my side, stuffing the pillow under my head. Soon the pillowcase is damp from my sideways tears.

The next morning, we sleep as late as DC lets us, which means Norah and I are up at six a.m. I start the coffee while Norah feeds the baby. We are still in our nightclothes. I have my hair wrapped in toilet paper. My hairdresser, Davina, at the *Salon de Paree*, swears the toilet paper in combination with my satin pillowcase keeps my set neat until my next appointment.

Norah looks like an old dishrag in her faded nightgown and stringy hair. She seems so much older than she did when I saw her at the beginning of this pregnancy. I feel kind of obvious in my red satin pajamas and black slippers decorated with feathers. Oh, well, this is what I sleep in. I'm not going to spend good money on flannel just to live down to my sister's wardrobe.

Clay comes into the kitchen, fresh from his shower. He looks handsome as he grabs a cup of coffee and a piece of toast. If he wasn't married to my sister, I could just sop him up with a biscuit, because nothing's sexier than a good husband and father.

He gives Norah a kiss and leaves for the plant. Ignoring a stab of jealousy, I crush my cigarette in the ashtray and get another cup of coffee.

After a few minutes, Norah is dozing on the sofa, nursing the baby. When he turns away from her breast, I take him, covering Norah with the extra blanket she keeps handy.

He smells like sweet cream, warm and rich. My arms are full and happy as I rock him gently back and forth. I close my eyes and hum softly, soaking in the feeling of a baby in my arms. For an hour, I'm so happy.

Saturday
October 20, 1962

MELANIE

"All right, Davina, I'm ready." Birdie sits in a dining room chair like a queen waiting for her servants to work their magic. We're playing Beauty Shop with Aunt Lola, who's gathered her rat-tail comb and hair lacquer.

"Can I have some make-up, too?" Birdie asks.

"You have to check with your mama." Aunt Lola finishes ratting Birdie's crown of fluff into a smooth bubble about twice the size of her little-girl head.

"I guess you can have a little lipstick," Mama says.

"I've got just the color right here." Lola digs in her gigantic cosmetic case. I can't believe she's got so much stuff. Mama only has two lipsticks and a compact.

"Pink Cotton Candy," Lola croons. "A sweet color for a sweetie-pie."

Birdie bounces from the chair, begging Mama for some perfume. "Please, please Mama? Just a little? An itty-bitty dab? I'm so pretty, all I need is perfume."

"If it will hush you up, go ahead. But just one short, short spray." Mama wrestles with DC, trying to give him a bath in the kitchen sink while he's screaming. "He's hungry, and I'm about to explode with all this milk." Her voice sounds tight and tired. DC screams again and Mama's hand slips. Water sloshes from the sink and soaks her blouse.

Lola steps up to the sink. "If you'd stop squeezing him like a rubber duck."

"Leave me alone. I'm almost finished."

"Norah. Stop." Aunt Lola wraps her arm around Mama's shoulders. "You're angry. You don't want to be this way. Let me finish."

They look at each other, and something passes between them. Their eyes get sad together and Mama rests her head against her sister's. With a sigh, she says. "Okay. I'll go change and take a breather."

Mama hasn't let anybody else bathe the baby since they came home. Something isn't right. I'm getting worried about her, but I don't know what to do. That's the hardest thing, when you see a problem and have no idea how to fix it. All of us are tired from DC's middle of the night crying, but Mama has it the worst. I wish she'd get DC started on the bottle so Daddy could help her out. Even I could get up in the middle of the night on weekends. But she keeps putting it off.

Daddy doesn't seem to notice that Mama's temper is getting shorter each day. He doesn't seem to care that until Lola got here and said something about it, Mama hadn't washed her hair in more than a week. In fact, just now he doesn't seem to care about much of anything except the beer that Lola bought at the liquor store this afternoon.

He holds the brown bottle by its neck between two fingers and stares at the television news like none of us are even in the house. Actually, I think it's weird that he can shut things out.

How can he ignore the baby crying, Birdie's screeching, Mama's anger, and Lola's noise? Seeing and hearing it all makes me exhausted.

Lola wraps DC in his towel and carries him to the bedroom. In a few minutes, Mama and Lola come back. Mama's wearing a clean white blouse and Lola is carrying DC, smiling and baby talking to him. Mama settles on the sofa, and Lola hands her the baby.

"Norah, I really wish you'd let me give him a bottle tonight and let you sleep. You look so tired."

"Okay. You've convinced me. We'll give him a bottle tonight."

"Great. It makes me feel good to help you out."

It seems like all the tension of last night is forgotten. Mama and Lola and have been laughing and having a good time today. Maybe I need to get over it, too. After all, Aunt Lola said she'd send me another present. I'm sure whatever it is will be better than that awful underwear. Still, I kind of wish I'd had a chance to put it on, just to see how the red satin feels.

Aunt Lola flaps the white bath towel she'd put around Birdie's shoulders. "Next?"

With a sigh of resignation, I sit in the dining chair. Lola clips the towel behind my neck. "What will it be this time, Mel? How about a nice beehive like mine? Your hair is perfect for that."

I scoot against the chair's back. "I don't care."

"Oh, but you have to care about your hair. It defines you, gives you style, pizzazz."

"If you say so."

Lola drags the brush through my thick hair. The brushstrokes pull at my scalp. I watch in the hand-held mirror as she teases every hair until it stands out from my head and I look like a character in a monster movie who's frightened out of her wits. I even open my eyes wide and shape my mouth like a scream to see if I could play the part. Oh, definitely.

But, when the ratty mess is sprayed and smoothed into a twirling high style, it does look nice. Then Aunt Lola pulls out her make-up case and does my face.

My eyes look larger with the blue eye shadow and mascara. Aunt Lola finishes the look with a lipstick that's called Hot Pink Passion. If passion were a color, I guess it would look like this. Or maybe red satin.

I wish Robert could see me all done up. Maybe he'd forget about Brooke and kiss me again.

Lola looks over my shoulder and the mirror reflects both of our faces. She made me into a duplicate of herself. Only the years etched into Lola's face make us look different behind the make-up and hair. She grins and removes the towel with a flourish. "Voilà!"

Birdie claps her hands. "You look so pretty, Mellie. Almost as pretty as me."

"Thanks. I think." I stand up and push my slacks down my calf with my foot.

"Norah, what do you think about your young ladies now?" Lola asks, as she carries the chair back to the dining room.

Mama opens her eyes and lifts her head off the back of the couch where she's been resting while DC nurses. She smiles at Birdie. Then Mama looks at me. Her smile turns down, and her eyes, focus on my face, fill with tears. Silently, they run down her cheeks while her lips tremble.

"Very pretty." She wipes her face with the back of her hand and looks back at DC. "Very pretty."

Seeing Mama tear up makes me want to cry too. I don't know why. Mama thinks I'm pretty. I can see the truth in her gaze. But somehow, it hurts her. And I don't want to hurt her. Helpless, I just stand there.

Back in the kitchen Aunt Lola cracks open ice trays. "Let's liven things up after all that Cuba mess on television." She cuts her gaze to Daddy like he shouldn't be watching the news. Like he should just ignore it.

But now I want to defend Daddy. I'm glad he pays attention to what's happening. He needs to be able to concentrate on the news and not worry about the ordinary stuff happening in our house. If he knows what's happening with Cuba and the missiles, he'll be able to take care of us. He'll be able to make decisions like letting Birdie and me stay home from school so we'll be safe.

Daddy turns the TV off. "The news is over now. Whether you like it or not, Lola, things are happening and I need to keep up with them."

Aunt Lola just stares at him, and says, "I think we should have a twist contest." Lola twists her hips and looks at me. "Why don't you call Stephanie and see if she wants to come over?"

"Can I, Mama?"

Mama yawns. "I guess so. But I'm not going to be able to stay up late."

"I know, Norah," Aunt Lola says. "You're completely exhausted. You should turn in early."

Mama sighs and leans her head on the back of the sofa. She shuts her eyes and nods.

I call Stephanie while Daddy moves the coffee table and chair to give us room for dancing.

Lola motions to Birdie with her hand, holding her cigarette with two fingers. "Honey, dig down in my suitcase and bring me those forty-fives, would you?"

I thumb through the records on the metal rack holding our meager collection. "We've got the 'Peppermint Twist'." The doorbell rings. Stephanie opens the door and pops her head in.

"Hey, honey, come on in." Aunt Lola kisses Stephanie on both cheeks. "You know, that's how they say hello in Europe."

"Really? Ooh-la-la!" Steph says in a high-pitched voice. "Do they say that, too?"

"*Oui, mademoiselle*," Lola says with a French accent.

Birdie comes back into the living room with Lola's forty-fives. She's slipped on a pair of Mama's high heels, so she walks slower than normal, the clicking heels announcing her arrival. Daddy brings the box of pretzels and the big, beige can of Charles Potato Chips from the kitchen, and puts them on the makeshift bar next to the vodka and orange juice. Aunt Lola is mixing screwdrivers.

"You girls can have drivers." She laughs and winks at Daddy. "We have to save the screw for the grown-ups."

I slip a record onto the fat spindle that holds forty-fives and set the speed adjustment.

Mama scoots to the edge of the couch. "Wait a minute, Mellie. Let me put DC in bed before you start the music." She groans as she pushes to stand up. "Maybe if I close the door he'll sleep through this."

Lola pours drinks into six glasses. When Mama comes back into the room, Lola pushes a drink at her, then one at Daddy. "Girls, get your glasses. We need to make a toast."

Stephanie sniffs hers and frowns. "It really is just orange juice."

"Yep."

"To family. What would we do without them?" Lola grins and clinks glasses with Mama, then kisses her cheek. She taps Daddy's and kisses his cheek. Then we all clink together.

It seems like we're all happy for the first time in days.

NORAH

The mix of vodka and orange juice tastes so good—a slow burn and a tart sweetness. It's a treat, and I didn't have to make it myself. I drink it too fast because I'm not used to drinking. I forget a screwdriver is not like iced tea.

Still full of energy after a day of shopping and entertaining the kids, Lola spins around and flips the switch on the record player.

The needle hisses on the vinyl for a second, then twist music fills the living room. "Contest begins now!" Lola cheers and moves into the center of the room. "I'll win, of course, since I am the reigning Twist Queen of American Legion Post 214 in Mud Springs, Georgia. But y'all might learn a thing or two, just by watching."

The party's begun. I guess I don't have a choice but to endure.

Lola puts her foot in front of her and moves in smooth gyrations to the music. "C'mon, Norah."

"No. I'll just watch. I'm going to bed soon."

Lola dances to where I'm sitting on the couch and takes my hand. "You can't go to bed until you dance."

"Okay. The sooner I do this the sooner I can sleep." I'm barely moving, but I'm up and dancing. I'm surprised that it feels good. Lola smiles at me. We move in sync. We're sisters, after all. Two sides of a coin, like our daddy used to say. We both tilt our hips slightly forward, and our hands are limp at the wrists. Most of our twisting motion comes from our waists.

It's kind of a lazy twist. "You know I've only got one dance in me."

Clay stands by the table with his arms crossed over his chest, watching us. He's smiling at me with that smile he saves just for me. I lift my hair off my neck and fan my face with one hand, all the while keeping my hips moving in time with the music. I feel my shirt rising, exposing my pregnancy-soft waist, but I don't care. Clay watches me with that look in his eye. I'm reminded of what it feels like to be a woman. Not a wife, not a mother, not a milk factory. Just a woman.

The girls join us. Birdie kicks off my high heels, grabs Lola's hands, and moves like a washing machine agitator. Steph and Melanie are concentrating too hard to be having fun.

"Keep doing this and you'll get your figure back real soon." Lola smoothes her hands over her slim, no-baby hips.

A snide remark is on the tip of my tongue, but I bite it back. Because, surprise, surprise, I'm having fun. Real fun. I put my shoulders back, which pulls my blouse tight across my breasts. The top button pops open. I glance down, taking in the magnificent cleavage that's purely functional. I lean toward Clay, giving him a peek. I crook my finger and he joins me, dancing close in the small area we've cleared. His eyes are dark, and I know that if DC were more than a week old, Clay would be leading me back to the bedroom pretty darn quick. I miss that look.

It makes me feel good that he wants me. But I'm also glad I've got doctor's orders to follow. Clay will have to wait a few weeks.

When the record stops, we all head for our drinks. The faint chill of the brief cold spell is gone, and we're hot and thirsty. I flap the hem of my shirt to move some air. "That's it for me, kiddos. I'm taking another shower and joining DC."

"C'mon, Baby." Clay finishes his drink and sets the glass on the table. He locks his fingers behind my neck and puts his forehead against mine. He smells warm and spicy. "We just got started."

"You have a good time." I take his face in my hands and kiss him. He tastes like beer and liquor and orange juice. It reminds me of those early days when we drank and danced and made love over and over. Sometimes I wish we could go back to that time, before we had children. When our focus was on each other, and all we worried about was saving enough money so we could go dancing on the weekends. I wonder if he'd do anything differently? I know I would.

I'd demand more of what *I* want from life. This vague notion that there's something better nags at me, though I can't put my finger on what it is I'm missing. I know it's more than just dancing on the weekends. I shouldn't waste precious energy thinking about it; it's too late to change anything now.

I end the kiss, hoping he can't taste my frustration. "Sorry, but I'm tired."

He gives me another quick kiss and I slip away, closing the hall door behind me.

Another record starts as I walk the dark hallway. Lola's voice follows me. "Melanie, you're hopeless."

In the shower, the hot water sprays over me for the second time in one day, and I feel like I'm at the gates of heaven. Heaven itself will be my nice, soft bed and deep sleep. Toweling dry, I'm so relaxed I feel boneless. I pull a clean nursing gown over my head and step into the bedroom. Clay sits on our bed, unbuttoning his shirt.

He can't be serious.

"What are you doing? You should go back out there with the girls."

"What if I want to stay in here with you? Lola's watching the kids."

"It's only eight-thirty, Clay. You're not ready to go to sleep."

He grips my hips and pulls me between his legs. He kisses my breasts at the top of the gown. "You smell so good." He buries his face in my cleavage. His voice low and muffled, he says, "Who said anything about sleep?"

I push him away. "I did. I need some sleep before DC wakes up again. And besides, you know we can't do it. It's too soon. The doctor said so."

"But we could still have some fun."

"You mean *you* could have some fun. No thank you." Wiggling free of his grip, I walk to my side of the bed. "I'm going to bed to sleep and you should go back to the living room."

I'm not sure if I'm angry or ashamed. I snap the bedspread back, and he stands up. I say, "You can end the party whenever you want. Come back when you're ready to *sleep*."

His lips tight, he buttons his shirt again as he heads for the bathroom door. "Goodnight, Norah."

Suddenly, I feel awful. I didn't set out to send a message I wouldn't follow through with. I was just having a good time. Feeling a tiny bit of the woman I used to be. And now I feel like the worst kind of tease.

"Goodnight."

LOLA

I swallow the shot of straight vodka I poured when Clay and Norah left the room. Putting the glass on the table, I say,

"C'mon, Mellie." I grab Melanie's hips to show her how to move. "You've got to relax and feel the music. This is supposed to be fun, not dental work."

Clay comes back in, closes the hall door behind him, and goes straight to the pitcher of screwdrivers, pouring himself a tall one. I didn't expect him to come back and join us.

His shoulders are rigid and his jaw clenches. I've known Clay for almost as long as Norah has. It's always been easy for me to read his moods. Right now, he's frustrated and tight with tension. Sexual tension, it seems to me. It must be tough on a guy to be on the abstinence wagon for a couple of months.

Pulling my gaze away from Clay, I focus on the girls again. "Steph, bend your knees and keep twisting." I'm giving a lesson on the low twist, showing the girls how to bring their bodies closer to their feet and then slowly rise back up. "This is the move that I won the last contest with."

I feel Clay's gaze on me. "C'mon," I say to him. "Let's show these kids how this is done."

He puts down the glass and rolls up his shirtsleeves. "All right."

I'm surprised at the flutter of excitement I feel when he stands just inches away from me. It's crazy. He's my brother-in-law. We're just dancing with the kids in his living room.

But when the music begins and we start to move together, I suddenly see that things could have been different. Clay could have been my husband, and these beautiful girls and that darling baby could have been mine. I could have had this life that seems to make Norah mad.

It's not fair. When we all met, Clay was up for grabs. But Michael caught my attention with his dangerous good looks and his bad boy attitude. Clay was so ordinary. Boring.

Look at us all now.

Michael is dead from that awful car crash. Norah is sleepwalking through life. And Clay isn't boring at all. He's a good husband, a good father. A very handsome man.

I move closer, almost close enough to "dirty twist." His gaze locks with mine, and I see that he's feeling vulnerable. Maybe he's thinking about the newscast, realizing that we all might be close to the end. That there may not be many more chances to really live.

I back away a bit. "You still haven't taken my car out for a spin."

"Maybe in the morning."

"Sure. There shouldn't be many cops out on a Sunday morning when all the fine folks are in church."

"Are you planning for us to go drag racing?"

Laughing, I shake my head. "A little time in the fast lane is all."

He smiles. I've made Clay smile, despite all his worries.

When the song ends, Birdie flops on the sofa. She's asleep in minutes. "Look. Li'l Bird is gone. Such a party pooper. It's only nine o'clock."

"Nine?" Steph says. "I've got to go home, too. Curfew stinks."

"Can I walk her halfway home, Daddy?"

"Sure, Mellie. I'll put Birdie to bed." Clay scoops his child up and carries her through the hall door.

When he returns, I'm fanning myself. "God, it keeps getting hotter in here."

"It does." Clay unbuttons his long sleeved shirt. His chest muscles are outlined beneath his white undershirt.

Mellie comes back in through the front door and cool air streams in behind her. I say, "Maybe we should leave the door open for a while.

"We still have mosquitoes here, Aunt Lola. Mama doesn't want DC to get bites." Mellie closes the door behind her.

"I hope you don't mind, Lola, but I'm going to take this shirt off."

"Go right ahead, Clay." I pour more vodka and orange juice into the pitcher. When I turn back to hand Clay a glass, I freeze for a second.

Clay's gaze drops from my eyes, roves slowly over my breasts and drops to my hips. The air changes. It seems thinner, compressed somehow, like it feels just before a storm.

Clay shoves his hair back from his forehead and sips his drink. Focusing on his daughter, he asks, "Are you hot too, Melanie?"

I know what he's doing. He's reminding himself that he has a family.

Mellie yawns. "A little. I think I'll rest for a minute." She grabs the folded newspaper from the floor and lies on the couch, fanning herself slowly.

Downing the rest of my screwdriver, I shuffle through the records. "Maybe we should slow things down a little. How about a samba, Clay?"

Clay walks over to Mellie and strokes her sweaty hair from her forehead. She gives him a sleepy smile.

"I should turn in now," he says. "It's been a long day."

He's reminding himself again. Power surges through me. I make him *need* to remember.

I don't want him to go to Norah. Not yet. "It's still early. You can't leave me to finish a whole pitcher of screwdrivers by myself." I put the record on. The music will make him stay for one more dance, I know. One more song I can pretend through. "Maybe if we turn some of these lights down it'll cool off a bit."

I switch off the lamp and the kitchen light. Only the TV lamp, the small light behind the horse statue, remains on. With its greenish glow and the softer music, the room does feel cooler.

I take his fingers in mine and stroke my other hand up his arm, finally resting my hand on his shoulder. Sighing, Clay puts his palm on my waist. I step closer until his heat surrounds me. My eyes drift closed, and I sway against his firm chest, his flat belly, his hard thighs.

MELANIE

I stop fanning myself with the folded newspaper. It doesn't really help. Since Lola turned out all the lights, I can't read the paper, either. I know from looking at it earlier in the day the words Castro and Cuba take up almost the whole top half of the front page. There are grainy photos of an island, supposedly taken by our spy planes. I can't believe the jets we see flying over us can take a picture from so far away. But, there's proof in black and white. The caption says the long tube-like things are missiles.

Bombs.

Just ninety miles from Florida's coastline. Only three hundred and fifty miles from my home.

I close my eyes. The sighing rhythm of the saxophone music almost lulls me to sleep. I open my eyes every few seconds to keep from nodding off. Flickering snapshot impressions of the room mix with the half dreams in my head.

In the first image, Daddy looks like a man I don't know. His tight, sleeveless undershirt sticks to his damp skin. The muscles in his arms and shoulders glisten with sweat. As he moves to the jazz tune, his hips sway in the pleated slacks he wore to work today.

I blink, and that snapshot changes to reveal Aunt Lola, her head tipped back, her lips moist and parted. She strokes her fingers up and down Daddy's arms, dragging her fingertips as if she can't bear to lose the feeling of his skin under her fingers.

I doze, and those glimpses give way to images of missiles resting in dark metal cradles beneath green palm trees. Brooke and Robert walk between the huge, sleeping monsters on their way to the beach. I can tell they're heading for a swim, because they trail beach towels behind them in the sand.

I don't want Robert to be with Brooke the same way I don't want Daddy to be with Lola. It's not right, but I can't do anything about it.

The music changes, and my eyes open a slit to see the next snapshot. Daddy and Lola stand so close together, no light shows between their bodies. They're a shadowy silhouette against the greenish light behind them. Lola's head rests on Daddy's shoulder; her lips brush his bare neck. Her hands trail up his arms until her fingertips slip into the short hair on the back of his head.

Daddy's hands rest low on the top of Lola's hips, his fingers making gentle indentations where he pulls her tight against him.

I struggle to stay awake but my heavy eyelids slide down again and again. The image of Daddy and Lola pressing against each other doesn't make sense, I think sleepily. What I want is Robert. My eyes close and my mind chases after him.

I want to see the Robert who sat on the porch with me. The Robert who walked me home and kissed me softly, like a real boyfriend. I know it wasn't real, but I want it to be, more than anything.

Love seems to be both real and imagined. After all, how do I know it exists? I mean I know I love my mother and father. I even love Birdie, most of the time, anyway. Maybe I love Robert. I *want* to love Robert.

I know Mama and Daddy love each other. What does it mean that my father is holding Aunt Lola so close? Letting her kiss his neck?

It isn't love.

I blink again, trying to keep my eyes open. I know this is important. I have to pay attention.

Lola eases away slightly, allowing the tiniest bit of space between her and Daddy, and whispers something I can't hear. Daddy nods. The music stops.

Okay. They aren't dancing anymore. I can rest. The silence lulls me back toward my dream of Robert. We sit on a porch, eating banana Popsicles and watching the waves roll up on the golden sand. There are no missiles, no roaring jets, no crying babies, just Robert's voice, rich like melting ice cream.

But there's a baby crying, pushing me out of the dream. It's DC.

I bolt up from the couch. The living room is dim and empty. The record player's needle popping and scratching is the only sound. Daddy and Lola are nowhere to be seen.

DC cries out again.

I close the hall door behind me and then tiptoe toward Mama's room, hoping Daddy is there to get DC before he wakes up Mama. But their door is still closed and no light shows beneath it.

When I swing it open, Mama's curled on her side, facing away from DC's bassinet, so tired she doesn't even hear the baby. Her lips puff with each snoring breath.

Tiptoeing to the bassinet, I lift DC and grab a clean, cloth diaper from the basket beside it. He quiets a little and snuffles against my neck, looking for his milk. We slip out of the room.

I change him on the sofa bed Aunt Lola uses. The overhead light glares, and I rub my eyes to clear away the sleep fog. Lola's red satin pajamas lie across the spread, and her black satin pillowcase gleams in the light. The room smells like her perfume and cigarettes.

DC squirms a little while I change his diaper.

Holding him close, I say silly words to him like Mama does and head to the kitchen to get him a bottle. I open the hall door and freeze.

What I see explodes through me as savagely as a bomb.

Daddy's kissing Aunt Lola.

He holds her tight in his arms. His hands push her blouse up and he fingers the black lace of her bra.

Lola's hands disappear into the waistband of Daddy's slacks, sliding around to the belt buckle.

All of this registers in a split second. I tense and squeeze DC. He wails, sending Daddy and Aunt Lola skidding apart.

They stare at me, eyes wide and slightly unfocused. Their lips glisten, red and damp. Their hands, at first dangling at their sides, flap into business. Daddy tucks in his undershirt and straightens his pants.

Lola adjusts her bra and blouse.

Aunt Lola speaks first. "We thought you'd gone to bed." Her words, low and husky, break the spell that froze me to the hallway floor.

The fear that was always outside my home, the fear of whistling missiles destroying my family, has been replaced with something more terrifying.

President Kennedy and the Navy can't defend me against

this. No guns can stop it. No peace treaty can change it.

Daddy shoves his hair back and comes toward me. I tuck DC closer, hunching my shoulders to protect him from this new, terrible danger.

I can't look at Daddy or Aunt Lola. It hurts too much, like looking at the sun too long. The sight of them kissing seems burned into my vision, because when I close my eyes, there they are, bright against my eyelids.

"I'll go check on Norah," Daddy says, and starts toward the hall, but Mama meets him at the half-opened door.

"What's happening?" Sleepily, she looks from Daddy to Lola to DC and me.

When no one answers, she strides through the room to the kitchen where I stand with DC wailing on my shoulder.

"Mel, why do you have DC?" She takes him out of my arms, automatically checking his diaper. "You already changed him?"

"Yes, ma'am." I duck my head and focus on setting up the bottle warmer. "I'm heating the bottle like you showed me this afternoon."

She holds DC and glances from me to Daddy, then to Lola. Lola drains the last of her drink. Mama looks like she's working hard to figure out what's going on, but she's awfully sleepy.

Finally, she nods. "I still need to nurse him a little, but bring the bottle back to my room when it's warm. Thank you for your help, Mellie. I can always count on you." She shuffles down the hall, patting DC on the back.

The three of us stand in the kitchen. We stare at each other.

I feel like words, horrible, hateful words—curses—the nastiest things I can think of, are shooting from my eyes like sparks. I wish I could do that. I wish I could burn both of them with the bolts of hate and anger blasting through my brain. They need to be punished.

But I don't know what to do.

Daddy's expression looks shattered. His shoulders slump and his body seems to shrink right before my eyes. His fingers stretch and curl like he needs to shake off the feel of Lola's skin.

I imagine—I hope—that the words bubbling in his mind are, *I'm sorry. I didn't want to.* But he doesn't say anything.

Aunt Lola looks like she does when she's about to cut a donut while driving her convertible. If Lola does it, it can't be wrong. Her expression says she was just having fun. She doesn't seem to understand what all the fuss is about.

She picks up her cigarette case from the counter and lights one. Exhaling a stream of white smoke, she plucks a loose shred of tobacco from her tongue. I know she thinks she never does anything dangerous enough to hurt anybody.

This time she did, and I don't think I'll ever be able to forgive her.

Finally, Daddy says, "You both go on to bed. I'll take the bottle to Norah and clean this up."

Aunt Lola touches the corner of her mouth. Her lipstick looks old and faded. "Well, goodnight, then." She crushes the just-lit cigarette in the ashtray and starts toward the bathroom.

Daddy leaves with the baby's bottle. I watch his bent back and caved-in shoulders as he passes through the door.

Licking my lips, I taste the gooey remains of Aunt Lola's Pink Passion lipstick. The image of our faces, side by side and identical in the hand mirror, flashes in my mind.

She did this. Like a rock dropped in a pond, the damage seems to grow in bigger and bigger circles. How will Mama bear the hurt and betrayal? Nothing will ever be the same.

Another surge of pure hatred flares through me.

I tear the pins from my hair and toss them on the kitchen counter, then scratch my fingers across my scalp to destroy Lola's ratting. Leaning over the sink, I splash water on my face. I rip a paper towel from the roll and scrub at the eye shadow and mascara, scour the lipstick from my mouth, until my lips feel raw. The white paper oozes with black and blue and faded scarlet.

I'm still in the kitchen when Daddy comes back. "Go on to bed," he says, like nothing happened. Like the whole world hasn't changed.

"Why?"

He sighs. "Because I said so."

Only a few minutes ago, I wouldn't have hesitated to do what he told me to. But everything's changed. Something has clicked inside me that tells me I don't have to do what he says any longer. He's lost that right.

I look at him, knowing my own face looks like a horror show. I feel like a horror show. Grimly, I say, "No."

Daddy stares at me. "What?" His face appears broken, but I can tell he's working hard to put the pieces back together. "I said go to bed, young lady."

I pick up the pitcher of orange juice and shove it in the refrigerator. "Why did you do that, Daddy?"

He braces his hands on the sink and hangs his head. He reminds me of a building in the movies about Germany after the war. You can tell it was once a building, but you can't decide what it looked like before the bombs.

He straightens and turns around, swiping his hand through his hair. "You're too young to understand, Melanie."

"Daddy, you did something wrong." I decide that since things are never going to be the same, I should say what I think.

"Listen, you can't understand this. There are things that happen that a man just can't control. Forces of nature."

"I don't think so."

"You're just a kid. Things happen between a man and woman. A man can't help himself. It's in his nature." He slams his hand against the edge of the sink. "Damn it, I didn't want to do it."

There! Those are the words I need to hear. But it doesn't help. It doesn't change anything. I just stare at him, trying to make sense of it all. If he didn't want to do it, then what happened? Is he blaming this all on Aunt Lola?

I know she can be cruel, even when she says she loves you. I know that from personal experience. But he could have stopped her. In my heart, I know that Daddy could have stopped, if he'd wanted to. He hadn't wanted to.

That thought breaks my last restraint. I need to lash out at him, to hurt him like he hurt me. Like Mama will be hurt.

Tears burn my eyes. "Are you saying this is all Aunt Lola's fault? That Aunt Lola did that all by herself?"

"Melanie, Lola just kept pushing and pushing. A woman who wears tight pants and rubs up against a man wants one thing. Like that damned red underwear: it's a signal, a sign. She's real damn lucky I didn't give her what she asked for."

"What was she asking for?" I want to grab the words back into my mouth. My belly tightens and I feel sick. I don't want to know anymore. I just want to forget tonight ever happened. If only I could.

"I swear, Mellie, I don't want to hurt your mama. Or you. Let's not say anything, okay? Some things are better kept secret." His pleading eyes glisten, like he's about to cry.

I've never seen Daddy cry. Ever. If he cries, I feel like...I don't know. It will be like day and night changed places. Like the world turned upside down.

He clears his throat and says, "I'll make Aunt Lola leave early in the morning." His gaze meets mine. "You need to go to bed, Mellie." He walks away.

I stand in the kitchen, scrubbing my face with paper towels until my skin feels raw.

LOLA

As I disappear into the girls' tiny pink bathroom, I wish I hadn't wasted that cigarette in the kitchen. I need it now. My hands are shaking and cold sweat trickles down my spine.

Oh, God. What did I just do?

The grim disappointment on Melanie's face haunts me. And Clay's shattered expression.

My God. What have I done?

I can't bear to look at myself in the mirror, so I gather my hairspray and perfume from the back of the toilet and toss them in the train case. I'll go back home tonight, after everyone's asleep. I'll creep out the front door and roll my car down the driveway so the engine won't wake anyone. I'll drive down the road without lights until I'm a safe distance away, then I'll put my foot down hard on the gas pedal.

I'll leave like the illicit, immoral bitch I am, skulking away in the dead of night.

I won't even change clothes. Biting my dry bottom lip, I dump make-up and lotions into the cosmetic case. Grabbing my toothbrush, I scrub at my mouth, brushing out the taste of Clay's kiss. Maybe I should take a shower to wash away the lingering scent of his cologne.

That would take too much time. I need to get in that spare bedroom and be quiet, so everyone will go to sleep.

Instead of washing away Clay's scent, I bring my forearm to my nose and inhale the mingling of our fragrances: his familiar Old Spice and my earthy Topaz. The smell of us together is wicked and so tempting. I can't help wondering what our finish would smell like. What would our sweat and sex together make? Something sinful and beautiful and destructive.

Melanie's girlish voice penetrates the thin wall between the kitchen and the bathroom. I clutch my arms around my middle to keep it from heaving. I really drank a lot tonight. I'm so drunk.

Clay's voice, a deep, indistinct rumble, answers Mellie's. What can he say? How can he defend himself against what I did to him? Well, it wasn't only my fault. He certainly didn't push me away. I should go back in there. I should say something to Mellie.

There's nothing to say, though. I want what I can't have. There's no way to explain this to my niece. My sweet, thoughtful, intelligent niece.

After snapping the latches on my case, I turn off the light and slip through the darkness to the middle bedroom. Cranking open the window, I breathe in the clean night air, amazed that anything is clean tonight. In the dark, I lie on the bedspread and smoke a cigarette. My hands quit shaking. A restless quiet slides through the house.

After three cigarettes, I get up and open the window wider. Folding my pajamas, I stuff them into my suitcase. I put the bed pillow over the clasps to muffle the click. Standing beside the crib, I smooth the sheet that waits for the day David Clayton will move from Norah and Clay's room to this one. I pick up the tiny pillow my mama embroidered for Melanie, the first grandchild. The colors are a little faded and the cloth has yellowed. But the old pillow is as soft as the dreams Mama had for all of her babies.

I press my face into the thin and worn fabric. Instead of Ivory Snow and sunshine, the baby pillow smells like cigarettes and Topaz.

Everything I touch is ruined. I leave the awful leftovers of me—ashy stink and stale perfume—like a trail of glass shards. For the first time tonight, I feel like crying. Why am I like this? Why must I ruin everything? Why do I always want what I can't have? I crave another cigarette.

Laying the pillow in the crib, I wipe my face with my hands. Out of habit, I'm careful not to smear my mascara. Like a perfect face will cover up the ugliness inside.

The glowing clock dial on Mama's old Baby Ben shows one-thirty. I pick it up off the small end table beside the sofa bed. It's heavy and cold in my hand. It feels like so much wasted time, just there, weighing me down.

Now. I should leave now. If I wait much longer, DC will be awake again. Suitcase in hand, I open the bedroom door.

Suddenly I see the next morning playing out in my mind. All the questions from Birdie and Norah. Questions that Clay and Melanie will have to answer with lies.

But staying won't make things better. Facing them in the morning won't change what happened. It won't change what Melanie saw. If I stay, it won't be insurance against Mellie telling her mother. And that would kill Norah and any chance she has to be happy in the future.

The clock ticks loudly, the luminescent hand jerking with every second that passes. I close the door as I leave.

Sunday
October 21, 1962

BIRDIE

I'm the first person to wake up this morning.

I like being first.

Except it's very quiet, and that means I have to be quiet, too. I don't like that. I want to turn on the television. The clock in the kitchen has the big hand on the six and the little hand is close to the seven. I can't remember if that's six-thirty or seven-thirty. We just started learning to tell time at school. Through the living room window, I see the sun isn't very bright so I think it might be six-thirty. If that's what time it is I have to be quiet for a long time.

Getting my crayons, I lie on the floor and color in my Huckleberry Hound coloring book. The two mouses, Pixie and Dixie, are my favorite. I think Dixie talks like Aunt Lola. He makes his words long and he talks kind of slow.

I wonder when Aunt Lola is going to wake up. Maybe she'll make pancakes again this morning. Oh! I just remembered she's going to take me for a ride in the convertible with the top down today, too. She promised.

The clock in the kitchen has the big hand on the nine and the little hand is still close to the seven. I have to be quiet a lot longer.

I've colored two pictures, staying in the lines pretty good, and using the right colors for grass and sky and mouses. Now I'm bored. I take the pink crayon and color Huckleberry Hound. He's supposed to be blue, but dogs aren't blue. I don't know why he's blue on the cover of my book. I don't even stay in the lines for this picture. I color fast and hard, pretending I'm an artist who doesn't have to be careful and stay in the lines. I can do whatever I want.

I hear Daddy cough, and I stand up. When he steps into the living room I jump out in front of him. He scoops me up in a hug. His face is scratchy and he doesn't smell nice like he does when he's going to work.

"Daddy, is it time for *Davey and Goliath*?"

"Shh. Everyone's still sleeping."

"We're not. Why are they still asleep?"

Putting me down, Daddy says, "Let me get the paper and make the coffee. Then I'll check the TV schedule and see when your show starts."

"I can get the paper."

"No. It's chilly outside. You'd need your shoes and your robe. I'll get the paper, so you won't bother Melanie by going back in your room."

"But Daddy, you don't have your shoes or robe. Won't you get cold?"

"Shh, Birdie. I'll be right back." He sounds kind of angry. Not really mad, but what Mama calls 'gravated. Daddy runs outside in his bare feet with no jacket or robe, just his shirt and pants. So I run right behind him. If he can go outside barefoot, then why can't I?

"Daddy! Where's Aunt Lola's car?"

Daddy grabs my hand. "Be quiet, Birdie. You're going to wake up your Mama and the whole neighborhood."

"But where's the convertible? Aunt Lola promised me a ride today."

"You never listen to me. Be quiet." His voice sounds hard, like sharp rocks hitting the ground, and his hand is tight around mine.

"But, Daddy—

"I said for you to hush up. I guess she went home."

I want to ask why Aunt Lola left in the dark, but I'm afraid to say anything.

Daddy closes the door behind us and tosses the newspaper on the table. He goes right to the kitchen and makes the coffee.

I really 'gravated him this time. I wish I knew what was going on. I'm 'gravated myself. Aunt Lola promised she'd take me for a ride with the top down today. I wanted to put the top down yesterday, but she said no. We'd have a special ride today. But now she's gone. Yes, I'm sure 'gravated. I want to throw a tantrum, but I'm not stupid. Daddy's already mad.

So, I need to be extra good for the rest of today, no matter how disappointed I am. I get my coloring book and crayons and sit at the dining room table. Maybe Daddy will be happier after he has some coffee. Grown-ups always take a sip of it and say *ahh*, like it makes them feel good.

I hope it makes him feel good, because right now, Daddy has his eyebrows pushed together. I guess he's still mad at me, but maybe it's because of what he's reading in the newspaper. He and Mama talk about the newspaper a lot. It takes me a long time to figure out the words in the newspaper, and if it makes them frown, I don't want to read it.

"Daddy, since Aunt Lola's gone home, who will make

pancakes for us this morning?"

Daddy stands up. "Birdie, you can turn on the TV now. I think your show will be on soon."

Now I don't really want to watch *Davey and Goliath*. "I'm hungry. What about the pancakes?"

"I'll make your pancakes."

"I'll help you, Daddy." I stand by him in the kitchen and finally he smiles at me. It's a sad smile, but he lifts me up to sit on the counter. He gets the flour and a bowl out of the cabinet.

Mama brings DC in. "Morning. Is Lola still sleeping?"

"She went home," I tell her. "She didn't even give me a ride in her car. She broke her promise."

Mama looks at Daddy. "What? Lola's gone?"

Daddy shrugs and measures out flour. "Guess she decided to get an early start."

Melanie is up now, standing at the kitchen door. She's staring hard at Daddy like she's never seen him make pancakes before. Well, I don't think I've ever seen him make pancakes either, but he seems to know what he's doing.

"She's gone?" Melanie asks.

Daddy doesn't look at her. He just cracks eggs in the bowl with one hand. Mama can't even do that.

"I guess," Mama says. "Clay, what did you say to her last night to make her mad?"

Daddy stops stirring for a minute and just stares at the bowl. Then he says, "Norah, I didn't say anything to make her mad."

Melanie is shaking her head. I guess she can't believe Aunt Lola broke her promise, either.

"Maybe somebody stole the convertible!" I jump off the counter. "I'll see if she's still in her bed."

Melanie follows me to the middle bedroom. But Aunt Lola

is really gone. The bed is made and her suitcase isn't there. Under the alarm clock is a note and two dollars. Melanie picks it up and reads it to me.

"It says, 'Sorry to leave so early, but I remembered I have a union meeting tonight. Birdie, please take a rain check on the ride, okay? Here's two dollars for a treat. Be sweet and maybe Melanie will take you to the store.'"

"What's a rain check?"

Mellie hands me the two dollars. "It's just a way of saying wait until next time."

"You mean Aunt Lola will take me for a ride with the top down while it's raining?"

Melanie is studying the piece of paper like it's got a secret code on it or something. "Yeah," she says, walking toward the kitchen. She hands the note to Mama.

"Well, I never heard of such," Mama sighs and studies the paper. "It must be a real important meeting for her to hightail it out of here so doggone early. I didn't even hear her leave. Did you, Clay?"

"Nope. Who wants the first pancakes?"

I jump up and down. "I do. I do."

Folkston, Georgia

LOLA

When that same, ugly cop catches me doing seventy-five miles an hour through Folkston, I figure maybe fate has decided to take care of settling the score. It's only been about forty-five minutes since I left Norah's, so I'm still a little drunk.

I've had enough to drink that the cop can throw me in jail for the night.

Instead, he suggests, quite nicely, that he buy me a cup of coffee at the truck stop. *Well, okay*, I think. He follows me to the truck stop on Highway 301. The lights inside are so bright they hurt my eyes. He orders coffee and the breakfast special for both us.

"Well, Miss Carter," he says, stirring sugar into his coffee. "I could run you in to the jail and let you sober up overnight. That might take care of your little speeding problem, too."

I take a sip of coffee and nod. I deserve to be put in jail. Hell, I deserve to be put in front of a firing squad and shot dead. But that would be too easy. After all, dead people don't have to think about all the evil they've done.

He folds he his hands on the tabletop and leans toward me. "Of course, if we make this official-like, I'll have to write you a ticket. You don't even want to know how much that fine will be."

"How much do you think?" I ask, but I don't really care. I'm broke no matter how I look at it. I'd just as soon go to jail.

"At least a hundred. And then there's the matter of the red light you ran on the other side of town."

"You were following me that long?"

"Yes, ma'am."

The waitress appears with two plates of eggs and grits. The smell sends me running for the bathroom.

I hear the waitress laughing as I round the corner.

"Wally, you sure do have a way with women," she says.

When I come back to the table, the officer is sopping his plate with his biscuit. He winks at me, "Feeling better?"

I put on a big smile. "Sure." I force myself to take a bite of eggs. My stomach is so empty, it's about to turn inside out.

After another sip of coffee, I manage to ask, "So, what's it going to be? Jail or a ticket?"

He just smiles, then motions for the waitress to pour another cup of coffee. She tops off our mugs and leaves us alone again.

I shove my plate away. I can't eat anything else. "If it's just the same to you, I'd rather not have a ticket. I'm broke."

"You'd rather go to jail?"

"I'd rather get on the road so I can get back home." I rub my thumb over the dribble of coffee running down the side of my mug. Looking into his ugly face, I say, "But I don't suppose you're gonna settle for that, are you?"

"Well, Miss Carter, I don't want to put a pretty little thing like you in jail." He frowns. "It's not a very nice place. Lots of the wrong kind of people in jail."

Wrong kind of people, just like me. "So, you're feeding me breakfast and sending me on my way, then?"

"After our, uh, encounter on Friday night, I thought you understood how I do business."

"I told you, I'm broke. I haven't gotten any more cash since I gave you that twenty-five. I don't have any money in the bank. You might as well put me in jail."

"You don't have anything you could, um, barter?"

Now I understand. I lower my head so he can't see how rattled I am. How could I have been stupid enough not to see where he was going with all this discussion, and buying me breakfast, and *not wanting to put a pretty little thing like me in jail?* But I'm not going to make it any easier for him. He's going to have to make the deal. So I bluff.

"Do you see me dripping diamonds?" I pull off the clunky costume jewelry earrings I'm wearing and throw them on the table. "Knock yourself out. Forty-nine cents at Woolworth's."

He just rolls the red plastic bead between his fingers and stares at me.

The sight of his stubby fingers on my earring fills me with disgust. My stomach rolls over once more, and I run for the bathroom. At this sink, I don't look at myself in the mirror, same as I couldn't at Norah's house.

This time when I come out, he's standing just outside the door. "I wouldn't want you to try to run away or anything. After all, in your condition, you present a danger to yourself and other drivers."

I don't deserve any better than this. I don't deserve any better than him. He follows me out to my car. "Here?" I choke out.

"There's a rest area with a picnic table about a mile up the road. It's nice and wooded. A real nice place for a picnic."

"I'll follow you."

He shakes his head. "I don't think so. I'll follow you, and if you lose your way, I'll be able to catch up with you real quick-like."

I crank the car and put my head on the steering wheel for a minute. How in the world did I get to this place in my life? He flashes his headlights, and I put the car in drive. I sure as hell take my time driving that mile.

He spreads me across the picnic table.

A leering grin contorts his ugly face as it comes toward me. I close my eyes and wish I were dead. His breath stinks of coffee and stale cigars. His wet, rubbery lips move over mine. Bile burns in my throat. His fingers reach under my blouse and grab at my breast. Pain shoots through me as he grinds into me, rocking the picnic table like a boat about to sink in rough water.

After, he zips his uniform pants, then wipes his hands and

face with his big, white handkerchief. "You drive safe, now, you hear?"

I throw up three more times before I can drive. I turn the car around and go back to the truck stop. I ask the waitress for some vinegar.

She gives me a look of pity, and fills a white coffee mug with vinegar.

"How much do I owe you?" I ask.

She waves me off. Doesn't say word.

I wonder if Wally the Cop brings all his *dates* here.

In the bathroom, I soak a paper towel with vinegar to improvise a douche. I don't want Wally's bastard. I wash up the best I can.

I drive as far as Perry, Georgia, then have to pull over to sleep.

Jacksonville, Florida

MELANIE

I sprawl on a sunny patch of grass in our back yard. The afternoon sun is warm on my face, the grass cool against my back. For the first time since last night, I feel like I can breathe without my chest breaking open. Around me, pine needles stick up out of the grass like tiny spears. Daddy says he's going to have the big pine tree cut down because it's too close to the house. A hurricane could make it crash and destroy the whole house.

It seems like danger is everywhere I look these days.

I hear footsteps and glance over to see Steph crossing the

yard. I pretend I don't know she's coming, closing my eyes.

I feel her standing beside me for a few seconds before she flops down on the grass. "Sure is quiet in your house." She kicks off her loafers and wiggles her sock-covered toes. "Where's Aunt Lola?"

And just like that my chest feels like there's a brick on it. Sitting up, I take a deep breath. "She left this morning. Real early."

Real early. I'd heard the front door click and checked my clock. Two o'clock. The middle of the night. I knew she was sneaking off like a… I can't even think of a bad enough word.

Part of me wants to believe that what I saw didn't mean anything. That it was just human nature, like Daddy tried to explain. But I can't buy it. I can't convince myself that people can behave like that and not understand how it hurts other people.

And no one, absolutely no one, can make be believe that a kiss is about the same as a handshake.

No, a kiss is more than that.

Lips are different from hands, and kisses on the lips aren't the same as pecks on the cheek. Daddy kisses Birdie and me on the cheek. Mama kisses us on the cheek. But Mama and Daddy kiss each other on the lips, on the neck, on the hand and on the cheek. I understand what I saw Daddy and Aunt Lola doing.

It was wrong.

Aunt Lola proved it by sneaking away in the middle of the night. Daddy proved it by not looking me in the eye this morning.

I yank up a handful of grass, then let it slide through my fingers like green rain. Choosing a fat blade, I hold it between my thumbs and blow. Nothing happens, except suddenly my chest feels lighter.

"You're still trying to learn how to do that?" Steph carefully places a blade of grass between her thumbs and blows. The shrill blatting sound sets the hair on my arms standing on end.

Slowing shredding the grass, Steph says, "Why did she leave so early? She usually stays until dinner time."

My stomach rolls and I prepare to tell the same lie Daddy has been telling. Only Birdie and Mama think it's the truth. "Lola needed to get home. She has a union meeting tonight that she forgot about."

Lying makes me feel heavy again. I'm disgusted with Aunt Lola, but truthfully, that isn't a completely new emotion. My feelings for her usually teeter between love and something else.

My disappointment with Daddy seems to be slowly crushing the life out of me.

I need to think about something else or I'll end up telling Steph what happened. And I can't do that. "Are you excited about becoming an auntie?" I say. I don't warn her not to be like Lola.

Steph exhales sharply through her lips, making them buzz. "I guess so."

"Cherie looked really pretty when she came to visit us the other day."

"Yeah, I guess she's okay. My mom acts like Cherie died or something. Mom keeps moaning about how Cherie's life is ruined. I don't get it."

"Do you think Cherie's happy?"

Steph shrugs. "Who knows? I went over to their apartment. It's really just a couple of rooms in an old house, but Cherie acted so proud."

"It must be pretty neat to have your own home."

Steph picks up a pine needle and begins to braid the three

pieces together. "I think Clint blames Cherie for getting pregnant. He never smiles. While I was there, he didn't even tease me. He just got his beer out of the fridge and went downstairs to sit on the hood of his car to smoke. He never sat on the hood of his car before."

"How can it be Cherie's fault? I specifically remember that part of *The Talk* where it takes two, a man and a woman, to make a baby."

Steph looks up and said, "Haven't you figured out that facts and reality are two different things?"

The truth of her words hits me like a rock between the eyes. I fall back on the grass and stare up at the clouds milling around in the bright blue sky. That's a lot like what Daddy said last night. I wonder if Clint feels like Cherie made him do something he didn't want to do? I'm so confused. All I really know is that none of this can be love. Not real love.

I think sometimes love seems like the prism we used in science class. In the same way the prism takes ordinary sunlight and throws out reflections of every color imaginable, from indigo to canary yellow, love seems to take ordinary life and cast it in different colors, shades bright and dark, depending on who is on the other side of the glass.

Steph rolls onto her stomach, props her chin in her hands, and stares through the chain link fence to the back of Marvin's house. We can hear his guitar. He's practicing again.

"What's new with Marvin?" I ask.

"Not much."

I roll over, too. "You never finished telling me about the kiss. What was it like?"

She shifts her gaze to me. "It was cool. Can you believe he even slipped his tongue in my mouth? That's called Frenching."

"Really?" I tried to imagine how that would feel.

Yucky.

Robert hadn't put his tongue in my mouth. But the way his kiss had made me feel—soft, and like I wanted more of something—makes me think that maybe I would like it. Only if it was Robert doing it. I can't imagine letting any other boy put his tongue in my mouth.

Was that what Daddy and Lola were doing? I shudder and try not to see it again in my head.

"Yep. Okay, now I've had my kiss. What about you? Just because Cherie killed our plans for the Sadie Hawkins Dance doesn't mean you're off the hook. Who are you thinking about for your first kiss?"

For Stephanie, kissing is like reaching President Kennedy's goal for the standard number of pull-ups or something. Kissing Robert was a lot more than that for me. It was all the best things about being grown-up. He made me feel special and beautiful.

Suddenly it's important for me to know that Steph has some feelings for Marvin. Because if she doesn't really *like* Marvin, then she's kind of like the women Daddy talked about: the ones who ask for it. Like maybe Cherie did? Would Steph turn out to be an aunt like Lola and give her niece red satin underwear? "Do you really like Marvin?"

"Sure. He's a good guy."

"I mean for a boyfriend."

"No! Hellfire, Mellie. He's, well, you know." Steph pauses and looks back toward Marvin's house. "He kind of scares me. He makes me think about stuff I don't want to think about. He makes me try to understand things. It's hard. It's like I'm small, and he's pulling and tugging to make me stretch."

It sure sounds like she has some feelings for him. I just can't tell what they are. "That's not all bad, is it?"

"I guess not." Steph stands up and brushes the back of her slacks. "I think I'll go over and see him. Want to come?" She sticks her feet into her loafers. "Maybe he has a friend over, and we can take care of your kissing too."

I stand up, too. Maybe I'll just make an excuse that I have to go help Mama. Only, I don't want to go back into the house. Guess I'll go to Marvin's with her. But I'm not kissing anybody.

NORAH

I'm taking the sheets off the bed in the middle bedroom when I hear Mellie come home. "I'm glad you're back," I call. Birdie flaps the top sheet like it's a parachute, then she dives beneath it. "You're supposed to be helping me, Birdie. Get out from under there."

Mellie stands silently in the doorway. I say, "You'll never guess who called this afternoon."

"Who?" She comes in and reaches across the foot of the bed to lift the last tucked corner, then tosses the sheet to Birdie at the head of the bed.

Birdie covers herself and walks around with her arms sticking out like a ghost. "These smell like Aunt Lola," she says. "Woooo. Wooooo. I'm the ghost of Aunt Lola. I only appear at night."

Again, I wonder what Clay said to make Lola mad enough to leave like that. I don't think Lola was still mad about my reaction to the underwear. We had a good day together on Saturday. I was so groggy when I took DC from Melanie last night, I can't remember what they were talking about. But, it seems like there was tension in the air.

I'm sure it's nothing serious. Lola had to get back for the union meeting like her note said. It's still strange that she drove off in the middle of the night.

Mellie unfolds a fresh sheet over the mattress. "Who called? Aunt Lola?"

"No. She's probably at her meeting. I'll give her a call tonight, I guess." I tuck the upper corners of the fresh sheet under the mattress while Mellie tucks the bottom. "Myra Mayfield called. You remember, our neighbors who got stationed in Cuba? They're coming to stay with us for a little while."

"You're kidding." Mellie stands at the foot of the bed with a look of disbelief on her face.

"No. Mr. Mayfield wants them out of Guantanamo, and they need a place to stay until they can get housing on the base. They'll be here sometime Tuesday or Wednesday."

"That sounds really bad. Mr. Mayfield doesn't think they're safe anymore?"

"Don't worry, sugar. I'm sure Joe is just being careful. But it is sad that Kevin and Brooke have to leave their home and their school."

"Where's everybody going to sleep?"

"We'll put Brooke and Myra in here on the fold-out sofa and Kevin will have to camp out on the couch in the living room. It's just for a few days."

I sit down on the freshly made sofa bed, and sigh. I wish I could take a nap, but I've still got a lot to do. I'm still not back to normal. Sometimes, I swear I'm walking around in my sleep. It didn't seem to take this long to recover after Birdie was born. I guess six years make a big difference.

I hope the Mayfields will only be here for a few days, but

from what I've seen, the Navy does things in its own sweet time. If a lot of families are evacuating—that's the word Myra used, but I don't want to scare the girls—there may not be much base housing available. I couldn't say no to Myra. She was my best friend before she moved away. Forcing a smile, I say, "Won't it be nice to see Kevin and Brooke again?"

Mellie shrugs and gathers up the dirty sheets. "What does Daddy think about this?" She sounds so much older than she did just a few days ago.

I smooth the coverlet on each side of me. Mellie doesn't need to know that Clay and I fired off a few angry words at each other after Myra's phone call. That's a few more angry words on top of arguing about Lola. He still won't tell me what set her off like that.

I take a deep breath and will myself to calm down. If I can't stay relaxed, my milk supply will be gone in just a few days. Maybe, that would be for the best. DC does well on a little formula every day, so he should adjust to all formula easily. Maybe I'll get some of my energy back if I quit nursing. Besides, bottles would be more modest with so many more people in the house, and Clay and Mellie could help out more.

I look up to see that Mellie is still waiting for my answer. I won't lie to her and tell her that Clay's approves. "It's okay. Everything will be fine."

She leaves with the dirty sheets bundled in her arms. Birdie struggles to put a fresh pillowcase on. I grab the other pillow and slide the case on.

I'd much rather see Birdie struggle with a pillowcase, than an unhappy husband. Some things never get easier.

I hear Melanie ask Clay what he thinks about this change in plans. I move to the hallway door to hear his reply. "Your mother says she can handle it."

I don't know why he's being this way. Myra would do the same thing for me, I'm sure.

Only Birdie has anything to say at dinner. Afterwards, Clay settles into his chair with the newspaper and watches the news on TV while I'm washing the dishes with Melanie.

The doorbell rings. Birdie runs from the kitchen. "I'll get it. I'll get it." She opens to the door to reveal Rachel Winston.

Mrs. Winston steps across the threshold with her miniature poodle squirming in her arms. "Hello, Norah. Clay. Hi, girls."

"Come in and have a seat, Rachel." Clay stands up and tosses the newspaper onto the floor.

Mrs. Winston sits on the edge of the sofa and places her Fifi on her lap. "I'm sorry to bother you. I'm sure you're busy with the new baby."

"No," I lie. "I was just finishing up the dishes."

DC begins to cry. He'll be ready to eat soon, and then he'll probably be awake for a while.

Clay lifts him out of the bassinet. "I'll change his diaper."

"Thanks, honey." I turn my attention to Rachel. "How are you?"

"Okay, I guess. Bob should be home in a day or so. You know he's been on special duty for a week now."

"I know. You must miss him."

From the corner of my eye, I see Melanie frown, not so much that anyone but I would notice, but I can't put up with her being disrespectful to adults. I lift my brow at her, and she looks down at her hands.

"Bob wants me to go visit my mother in New York until this whole Castro thing blows over. He's worried about me being so near the bases here in case something happens."

I hear Melanie suck in a panicked breath and look at her. She's pale. I know how worried she is about the Cuban situation, and she's been exposed to a lot of bad news tonight: the Mayfields evacuating, and now Rachel Winston leaving Jacksonville for safety. It seems like an awful lot. Even I'm feeling edgy. "Mellie, why don't you go see what Birdie's up to?"

"Yes, ma'am."

Rachel says, "I hope I didn't upset her. I know Melanie is the sensitive sort."

When Melanie is out of the room, I say, "Things must be pretty serious if Bob wants you to go to New York. Does that mean he knows something we ordinary civilians don't?"

Rachel lifts her slim shoulders and rubs her hand down the poodle's back. "He won't say much about it, really. I'm just glad to go see my mother."

Come to think of it, Stephanie's father has to report to his ship tomorrow. I wonder how many families are preparing to tell husbands and fathers good-bye tomorrow morning.

"I was wondering if Melanie would get our mail for a few days. I'm leaving first thing in the morning, and Bob won't be back until Thursday." Rachel pulls a five-dollar bill and a key out of her pocket. "I'll pay her, of course."

"Rachel, put that away. Of course, Mellie will get your mail for you. We're neighbors. You don't need to pay her."

Melanie comes back to the living room with Birdie following closely behind her. Birdie kneels in front of Rachel so she can pet her dog. The dog snarls and Birdie yanks her hand back.

"I was just telling Mrs. Winston you'd be happy to collect their mail while she's gone."

"Yes, ma'am, I heard."

"Thanks. I'll bring you back something nice from the city."

"Thank you, Mrs. Winston." Mellie goes into the kitchen

to put the key in the drawer where we keep stuff like that.

Rachel doesn't get up to leave. I have to make more small talk, I guess. "You're going to miss seeing the Mayfields. They're coming to stay with us for a few days until they can get base housing."

"Frankly, I'm surprised they are coming to Jacksonville," Rachel says. "It seems like Joe would want them to go further north. Doesn't Myra have family in Ohio?"

"I don't think Myra wants to go back to the cold weather. She said something about the kids not having coats anymore, since they haven't been back to Cincinnati in a while."

"But still, they would be safer there."

"Rachel, you know we'll be perfectly fine here. Nothing is going to happen." Can't she see my two girls right here?

"Well, I wouldn't—"

"Listen, I know you have a lot of packing to do, and I've got to get the girls ready for school tomorrow." I've had enough of her doomsday. "We'll take care of the mail for you."

Rachel rises. "I should be going. Tell Myra I said hello, okay?"

"I will. Have a safe trip."

Finally, she's gone.

Clay enters the living room and glances from me to the girls with a worried look on his face. "What's going on?"

I reach out for DC and walk to the couch. "Nothing really. Girls, will you please finish the dishes?"

Finally, I can close my eyes and have a moment of peace. After I put DC to bed, I'm going to call Lola and find out why she left us like she did. Somehow, I'm sure Clay did something to upset her.

Atlanta, Georgia

LOLA

It's eight o'clock. I pour myself another drink. Of course, I'm already so drunk I can barely keep my eyes open. Too bad the liquor won't slow down my thoughts. I haven't really slept since I left Norah's, only that nap in the car.

I'm still raw from the cop's *picnic*.

I throw back the rest of my drink, fill up the glass again and reach for the bottle of Seconal. I take one, washing it down with the booze. Instead of replacing the cap, I pour out the pills on the counter.

The capsules look like red jewels on the white countertop. I push them around with my finger. Are there enough?

They really are pretty: oblong and shiny red, like red patent leather. One, two, three, four, five… I've only got twenty left and can't refill my prescription for another three weeks.

How many did Marilyn Monroe take?

I can't remember. I could take the twenty pills, open my last bottle of vodka and get in the bathtub. Nice hot water. I'd be so relaxed. Maybe I'd fall asleep. Slide down and down and down.

I line the pills up: four rows with five pills in each row.

The water would come up over my face. Would I wake up when my nose filled? Would I come splashing out of the water, gasping for air? That would be a waste of these red beauties and a good bottle of liquor.

I open the drawer right in front of me and take out a butcher knife. It's too big. It looks frightening. If it looks scary just resting on the counter, how will I be able to make myself drag it across my wrist?

The paring knife looks more manageable. I lay it on the counter and put the butcher knife away. I move the twenty red capsules to a straight line beside the small knife, then I push the knife into the middle of the line, making a scraggly arrow.

Pointing the way to where?

Hell, for sure.

Mama always said that suicide was the one unforgivable sin.

Like the rest of my sins can be forgiven.

Like it matters. I'm already in hell.

Can I just check out? Can I leave without ever talking to Norah again? Without telling her how much I love her? Can I stop my suffering without asking Mellie, sweet Mellie, for forgiveness?

She's only twelve. Can she understand enough to begin to forgive me? She knows about Michael and the car crash, but nobody knows how much pain I've lived through since then. Not even Norah.

Oh, she understands that my heart was broken and my back was injured. She knows I take medicine to help with the physical pain.

Even if I could explain to her how I feel inside, she wouldn't get it. How could she? Her life is perfect. She has her children. She has Clay.

I pick up the knife. Hold the point to the bluish vein in my wrist.

Press.

My flesh resists, like a thick-skinned tomato against a dull knife. I push the point in about an eighth of an inch before I feel the burn, the pain just before it punctures. I pull the knife away.

Norah has never felt the point of a knife on her wrist and wondered what it would be like to push it all the way through, to watch the blood well up, to make the cut deeper and wider. No, Norah has never hurt like this.

But she would hurt like this if she knew what I'd done on Saturday night, what I'd wanted to do on Saturday night. What Clay almost did to her. Yeah, she'd understand a little bit then.

If Norah had spread herself on a picnic table and let an ugly cop use her body so she wouldn't have to pay a ticket or go to jail, Norah would understand this pain.

I gather up the pills in the palm of my left hand. They look like candy. How many can I swallow at one time? Maybe four at time. Five swallows and they'll be gone. Then I'd fill up the bathtub. Maybe put in some bubbles. That would feel nice.

The last thing I'd feel is warm water and tiny bubbles bursting against my skin. The last thing I'd hear is that crinkling, popping sound of bubbles around my ears.

No, I think I want to hear music. I put the pills back on the counter and go to my records. I choose five and stack them on the spindle, turn on the record player. The sound fills the room, but I turn it louder. It needs to be louder for me to hear it in the bathtub.

In the kitchen I gather up the pills again, top off my glass. I balance my hands like I'm weighing something on a scale. Red sins in one hand, amber sins in the other. All heavy, so heavy.

The shrill ringing of the phone scares me out my skin. I scream. The pills jump from my hand to scatter across the kitchen floor. My drink sloshes all over.

The ringing continues as I kneel on the floor to pick up all my pretty red pills. One, two, three…seventeen. Three missing. They probably went under the stove. I stand up, place my seventeen pills on the counter and get the flashlight out of the drawer.

Finally, the phone stops ringing.

I gather the last, lost pills from beneath the edge of the stove and blow the dust from them. I can't throw them away. I don't want to put them back in the bottle. I fill my glass again and put the three pills in my mouth. Swallow. I'll only have four more swallows to finish the job.

My head is floating like a balloon with no string attached. I need to go to bed. I'll think about sins tomorrow. The phone rings again. It seems like it's going to ring all night if I don't answer it.

"Hello?" My voice sounds weak.

"Lola? Are you okay?"

"Who is this?" The voice sounds so far away. "Norah? Is that you?"

"Yes, it's Norah. Tell me, are you all right? You sound terrible."

"I'm okay. I'm just tired. I'm so tired."

"I imagine so, leaving my house and driving so late at night. Or should I say early in the morning?"

"Both, I guess."

"Well, I'm glad you got home safely."

"Yeah." I lean against the wall and slide down to sit on the floor. My eyes just won't stay open.

"Listen, I'm sorry for whatever Clay said or did to make angry enough to leave like that."

Adrenaline shoots through me and my eyes flash open. "What did Clay say?"

"Nothing. He wouldn't tell me what he said to make you mad, but he's been such a bear all day. If he was like this after I went to bed last night, no wonder you took off in the middle of the night."

I need to focus. I have to keep talking, make sure the lie keeps going. "I remembered this meeting today. You know I have trouble sleeping. I decided to hit the road."

"It doesn't sound like you'll have any trouble sleeping tonight."

"No."

"Lola."

Norah stops talking and once more that hot energy surges through me. It's that feeling of being caught doing something wrong and it makes me feel like such a child. What I did wasn't the crime of a child.

"What?" I need to know that things are all right there. That the damage I caused isn't permanent. That Clay still loves my sister. That someday Mellie can forgive me, even if she can never understand what was going on between her Daddy and me. I want my sister's family to settle back into their routine, somehow.

"It's just that nothing seems to be right. Nothing is normal. Did you watch the news?"

I can't help but sigh with relief. She's upset about the Cuban situation. "I missed the news because I was at my meeting," I lie. Again. One more can't hurt. I was sitting in my living room drinking, instead of watching the nightly news broadcast.

"It seems to be getting serious. Myra Mayfield called this afternoon. They're being evacuated from the base in Guantanamo Bay. She asked if she and the two kids could stay with us."

"Evacuated?"

"Of course, I told her they could stay with us. They have no place else to go right now. They've been promised base housing as soon as it's available. That's one of the reasons Clay is so grouchy. He doesn't want them to stay here."

"Oh." It's all I can think to say, my head is so fuzzy.

"I just wanted to let you know how much I love you, Lola. I wish you were still here. The girls missed you all day today."

"Really?" I know Mellie was glad I'd left and she didn't have to see me again. "Was Birdie too disappointed about not getting a ride in the convertible?"

Norah manages a bit of a laugh. "What do you think? She was convinced someone stole your car until she found the note in your room."

"I'm sorry, Norah. I'm so sorry for…" I swallow back the sob pushing up through me. "I'm sorry for everything."

"You don't have to be sorry. We're sisters. We love each other, no matter what."

I put my hand over the receiver so she won't hear the sob I can't keep back any longer.

"Lola? Are you still there?"

"Yes. I'm here."

"Well, I just wanted to talk to you. You know, before everything gets too crazy with the Mayfields here. I wanted you to know how much I love you."

"Oh, Norah. I love you, too. You and your family, you're all I've got."

Norah is crying now. "If—you know—if things get out of hand, with…"

"Kennedy is going to take care of it. We shouldn't worry."

"I just wanted you to know, in case we don't get a chance to talk again."

I hear Clay's voice in the background. Norah says, "I need to go now. Birdie is upset about something, and you need to get to bed."

"Yes, I do. Bye, Norah."

"Bye, Lola."

I sit on the floor for several more minutes, letting my thoughts—not quite so drunken anymore— ramble. Thoughts of weighty things like love and whether it can stand some of the awful things people can do to each other. Finally, I lay down on the cool, wood floor of the living room. My eyes won't stay open any longer.

Monday
October 22,1962

Jacksonville, Florida

MELANIE

Everybody's edgy this morning. I still feel sick when I think about what Aunt Lola and Daddy did, so I try not to think about it.

Birdie's baby-talking to DC in the living room, while I'm trying to fix my hair for school. Birdie and DC seem to be the only ones in a good mood. Mama and Daddy are discussing the arrival of the Mayfields. Loudly.

Daddy's voice sounds clearly all the way from the dining room. "It's just too much for you. Why don't you give yourself a chance to rest and recover? DC is only two weeks old." I hear Daddy's coffee cup land in the saucer harder than usual.

"I'm fine. Besides, Myra and the kids need someplace to stay. She said Brooke and Kevin are really looking forward to seeing their old friends again."

"I'm sure they are. But we need to think about our own family."

Yeah, Daddy. You should've thought about your family on Saturday.

I hate it that I feel that way about my father. When will I ever be able to think of him as my good old Daddy again?

He continues, "How will our kids feel about it?"

I hear Mama's chair scrape. "They're looking forward to it. Melanie and Kevin were practically best friends. And Brooke is so sweet, she'll be a big help with DC."

"What about feeding everyone?" It sounds like Daddy slid his plate into the sink. I stand quietly in the bathroom, waiting for this discussion to end. I don't like the way the tension is building.

Daddy's voice continues over the sound of running water in the kitchen. "How are you going to take care of DC, do the wash, and cook for three extra people? Just think about it."

"Myra will help me out, you know that. Stop worrying."

"I'm afraid it'll be too much for you. And the minute it is, I'll have to tell them to leave."

"Just like whatever you said to make Lola leave here before dawn?"

"What did she say?" Daddy's voice sounds even more harsh. It doesn't sound like Aunt Lola told Mama what happened. I can't imagine Mama being this calm and only arguing about the Mayfields if Lola had told what she did, what I saw. After I fumed for a while, what Daddy said about not telling Mama made some sense to me. I don't want Mama to be hurt.

"All Lola said was that she had a union meeting to attend and that she couldn't sleep. She thought she'd get a head start. Not sleeping took its toll on her. She sounded so tired last night. She could barely talk."

The refrigerator opens and closes. More dishes clink against the sink.

Daddy shouts good-bye to us, then slams the front door.

"Mama, DC stinks," Birdie sings.

I creep out of the bathroom, and peek around the kitchen wall to see Mama. Her shoulders are shaking. She's crying.

This morning, the dark circles under her eyes look like bruises. "I'm coming," she mutters under her breath. "I'm coming."

I feel so sorry for her. She's tired and sad and I don't know how to help her. But I can change DC's diaper.

"Mama, I'll change him. I've got time."

"Thanks, sweetie."

Distracted, Mama says, "How about corn flakes for breakfast this morning?"

"Goody. I love cereal for breakfast." Birdie dances around the playpen when I put a fresh-smelling DC in it, placing him on his back, like I'm supposed to. He watches her with big eyes. I wonder when he'll understand that he has his own personal circus.

I open the cabinet and get two bowls. "I'll fix it."

Mama stands behind me and kisses the top of my head. "You're a big help, you know that?"

She walks out of the kitchen before I can answer.

There's a knock on the door.

Thank goodness. Flossie is here.

FLOSSIE

Birdie runs to meet me at the door and hugs me around my legs, just like she's done every time she's seen me since that awful first day of school. Melanie stands in the kitchen with two bowls in her hands. The baby's lying in the playpen. I don't see Miz Adams anywhere.

"Hey, Flossie," Birdie says. "We're having cereal for breakfast this morning. We never get to have cereal on school mornings."

"I'm guessing Miss Birdie likes cereal?" I laugh as I take off my hat and put it in my shopping bag. "How about you, Melanie? Do you like cereal?"

She shrugs. "Mama's really tired today." Her expression says a whole lot more.

"Well, I can cook some breakfast for you girls. Want some bacon and eggs?"

Birdie jumps up and down, making her full skirt flounce. "No! I want cereal. I want cereal."

"Cereal's fine with me, too," Melanie says. She walks over to stand real close to me. "Try to help Mama rest today if you can, Flossie." Her voice is low and so grown up. "We had a busy weekend and company is coming tomorrow."

"More company? I don't understand why folks think a new mama and baby need visitors all the time."

"Not that kind of company. The Mayfields are leaving Guantanamo Navy Base because of all the Cuban stuff. They don't have any place else to stay."

"Well, now, isn't that something? I'll do my best to get your mama to rest some. It does sound like she's gonna need it."

I can't help but think how odd it is that Miz Adams hasn't come back to the kitchen. It's not like her to leave her children to get ready for school by themselves. I haven't been working here for long, but it doesn't take all that long to understand how a family does things.

Cleaning folks' houses is a quick way to get know people

real well. I see their dirty laundry, the dust under their beds, and bills left lying around. And I know this isn't the way Miz Adams usually does things.

I also understand that Melanie is feeling bad about something.

When I started this job, I knew it was short term. I swore I wasn't going to get attached. Honestly, with some families there's no temptation to think of them as any more than a job. But the Adams' aren't that kind of family.

I'm near to lovin' these girls, whether I want to or not.

The baby starts to cry, and I lean over to lift him out of the playpen. Miz Adams comes up behind me.

"Good morning, Flossie." She sounds like she's struggling just to get the words out. "I'll take him. He's ready for a bottle."

"You got him started on formula?"

Birdie pauses, before spooning cereal into her mouth. "DC had bottles this weekend. I gave him part of one. He really liked it."

Studying Miz Adams, I notice that her skin is pale and she has dark circles under her eyes. Her hair is kinda lank. Mellie's right, this woman is plum wore out.

"Miz Adams, why don't we rearrange our work schedule a bit? I'm all caught up on the dusting and such. Let me take care of feeding the baby this morning while you take a shower. Then he'll be ready for a nap, and you can lie down with him and rest while I take care of the laundry and the kitchen. How does that sound?"

"That sounds like a really good idea, Mama," Melanie says.

Mis Adams shakes her head. "I don't need to sleep."

Melanie gets up from the table and puts her arms around her mama. "Please, Mama. You need to rest up before the

Mayfields get here. Please." The poor girl sounds like she's 'bout to cry. I can't help but wonder what went on this weekend.

Miz Adams pats Mellie on the back, and clears her throat. "I guess it wouldn't hurt me to have an extra nap today. But it's time for you girls to get going. Birdie, do you have your lunch box?"

Birdie jumps up. "Yes, ma'am. I just need to brush my teeth."

I pat the baby's back. "You go ahead and take your shower. I'll make sure they get going. Miss Mellie and I have things under control, don't we?"

Pure thankfulness wells up in Mellie's face. She kisses her mama's cheek. "Bye, Mama. I'll see you this afternoon."

Miz Adams walks down the hall, her shoulders slumped with tiredness. Poor thing. And company coming, too.

"Flossie," Melanie says.

Her voice is soft and strained. "What's on your mind, honey?"

"Just," Melanie looks down at the floor and then up to my face. Her eyes are filling with tears, but she blinks them back. "I just want to say thank you."

I pat the baby and sway back and forth with him, wishing I could do the same with Melanie to make her feel better. "You know I'm here to help out however I can."

"I know."

Then Melanie throws her arms around my neck, squeezing her baby brother between us in a fierce hug. "I'll see you this afternoon."

Birdie grabs my legs in a hug like she usually does. "Bye, Flossie."

Then both girls are out the door and the house feels so

empty. I get the baby's bottle from the warmer and we settle in the rocking chair. He latches onto that bottle like he's been starving for days on end.

Sometimes I can feel when things are out of kilter and it sure feels like something's out of kilter here. I can't help but wonder what happened in this house since I was here on Thursday.

Atlanta, Georgia

LOLA

The damn phone is ringing again. Why can't they just leave me alone?

My eyelids feel like they've got weights on them, and I hurt all over, like I've been beat up. Slowly it comes to me that I'm still lying on the kitchen floor.

I haven't moved since I talked to Norah on the phone. Is she calling me again so soon?

My eyes open and it's daylight. I slept on the floor the whole night. Shit. No wonder I feel like I've been run over by a truck.

My stomach churns and I lurch toward the bathroom. I've got the mother of all hangovers. After retching myself inside out, I rinse my face with cold water. Then it comes to me.

The pills.

The booze.

The knife.

Norah's phone call kept me from taking the rest of the pills. I fell asleep as soon as we hung up.

Of course, now I remember *why* I had counted out the pills. *Why* I'd put the knife on the counter.

The shame remains, like a stone pressing on my heart.

Even though I wanted to, I didn't sleep with Clay. Melanie saved Clay and me from hurting the person we love most in the world.

I'll always regret what happened while we danced on Saturday night. It will never happen again, but in the light of day, without the fog of drunkenness, it seems that I may be able to live with myself.

Now that I'm seeing clearly, it occurs to me that the light isn't right for early in the morning. I check the clock.

Oh, my God! It's one-thirty in the afternoon. That must have been my foreman calling. I grab the phone and dial.

"This is Lola Carter." My voice sounds like a cement mixer. When I tell the foreman I'm sick, he won't have any doubts. "I caught a terrible bug over the weekend. I'm running a fever and that's why I didn't call in before this. If I'm not able to come in tomorrow, I'll get a doctor's excuse."

"I'll make sure the foreman gets the message, Miss Carter," the perky receptionist says. "You take care of yourself now. Get some Coca-Cola syrup from the drug store. That's what my mama always gave me when I got sick."

"I will. Thanks for the tip." The thought of uncarbonated Coke syrup sends me back to bathroom. This time I shower.

Aches radiate from head to toe, like I've tumbled through a grist mill. Now I remember the other reason I wanted to die.

The cop.

The washcloth brushes across the tender area between my legs.

The heavy stone of shame weighing on my heart bursts into flame, a hot coal of disgust and anger burning within me. I can't believe I didn't fight the S.O.B. Why didn't I hand over the few dollars I had in my purse? Why didn't I beg him to take me to the police station?

Instead, I took the punishment. I'd acted like a whore with Clay. What was the difference? I scrub harder at my skin. I lather the wash cloth again, and bathe my whole body once more. Another glob of shampoo, and my fingers attack my scalp, scrubbing away the stench of stale cigarettes, the liquor oozing from my pores.

I will be clean.

It's seven o'clock when I wake up, clean and dry in my own bed. I go to my kitchen, slather a slice of white bread with peanut butter, and drink a glass of water. I'm so thirsty. After gulping another glass of water by the sink, I put ice cubes in the glass and add more water, to drink slowly this time.

I turn on the television. President Kennedy is talking.

Jacksonville, Florida

MELANIE

After dinner, we all gather around the television to hear what President Kennedy has to say. The president's handsome face looks tired and worried.

After saying, "Good evening, my fellow citizens," President Kennedy talks about the *unmistakable evidence that a series of offensive missile sites is now in preparation* in Cuba. He tells us that some of the missiles have ranges of 1,000 miles and others more than 2,000 miles. The Russians could wipe out the whole southeastern United States.

The president has a plan, though.

"First: to halt this offensive buildup, a strict quarantine on all offensive military equipment under shipment to Cuba is being initiated."

I glance at Daddy. His jaw is clenched tight. Mama is frowning while she pats DC on the back. Birdie is sitting so still I'm not sure she's even breathing.

"Second: I have directed the continued and increased close surveillance of Cuba and its military buildup.

Third: It shall be the policy of this Nation to regard any nuclear missile launched from Cuba against any nation in the Western hemisphere as an attack by the Soviet Union on the United States, requiring a full retaliatory response upon the Soviet Union."

My stomach is in knots.

"Fourth: As a necessary military precaution I have reinforced our base at Guantanamo, evacuated today the dependents of our personnel there, and ordered additional military units to be on standby alert basis."

Of course, we knew this when Mrs. Mayfield called on Sunday. In fact, they'll probably arrive tomorrow. Daddy's still mad about it, but he's not saying much. He's focused on the television.

I can't help but wonder if Caroline and John-John are scared like me? Do they have their toys in the bomb shelter that must be somewhere in the White House?

I wonder what Mrs. Kennedy is telling them.

Mama and Daddy aren't telling me anything but what I hear on the news. That's enough to scare me.

Last night, the only way I could fall asleep was with my favorite stuffed toy, Heidi the rabbit, resting on my chest, her floppy ears lightly brushing my cheeks. When I closed my eyes,

I pictured Heidi as a real rabbit hopping down a curving path. Butterflies danced over brightly colored wildflowers and bluebirds sang in the weeping willows that trailed their branches in the bubbling silver stream.

Yes, it's like something out of the movie *Bambi,* but it's better than what I saw on the news. Walter Cronkite said that most Americans believe World War III will start soon.

I'll sleep with Heidi again tonight.

The phone rings and I answer. "Hello?"

"Hi, Mellie. It's Lola."

"I'll get Mama."

"Wait a second, okay?" Aunt Lola's voice sounds different, kind of scratchy like she's sick, soft like she's whispering.

I don't want to talk to her. There's nothing to say.

"Mama's right here." I hand the phone to Mama when she walks in. "It's Aunt Lola."

Tuesday
October 23, 1962

NORAH

Last night, Lola asked me and the kids to come stay with her until this Cuban stuff is over.

Looking at Melanie's worried expression and Birdie's raw, chapped mouth was enough to make me seriously consider it. Maybe the kids could relax a bit if we were further away.

But then, if the unthinkable happens, if the missiles are fired, we'd be away from Clay.

I shiver.

The decision is made. We're staying in our home. I've already told Myra they are welcome to stay with us. I can't change my mind now.

Lola wasn't happy about that. In fact, she began to cry. Once more, we assured each other that nothing would happen, that the whole thing would blow over.

We said we loved each other again, and hung up.

I'm in the utility room beside the carport, putting dirty diapers in the washer, when a shiny car pulls into the driveway. Sticking my head around the door, I see Myra Mayfield step out of the car dressed in a straight pink skirt with matching jacket and hat, *à la* Jackie Kennedy. Her ever-present cigarette dangles from the corner of her mouth.

"Norah!" she shouts, clicking up the driveway in her high heels. She looks so sophisticated and neat. I must look like something the dog dug up in comparison.

"Myra! I'm glad to see you. I was hoping to have a chance to change clothes before you arrived, though."

"You look fine." Myra takes the cigarette out of her mouth and kisses my cheek. "I'm sure our barging in on you has increased your work load about a hundred percent, especially after having a baby. Is he sleeping now?"

"Yes, thank goodness. I was just getting a load of laundry started. Let's go in the house."

Brooke, Myra's beautiful daughter, climbs out of the passenger door. She's so grown up now, I just can't believe it. Her curvy figure is belted into a pretty blue shirtwaist dress.

"Hi, Mrs. Adams," Brooke says, patting her blonde, flip-styled hair.

"Hi, Brooke. Don't you look pretty?" I clap my hands to my cheeks. "This can't be Kevin. He hardly looks like the boy who lived next door just a year ago. My lord, he's so tall."

"Isn't he, though?" Myra says with pride. "Say hello to Mrs. Adams, son."

Kevin gives his mother a sulky look then mumbles, "Hello."

I smile at both of the children. "Hi, Kevin. I know it must be hard having to leave your school and your friends. We'll do our best to make you both happy while you're here. Now, come on, let's go in."

Myra turns to Brooke and Kevin. "Bring in the suitcases, children."

"It'll be a couple of hours before Melanie will be home from school. Would you like some iced tea?"

"Actually, do you have something a little stronger? My nerves are worn to a frazzle. I just hate to fly."

When I open the door, the odor of burning rubber nearly knocks us over. Myra covers her mouth and coughs. Smoke rises from the bottle sterilizer on the stove. The burner is glowing red hot, and the bottom of the pan is turning black.

I've almost burned the house down. I grab a towel, pull the big pan off the burner, and turn the control knob to off. When I lift the lid, I see the rubber nipples have melted and dripped in contorted shapes over and through the metal rack to drape onto the glass bottles below. There's no water left in the pan at all.

Myra stands beside me. "I remember how it was, Norah." She pats my shoulder. "Don't worry, we'll help you as much as we can. I'll stop at Woolworth's and pick up another bottle sterilizer and a set of bottles for you."

"No, Myra. That's too much."

"Pshaw. I've got to take Kevin to the school to get registered, anyway. It won't be any trouble at all."

It would be nearly impossible for me, so I have to give in graciously. "That would be a big help, Myra, if you wouldn't mind."

MELANIE

The afternoon air seems heavy when I get off the school bus. It's almost enough to choke me. Maybe it's just the apprehension that's been growing in me all day. The Mayfields might be at my house when I get there, and who knows how that's going to be.

Like Daddy, I have a feeling it's not going to be good.

"I just had a great idea," Steph says. "Kevin. He can give you your first kiss." She grins like she just won a prize or something.

"Are you crazy?"

"Like a fox. Think about it, Mel. It's perfect. Kevin's going to be hanging around your house. He doesn't really have any friends here anymore, except you and me. And you like him, don't you?"

"Like him? We played kickball together. It's not the same thing." My patience with Stephanie gets thinner every time we talk about this kissing stuff. The whole country is going to hell in a hand basket—yes, I can think that, even though Mama would wash my mouth out with soap if I said it out loud—on the verge of possible total destruction, and Steph's worried about kissing. I wish she would just give up.

"I'll bet you'd rather kiss Kevin than that ugly boy who has his locker next to yours." Her grin turns wicked. "All I have to do is hint to him that you think he's cute, and you'll be lip-locked, for sure."

Sometimes Stephanie's grin is just plain evil. This is one of those times.

"You wouldn't dare."

She wags her fingers my way and waltzes up her driveway. "You know I'm just looking out for you. You'll never get kissed on your own."

Under my breath I mutter, "The things you don't know, Miss Smarty Pants." I'm tempted to tell her about the night of Robert's going away party. It would save me a lot of trouble.

But I won't. Robert's kiss is still the most precious thing

that's happened to me the whole year. I know Steph looks at kissing like wearing your first pair of stockings or something. It's just one of those things a girl does as she's growing up.

When I open my front door, I feel like I walked into somebody else's house. Instead of cartoons on the television, "Big Girls Don't Cry" plays on the record player. Instead of Birdie playing with Tinker Toys, Brooke Mayfield lounges on the sofa.

She looks up from the magazine she's reading. She's wearing her black, rhinestone-trimmed glasses. "Hi, Melanie."

"Hello, Brooke. When did you get here?"

She flips a page. "After lunch. The flight from Cuba isn't very long, but we had to rent a car."

Since lunchtime, she's been sprawled on my sofa? Instead of being happy to see her, all I can think of is the photo of her and Robert on the beach. I want to say something mean to her, but instead I ask, "Where's Kevin?"

"He and Mom went to the school to get him registered."

I'd forgotten about Brooke's soft lisp until she said *thool*. She pronounces every *s* like a soft, furry *th* sound. That makes her words like a whisper, and her lips pucker into a little pout.

The record stops and Brooke sits up.

Waving her off, I say, "Never mind. I'll get it."

"Just thart it over, okay?"

I *thart* the record at the beginning. Through the back window, I see Mama hanging diapers on the line. I guess DC's napping. "Since Kevin's registering for school, I guess y'all are going to be here a while."

Brooke pushes her glasses up on her nose. "I hope not. I only have a few more weeks until I graduate from the base high school." She sits up, smoothing her hands down her skirt. "Does your mom have any soda pop?" She strolls to the kitchen and opens the fridge. She's made herself right at home.

I have an ugly premonition that this is going to be a long visit from the Mayfield's, even if it only lasts a few days.

Mama comes in with the empty laundry basket. "Hi, Mellie. How was your day?"

"Pretty good. What smells so funny?"

"Did Brooke tell you what a stupid thing I did?" Mama shakes her head. "I let the water boil all the way out of the sterilizer." She puts the basket on the table. "If these clouds and humidity don't clear up, I'll need to use the dryer at the laundromat tonight."

"Mrs. Adams, when Mom gets back with car, I'll take those to the laundromat for you. You won't have to wait until tonight."

"Thanks, Brooke. That's awfully thoughtful."

"There's probably more happening at the laundromat, anyway," she says, spoiling her nice gesture. "When did you say Cherie usually visits her mom? I just can't get over the fact that she's married. Gee."

The doorbell rings. "That's probably Steph," I say, adding "Cherie usually visits her mom on Wednesdays to do laundry."

Brooke sighs. "Imagine that. Washing your husband's clothes." She looks dreamy as she leans against the refrigerator, sipping a Coke.

I open the front door. Over Steph's shoulder, I see the Mayfield's car pull into the driveway. Kevin gets out of the passenger side. I wonder if Steph is as amazed as I am at how tall he's gotten in just a year.

Mrs. Mayfield shouts, "Hello, girls. You both look good enough to eat."

Steph leans toward me. "Gee whiz. He sure did grow," she says under her breath.

"Yeah." When he'd left the year before, Kevin had been short and pudgy with freckles all over his face. The boy standing beside the rental car is tall, with new muscles clustered on his wiry arms. His hair and eyebrows are thick and dark. The freckles are gone, replaced by a smattering of acne across his chin.

Kevin smiles at us. His smile is still kind of cocky, kind of know-it-all. Almost a bully smile, but I know Kevin isn't a bully. He's a nice guy.

After tucking his plaid shirt into his navy slacks, he waves. "Hi, Melanie. Hi, Steph."

"How are you?" Steph says with a huge grin on her face.

"You girls just can't understand how happy we are to be here. Well, not happy. No, these aren't the happiest circumstances, at all." Mrs. Mayfield grabs my shoulders and pulls me to her chest. She smells like stale cigarette smoke and hairspray. I don't recognize the cologne she's wearing, but it rivals the hairspray in strength.

Releasing me, she turns to Steph. "And look at what a pretty girl you turned out to be." She takes Steph's shoulders and spins her around, giving her a head to toe inspection. "Norah, our babies are growing up."

Mama stands in the doorway and smiles. "They sure are. I still can't believe how tall Kevin is." Mama glances at Brooke standing beside her in the doorway. "And Brooke is practically a woman."

Brooke preens at Mama's compliment, but Mrs. Mayfield shoots a glare her way. I interpret the look to say *don't think you're such a big shot, missy.*

Isn't this great? We start out living together with tension between Daddy and Mama, Brooke and her mom, and me and Brooke. I can't help thinking that if we don't get comfortable with each other pretty soon, we won't be using all the food Mama bought. Or maybe I'm just being hopeful.

Thursday
October 25, 1962

FLOSSIE

When Birdie opens the door for me, the Adams' house is as busy as the downtown bus station when all us maids are going to work. It seems like there's people everywhere, making the house seem tiny.

"Good mornin', Miss Birdie." I pat her back and pry her arms from around my legs. I notice that woman, must be Miz Mayfield, is frowning at me. Long time ago, Miz Adams relaxed with me and she's never said a word about Birdie hugging me every morning when I arrive and every evening when I leave. It's clear from the sour look on this Miz Mayfield's face that she doesn't like the touching, much less the affection, between me and Birdie, that's for sure. So, I ease away from Birdie, but I give her an extra big smile.

Miz Adams steps out of the kitchen with the baby in her arm. "Hello, Flossie. This is my friend Mrs. Mayfield, and her children, Brooke and Kevin. From Guantanamo. I told you they'd be staying with us for a while."

"Yes'm. Sorry you folks had to leave your home and all, but

it's nice to meet you."

Miz Mayfield steps forward. "I've put some laundry beside the washer. Make sure to wash the delicate items by hand."

Miz Adams looks at the woman like she's from another planet. Miz Adams has never asked me to wash anything by hand. In fact, she usually puts the clothes in the washer herself, and even hangs them on the line most times. Miz Adams and I work more like a team than other women I work for, 'cause she's still not quite used to having any help. Sure seems that Miz Mayfield is used to having help, though.

"Myra, Flossie won't have time to do any hand laundry. We've got so many towels and diapers to get on the line today, and there's ironing, too." Miz Adams turns to me. "I was hoping you'd help me with some cooking this afternoon, too. Melanie said your fried chicken was so good, I thought maybe you'd cook some up for us. Of course, I'll help."

Miz Mayfield is looking at us like she's never heard folks talk before. She gives me a look. "I suppose every maid works at a different pace. I'm glad my girl manages the hand laundry as well as everything else." With her nose in the air, Miz Mayfield gathers her purse and coat. "Well, Norah, you can tell Flossie where to put our clean laundry, then. I've got a meeting on base this morning, and then I'm joining my old bridge club for lunch this afternoon. I'll see you tonight. Have a good day at school, kids." She leaves while her children still sit at the breakfast table.

Miz Adams stares as the front door closes. Under her breath, she mutters, "Well, I never."

Miz Mayfield's attitude might be something new for Miz Adams, but it isn't new to me. No, ma'am.

With the baby still in her arm, Miz Adams stalks back into the kitchen and slams the top down on Birdie's lunch box.

"Does everybody have their lunch money?"

"I've got mine, Mama." Melanie kisses her mama's cheek. "Bye. Time for us to go, Kevin."

He doesn't say a word as he walks out the door with Melanie. Birdie grabs her lunch box, hugs Miz Adams, and plants a big wet kiss on the baby's head. "Bye-bye, Mama. Bye-bye, DC." She hugs my legs one more time. "Bye, Flossie. I'll show you my pictures when I get home today."

Now it's just me, Miz Adams and the baby, and the older girl, Brooke. She's sipping a cup of coffee and reading the paper through her fancy eyeglasses. At first, I think she must be a real serious girl, but then she turns the paper over and I realize she's reading the funny pages.

I walk into the kitchen and fill up the sink with hot water. "Miz Adams, I'll put the breakfast dishes in hot water and then I'll go start the laundry. You want me to heat up a bottle for the baby?"

"Would you, please? His diaper needs changing again."

I get busy with things in the kitchen and sneak a peek at Miss Brooke every now and then. "Don't you have school today, Miss?"

"Not that it's any of your business, but, no, I'm not in school here." She pushes back from the table and tosses her paper napkin onto her plate. "I'm playing golf with some friends on the base today. They're picking me up in an hour."

Hmm. Seems to me like Miz Adams started running herself a hotel. Miz Mayfield off to play bridge, Miss Brooke off to play golf, and Miz Adams here to take care of their boy when he gets home from school, then put dinner on the table.

Lord have mercy.

These Mayfields must be the kind of white folks who think everybody, most especially colored folks, are alive to make their life easy.

That Brooke's expression is downright nasty. It's not a stretch for me to imagine this mean girl roaming with a bunch of hateful boys carrying baseball bats and ax handles.

I shiver and push that memory to the back of my mind.

There's work to be done, for sure. I gather up the piles of dirty towels and head out to the washing machine.

After a nice, quiet workday, all those folks come home about the same time. Birdie comes in first, happy as always to be home again.

"Flossie, look at the picture I drew for you. You can take it home with you."

I'm ironing Mr. Adams' dress shirts, but I put the iron on the resting plate and hold that crayon picture like it's a priceless work of art.

"See? It's you and me, Flossie. Do you like it?"

I'm about to cry, 'cause she's drawn a big woman colored with a brown crayon and white dress and a little girl with yellow hair and a big smile.

They're holding hands.

"Well, Miss Birdie, this is about the most beautiful picture I have ever seen." I hope that the tears don't run down my face. "Let me put it in my shopping bag so I won't forget it." While I'm bent over in the closet, I take a minute to pull myself together, act like I'm just blowin' my nose with my handkerchief. Then I'm back to the ironing.

By the time I finish the last cuff on the last shirt, Mellie, Birdie, the boy, and that Miss Brooke are all back in the house because a little rain shower came up. The noise of Birdie's cartoons in the living room and the loud radio coming from the middle bedroom is nearly enough to drive me crazy, but I go ahead and get the fixin's for the chicken ready.

Miz Mayfield gets home about that time, breezing in with a cloud of cigarette smoke behind her. She stops by the kitchen door and says to me, "Make some coffee for us," just like she's the boss of the house.

Miz Adams is in her bedroom folding towels. That's the only space she could find to do it. If she'd heard that order to make coffee, I'm not exactly sure what would have happened. She commented several times today about *hand washing clothes* and *you can tell Flossie where to put our clean laundry*. I've got the feeling her patience won't last too long.

Birdie's playing with some little cars in front of the TV, not bothering a soul. Melanie and the boy are doing homework at the table. It sounds like Brooke and Miz Mayfield are havin' words about something. Everybody seems to have a found a place to be.

I put on the coffee pot and melt the shortening in the two skillets it's gonna take to cook enough chicken to feed this bunch. Since the stove is right by the kitchen door, I can watch Birdie and cook at the same time. She's buzzing her lips and lining up the cars just so. Having a good time, she is.

I get the skillets sizzling with chicken, then I go over to the sink to wash up my hands and get started on the biscuits. When I step over to the cabinet to get the flour, my foot hits one of those little cars. That foot turns over so bad, I feel like my ankle catches on fire.

I manage to hold onto the counter so I don't land on my backside, but I know sure as the sun rises that I'm not going to be walking to the bus in a couple of hours.

Birdie comes running up to me. "I'm sorry, Flossie. That car is just too fast." She snatches it up off the floor and runs back to her little game. She doesn't realize that I've gone and hurt myself.

I don't rightly know what to do. I've never really been hurt on the job before, aside from a little burn or a knife nick. I lean on the counter and think for a minute. Then Melanie looks up from where she's doing her homework. She sees me leaning on the counter with my foot kind of up in the air. "Flossie, are you okay?"

"Well, I don't think I am. I've hurt my foot."

She jumps up and runs to me. "Oh, no! Come sit down." She helps me to a dining room chair, and I'm happy to sit down. She says, "I'll go get Mama."

Miz Adams and Miz Mayfield come running to where I'm sitting. By now I'm realizing that the chicken needs turning, or it's gonna burn.

"What on earth happened?" Miz Adams says. She looks all worried about me. I appreciate that, I do.

"Before we talk about this, that chicken needs to be turned." I nod in the direction of the stove. The house is beginning to smell like dinner.

Miz Adams turns the chicken in both skillets, then rushes back to me.

I hold out my foot and we all study it for a bit. "I turned my ankle. It's already beginnin' to swell, I'm afraid."

Miz Mayfield puffs on her cigarette and nods. "I'm sure it's just a sprain. You should put some ice on it."

"I'll get the ice," Mellie says.

"Do you think it might be broken?" Miz Adams is looking really worried now.

"No, ma'am. I don't believe it is. Probably a sprain, like Miz Mayfield says. Trouble is, I'm not gonna be able to take the bus home tonight."

Mellie's here with some ice cubes wrapped up in a kitchen towel. She pulls a chair up so I can rest my foot and places the ice on my foot, careful as can be.

"No need to worry about that. We'll take you home." Miz Adams looks like she just had a grand idea. "Could Brooke and Mellie drive Flossie home in your car, Myra?"

Miz Mayfield looks like Miz Adams is talking in Japanese or something.

"Absolutely not. My daughter is not driving into colored town. Frankly, I don't think it would be safe for any of us women to drive down there. I'm sure she'll be fine until Clay gets home. All that can be done for a sprain is ice, and you've done that." Miz Mayfield blows a cloud of smoke and goes back to the room the baby will sleep in, once all this Cuban evacuation business is over with.

Miz Adams is studying my foot. Mellie is looking back and forth between me and her mama, waiting for one of us to say something.

"I'll be fine, Miz Adams. We just need to tend the chicken. Maybe Mellie could help me with that? I can sit here and talk her through what needs to be done, if that's okay with you?"

Now, Miz Adams is looking between me and Mellie.

"I can do that, Mama. I'm almost finished with my homework, anyway."

"Would you rather cook or take care of DC while I finish up dinner?"

"I don't care. Why don't you rest some while you feed DC?"

Miz Adams smiles. "Okay. Be careful, though."

"I will, Mama."

I feel kinda like the Queen of England, sitting in a chair with my foot up. Birdie brings me a glass of ice water and sits next to me at the table, coloring.

Mellie gets over being scared of getting spattered by the hot grease. She's doin' a fine job with the chicken.

But soon as Mr. Adams comes through the door, he sees things aren't right. Mellie's at the stove and Miz Adams is at the sink, finishing up some dishes. I'm usually putting on my hat and getting ready to leave by now.

Birdie runs up and grabs his hand. "Daddy, you have to take Flossie home, 'cause she hurt her foot so bad, she can't walk to the bus stop. We had to put ice on it just like on my hand. Do you think she'll get a cast like me?"

"Hold on a minute, sweet pea." He glances at his wife and she nods.

"Flossie, do you want me to take you to the hospital?"

"Oh no, Mr. Adams. I'm gonna be fine. I'll call my doctor when I get home, and he'll come by the house and check on me."

"Are you sure? St. Vincent's hospital is really close by."

I shake my head. He doesn't realize that even if he drove me to St. Vincent's hospital and told them I was his mother, they wouldn't treat me. They'd send me to the colored hospital downtown. I don't want to say nothin', though. These four Adams' can't change things.

"If you can give me a ride home, that'll be just fine. I would've called Max, but his truck is in the shop, and he's been takin' the bus himself."

"Daddy, can I go with you?" Birdie tugs on her daddy's arm.

"Clay, why don't you take both the girls with you? It'll get them out of the house for a bit. By the time you get home dinner will be on the table."

"Fine with me. You girls ready to go?"

Now this is a surprise to me. I think back to this morning and wonder if I put my coffee cup in my kitchen sink like I usually do before I come here. I sure I hope I haven't left anything laying around, since I'm going to have visitors for at least a few minutes this evenin'.

Friday
October 26, 1962

MELANIE

"Why don't we go to the park this afternoon?" Steph suggests to Kevin. "I'll ask Marvin. He'll probably bring his guitar, if we want him to."

She's walking between me and Kevin on the way home from the school bus stop.

He shrugs. "I guess. It'll be more fun than sitting around Mellie's house, listening to the baby cry."

"DC doesn't cry that much," I snap at him.

"Really? Seems like he cries all the time to me."

Steph looks from me to Kevin. "We'll go to the park, then. I can bring some brownies." Steph hurries up her driveway. "I'll be over in a few minutes, and we can go get Marvin."

"I've got to get Mrs. Winston's mail," I say.

"I'll go with you." Kevin strides up to the double gate on the Winston's driveway and opens it for me.

I gather the mail from the box and squeeze between Kevin and the gatepost. "You don't have to. I just put the mail on the table and go straight home."

He clanks the gate back in place and follows me. "Have you got a key?"

I flip up the corner of the doormat and get the key. The door swings open, and we walk into the Winston's dim living room. The matching white sofas and the gold trimmed lamps overpower the small room.

Rachel Winston's house looks like her.

Kevin looks around and walks over to the shelf where two white and gold figurines stand. "Wow, it's quiet over here."

"Yep." I put the mail on the table. "Come on. Let's go."

Kevin puts the figurine down and turns toward the hall. "I just want to look around."

"Steph's waiting for us."

"It won't kill her to wait a minute or two."

I follow Kevin to the doorway of the Winston's bedroom. "We should go." The huge bed is covered with a gold satin spread. Big pillows rest against the white padded headboard. Matching nightstands hug the sides of the bed and long, flowing drapes darken the room and make it look like midnight, even in the middle of the afternoon.

I shiver. Everything about Rachel Winston gives me the creeps. "Come on, Kevin. This isn't right."

"You're afraid of your own shadow."

"I am not. It's not right to go rambling through other people's stuff."

"I'm not rambling. I'm just looking." Kevin walks to the nightstand and opens the drawer. He grins at me, points. "This is rambling." He sucks in a breath, focusing his attention on the contents of the drawer. Like he's in a trance, he reaches into the drawer and lifts out a magazine. He seems to forget I'm even there as he stares at the cover.

I'm peeved. "Kevin. Let's go."

"Cool your jets." He sticks the magazine inside his notebook.

"Put that back."

"Aw, Captain Winston won't mind if I borrow it." He grins and licks his lips. "I'll put it back tomorrow and he'll never even know, unless someone spills the beans." Kevin grabs my elbow and pushes me toward the door. "I thought you wanted to go."

Outside, I shake off his hand and slide the key into my pocket. I'm not leaving it under the mat anymore.

Kevin opens the gate. He says, "Look, there's Steph. You're not late at all."

The three of us go to my house, so Kevin and I can drop off our stuff.

"I've got a lot of homework," Kevin says. "I think I'll go ahead and get to work on it." He goes to the middle bedroom and closes the door. I hear the lock click. Just as well. I'm so mad at him right now, I don't even want him around.

"Huh. I guess I won't bother Marvin," Steph says. "Are you ready to go?"

"Where are you going?" Birdie asks.

"To the park."

"Can I go? Please?"

I look at Steph. "I don't care," she says. So Steph and I let Birdie and her friends, Mary and Ramona, tag along with us to the park.

We sit on the carousel while the girls play on the monkey bars. Steph pushes at the ground with her foot and sets us to spinning slowly. "Have you thought anymore about getting Kevin to kiss you?"

Anger flares and I feel my face go hot. "Not that again."

"Well, have you? That's why I wanted Marvin and Kevin to

come with us today. I figured Marvin and I would start kissing and then Kevin would get the idea, then you'd have your kiss."

"Will you give it a rest?"

Steph drags her foot in the sand, slowing the carousel to a stop. "What's the matter? Don't you want to be kissed?"

"I guess so."

"It sure doesn't seem like it."

I jump off the spin-around. "Maybe I want to wait until a boy I really like kisses me. Maybe I want my first kiss to really mean something."

Steph frowns at me. "Are you saying that Marvin's kiss doesn't mean anything?"

"I'm sorry, Steph. It's just that sometimes you act like you don't even like him."

"So, you think I'm cheap and slutty like my sister, huh?"

"No!" Poor Steph is being punished even more than Cherie for what Cherie did. "No. I'm sorry I didn't mean to hurt your feelings."

She shrugs and stares at the ground.

I wasn't fair. We made this pact together, and she kept her end of it. I'm not ready to tell Steph the truth, but I have to make it up to her. To make her feel better, I say, "Listen. I did take your advice about Kevin."

Her eyes light up. It's that easy to make her happy again. So I keep going.

"Yeah. He went with me to put Mrs. Winston's mail in her house today, and well…" I can't bring myself to actually say the lie out loud. I'll let Steph draw her own conclusion.

"Really? He kissed you?" She moves closer and links her arm with mine.

I nod.

"Wasn't it nice?" She sounds dreamy. More dreamy than

she had the first time she told me Marvin kissed her. It's obviously become better as she remembers it. That makes me wonder if I'm remembering my kiss with Robert better than it actually was.

She sighs. "Isn't it the greatest?"

Again, I just nod. If I don't say the words, I'm not really lying, right? Not technically, anyway. I could truthfully say, *I never said that.* I cross my fingers for good measure.

"Tell me what it was like." She pulls me back down on the carousel.

Still, I can't share the only kiss I've ever known. I just can't. So I invent one. "He just put his lips on mine. They were kind of wet and warm. Maybe a little hard."

"But wasn't it nice? Didn't it make you feel special?"

Memories of Robert's kiss spread warmth through me and over me, like it feels to sink into a warm bubble bath.

"Hellfire, Mellie. You're blushing." She slaps me on the back. "I'd say you've really been kissed."

BIRDIE

When the news is over, I decide to stay out of everybody's way. In my bedroom, I play with my dolls on my bed. I pretend like they are all in the hospital. And maybe they don't have any parents anymore. Mellie is on her bed reading a big book.

"Mellie, where do babies live when they don't have a Mommy or Daddy?"

"An orphanage. If you don't have a Mommy or Daddy, you are an orphan."

"Oh. Orphan." That's a funny word. I whisper it over and over, while I'm covering up my baby dolls. I don't want to 'gravate Mellie. There's enough 'gravation in our house tonight.

Mrs. Mayfield is talking loud to Brooke, and Brooke is being sassy. Mama would spank me for talking to her like that. I look at Mellie to see if she hears. She's frowning, so I think she does.

After we turn out the lights, I listen to the sounds of our crowded house. Brooke and Mrs. Mayfield are still talking, but quieter now. In the living room, a record is playing real low. Kevin's not very happy that we got his bed on the living room sofa ready so early. He'd said he doesn't go to bed until eleven at his house. I wonder how late eleven o'clock is. I turn to face Mellie's bed. "Mellie, are you asleep"?"

"No."

"How late is eleven o'clock?"

"Remember when Aunt Lola came to visit, and we'd all been sleeping on the couch? That was after eleven o'clock. Eleven o'clock is late. Are you thinking about what Kevin said about his bedtime?"

"Yeah." I think about all the changes as I lay in my bed. I can't seem to keep my legs still. The sheets make a crinkly noise every time I move. The jets just keep blasting by over our house. We don't run into the living room when the jets fly over anymore. I do cover up my ears, though. I don't like the sound at all.

I still have all my babies on my bed. I was surprised Mama didn't make me put them away like she usually does. Mellie has her rabbit, Heidi, hugged to her chest now. I can tell she's trying to go to sleep. Sometimes I'm afraid to fall asleep. I have bad dreams. I think Mellie has bad dreams, too, but we don't talk about them.

I lick my chapped lips because they are burning. Mama put Vaseline on them after she kissed me goodnight and that made them feel better for a little while. Then my mouth felt sticky and the Vaseline tastes so yucky. I wiped it off with my sheet. Now my lips are burning again.

Mama says it's a nervous habit I have, licking my lips, but I can't stop doing it. She tells me to stop all the time, though.

I close my eyes and try to fall asleep. I hear Mrs. Mayfield cough. Brooke sneezes and blows her nose. DC cries, and I hear Mama speaking softly to him. Melanie flops over in her bed and huffs out a breath. The refrigerator door opens with that sucking sound. Kevin's getting a drink, probably.

"Mellie? Are you asleep?"

"No."

"Can I get in your bed?"

She's quiet for a few minutes. She's going to tell me no.

"Sure. Come on."

I'm surprised and happy. I jump up and skip to her bed. I snuggle up against her. "Can I hold Heidi, too?"

"Okay."

Mellie moves the stuffed toy so that Heidi rests between us. I take one of her rabbit ears and rub it back and forth over my hurting mouth.

"Do you think Kevin will eat all of our bread?" I ask.

"Why would he eat all of the bread?"

"In that movie we saw about the people who were hiding in the attic to be safe from the bad guys who wanted to take them away, the mean man ate all the bread and everyone got mad at him. I don't want Kevin to be selfish and eat all the bread."

Mellie is quiet.

"Are you talking about *The Diary of Anne Frank*? The girl

had dark hair and she was upstairs with her mom and dad and some other people. And a boy?"

"Yeah. That one. We saw it at the drive-in."

"We thought you were asleep."

"I slept some, but I remember seeing the part about the man eating all the bread."

"You don't need to worry. Kevin won't eat all of our bread. And even if he did, we'd go buy some more."

"Why couldn't those people buy some more bread?"

"Because if they left their hiding place, the bad guys would get them and take them away."

"Like hide and seek?"

"Sort of. Only it wasn't a game."

I think about this. "Now our house is kind of like that place where they hid, isn't it? We're all crowded together and we can hear all the noises people make at night."

I feel Mellie move. "I guess so. Kind of."

"I don't like it, Mellie."

She wraps me up in her arms. "I don't like it, either, Birdie. But it won't be like this for long. We just have to wait."

"Okay. I'll wait. I'll try to be good. I'll try not to be afraid."

"Me, too, Birdie. Me, too."

Saturday
October 27, 1962

MELANIE

Kevin is at his old friend Dan's house. I didn't expect them to hit it off again. Dan has changed even more than Kevin, and in the opposite direction. Where Kevin has grown taller and looks almost cool, Dan is still short, fat, and goofy. But Dan is also really smart, almost a genius. At least I won't have to worry about entertaining Kevin for the afternoon.

Once again, Brooke is sprawled on the sofa. A stack of records are on the record player. She has a new magazine.

"Where's Mama?" I ask.

Without looking at me, Brooke says, "They all went to Mrs. Schultz's house. Mom wanted to see her."

"Oh." I pour a glass of milk. A bag of cookies lay on the counter top, so I grab few. "What're you reading?"

"Nothin'." Brooke licks her finger and flips a page. She sighs, and it sounds like the very definition of boredom.

I dip the cookie in my milk and stick the whole thing in my mouth. Mama would yell at me for that if she were at home, but she isn't. Brooke doesn't even notice. She's buried behind her magazine.

Suddenly, Brooke throws the magazine down on the floor and sits up. "I'm going out of my mind, I'm so bored. How can you stand it around here?"

Swallowing the cookie, I choke out, "I've always got plenty to do."

"Well, you're a dopey kid."

"I am not."

"Maybe we should play a little True Confessions and see just how dopey you really are, sweet little Melanie." Brooke narrows her eyes, and I feel like a bug under a microscope.

What's with Steph and Brooke? What do they want from me?

"Okay. Here's the first True Confession. You have to confess and name names. If you haven't done the thing, you lose and have to take a dare. Okay?"

"What's the dare?"

Brooke's grin turns evil. "You smoke a cigarette with me."

I look at my shoes, calculating my odds. What kind of things will she come up with for this silly game? How badly do I want to fit in?

Strangely enough, I want to fit in with Brooke. She's spoiled and shallow, but so pretty with her flipped blonde hair and glamorous cat-eyed glasses that make her look older. And I really want to talk like her. The lisp sounds so, I don't know, pouty. No, sexy. I think her lisp sounds sexy. I figure boys think so, too. I bet Robert likes that soft whispery sound. Yeah, I want to play Brooke's game, and I want to belong. "Okay. I'll play."

Brooke grins. "Have you ever seen a penis?"

"Of course, I've seen a penis."

"When?" Her voice echoes with doubt.

"Gosh, Brooke, I have a baby brother. Did you forget?"

"You can't count a baby's wiener."

"You didn't say how old or how big. You only said *a penis*. I've seen *a penis*. I win."

"I still say you cheated. At best, that one's a draw. But you can have your turn now. What you got?"

I thought for a minute. "Have you ever French kissed?"

"Please, Mellie, I'm seventeen. Of course, I have. With Robert Taylor before we moved to Cuba, and that was only the first time. You've got to do better than that. How about you? Have you ever even been kissed at all?"

I just sit there, her words roaring in my head. How could his kiss with me have meant something if he'd French kissed Brooke? The milk I just drank churns in my belly and I feel my face turning red. I have to tell her something, but I'm not about to tell her that I kissed Robert, too.

I shake my head.

"Well, that was a short game. I just happen to have some cigarettes right here." Brooke pulls a crumpled pack of Pall Malls from her purse and hands one to me.

I roll the cigarette between my fingers. All I can think about, all I can picture in my mind, is Robert kissing Brooke.

"Here, I'll light it for you. Put it in your mouth." When I do, Brooke leans forward with a match and lights the cigarette. The heat so close to my face is surprising, and I move the cigarette away immediately.

"You have to draw on it to keep it lit. Like this." Brooke takes it away from me, and sucks in a deep draw, then blows a long, thin stream of smoke above her head. "Don't you think it's sexy? I love the way it looks in the movies." She holds the cigarette between her first two fingers, watching the curl of smoke drift upward, then hands it back to me.

I bring the cigarette to my lips and take a big puff. It feels like fire burning down my throat and through my lungs. I choke and cough.

Brooke laughs. "That's the worst. Take another puff. You'll like it better."

I try again. At least this time I don't cough so much. Clearing my throat, I whisper, "What's that noise? Turn off the records." I hand the cigarette to Brooke.

"I don't hear anything." Brooke switches off the record player and strolls back to the sofa, puffing away on the cigarette like a small, elegant steam engine.

Birdie's voice rings through the window.

"Oh, my gosh. Mama." I jump up, grab the cigarette from Brooke, and run for the kitchen. I toss the cigarette into the garbage can.

Brooke is behind me. "Wait. Water. Run water over it."

But it's too late. The cigarette catches fire to the paper napkins and tissues the trashcan. Smoke is already billowing up from the top of the can.

Panic grips me. "It's going to catch the house on fire."

The front door opens and Birdie charges inside. "Pee-yoo, what's burning?"

Mama dashes in with DC in her arms. "What is it? Did I leave something burning on the stove again?"

She screeches to a halt beside the trashcan just as I douse it with a glass of water. The smoke stops, but the smell grows worse.

Mama looks from me to Brooke. When she brings her gaze back to me, I can tell she knows what's been going on. Her expression cracks with disappointment then glues itself back together with anger. The anger slowly grows.

But she doesn't yell. "Melanie, I can't believe you'd do this.

What a foolish thing to do. You put the whole household in danger with your recklessness."

Her voice gets louder. "I've always trusted you. I always thought you knew right from wrong, and I never doubted for a minute that you wouldn't choose the right thing."

Now she's yelling. "But I was wrong, wasn't I? I can't trust you at all. I leave you alone for an hour and what happens? You practically burn the house down. Smoking! You know how I feel about women smoking."

Mama's face breaks a little more. I don't know how much more I can stand. Mrs. Mayfield, Brooke, and Birdie are all standing there, watching Mama yell at me.

I feel so ashamed and stupid. Why did I ever let Brooke talk me into doing something so dumb?

"The worst thing is, I don't know if I'll ever be able to trust you again, Mellie." She sighs and turns around. With her back to me, she says, "You'll have to earn my trust."

Mama walks out of the kitchen.

The next sound I hear is the door to her bedroom closing. She never closes her bedroom door during the day.

I want to cry. I want to run after Mama and grab onto her skirt like a two year old.

But even more, I want to hit Brooke. I want to smack her right in her stupid face. I want knock her stupid glasses off and give her a black eye. It's all her fault. I wouldn't have ever smoked a cigarette, but I wanted to try being like her, to try growing up a little.

Mrs. Mayfield interrupts my furious thoughts. "Melanie, I can't believe you'd do such a thing to your mother at a time like this. She's going through so much with the baby. You should be more considerate. Wash out the trashcan and clean up the kitchen. Brooke and I will go to the Italian restaurant and bring back pizza and spaghetti for everyone for dinner tonight."

Brooke rolls her eyes at me behind her cat-eye glasses and follows her mother out the door.

Birdie stares at me for a minute, then she leaves me alone with the smoky mess in the kitchen. I don't know where to start to make things right again.

NORAH

For the first time since Myra and the kids arrived, I'm thinking Clay was probably right. Having so many people in the house is just too much. Too much for the girls. Too much for me.

I never thought that Melanie would do something so disappointing. Sneaking cigarettes right in the house. Brooke must have encouraged her. My Melanie just wouldn't go behind my back like that. But, I can't blame Brooke. After all, only Melanie admitted she was smoking.

What should I do now? I lay on my bed, trying to rest for a bit while DC naps. My mind just won't slow down. On the one hand, sneaking a cigarette isn't that awful. There are so many worse things she could have done. She could have gotten into the liquor. She could steal. Yes, so many other bad things she could have done.

My problem is how to handle her punishment. I can't just let this slide, as much as I want to. No, I need to make sure she learns her lesson. We make rules for a reason: to protect our children. I have to enforce those rules if I want to keep her safe.

Of course, I saw the worry and hurt in her eyes when I said

I wouldn't be able to trust her anymore. Maybe that will be enough punishment. I just don't know.

I turn onto my side, burying my face in my pillow. I wish Clay wasn't working Saturdays, even if we do need the money. I need him more than I used to. I just don't know how to handle things anymore.

Monday
October 29, 1962

MELANIE

I have the house to myself for a change.

Mrs. Mayfield and Mama took Birdie and DC to the grocery store. Flossie didn't come to clean today because her foot's still hurt. Kevin's at Marvin's house, and Brooke has gone out to have milkshakes with one of her old girlfriends.

I can do whatever I want without having to worry about anyone else. I put on a stack of records and have a Coke. Stretching out on the couch, I open my English book to the story I have to read for homework. Steph complained all the way home today about having to read so many pages tonight, but I'm looking forward to it. I like stories by Jack London.

Kevin comes in.

I look at him over the top of my book, trying not to look as surprised and disappointed as I feel. "Hi."

"Hi, yourself." He just stands there by the front door with that almost-bully look on his face.

"I thought you were at Marvin's." I put my Coke bottle on the floor and turn a page in my book. Maybe if I keep reading, he'll go away.

Kevin flops on the green chair next to the sofa. "Yeah, I was."

The records switch and Bobby Vinton begins singing "Roses are Red, Violets Are Blue." I glance at Kevin. His brows are knit together in a frown.

I'm not going to let his sour mood ruin my afternoon. Maybe I can get rid of him. "Do you want a Coke? There's more in the fridge. You can take it with you."

"I'm not going anywhere." He looks around. "Where is everybody?"

"They've gone to get trick-or-treat candy."

"Even Brooke?"

"Yep. Well, she's with her friend, Susan."

"Oh." He sits there, staring at me for a few minutes. "I think I'll have that Coke."

"They're nice and cold." I hear him moving around in the kitchen, but go back to my reading, hoping he'll take the hint and hit the road.

"So, you told Stephanie I kissed you, huh?"

I jerk my head up.

Damn, damn, damn.

Anger and embarrassment rush in my veins like flames of a forest fire. I swallow. I'll try to bluff my way out of this. "What?"

"You heard me," he snaps.

I stare at him for a few seconds. I can't believe Steph's big mouth. With friends like her, who needs enemies?

I don't know what to say. Kevin sounds pretty serious, like he's mad about it. Am I too awful to kiss? Don't guys like to be talked about? Don't they want everyone to know how many girls they've kissed? I keep up my bluff, pretending I'm not bothered. I shrug. "So?"

What do I have to worry about, anyway? This is just Kevin. He's a nice boy. An old friend. He'll understand, if I can somehow explain to him.

He swallows a mouthful of Coke. "Well, did you or didn't you?"

I'm such a bad liar. I should've known the lie would come back to haunt me. I swallow the lump in my throat. Maybe if I don't say the words it won't be another lie. I'll make it seem like a silly girls' joke. After all, Kevin does think Steph and I are goofy. He said so. I tilt my head to one side, give him a stupid grin and shrug again, hoping I look like a stupid girl.

He leans forward in the chair, props his elbows on his knees with the Coke bottle grasped loosely in his fingers. He's not smiling. "What does that goofy look mean?"

I sit up and put the book on the floor next to my feet. "Well, I might have said something like that to Steph."

"Why?"

"C'mon, Kev. You know her." I guess I might as well tell the truth. "She kept bugging me and I had to tell her something. She's the one who suggested that you kiss me."

He lifts his left eyebrow. "What?"

The word seems to suck all the air out of the room. I draw my knees up to my chest, dangling my toes off the edge of the sofa. Taking a deep breath, I try to explain. "Steph got this crazy idea that we should have our first kiss by the Sadie Hawkins Dance, but then Cherie ran off and we didn't go to the dance." I give him a weak grin. "She's been bugging me ever since."

"So, how did I get into this?"

"When you got here…" I pause. He's scowling across the room at me. Steph's big mouth is going to cause big trouble this time. I swallow again. "Steph said you'd probably kiss me."

He leans back in his chair and takes another drink of his Coke.

I try to laugh, but it sounds like a croak. "You know, stupid girl stuff. Just kidding around. Besides, I thought guys liked having a reputation." Maybe I'm on to something here. I rush on. "If you think about it, I just helped you get yours going a little, that's all." I get up and carry my Coke bottle to the kitchen and put it in the carton with the other empties, so we can return them and get our deposit money back.

He follows me.

I turn to face him. "Look, I'm sorry if it upset you. I'll tell anybody you want me to that you didn't kiss me. I don't want to embarrass you or anything. I swear, I didn't think Stephanie would tell anyone at all."

"It's not a big deal." He puts his Coke bottle in the carton next to mine. He takes a step toward me. "Do you want me to kiss you, Melanie?"

My heart stops for a second, then beats double time. I shake my head.

"If you need to be kissed so bad, if you've never had a kiss, I guess I could help you out." He touches my cheek. "You're not really bad-looking."

"Gee, thanks." Giggles fizz inside me, but I manage to hold them back to a small laugh. "You're not that bad yourself."

He steps closer. "You do need to be kissed." He slips his hand behind my head and pulls me toward him.

Yeah, I think. I do want Kevin to kiss me. I know it won't be like Robert's kiss, but that kiss seems like a fairy tale, now that I know Robert gave Brooke *her* first French kiss.

Kevin's kiss would be real, not a fairy tale. A real kiss from a boy my own age.

My heart slows, pounding steadily against my ribs. I feel bold. This must be what Aunt Lola feels like, I think. She knows what she wants, and she goes after it.

Yeah, I do want to be kissed. Right now.

Suddenly, the air seems thinner. Tension stretches from where Kevin's fingers touch my neck, all the way through me, to deep inside. To the same place that had come alive when Robert's lips had touched mine.

I want that feeling again. I want that feeling to grow, to expand and fill me, like I expect it will. Like it didn't have a chance to when Robert kissed me. I close my eyes for a second and think about the color red.

This feeling inside me must be what the red satin panties are like. Warm, smooth, slippery. Waiting for a surprise.

When I open my eyes, Kevin's face is closer, so close it's almost like looking through a magnifying glass. Everything seems so clear and sharp, my eyes hurt. Every scent so strong, my nose burns. Kevin's breath is syrupy, sweet and thick, like Coca Cola. I can see the slivers of black in his brown irises, even though his lids are half-closed.

He puts his other hand on my shoulder and jerks me flat against him. His lips come down over mine. They're hard, just like I told Steph in my lie.

I wait a second, not moving, hoping that he'll soften a little. The sensation that had begun to bloom inside me shrinks.

His hard mouth presses against mine until I feel my teeth cutting into the puffy inside of my lips. I move, trying to release the pressure.

He squirms against me, shoves me back against the counter until it presses into my hips.

This isn't right. I can't breathe. I turn my face, trying to gulp some air.

Kevin turns too, smashing his mouth down even harder. Grinding his lips against mine, until he opens his mouth and pushes his tongue against my tightly-pursed lips.

I want him to stop. He needs to stop. I try to lift my arms to push him away, but they're pinned against my side as he slides his arms from my shoulders, drawing me away from the counter and pressing me closer against him. His hand moves down my back to my bottom.

He pinches me. Hard.

I jerk backward against the counter top, feeling the edge bite into my waist. Needle pricks of pain dart over my hips and legs. He grinds his hard *thing* against my belly. Nausea rolls through me.

My mouth opens on a reflex. I need to scream, but he smothers my cry. He shoves his tongue into my open mouth. My throat closes. I'm choking and gagging. I try to breathe, to draw air into my lungs. My eyes burn with tears as I stare at him.

I can't believe this is happening. Finally, he breaks the kiss and pulls away, panting.

"Is that what you wanted?" He's breathing shallow and fast. His lips are wet and shiny, lifted at the edges in an ugly sneer. "How's that for a first kiss?" He slides his hand up my rib cage until his thumb rests just beneath my breast. "Now, I'll let you know what else happens when boys kiss girls. Especially girls like you and Stephanie. Girls who ask for it. Girls who end up like Cherie."

I try to shake my head, to deny his accusation. He's wrong. Stephanie talks big, but she's a nice girl. Before I can speak, his mouth slams against mine again, bending my head back. My stomach turns over and cold chills race along my arms. A sick feeling washes through me and I groan.

"You like it, don't you?" he snarls against my mouth.

The counter digs deeper into my back. He moves his whole hand over my left breast and squeezes.

I hate it!

"Too much," he mutters and slides his hand beneath my shirt. His fingers feel like ice needles against my skin. "All boys want to do this, Melanie."

I shove against his shoulders, but he's got all his weight pushing me against the counter. I can't make him move. I punch at him, my fists pounding against his arms and back.

He ignores my hits. His hands run over my ribcage, and then he slides his fingers under my bra. His skin feels rough, like sandpaper. His ragged, chewed fingernails dig into my tender flesh. My skin prickles and shrinks at his touch.

"Stop," I hiss. But his mouth crashes down again. His hips grind against me, pushing me even harder against the counter top until the edge knifes into my back. I arch backward. He presses against me with such force, I can't move.

Still holding his mouth on mine, Kevin moves his body away slightly. He grasps the neck of my shirt and pulls. Buttons fly, launching into the air then exploding onto the tile floor and counter top with precise ticks and taps. Air rushes against my skin, making me shiver.

Or is it fear that makes me shake? Because I'm afraid. I'm afraid of what Kevin's going to do. Something that I know will be terrible. Something that I'm afraid will change me forever.

I have to do something. He has to stop. I dig my fingers into his shoulders, and push against him. He pushes back, forcing me against the counter with his weight. The hard bulge in his pants grinds against me, hot and threatening.

My mind goes blank. It's like I'm watching this happen to

someone else.

He sweeps his tongue around in my mouth and a bitter tide of nausea rises in my throat. I want the sour rush of vomit to spew at him. I want the stinking, hot stream of puke to send him reeling backward. That vomit would save me. But it remains clogged in my throat, burning like acid.

He lifts my bra and with his raspy fingers pinches my nipple until I cry; a muffled, pitiful sound. He swallows it.

Barely lifting his mouth from mine, he whispers, "Feel that? How nubby it is? That means you really like this."

I suck in a breath, urgent to deny that horrible lie, to scream at him that I hate it. I hate him. But he slides his wet lips across my face, smashes his mouth against mine again and thrusts his tongue between my teeth.

I want to hurt him. Hurt him as badly as he's hurting me. My jaw locks. I can't move.

Shame at my weakness washes over me. I should be stronger. I should be able to stop this.

I should be able to stop all of these feelings rushing through me. I should be able to control the way my body reacts. I should be able to make myself numb.

Instead, electricity pulses through me, every nerve on alert, eager to warn me of each new danger, each new threat. And worse, every nerve still seems hungry for something that had been promised but not delivered.

That's the worst shame, the biggest betrayal.

Pressing his hot mouth against my neck, he runs his tongue along the rigid muscles tightening around my throat. I don't think I can hold up much longer. I feel wilted inside, shrunken and small.

Like a steam iron hissing over my throat, his breath burns as he whispers, "I could give you a hickey. You'd like that, too.

But then it would be hard to keep our secret." He lifts his head and stares at me. "But no one will see this unless you show them. That would mean you're proud of it."

His fingers squeeze again and he lowers his mouth to my exposed breast. He sucks hard, so hard it feels like his teeth are sinking into it. His breath is hot against my skin his rough fingers pinch my nipple.

Sensations rush over me. Pain. Shame. It seems that deep inside me, the place where my soul is, denies the vibrations thrumming through me. My soul slams closed.

Kevin slips his other fingers into the waistband of my slacks. He fumbles with one hand to lower the side zipper.

I wiggle sideways against the counter, trying to slide away from him. But he braces his arm on the counter beside me while he shoves his other hand into the gaping opening of my slacks, beneath the waistband of my white cotton panties. Suddenly, his fingers are digging into the tender skin between my legs.

Tears flood my eyes. "No!" I shift my weight, shoving against him with my whole body. I manage to gain some space between me and the counter, but before I can break free, he lurches against me, forcing my back against the counter once more.

"I know this is what you want," he hisses against my mouth, his fingers hard and rough in a place I don't even touch myself. "Robert and Brooke do this. It's what all of you sluts want."

An image of Robert and Brooke tangled with each other blooms in my mind. So ugly. So awful. I feel myself fold and shatter into a million shards of hurt. There's no air, no muscle, no bones in me.

The telephone rings.

Kevin jumps like he's been struck by lightning. He steps away from me, rubbing the back of his hand across his mouth.

I clutch my shirt together with trembling fingers. I move away from the counter, into the open, where I can run and not be trapped. I take a step, ready to escape.

The phone rings again.

Panting, he grabs my arm, shoving me toward the phone. "If you say anything, I swear I'll make it sound like you started it, like you wanted it." He swallows hard. "Because you did."

Oh my God. I had wanted his kiss in the beginning. How could this big, horrible lie have a grain of truth in it?

The phone rings again.

His fingers dig into my arm. "You hang around with Steph, who's a slut like her sister. Everyone will believe me."

I lift my head, anger rising beneath the hurt. My parents will never believe him. They love me. They trust me.

Or they had trusted me until Brooke talked me into smoking. I blink back tears. Never would I let Kevin see me cry.

Another ring.

As if he read my mind, he says, "Even your folks. They know the score, Mellie." He shoves me toward the phone.

The shrill, insistent phone cuts through the fog in my mind. I'll be able to get help now. I grab the receiver off the wall, the other hand clutching the front of my blouse together. The waistband of my pants hangs open. Shame burns through me. "Hello?" My voice is shaky.

"Hi, sweetheart."

I whimper, "Daddy."

"Are you okay?"

I swallow and open my mouth to scream *no*, but he starts

talking again. "Listen, I've got to run, but tell Mama I have to work late, okay? I should be home by seven."

He pauses a second and says something to someone in his office. "Okay, bye." And he hangs up.

How could he not know how much I need him? How did he miss it?

Kevin stares at me, waiting for the phone call to end. I know he's standing there to make certain I don't tell Daddy what happened. But Kevin doesn't know Daddy hung up. Kevin doesn't know that Daddy's working late. I can make Kevin leave now.

I look away from him so he can't read my face. "You're on your way home now, Daddy? You'll be here in a few minutes? Great. Bye."

My whole body shakes as I hang up the phone. Swallowing hard, I turn to face Kevin, my blouse still clutched closed in my trembling fingers.

He looks shaken. His eyes are wide with fear. He rubs his hand across his forehead as if he can erase what he's done. He turns and runs out of the house.

I stand in the dimly lit kitchen. Kneeling to scoop up the tiny white buttons from the floor, I wonder where Mama is. Why isn't she home yet?

Words swirl in my head like trash caught in a tornado. Kevin saying, *"Your folks know the score."* Daddy saying, *"She's lucky I didn't give her what she wanted."* My lie to Steph. *"Kevin kissed me."* Maybe somehow I started this.

I remember every nasty joke I've ever heard. Every wicked comment about sex and trashy women floods through me, making me feel dirty and damaged. Then I hear my mother screaming at me, *"Melanie, I'm so disappointed in you. How could do such a thing?"*

In the bathroom I look at myself in the mirror.

My stomach pitches and bile crowds my throat. I vomit until I have dry heaves.

I need help. I have to talk to somebody. There has to be someone.

I can never talk to Steph about this. Never. I want to blame the whole thing on her big mouth. I want this to be all her fault, but inside, I know that isn't fair. I told the first lie.

I wash my face and brush my teeth. I scrub my face dry with the towel.

How long before Mama gets home? How can I tell her? She'll think I'm terrible. And I am.

I am like Aunt Lola.

I need to talk to someone. And then, as though a chime rings in my head, I know.

Flossie.

I toss the towel onto the floor. I need to talk to Flossie.

I march down the hall to my parents' room. I scoop all the change from Daddy's dresser. I glance at the alarm clock. If I run, there is still time to catch the five o'clock bus.

I shove the change into my pocket along with the buttons and dash into my room, tearing the destroyed shirt from my shoulders. I stuff it under my bed, way back against the wall, where I'll never have to see it again. I grab a sweatshirt from the bottom dresser drawer and pull the warm softness over my tender skin.

Slamming the front door behind me, I run down the street, stretching my stride and pumping my arms, running harder than I ever have in my life. After four blocks, I arrive at the city bus stop, breathless and sobbing, skidding to a halt just as the driver pulls up.

Flossie will be able to help me. I just have to find her.

MELANIE

The city bus stops at the curb, its engine belching diesel exhaust. When the driver opens the door, the inside of the bus lights up like a stage full of silent actors, their lines recited for the day, as they wait for the curtain of night to fall.

As I march down the narrow aisle, I feel like I've entered another country. These people don't live in my world. They travel into it and through it. They earn their living in my neighborhood, but they live somewhere else.

As I pass each row, heads turn and gazes follow me. I lower my head and drop into a seat, trying to hide my swollen eyes and red nose. The driver closes the door with a hiss, and the lights dim. With a mechanical sigh, the brakes release and the engine roars as we merge into traffic.

Streetlights and headlights strobe through the bus, slicing time into light and dark, like the thoughts that keep cutting into my mind.

In the dark, I remember Daddy and Lola, dancing, touching, kissing.

In the light, I remember Mama and Daddy, laughing, holding each other, loving one another.

In the dark, Mrs. Winston and Robert, her hunger, his shame.

In the light, Robert kissing me, the quivering in my soul, the weightless feeling that lifted me above the earth.

Soon, the driver turns off Northern Boulevard onto Ridgewood Avenue. Not so much traffic, more sparsely spaced streetlights. More darkness. Longer darkness.

In the dark, Kevin.

In the dark, his bruising fingers.

In the dark, his pushing, probing tongue.

In the dark, Kevin's words. *Robert does this to Brooke. You like this, don't you?*

In the light, that was the darkest hurt, the deepest wound, the thing that drains the soul out of me.

In the light, those words kindle a fiery anger. I did not like it. I did not want it. I did not ask for it.

Tears burn my eyes. A hot lump scorches my throat. I clench my fists and pound my legs in silent fury.

I think about what Robert had said when he'd tried to explain about Mrs. Winston. *She's too hungry. I'm afraid she won't leave anything for me.*

It's like everything in my body stops.

I don't think I've ever really known a truth, not until this very moment on the bus, as I remember his words. Believing something is true is different from knowing it all the way through you.

Believing is in your head, somehow confined and contained in your brain. But understanding a truth must touch your heart, your soul. Understanding wedges into you and becomes a part of you, so that you can't forget.

The bus works through the maze of short blocks that make up downtown. Adams and State Street. Eighth and Main. Duval and Monroe. At each corner we stop, and the cast of passengers follow the driver's cue. Doors open, lights flick on, people rise, people walk, people sit. Lights off. Travel to the next block.

I read each street sign through watery eyes, and listen for the name of Flossie's stop. Finally, the driver pulls up to the curb and announces Pearl and Union.

That's what I've been waiting for. I grip the handrail and

dangle one foot over the step, hesitant. In the street light's yellow glow, the corner looks dingy and crowded. Three different groups of colored men stand outside the store that occupies the triangular building on the corner. Their cigarette tips glow red.

"You sure you want to get off here, Miss?" the driver asks in a soft, rolling voice. His hands look like wrinkled white paper wrapped around the steering wheel. "I don't have many young white girls traveling to this corner." He nods his head toward the shuffling crowd in front of the store.

A rush of fear sweeps through me. What have I done? I've never been to this part of town, unless I was riding in the car. Maybe I should just turn around and go back to my seat. I'll be safe there.

The thought that safety is just a lie explodes in my mind. I hadn't been safe from Kevin an hour ago in my own house. I have to look out for myself. I push the fear down.

Looking over my shoulder, I say, "I'll be okay. I'm going to someone's house."

"Yeah?" The driver lifts both eyebrows and makes his eyes big and round. "Who would that be?"

"Flossie…" My voice fades as I realize I don't even know Flossie's last name.

"Flossie? Johnson?"

I duck my head. "I'm not sure."

"How do you know this Flossie?"

"She cleans for us."

"Must be Flossie Johnson. She catches this bus from your neighborhood."

"Yes, sir. On Mondays and Thursdays."

From the back of the bus, a man shouts "Let's get going. Let her get off the damn bus if she wants."

"Hold your horses back there." The driver nods at me. "One block down Pearl is where Miz Johnson lives. Be careful, and you call your folks when you get there."

"Thank you." I step off the bus and wait for it to pull itself together with moans and grinding hisses before it leaves the curb.

The street corner quiets. The men smoke and stop shuffling their feet. I feel like their stares are blistering my back. I quickly cross the street.

Still no sound, no footsteps behind me. I wiggle my shoulders, trying to shake off the strange feeling. Soon, I hear voices, followed by laughter. I turn and see the men still standing outside the store. No one is paying any attention to me as I continue down the sidewalk.

My hands shake so badly, I stick them in my pockets.

I find a house with Johnson painted in white letters on the faded black mailbox. I stand on the sidewalk for a long time, staring at the narrow wooden building. A single lamp shines in the front window, but no sound comes from the house at all. A pot of red geraniums bloom next to the porch steps and one rocking chair, brown and battered wicker, waits by the door. I sit on the lowest step.

It's full dark now. Waiting, I watch the traffic zip up and down Union Street. Not many cars stop. They're all passing through, going someplace else, just like I've always done.

Until tonight.

Sounds drift through the doors and windows of the houses around me. Voices, clanging pots and pans, radio music, TV news. The houses sit close together, long wooden shotgun houses with narrow alleyways between them. Some of the people keep a little patch of green grass in front of their house, like Flossie does, but most just live with weeds cluttering the dirt.

I pluck a long stem of grass and twirl it between my fingers. I'm not quite sure what I'll say to Flossie, but the thought of telling Mama and Daddy makes me sick. I want them to believe me when I tell them I didn't ask for it, but I can't help thinking of what Daddy said about Aunt Lola. About how a man can only stand so much.

Everything is horribly confusing. Will Mama blame me, too? Will she say I should have gone shopping with her? Suddenly, I remember what Mama had said when Birdie went to the hospital.

It isn't proper for you to be alone in the house with Robert.

Now, I understand why I shouldn't be alone in the house with a boy. But Robert wouldn't have done what Kevin did.

Would he?

Robert and Brooke did this.

Besides Brooke being older, what was the difference between us? I knew there must be a difference somewhere, somehow. Just a few months ago, everything had been so clear. I knew what was expected of me. I knew what to expect of everyone else.

I never thought I would live with such fear. I never thought the sound of a jet could make my belly burn or Daddy could make my heart ache. I never thought Mama would turn her back on me.

And never, ever would I have expected that someone would touch me in a way that would make every molecule of my body crawl.

I want things to be like they were before my birthday.

Suddenly the porch light comes on. I stand and hold my breath.

Maybe she didn't want me to come to her house. What if

she sends me home because she's angry? Twisting my hands in the hem of my sweatshirt, I fret about what to do.

"Who's out there?" Flossie says. I can see her looking out the front window.

I clear my throat and croak, "Flossie, it's me, Mellie."

She opens the door. "Child, what are you doing here?" She sounds more concerned than angry, and I take a tentative step toward her.

The tears break and roll down my face. Flossie doesn't say anything else. She motions for me to come inside.

Nervously, I glance around. Her living room looks like a faded golden photograph or a page in an old magazine, neat and clean with doilies on the chair backs and books on the coffee table. Odd that the room looks like a snapshot, but there are no photographs or paintings on the walls.

A frown knits Flossie's brows. The lines around her mouth appear deeper, sadder. "What are you doin' here?"

I shuffle my feet. "I had to talk to you."

She puffs out a breath. "Do your Mama and Daddy know you're here?"

"No, ma'am."

"You catch the bus?"

Studying the pattern in the wood floor, I mumble, "Yes, ma'am."

"Child, this must be serious." She rubs her hands together and I notice how swollen and chapped her knuckles are. She sighs. "I hope it don't cause no problems. You shouldn't have done that, riding the bus by yourself."

"I had to."

"Well, sit down on that couch and tell me what in the world is going on." Flossie doesn't actually sound angry, but she doesn't sound happy, either.

I begin to think I must have done something really awful—something besides kiss Kevin—without even knowing. She sits next to me and puts her sore foot on the table.

"How's your foot today?"

"It's a bit better. I should be able to get back to work next week."

"I hope so. I sure do miss you."

"Are you saying that's why you took the bus all the way here? Because you miss me?"

She's smiling, so I know she's teasing. I think she understands that I really need help. *Please, God, let her help me with this mess.*

Taking a deep breath, she leans back and folds her hands in her lap. "Well? What is it, Mellie? Your Mama all right?"

"Yes, ma'am."

"Y'all gettin' on with the Mayfields?"

The mention of the Mayfields makes my stomach clench and I curl my knuckles against it without thinking. I glance up at Flossie.

She nods. "Uh-huh. Mayfields brought a problem with them, huh?"

I nod. The words pile up on my tongue, but I can't seem to open my mouth to let them out. Those words belong in that dark place.

"Let's see. Miz Mayfield, she's always got somethin' to be put out about, but she doesn't mean anythin' by it. Now, Missy Brooke is spoiled and too busy with her own self to think about anything else, so I don't guess it's her. That leaves Kevin, doesn't it?"

I nod again. I wait for Flossie to keep talking. Maybe she'll say the words for me, and I won't have to. But she just sits there with her eyes closed and hums under her breath.

"It's Kevin," I whisper. "He kissed me."

"Uh-huh. And?"

"He grabbed me. He hurt me." Hot tears start to flow, burning trails down my cheeks. "He said awful things." After that the words just tumble out.

With her eyes still closed and the humming wrapping around us, she reaches out and pulls me up against her.

I sob. I shake until I think I'll shake apart, like a wooden house in a hurricane. Flossie rocks me, humming and patting my back, stroking my hair. She waits and waits, until my sobbing quiets.

FLOSSIE

I put my hands on this poor girl's cheeks and kiss her forehead. I know she come to my house for help. Before I can give her what she needs, Mellie is going to have to answer some hard questions for me.

"Listen to me, Miz Mellie," I says. "You got to tell me the truth here. It's real important that you tell me the whole truth, understand?"

She bites her lip and nods.

"Did you bleed?"

She wrinkles her forehead in confusion. I can tell she don't know what I'm talking about. A bit of relief comes to me.

Shaking her head, Mellie says, "No. It's not that time of the month."

"Did that boy take off your clothes?"

A furious blush covers her face. She drops her gaze to her lap, shakes her head.

I can wait. I can wait as long it takes for to find her words to answer me.

She looks up and whispers, "He ripped my shirt, reached under my bra and pinched me. It hurt." The tears roll down her cheeks, and I'm on fire with anger at this boy who hurt this sweet girl.

"Sugar." I cradle her against me and rock her back and forth. "Poor baby. I know. What else?"

"He…he put his hand inside my…"

I hug her harder. I can't help myself. I put my lips against this sweet girl's hair. I wish I could make this all go away. But wishin' don't make it so.

She sobs. "He said I wanted him to do that. That I liked it."

I draw back so I can have a look at her. She's gone pale. Her tears have made shiny streaks on her face.

"I think he would have done more if the phone hadn't rung. He said he knew what to do because of Robert and Brooke."

She cries and I rock her. She cries some more and I hum. Outside, the crickets begin to sing. They sound like whispers between the rushing traffic.

"Child, sometimes words cut deeper than any knife." I stop, clear my throat. "I'm sorry for that. Your bruises are gonna heal and your flesh won't remember that hurt. But, Honey, your mind is always gonna remember those words, those lies he told you."

I stand up, easing my weight off my hurt foot. I lift my arms out from my sides. "Look at me, girl."

Mellie wipes her eyes and looks into my face.

"I'm a colored woman. That's a fact. But I ain't a nigger."

Shock sweeps over Mellie's face. She can't believe I'd use

that word.

"Don't be so scandalized, girl. That ugly word is part of life. It's a part of *my* life. It's one of the lies of *my* life. I've lived with it in my head, had it ringing in my ears sometimes, but I never let it get to my heart. It never changed who I really am. Do you believe that?"

She nods.

"What Kevin said to you is one of the lies of life. It's become one of the lies of *your* life. People blame others for the ugliness they know is in their own heart. Men who use women like Kevin used you always say the women were sluts, the women asked for it. Ain't so, though. You know that."

She nods again. The clouds of shame in her eyes begin to clear. I must be making some sense to the poor girl.

"The thing you gotta know and understand is that Kevin was wrong. You didn't ask for what he did. You didn't make him do it. It was inside him. What he did to you can't change who you are unless you let it. Just like calling me a nigger doesn't make me one. You understand?"

I watch as she twists her hands together in her lap. She's got more to tell. I can see it in her face. "What is it, child?"

"Well, in the beginning, when Kevin was just talking to me, I thought to myself, I do want him to kiss me. I wanted to know what it was like. So, he was right. I did want it. Does that make me all those things he said?"

I open my arms and smile at her. "What do you think, child? Come here." She steps into my embrace. "No, missy. Wanting a kiss from a boy don't make you bad. It makes you human." I sigh, thinking about the heartache we peoples cause each other. "Mellie, one day you'll understand that a woman wants a man and man wants a woman. They want to touch and be touched and when it's done with love, it is a true wonder.

"You been hurt, in your body and in your soul, but only you can let it change you. Your body gonna heal quick. Them bruises gonna be gone in a day or two. Your soul gonna take longer. You got to be patient and help your soul get better. You got to remember who and what you are. You're Melanie Adams. You're a smart girl, a loving girl, a good girl in your soul, Melanie." I put my hand over my heart. "Right here in your soul."

"Flossie, how do you know all this?"

I rock her back and forth, wrapped in my arms and pressed against my softness. I'm wishing I could've stopped this thing from happening to her. I'm remembering the first time some man thought he could do whatever he wanted to with me. "I reckon most all women had something like this or worse happen to them."

"Flossie, were you ever married?"

"Nope, never got married."

She's studying my face. After a little spell, she says, "But you loved a boy, didn't you?"

I can't hold back a sigh. "If you want to hear this story, we best sit down again."

"What happened?"

"You guessed right, child. I did love a boy. We were gonna get married, but he wanted a better job first. He went over to the big mill and asked for a job. The foreman laughed at him and told him they didn't hire no niggers."

I stare at the wall for a long time, seeing those scenes playing over in my mind. Remembering the pain. "He went back to his job at the packing house on the river. The foreman there called him into his office after work that day. He didn't like his *boys* lookin' for work nowhere else. The foreman said he always did think my man was uppity and that he needed to be taught a lesson."

Mellie swallows hard. I know that for the first time in her protected life, she's learning how cruel people can be. That cruelty isn't limited to one mean boy. She's seeing that folks are capable of all kinds of hateful, hurtful, merciless acts against each other.

She says, "That's enough. You don't have to tell me anymore."

I turn and give her a hard look. "I think you need to know, Melanie. There's a lot of ugliness in life. But like I told you before, it's up to you whether you let it change you or not. You need to hear this to understand about a lot of things."

There is a long pause. Mellie studies me for a minute, then nods.

I take a deep breath and tell my story. "That foreman and his men beat my Clyde. They beat him so bad, he bled inside. He died in my arms. Then they came after me."

She sucks in a breath, her eyes wide. "No."

"Yes. They kicked me around, too. Said, Who did we think we were, me and Clyde? Always too big for our britches."

I close my eyes against the remembering. "Thing is, I was expectin' at the time. I lost the baby." Big, fat tears run down my cheeks, even after all these years. After all these years, I still cry for my lost baby. "My brother came and got me, and we moved to Jacksonville. Been here ever since."

"How do you stand it? Why don't you hate white people?"

I take her hand in mine. "Child, the way I see it, you have two choices in this life. You live or you die. Some people, they're so filled up with hate and meanness that they die inside. I choose to live. If I'd let those men make me like them— hateful and bitter—they would have won. So I pray every day to learn to love and forgive. Not for them, but for me. So I can live and see some joy, some happiness in this life. So I can enjoy being with good people like you and your little sister and your mama, who loves you both so much."

She closes her eyes. I move the hair away from her cheeks. "I told you, sugar. It's all up to you. What are you gonna choose? Are you gonna let this eat you up or are you gonna make yourself a life?"

Mellie smiles at me, understanding shining in her eyes.

"Well, then. Let's get some milk and cornbread. We need to call your Mama, too. She must be worried sick."

MELANIE

On the drive home, Daddy and I are both quiet. I don't suppose either of us knows what to say. I've never left home without permission before.

"Why did you go to Flossie's?" Daddy almost whispers the question, like he's afraid of the answer.

My eyes burn as I stare at the road ahead of us. Flossie and I had decided that I should tell Mama and Daddy what happened, but I just can't right then. I can't. I swallow hard and shrug.

"It's the Mayfields, right?"

I suck in a sharp breath. Did he guess what happened? I wonder if there's a mark on me somewhere, but then I remember what Flossie said about that being part of the lie and the hurt: I might feel like everyone could see on the outside what had happened to me. But it's not true. Nothing shows on the outside of me. I have to remember that.

I'm not marked. I'm not bad. But still, I can't answer

Daddy.

He hits the steering wheel with his fist. "I knew it. This was a bad idea from the beginning. I should have stood up for my family and told Myra Mayfield to find someplace else to stay. I knew from that first night when Kevin threw a tantrum about going to bed that this just wasn't going to work out."

He glances over at me, studying my face in the light of the dashboard. "The house is too crowded, isn't it? I know your mama is going crazy trying to take care of everyone. Well, she just can't do it."

He drives in silence for a few miles. "Tomorrow. They have to go tomorrow. That's it."

I sigh and lean my head against the cool glass of the car window. I know he's trying to make things right. "Thanks, Daddy."

We turn onto Highway 13, and the tires settle into the clickety rhythm of the concrete road. Pine trees loom tall and shadowy beyond the road's shoulders. The sad call of a peacock, those poor, displaced peacocks who roam around the little creek, wavers through the night. The tires bump over the joints in the narrow bridge.

Daddy clears his throat. "I love you, sweetheart. There's just been too much happening." He blows a harsh breath between his lips, and I look over at him. His shoulders slump. "I'm sorry I let you down. Again."

In the glow of the dashboard lights, I see him chew his lower lip.

It's true. He did let me down.

It's true that I'm still furious with him and Aunt Lola. But I think about Flossie praying every day to learn to love and forgive. Right now, it seems like it will be impossible for me to forgive Daddy or Lola. Especially Kevin.

But I'll try. If Flossie can learn to forgive those horrible men who took so much from her, I can try to learn to forgive Daddy and Lola. I can try to love them again.

But the matter of Kevin is still up in the air. I don't see how I'll be able to forgive him. I'll try, just maybe not tonight.

NORAH

The slamming car doors announce that Clay is back with my daughter. I swing the front door wide open, covering my mouth with my hands as I run toward the car. I can't wait to hold my baby.

"Oh, Mellie, baby. Why did you leave like that? What were you thinking?" I pull her into my arms, squeezing and hugging and kissing her, but she doesn't say a word.

Clay stands beside us. He kisses my cheek, then Mellie's. "The Mayfields have to leave."

I nod, tucking a stray hair into Mellie's ponytail. "They're packing right now. They'll leave in the morning."

Clay stuffs his fists into his pants pockets. "Norah, I was going to tell them."

"You were right from the beginning, but I wouldn't listen to you. I made the mistake. It was my place to tell them."

"We just can't handle it anymore."

I lift Mellie's chin with my fingers so I can study her. She doesn't seem to be hurt, but her eyes have a haunted look to them.

"What happened, sweetheart? Why did you leave like that?"

Clay puts an arm around the both of us. "It was just too

much, Norah. The Mayfields, the missiles, everything. Too much for a girl to handle."

Melanie is looking over my shoulder. I turn to see Kevin leaning against the doorframe, his arms crossed over his chest. Birdie shoves past him and runs outside to squeeze between Clay and me. She grabs Mellie's hand and says, "You didn't really run away, did you, Mellie?"

"Of course, she didn't run away, Birdie." I smile and run my fingers through her hair, but on the inside I'm a bundle of doubts. Did Mellie actually run away, or did she just need some time alone? That's a fine distinction to make, but somehow in my mind, the two things are worlds apart.

And why did she go to Flossie's house?

I shudder to think of her on the bus alone, all way over in that part of town. I don't let any of this show, though. Putting on a big smile, I say to Birdie, "Only people who are very sad or very mad or in a lot of trouble run away. Melanie just went to visit with Flossie."

The words spill out of me in a rush, like I needed to say them before they change to mean something else. I'm scared. My daughter didn't run away. My daughter isn't sad or mad or in trouble.

Is she?

The four of us walk inside, and Kevin closes the door behind us. Myra and Brooke are doing the dishes. Kevin returns to his place at the table, and finishes his bowl of ice cream.

"Melanie, dear," Myra says, while she dries her hands. "I know how difficult this has been for all of us. I'm so sorry you got upset." She puts her hands on Mellie's shoulders and lowers her voice a touch, like she's telling my daughter a secret. "It's always hard when there's a new baby in the house. But your mother needs you to be a big girl now. No more of these tantrums. They don't help anyone."

How dare she accuse my Mellie of behaving like a spoiled brat? I want to shout that my girls don't throw tantrums like her spoiled brats. I remind myself that Myra and the kids will be gone in the morning. There's no need to make things worse. Calmly, I say, "Myra, thanks for taking care of the dishes. I'm going to put the girls to bed now. It's been a busy day."

I close the girl's bedroom door behind us and lift my face to the ceiling. "Well, I never heard such in my life. The nerve of that woman. To think that you would throw a tantrum over DC. You would never do something like that," I sputter. "Melanie, you are nothing like her stinking, rotten kids, you hear me?"

Melanie and Birdie both look at me with wide eyes. Melanie whispers, "Yes, ma'am."

I pull Birdie's bedspread back with such force, the ballerina pictures on the wall shake. I am so furious that I want to break something. With more force that I intend, I yank Mellie's bedspread back. It seems to take forever for the curtains to settle back against the window frame. I look over at Birdie. Her bottom is lip trembling. Now, I've frightened her.

She tugs on the bottom of my blouse. "Mama, it's all right. I'll never throw another fit."

"Oh, sweetie." I hug her. "I'm sorry. I'm just, just…" I can't find the words to explain to my six-year-old what I'm feeling. We all three begin to cry in each other's arms. In the distance, I hear the whine of a jet and we brace for the roar and the boom. Soon, the windows rattle. DC wails. I hear Clay trying to soothe him.

"Time for bed, girls." I tuck Birdie in bed and give her a quick kiss.

I sit down on the side of Melanie's bed and hold her hand in mine. Her eyes look full of dark secrets. I won't try to pry them out of her tonight. I'll wait until she wants to talk. Surely, tomorrow, when the Mayfields are gone and we have our home to ourselves, she'll feel better.

"Mama?"

"What, Sweetie?"

"Can I stay home from school tomorrow?"

I put my hand on her forehead, checking to see if she has a fever. Her skin is cool. She's not physically sick, but a day home from school wouldn't hurt her. "Sure. Do you feel okay?"

She nods. "I'm just really tired."

"I understand." I kiss her, and she rises up and hugs me hard. "Sleep well, sweetheart. I love you. Everything will be better in the morning."

MELANIE

I lay on my back with the sheet tucked tight under my arms, stiff like a statue. At least I don't have to worry about facing Kevin at school.

I think about how mad Mama was that Mrs. Mayfield said I ran away.

She didn't even let me explain why I went to Flossie's house. She just took Daddy's word that the problem was tension about the missiles and the Mayfields.

I understand now. I'll never tell Mama what Kevin did. I'll never tell Mama about Aunt Lola and Daddy, either. I have two things to protect Mama from, two dark secrets that she'll never hear from me.

I have to save Mama from being hurt in a way I know will change her forever. I don't want Mama to change anymore than she has already. I don't want her to think that she can't keep me safe any longer, that she can't keep me from being hurt or sad or mad.

It seems like hours later I'm still awake, even though I'm tired. I concentrate on breathing. Soon my belly rumbles. My mouth feels hot and dry, like it's stuffed with wads of cotton. I'm hungry and thirsty. I think of the ice cream Kevin had been eating earlier.

After what he did, he ate ice cream, my ice cream, in my house. Anger and frustration flare through me until sweat beads under my arms and behind my knees.

I fling off the sheet and sit on the side of my bed. I want ice cream. I deserve ice cream.

Like Flossie said, I didn't do anything wrong.

Thinking about the taste, so cold and sweet and creamy, makes my stomach rumble more. I open the bedroom door, careful not to let the hinges creak, and tip-toe into the hall. I freeze.

Kevin is sleeping on the sofa, a lumpy shadow in the dark room.

The ice cream is in the freezer, in the kitchen.

I will have to pass Kevin. I'll have to get a bowl out of the cabinet. I'll have to lean against the counter. I'll have to feel the sharp edge knife into my skin like it did earlier today.

I can't feel that again. I can't go in there.

In the bathroom I lower my head, turn on the water, and drink out of the faucet.

Back in my dark room, I reach under my bed and tug out Heidi the rabbit. Buttons slide on the tile. The hard little sound sends new shivers through me. My torn shirt.

My secret seems to want to escape from hiding, to run from the darkness. I stuff the shirt back under the bed and wedge myself against the mattress. Gnawing uncertainty growls like a monster in my stomach.

I close my eyes and wait for the magic vision of Heidi to appear. It doesn't. Instead, I see Kevin's face looming over me. I feel the bruised mark on my breast. There is still a raw sensation between my legs.

I shiver as I imagine Flossie's boyfriend, beaten and bleeding, dying. Dead. I wonder how Flossie's lost baby might have looked.

I toss and turn until the sheets twist around me like ropes. My hands clutch Heidi's patched fur, my fingers digging into the softness, until I feel threads pop and stuffing ooze up to snag on my nails. Now Heidi is hurt, too.

Furiously, I work my fingers back and forth, trying to repair the tear, but I can't. Hot tears stream from my eyes until my pillow is wet.

I don't make a sound.

Tuesday
October 30, 1962

MELANIE

In the morning, Birdie gently wakes me up. "Mellie. Breakfast is ready. Mama wants you."

I pull on some clothes and drag the brush though my hair. In the kitchen, Daddy is pouring a cup of coffee. "Morning, sweetie."

"Hi, Daddy."

Mama reaches over and pats Birdie's hand. "Are you excited about school today?"

"Yes, ma'am." Birdie's face lights up. "Tomorrow's Halloween, and Mrs. Blake said we were going to start learning our Thanksgiving play. I want to be an Indian."

Kevin keeps his eyes focused on his plate while he shovels eggs into his mouth.

This morning, I can look at him. In fact, I stare at him until he darts a glance at me and squirms in his chair.

It feels good to see him squirming with nerves. Does he think I told Mama what happened? Is he scared? I continue to look at him until he shoves his chair back.

He stands. "I've got to pack a couple of things. Thank you for the breakfast, Mrs. Adams." He nearly runs from the dining room.

Filled with a sense of power, I take Rachel Winston's key from the miniature pegboard next to the telephone. "Mama, I forgot to get the Winston's mail yesterday. I'm going to put it in their house."

The Winston's house is as dim and quiet as a tomb. I straighten the stack of mail on the table and noticed the film of dust. I get a paper towel from the kitchen and begin wiping off the table. The front door clicks, and I spin around. Kevin is standing in the open doorway.

I freeze, my hands clutching the paper towel. Slowly, he closes the door behind him. He tugs a girly magazine out of his notebook and holds it up for me to see.

Kevin glances from my face to the magazine cover. "Why are you so shocked? Everybody reads these." He steps closer to me, reaches out as if he's going to touch me.

I shove the dining room chair in front of me. My heart pounds, and I hear the blood rushing in my ears. I hate that he can make me feel this way.

He grins like he knows I'm frightened, then walks down the hall to the Winston's bedroom.

I drop my head and suck in a deep breath. Flossie's words come rushing back to me. He can only change me if I let him. His words can't touch my soul.

I feel my courage rising.

I shove the chair back under the table and wait for him to come back to the dining room.

Whistling through his teeth, he stops beside me. "Waiting for me, huh?"

"I have to lock up."

His grin turns evil. "I think you're sorry I'm leaving. I'll bet you want a good bye kiss." He reaches out to touch the hair that's fallen over my shoulder.

"Get your hands off me," I hiss. I'm steaming mad that he'd even think to come near me. Fury flares in my belly, burning and urgent. I want to spew flames at him. I want to sear him with the anger I feel. "Don't you dare even think about touching me again like that, Kevin. Don't you touch me again, ever."

Kevin shifts his feet like he wants to move away, but he keeps that bully look on his face. "Don't be so dramatic, you sissy baby. We just fooled around a little. That's all. Everybody does."

"You've turned into a mean bully, Kevin Mayfield."

"Oh, come one. You wanted it. You know it."

"All bullies blame someone else. Well, I won't take the blame for the meanness inside you."

His mouth stretches into a sneer. "You can't tell anyone, you know. They'll never believe you."

He's sweating.

"You're scared, aren't you?" I'm certain I'm right.

"I'm not scared."

"You are. You're scared right down to your toes."

"Oh, yeah, I'm so scared." He puts his hands out in front of him and makes them shake like he's trembling with fear. "The guys will really like hearing all about how much you liked it. They'll be eager to have their chance."

"Your lies can't change me. I won't let them. You should've stopped when I told you to. You had no right."

"Oh, you liked it."

"No, I didn't," I almost shout. I pick up his notebook from the coffee table and shove it at him. His arms wrap around it on reflex. I stride to the front door and swing it open. "I hope you decide to change and grow up."

"I'll see you at school, you know." He saunters out the door.

I slam the door behind him, flop down on Mrs. Winston's gold velvet chair, and press my fingers over my eyes. Unfortunately, Kevin is right. I will see him at school.

But Flossie is right, too. Kevin's lies are never going to change me. Not deep down in my soul, where it counts. It might not be easy, but there is strength in me.

A sense of freedom washes over me.

I finish dusting the table, straighten the stack of mail, turn off the lights, and go home.

MELANIE

Before supper, I'm reading a homework assignment when Mama says, "Stephanie's here."

Steph follows Mama into my room. "I'll be out of here in a minute. I just need to gather all the laundry, so I can get a head start on it tomorrow. I feel like things have gotten out of hand for the last few weeks." She kneels on the floor and lifts Birdie's bedspread, sweeping her arm beneath the bed, looking for lost socks.

All the blood drains from my face and I feel cold sweat bead along my hairline. *Not under my bed. Don't look under my bed, Mama.* I kneel in the cramped space between the two beds.

Our faces level, Mama grins at me. "Mellie, sweetie, you visit with Steph. I'll take care of this."

"I want to help. I'll get the stuff from under here." I pull out Heidi, remembering too late about the tear.

My heart stops. Mama will see the rip in Heidi and she'll know something has really upset me. She takes Heidi from me. Sitting back on her heels, she stares at it. "Now what in heaven's name…"

She touches the tear in the stuffed animal's fur, examining the snapped threads, her fingers gently probing the exposed stuffing. "Really, Melanie." She stares at the rabbit and her hands began to shake. She never once looks up at me.

Instead, she pushes to her feet. Still holding my stuffed toy, she says, "I don't think I can fix this. I don't know how." With the rabbit in her arms, she turns and leaves the room. The pile of dirty clothes is still on the floor.

Steph kneels beside me on the floor. She slides her arm around my shoulder. "Mellie, what's the matter? Are you getting your period again?"

If only things were as simple as getting my period. I shake my head. "No. That's not it."

Steph leads me over to my bed. She closes the door and snaps the lock. Her brow wrinkles with concern as she comes to sit beside me.

She hands me a tissue. "Listen, we're best friends. You can tell me what's going on."

I blow my nose, then study the folds on the damp tissue. Steph is my best friend, and she has been through almost as much as I have.

The kids at school tease her terribly about Cherie getting pregnant. Her mom has just about gone crazy with grief and has taken it out on Steph. Clint must have stopped championing her, because now Buzz has been saying nasty things to her for weeks, but Steph just raises her chin a notch and doesn't seem to pay any attention to him. Even I don't know what's really going on at her house, when they're all shouting and banging things around.

But Steph and I have always had each other. Before I realize it, I'm talking. My voice sounds serious, almost like a news reporter talking about an important event. It's like I'm telling Stephanie about something that happened to someone else.

I tell her about me being alone in the house with Kevin. I tell her about the awful feeling of the counter cutting into my back, how I couldn't move.

I tell how Daddy hung up on me before I could tell him I needed help.

I tell her about riding the bus alone to the colored part of town. About how scary it was to be where I'm the different one.

I explain as best as I can what Flossie taught me.

Steph is crying. Big, fat tears roll down her cheeks and her bottom lip trembles. She stares at me, then grabs me in a hard hug.

"Oh, God," she says. "Oh, God." Her fingers dig into my back. "I'm so sorry, Mellie. I'm sorry."

"It's okay."

She grabs my shoulders and holds my gaze with hers. "It's all my fault. Me and my big mouth."

"It's not your fault, none of it is your fault. At first, I thought I did want Kevin to kiss me."

"No, you didn't. Not really. You only thought that because I kept nagging." She shook her head. "Oh, Mel, I've ruined everything. All the boys at school say horrible things to me. They think I'm slut because Cherie got pregnant and had to get married. I didn't help matters by flirting with all the boys and trying to get Buzz to kiss me. I was so stupid."

"You're not a slut, Steph. I don't think Cherie is, either. People are just small-minded and mean. You know what Flossie told me? She said that we aren't to blame for the meanness in other people." I take a deep breath. "Their lies can't change us unless we let them. And, Steph, we won't let them change us. We're both smart. We're both strong."

She blows her nose. "So, are you okay? You didn't have to go to the doctor or anything?"

"No." I swallow, realizing that I really am lucky. Even though Kevin hurt and scared me, so much worse could have happened.

"Listen, Steph. I didn't tell Mama what happened."

"But, Mellie—"

"No, I can't. I'm not hurt, not physically, anyway. She was so upset and afraid when I came home from Flossie's." I shrug. "There's nothing she can do to change what happened."

I glance toward the door, and in my mind see Mama clutching my favorite toy.

Steph watches me in silence.

"Just like the torn rabbit, Mama can't fix it. She's had a hard time with the baby and being so sad and all. She just couldn't take it, you know?"

Looking at Steph, I notice for the first time how different her eyes look, so much older. We're different girls than we were back when school started.

She takes my hand and nods. "Yeah, she doesn't need to be hurt like that. Sometimes I think stuff like this is harder for moms than for us. I know Cherie is doing a lot better than my mom."

Kneeling on the floor again, I reach under my bed and drag out my torn shirt. "Will you do me a favor, then?"

She stares at the shirt. Slowly, she nods.

"Can you get rid of this somehow? I don't want Mama to see it."

Our fingers touch as she takes the shirt from me. We look into each other's eyes and for an instant, it seems like we see in each other the long road of hurt and happiness that lies ahead.

Steph wads up the shirt.

Friday
November 2, 1962

MELANIE

Birdie bangs on the bedroom door and shouts, "Mama said to come watch the news. President Kennedy is on."

Stephanie and I leave our homework on my bed and follow Birdie into the living room. The familiar knots of nerves are tight in my gut.

Mama and Daddy are holding hands with their eyes glued to the TV. Steph and I sit on the floor in front of the television.

The president says that progress is now being made toward the restoration of peace. The missile bases are being dismantled.

"Daddy," I whisper, "does this mean it's over? That we won't have a war?"

He puts his finger to his mouth for me to be quiet.

The president is saying he will follow closely the completion of this work through a variety of means, including aerial surveillance, until such time as an equally satisfactory international means of verification is effected.

Daddy looks at us all and smiles. "I think it might be over, girls. But it seems like the jets are still going to be making a lot of noise."

I can't believe it. I feel like I can really breathe for the first time since DC was born. Maybe everything *will* get back to normal now. Mama reaches over and gives me a big hug.

So much has happened, and now it's really all over. I wonder about all the stuff we have stored in our classrooms at school. I guess we'll bring it all home, huh? I picture us carrying blankets on the bus, and smile.

Birdie tiptoes across the floor, waving her Halloween magic wand, bouncing to make her tulle skirt float up and down. She stops in front of me and Steph. She trills, "I've made everything wonderful with my magic touch." She taps my head three times with the baton wrapped with ribbon and topped with a tin-foil star.

"Ouch." I rub my head. "Hey, knock it off, Tinkerbell."

Birdie spins around and dances out of the room.

With a much lighter step, Steph and I go back to my room. "See," she says, "I told you that Russia wouldn't do anything."

"I think we were just plain lucky. I'm just glad it's all over."

We haven't really talked about much since Tuesday, when I told her about what Kevin did. But, I have one more thing to tell her. Something I didn't think I would ever share, because it was too special, too precious.

Now, I need to bring it into the light and let it shine. I need to see how it really looks next to the dark things that have happened.

"Steph, there's one more thing I want to tell you."

Her eyes get round, like she's scared. Then I see her pull something together inside her, that same thing that I know is inside me. She's ready for whatever I have to tell her.

I smile, and she relaxes a little.

"Well, come on," she huffs. "Don't let me die of exasperation. What else do you have to tell me?" She pauses for a second. "It must not be all bad because you're smiling a little."

"I did have a special kiss."

Steph shakes her head. "I don't want to talk about that stuff anymore. I was stupid."

"No, Steph. This is different. Really."

She looks at me, waiting.

Thinking about Robert's kiss, I realize that it was special, no matter what Brooke said about Robert kissing her, no matter what Kevin said about what he saw Brooke and Robert doing.

I know what I felt like when Robert kissed me and it was… indescribable. The glow of it rises up in me. I feel it shining all through me.

"Robert kissed me."

Steph's mouth drops open. For once, she's speechless.

"The night of his going away party. He walked me home."

Steph shakes her head. "Wow, I can't believe you kept a kiss from Robert Taylor a secret for so long!"

As I tell her about Robert's kiss, I know that I'll find something that special again one day.

Even though I was changed by Kevin's kiss, and still hurting from it, I've been changed by Robert's kiss, too.

I'll figure everything out some day. Right now, it's enough for me to understand that I experienced a good thing before a bad thing.

I know the good thing will last forever.

THE END

Bibliography

Blum, John Morton. *Years of Discord: American Politics and Society,* 1961-1974. New York: W. W. Norton and Company, 1991.

Epstein, Dan. *Twentieth Century Pop Culture.* London: Carlton Books, Limited, 1999.

Freedman, Lawrence. *Kennedy's Wars: Berlin, Cuba, Laos, and Vietnam.* New York: Oxford University Press, 2000.

Hurst, Sr., Rodney L., *It Was Never About a Hot Dog and a Coke.* Livermore: WingSpan Press, 2008.

Medina, Loreta M., ed. *The Cuban Missile Crisis.* San Diego: Greenhaven Press, 2002.

Olian, JoAnne. *Everyday Fashions of the Sixties: As Pictured in the Sears Catalog.* Mineola: Dover Publications, 1999.

Wright, E. Lynne. *It Happened in Florida.* Guilford: The Globe Pequot Press, 2002.